USA TODAY BESTSELLING AUTHOR

Dale Mayer

SEALS OF HONOR

BOOKS 23-25

SEALS OF HONOR, BOOKS 23–25
Beverly Dale Mayer
Valley Publishing Ltd.

ISBN-13: 978-1-773364-06-3
Print Edition

Books in This Series:

About This Boxed Set

Troy

When a friend of Tesla's sends out an SOS on the lowdown on an oil rig in trouble, Troy has a good idea what he's getting into. As far as he is concerned, the maximum danger, the potential for betrayal, and the chances of not coming home sounded like the right kind of job for him.

After all, he lived alone. So going into these situations with no family to worry about him made him the ideal candidate—until he meets someone at the oil rig who suddenly makes him see his future in a different life.

Berkley knew something dangerous was going on. No way this oil rig hadn't been sabotaged. She'd requested to remain with the skeleton crew until her help arrived. And was surprised at the size of the team that showed up to assist her.

Who knew it would take all of them to get to the bottom of this mess and to keep them alive, as human nature and Mother Nature combined to take them all out.

Axel

Life was never boring, but, for Axel, things kick up a notch when he helps in an underwater rescue of a downed submarine that's low on oxygen. What they find is nothing like what they expected. All the crew but one was dead—as in shot to death. The last remaining crew member was alive but in rough shape. What the hell happened here?

Allee woke up in the hospital and barely remembers how she got here. But a fuzzy memory only compounds the horror when the investigation ranks her as their number one suspect in the nightmare that won't quit.

As the investigation takes a darker turn, so does her life, as someone decides a dead patsy is better than one who can talk …

Sign up to be notified of all Dale's releases here!
https://geni.us/DaleNews

Dale Mayer

SEALS OF HONOR

Colton

BOOK-23

PROLOGUE

COLTON EDGEWOOD BOARDED the military plane at Coronado, on the first leg of his journey overseas to the Thule Air Base in Greenland. He was okay with that, but, at the same time, he hadn't been home long enough to really get his feet under him. And, after helping Taylor these last few days, it seemed like such a rush job. Colton had really planned on staying on base for a week at least.

He'd served in a unique position in Afghanistan—as a liaison for one of the joint military teams, pulling together group training of "friendly" wars, all in a mission to foster peace and to further everybody's education and skills. So now he was headed to Greenland for a similar operation.

Greenland was a strategic site for the Thule Air Base. He didn't expect to be there for too long and would head off to Africa afterward, at least as far as he understood. For now. His orders were never firm for long. He'd get one step on a journey but would never quite know where he would go from there.

Still, he'd never been to Greenland and was looking forward to it. With a population of fewer than sixty thousand on the whole island, it was a unique corner of the world, where nobody owned their own land. Instead buyers were granted the right to use it, and everybody worked together to make their society the way they wanted it. The population was mostly native people, and Colton really appreciated the different viewpoint they brought.

He shifted position. He was the only one on this military flight, along with a ton of cargo. He wished he could have ridden in the cockpit, but, with room only for a pilot and a copilot, Colton definitely wasn't small enough to squeeze between them up there. The trip was long but uneventful.

Just as they prepared for a landing, he heard a large explosion on the left side of the plane. He bolted from his seat and stuck his head in the cockpit to take a look in that direction. The left engine was on fire. He swore.

The copilot glanced at him and said, "Take your seat."

He nodded but grabbed three parachutes instead, in case they had to abandon the plane. He made his way forward again to see the pilots calm and controlled but issuing updates to the base as they approached. "I've got two extra parachutes here, in case you guys need them."

The copilot nodded. "Hopefully not," she said.

Kate. Kate Winnows. Somebody he'd known for many years, had flown with a couple times and once had shared an overnight stay. That had been a hot and heavy night—then they had both showered the next morning and carried on with their individual lives. But to see her here and now just put another human face on this. He didn't recognize the pilot.

Kate looked at him again and said, "Take your seat, Colton."

At that, he nodded, grabbed his parachute and fastened it on, then took a seat. He couldn't buckle in with the chute on, but he wasn't letting go of it. At the moment, the parachute seemed more critical than the seat belt.

The plane careened to the side and slipped downward at

a rate that was more than a little nauseating. He caught his breath, following the safety procedures he knew they would go through now. He had been in similar situations before. Not exactly this but … He leaned forward to look out the cockpit window, hoping to see land in the distance. Regardless, if the pilots had put out a Mayday call, they could now jump and get free and clear of the plane, if headed for a crash.

Kate joined him in the cargo bay, holding onto a nearby strap, and said in a curt but controlled tone, "We have to bail."

"Understood." When he rose, he immediately fell as the plane listed again to the side. "What about the pilot?" he yelled over the loud din, scrambling to his feet once more.

"He's coming," she said, righting herself as well. She grabbed her parachute, and he helped her strap it on.

The two made their way to the cockpit, where the pilot still tried to guide the plane. She called out to him, "George, come on. We're done."

He nodded. "I know," he said. "I just wanted to make sure we got out to the ocean, where this doesn't come down on anybody." Finally he bolted toward them and, with their help, got buckled into his parachute. He looked around the plane and said, "It won't be that easy to get out of here. It'll be hard to get clear of the plane."

"I know," Colton said, as he struggled against the downward angle of the plane to reach the emergency door, kicked it open and basically tossed Kate out.

The pilot raised his eyebrows and shook his head. "Damn, this is the first time for me."

He didn't get a chance to say more because Colton already had pushed the pilot outside in the frigid air. Colton jumped out behind them. Colton watched as the plane dove, flames shooting out behind it, as it beelined for the deep dark ocean below.

They'd gone from an ugly and dangerous situation to an uglier and deadlier one.

Nothing was easy about landing in the Arctic Ocean. Hypothermia would set in within ten to twelve minutes. After that? Then it wouldn't matter who came to rescue them—it would already be too late.

CHAPTER 1

COLTON PULLED HIS cord and watched his parachute billow above him, tugging him upward with a sudden jolt that gave him a better view of the other two. Kate appeared to be fine, but George struggled. It looked like his first chute didn't deploy.

"Pull the second one! Pull the second one!" Colton shouted. The pilot did, and, thank God, that one deployed.

With the three of them now drifting toward the ocean below, the plane careened off to the side and hit the hard surface of the ocean full-on, exploding on impact, sending fire and metal parts everywhere. Soon it was just wreckage burning on the surface of the ocean. Kate was still a ways away.

Colton shifted to direct his descent toward her, so he could keep an eye on the two of them below him. Part of the problem with a chute was the fact you had to get rid of it once you hit the water. The chutes were heavy and could pull you down easily. He could see ships coming toward them already, which was good, but now he and the pilots had to stay alive long enough for the rescuers to reach them.

The trio had avoided the plane crash but were still ill prepared for the icy water waiting for them. More than that, the parachute lines were even more dangerous than the parachute itself once in the water, it was easy to get tangled up in the lines and drown. Colton would ditch his chute as soon as he got close enough to jump into the water because he hated the dangers inherent in those lines. Plus he had to be free and clear to help the pilots. Yet he had to time the cutting of his lines just right. He didn't want to do that too soon, extending his time in the frigid water. Yet he had to cut his lines at the last possible moment before he hit the water. But then, he'd done this many, many times. He wasn't so sure about the other two.

They were military, but not navy, and water was his element, not necessarily theirs. Ever since he was a kid, he'd wanted to be a Navy SEAL, and achieving that status had been a crowning glory in his life. Absolutely nothing had the same sense of achievement since then.

But he knew the dangers of this crash-landing. As long as the rescue boats moved toward them, they wouldn't be in the freezing water for too long. Judging the distance of the boats coming toward them, he realized their arrival would cut it close to that ten-to-twelve-minute hypothermia mark.

He maneuvered his position so he was between Kate and George. George looked to be less comfortable up here in the air, whereas Kate hung on like a trooper, studying the water below. Colton was less worried about any sea life in the ocean than the actual temperature of the water itself. They were also heavily geared up, and the work boots they wore would feel like fifty pounds by the time they soaked up water.

Just ten feet above the water he quickly unbuckled his chute and dropped it. Kate had hit the surface on his left, and George had splashed down on his right. He was in between them. Closing his legs, he slammed into the water and kicked hard to resurface.

Breaking through the ocean, he checked on the others. George was closest and still struggling. Colton headed toward him first. "Stay calm. I'll cut your lines." With his knife, Colton cut the buckles, pulling the lines away. "Can you swim?"

George nodded. "Just not well."

"Try to float," Colton said. "I've got to get Kate." And he headed to where Kate was, trying to undo her buckles. Once everything got soaking wet, it was that much harder to maneuver. He knew her fingers would start to freeze soon, faster if she panicked.

He called out to her, "I'm here. Calm down. Control the panic."

She took several deep breaths, and he could see the fear in her eyes as she looked at him. "Tread water gently," he said. "I'll cut you free."

Then he quickly got her buckles cut and helped her get out of the harness. "Can you swim?"

She nodded and started to strike out hard.

"Don't swim too hard or too fast," he said. "You'll burn up your energy. Hypothermia is our demon to beat."

She shot him a look.

George still struggled. Colton's SEALs training kicked in, and he put George into an assisted floating position. With Kate at his side, he told George, "Stay strong. The boats are coming."

George's teeth were already chattering. "I didn't expect to go out like this."

"You're *not* going out like this," Colton said fiercely. "*Fight*. We just have to stay afloat until they get here."

They floated, looped together, trying to preserve their strength and heat.

"What happened to the plane that caused the fire?" Colton asked after a moment.

Kate shook her head. "Explosion in the left engine. None of our diagnostics gave a reason. It was all fine, and then it wasn't."

"A bomb?" he asked.

"Possibly," George said, "but it easily could have been a damaged fuel line. I don't know. But something caused it to explode, and now nothing will be left for the military to discern what happened."

"Sounds like you guys have enemies," Colton joked.

"Yes," George said, his teeth still chattering.

Colton hated to say it, but George wasn't doing well. "George, you have to hang on. The boats will be here in a few minutes. Tell me about this enemy you're talking about."

"I'm supposed to testify against two coworkers—two pilots," he said. "They were smuggling drugs."

Colton's breath gushed out in a *whoosh*. "Wow," he said. "Didn't see that coming."

"Yeah, I know," George whispered.

Colton looked over at Kate to see a hard look in her eyes. "Did you know about it?"

She nodded. "Yes. Both men have been removed from active duty and are awaiting trial."

"Of course they are," Colton said. "Court-martialed and the military police are involved, right?"

"Yes, on both counts," she said. "The military trial isn't for another four months though."

"Right, and, if they can get rid of George, then, of course, they walk free."

"Exactly," George said. "And I've got a sorry-ass feeling

they'll be right about that."

"Do you want to see them walk free?" Colton asked, as he tried to keep George floating and fighting for his life, while Colton kept an eye on Kate. "I can hear the boats, George. Stay calm." But George wasn't answering. Colton gave him a shake and smacked him hard on the cheek.

George groaned.

"Did you hear me, George?"

"I don't want to hear you," he said. "I'm so cold."

"Soldier, buck up!" Colton snapped. "That's an order."

George's eyes flew open, and he stared up at the blue sky. "One of these days those orders can't be followed."

"It won't be today, dammit," Colton roared. "Stay awake, soldier. You can hear the boats. They're here." He twisted George's head so he could see the approaching cruiser.

"Oh, wow," George said. "You were serious."

"I saw them up above," Colton said, "but we still have to get somebody from the cruiser to us." Colton looked over at Kate. She was desperate to hang on but fading.

Nobody could keep this up for long, so Colton knew it would be close. "If you can't stay on the surface," he said to her, "you let me know."

She just glared at him. "Like hell," she said. "George needs to be rescued so those two assholes who did this don't get away with it."

"Are they the kind of assholes who would do this?" Colton asked.

"Who knows? But, if this was sabotage, George is likely the target."

"What about you?" Colton asked. "Do you have any enemies?"

"Not that I know of."

George gave a broken laugh. "Your ex-boyfriend would do this, Kate. Remember? He said he would make sure you paid."

"It was one of the reasons why I was okay to fly with you," she said, a weak attempt at a joke. "We were both targeted."

Colton swore. "How come I didn't get any warning to not fly with either of you?"

"Because you were tossed on at the last minute," she said, "but it's not like we could have warned you anyway. But I'm sorry you're involved."

"I'm not involved, but I am caught up in it. And I'll be damned if I'll let either of you die. We have a rescue right here, right now." He could see men getting into a Zodiac. "Come on. They're in the Zodiac. We've got minutes to go. That's it."

"Too late," George said, his voice slurred. "So cold. C-Can't feel anything."

"You'll feel it all soon enough," Colton said urgently. "It'll hurt like shit when the blood starts moving back through your body."

"Maybe it's better this way," George murmured, his eyes falling shut again. Colton reached over and smacked him hard. George groaned again but didn't open his eyes.

Colton looked over at Kate.

"Don't waste the energy on me," she said. "I'm still here."

But she was failing. He could see it. Her feet and arms were moving much slower, and her body was sinking, then popping back up again. He knew that, somewhere in the next few moments, she would go down and not pop back up again. He could hold out for another five or ten minutes, maybe fifteen, but that would be his max too.

As good as he was, and he knew what he could do, the temperature here would slowly sap away his own strength. He hadn't come prepared for an Arctic Ocean mission. Not one out in the freezing cold water itself. He was doing everything he could to preserve his own body heat, but he expended some of his energy to keep George afloat. Colton caught George slipping under again and smacked him hard once more. "We're almost there. Hang on, George."

But George was past responding.

Shit! Colton was using the standard rescue position to keep George floating beside him, but, as he watched, Kate went under and didn't come back up. He reached down with his boot and tossed her higher up in the water and grabbed her by the back of her jacket. He yelled for help. He could hear their rescuers coming, and so Colton started moving toward them as quickly as possible but still in control. Slow and steady won the race, but Mother Nature could be a bitch, and she always tried to trump everything else.

Sometimes humanity won too.

Suddenly the Zodiac was here, and hands reached for him. He passed up George first because that was the side they were on, then moved to get Kate up. Afterward, as he tried to pull himself up into the Zodiac, he could feel the slow effect of the cold as his legs didn't want to work and his hands fumbled. Willing arms caught him and yanked him aboard, dumping him into the bottom of the boat.

"Perfect timing, guys," he said, his teeth chattering. "Perfect timing." Colton stared up at the sky. "But it would have been really nice if you'd gotten here about five minutes earlier."

He could hear the men shouting orders as they raced toward the cruiser. George was unloaded first, and then Kate was carried up next, conscious but shivering badly. Colton had taken a few minutes to pump some oxygen through his body, but his body was cold, and he knew it needed to reheat fast. One of the men reached down, grabbed him by the shoulder and helped him to his feet. He stumbled forward.

"You okay, soldier?"

"Always," he said, right before he collapsed to the deck.

KATE WINNOWS WOKE up and stared around the small room. Everything was white, and she lay on a medical bed, yet the room seemed to rock. *I must still be on the destroyer.* The memories came crushing back, causing her to shudder. The plane went down, and the water had been so damn cold. Of everything that had to be the worst. Sure, she had an initial panic, knowing the plane was going down, but realizing they had the chutes gave her a course of action to focus on.

Once she was buckled in to her chute, it was a matter of getting George strapped up and deplaning. Floating down was an experience like nothing she remembered. She'd done parachute training, but it was always under calm conditions. Never like this. She knew, in theory, what landing in the ocean would be like, but she wasn't prepared for how quickly the ocean zapped the heat from her bones and the blood from her vessels, leaving her body as a block of ice, like the glaciers all around them.

She knew that, if it hadn't been for Colton, neither she nor George would have survived. At that, she sat up and looked around. She saw several other beds, but only one was occupied, where two men were working on that patient.

George. "Is he okay?"

One of the men walked to her, checking her temperature. "He's dealing with severe hypothermia," the doctor said. "We're treating him. You are suffering from hypothermia yourself, so let's keep your movements to a minimum, please."

She noted she had been wrapped up in special blankets, and her body, although it should have been warm, was not. "I'm still so cold," she whispered, and almost immediately her body started to shiver. "Colton?" she asked.

"He's fine," the doctor said. "He's probably in the mess hall, tanking up on hot coffee right now."

"I wish I was there," she muttered, her teeth chattering.

The man tucked yet another warm blanket around her. "Give yourself a chance to warm up," he said, then went back to George's side.

Kate knew from their discussions that it was not good news for George. He was suffering a lot more than she was. When the doctor finally returned to her again, she said, "The plane was sabotaged."

His gaze sharpened. "Does Colton know?"

"Yes," she said. "He does."

"Then trust us to look after it," he said.

"I'm worried George won't make it. And that whoever did this will have succeeded in killing him."

"We're working on it," the doctor said quietly. "You have to look after yourself. We can't have two of you not making it." And, with that, Kate's heart sank, as she realized just how bad George's situation was. He was a family man, who had come to marriage late in life, and now had three teenage boys. They needed him. He must keep fighting.

Mentally she sent out a message. *Come on, George. Fight. Colton kept you alive out there. I need you to stay alive in here.*

Even if he lost some fingers or toes, he had to stay alive. Even minus his legs, his sons still needed him. And, with that thought, she turned to her own healing, telling her body to warm up fast. She wanted to see whoever had done this to them soon caught so they would pay for their crimes. And finally, to Colton, she sent out a message, whispering, "Thank you, love."

She'd always known he was honorable. And that one night they'd come together in a heated flash had been nothing like she'd ever experienced before. She didn't even really understand who he was at first. But when she realized he was one of Mason's SEALs, she'd shaken her head and had stepped back. At the time she hadn't been interested in permanency.

Obviously he hadn't been either because he had walked away with nothing but a wave and a smile. Just another ship in the night. She didn't know if he'd felt the same crash and burn when they made love that she had or not—all her senses had been fired up, almost like a homecoming. But, when he left, it turned out to be a rude awakening, as she could never forget him.

She had heard about him every once in a while, that he'd been rising up the ranks, but they hadn't crossed paths until today. And this was something she desperately wished hadn't happened. Who needed this kind of crap?

After a life-and-death event like this one, it had Kate thinking. She had already been looking to settle down lately. Yet she hadn't found that special someone, at least not in a permanent way. Only in the last couple years did it really bother her, as she saw others having families. But not her.

She never had a relationship last long enough. She thought it was her fault mostly. Part of it was her circumstances as a navy pilot. She was here, then she was gone; she was there, and then she was gone. This type of job didn't foster permanency.

Those who had come into the military with a stable relationship seemed to go home to them. She hadn't had that. She had a vagabond aspect to her life that she probably couldn't change until she either transferred stateside or decided to ground herself—because the competition for pilots in places like Coronado was huge. And she didn't have the same seniority others did.

Or maybe she needed to change divisions and do something else. Maybe work in the private sector as a commercial pilot. She'd certainly been tempted to do that. She'd had offers she was reconsidering now, since she had about three months left on her current contract. Now if only she could figure out what she wanted to do after that.

CHAPTER 2

AFTER WHAT SEEMED like a long sleep, Kate woke up to find Colton standing at the end of her hospital bed. She started. "Wow," she said. "What a way to wake up."

"You okay?" he asked, grabbing a chair, spinning it around and sitting on it backward. He always had that easy grace she loved.

"I'm alive," she said. "How's George?"

"Stable, but in serious condition. He's no longer here. They airlifted him to the base hospital a few hours ago. They have better facilities for him."

Her eyebrows shot up. "I didn't even wake up," she wailed. "I wanted to say goodbye."

"Let's hope you get a chance to say hello instead," he said with a gentle smile.

She winced at that. "I gather he's in pretty rough shape still?"

"He is," Colton said. "How are you doing?"

"I've been better, but I'm not as cold anymore."

"The doc will check you over again, but I wanted to sneak in beforehand."

"Why?" she asked.

"I wanted as many details as you could give me. I want to make sure we find out who did this."

"You won't be allowed to do anything about it. You

know the military police will be handling it."

"Yep," he said, "I know that. But I also know Mason's team was brought in on several special investigations. Nobody knows about it, but it's been happening for the last year or so."

"I heard rumors too," she said, "but I don't always have access to the same info you guys get."

"I hear you," he said. "You're a hell of a pilot, and I appreciate you keeping me alive up there."

She snorted. "Not sure about being a hell of a pilot. George was at the controls there at the end."

"Nicely done by both of you, but I don't leave alone," Colton said. "I make sure everybody goes with me."

"Yeah, I seem to recall you pitching me from the plane."

"Oh, come on. I—"

She laughed. "Well, George's still alive, and so am I because of you, so thanks."

"Ditto." The two of them just stared at each other, neither mentioning their past. She was unsure how to even bring it up or if she should just move on from it.

Finally Colton asked, "How have you been?"

She shrugged. "Not too bad. And you?" She hated the stilted semiformal tone to their voices.

He cracked a smile. "Never better. Life has been really busy. I just came back from months in Afghanistan. I was hoping to stay in Coronado for a while, but I was asked to go to Greenland to impart some tips and tricks for a training session here," he said with a wry smile.

"So you weren't supposed to be here long?"

"No. Some training here, then to Africa."

"Ah," she said. "I heard you were doing a lot more training these days."

"Yeah, it's definitely shifting my world."

"But you're still an active SEAL?"

"Yes." He tilted his head in a nod, but she could see his eyes studying her, checking her color and making sure she was moving and awake. She shifted in the bed and groaned. "So, how come, even though we didn't hit anything, I feel like my body just got run over by a semi-truck?"

"But you did hit something. You hit the great big ocean. But some of that physical pain is due to the exhaustion from the extreme cold," Colton said. "There's nothing quite like it. It'll take time to recover."

"It feels like I'll never recover," Kate said, collapsing back down again.

"How about some hot drinks?"

"I feel like they damn-near funneled that stuff right into my stomach," she said, "and bypassed my throat."

At that, he burst out laughing. "How about I get you some warm coffee? We'll see if you can drink that."

"Sounds good," she said. And she closed her eyes as he got up and left.

KATE HADN'T LOOKED too bad, which was a blessing because he'd had a look at George, who hadn't looked great. The doctors had high hopes for him to recover, but they weren't sure if he would end up with all his fingers and toes and potentially even his limbs. However, Colton didn't want to look at those problems until necessary. At the moment, he was all about making sure Kate was as good as she could be. Because he needed to know everything she could tell him. He'd wanted to get details, but it was obvious she wasn't doing as well as she could, and he didn't want to impact her healing by revisiting the crash and stirring up unpleasant memories.

He headed into the cafeteria area, picked up two coffees, adding cream and a little bit of sugar to the one for her—it was the way she used to take it—and he knew the sugar wouldn't be a bad thing right now, given her condition. Then he saw fresh muffins. He plated four, added several pats of butter, and, with two knives in his hand, he carried the plate on top of one of the cups and made his way back to the sick bay.

The doctor sitting at a desk to the side looked up and smiled as Colton walked in. "Hopefully some sugar is in that coffee," he said.

Colton nodded and said, "There's a little, but I can get more if need be."

"No," Kate said, "a little is fine."

The doctor helped her raise the upper half of her bed, and, when he stepped back, Colton asked, "How is she?"

"A very lucky lady," he said. "She cheated death twice, both times barely beating it."

"Isn't that the truth?" she murmured. "I'll take barely beating death any day over the alternative." She looked at Colton. "And I owe one of them to you."

"Well, I owe one of them to you, so we're even," Colton said, as he moved a small table beside her and swung it around so it was over her lap. "Here. Get some of this down."

"I wonder how long I'll be cold for," she muttered, hugging the cup.

"Hours, if not days," the doctor said. "Hypothermia, for all that we know about it, can present as different symptoms in different people."

"Interesting," she murmured. "I guess you don't have all that many cases to study."

"Exactly," he said. "At least not severe cases who survived." With that, he gave her a smile and headed off.

Colton sat down at the edge of the bed and said, "Did he give you a free pass?"

"You heard him. I'm doing okay. As long as that continues, I can leave soon."

"We can hope so," Colton said, studying her color. She looked so much better.

"Well, they know we survived, I presume."

"Yes," he said, and then he lowered his voice. "But we haven't spread the word as to what happened."

"Why is that?" she asked.

"Because somebody tried to kill us. We don't want whoever it was to know they didn't succeed. The news is that the plane went down, but not a whole lot has been shared otherwise."

"Great," she said. "I hadn't really considered that." She took a sip of her coffee, wincing as the hot brew hit her throat.

He watched when she settled back. Now she had even more color and a brighter smile. It was her smile that had caught his attention when he had first met her. They'd been an inferno together, and he'd basked in that fire willingly. He'd left the following morning, fully planning on calling her, but his next mission had him gone for months that time. And then his opportunity to reconnect in a timely fashion was gone.

When she didn't take more sips of her coffee, he asked, "Is it too hot?"

"No. It's fine," she said. "It's just that everything is so

sensitive. My lips, tongue, … fingers." She wiggled them at him playfully.

"They will be for a while," he said. "We are being airlifted out today," he said. "We'll leave the destroyer in a few hours. The question is whether you need to go to a specialized medical facility from here or if you will be fine to walk off on your own."

"I'll walk," she said, "but I don't know where my clothes went."

"I'll see what I can find for you." Colton stood and took a sip of coffee. "How many of those muffins will you eat?"

"If you sit down in that chair," she said, "we could share them."

He hesitated.

"Come on. Clothing will wait," she said, "unless you're telling me that we're flying out right now?"

"No," he said. "Not for a few hours yet."

"Then let's eat. I'm starved."

<h1 style="text-align:center">CHAPTER 3</h1>

AFTER COLTON LEFT and returned just long enough to drop off a set of clothing for her, Kate got up slowly, her body shaky and weak. Once she was dressed, she made her way to the facilities and back, sitting on her hospital bed again. She hated to say it, but the cold had taken more from her than she had realized. Plus the rocking movement of the destroyer didn't help her balance any.

When the doctor returned once more, he smiled to see her dressed. "Well, that's a good sign."

She nodded. "I just wasn't expecting to feel quite so weak."

"Your body has taken a huge hit. It's amazing that it can even recover so fast from the stresses you went through. But, in another day or two, I think you'll be right as rain."

"Any update on George?"

"He's still alive," the doctor said cheerfully. "It'll be a few days yet."

She nodded sadly. "Well, let's hope he makes it. He's got three teenage boys, and they need their dad."

The doctor's face sobered. "That they do."

Looking around, she said, "I know Colton is heading out soon, and I was hoping to go with him."

"You can. In about two hours," he said, "so you might as well sit back and relax. We'll have to see if we've got some boots for you."

She looked down at the socks on her feet and smiled. "Did everything get cut off of us?"

He nodded. "Not your boots, but I don't know that we'll get them dry in time."

She nodded, saying, "Even if they're wet, at least they fit."

"I've got people working on it," he said. "We did have to cut everything else off though. Sorry."

"Understood," she said. "I've got on layers of clothing now, so that's at least something." When she shivered again, she shifted back onto the bed and pulled the blanket up around her. "Such a weird feeling," she murmured sleepily.

"Just rest. You'll be out of here in no time." And, with that, the doctor turned and disappeared.

She fell into a light dozing nap, surfacing and waking, going back under again. But, when she woke the next time, she saw her boots sitting beside her. They were partially dry, though not completely, but efforts were ongoing to soak up the moisture. Newspaper had been stuffed inside to absorb a little more too. As she sat up slowly and reached for them, Colton came in.

"Perfect," he said. "I was figuring out what to do about your footwear."

"They cut off everything else," she said, "but apparently not these."

"Which is a good thing," he said. "If they're anything like mine, they'll feel like they're superheavy, unless they're completely dry." He picked them up, pulled out the newspaper and shook his head. "Nope, they sure aren't."

"But they do fit," she said, "so it is what it is."

"Agreed." He waited while she tied up her boots.

Then she looked at him and said, "I gather we're leaving now?"

"We sure are," he said.

Once her boots were tied, she stood. She was still a little woozy, and, with his arms half supporting her, she took several steps forward.

"Let me try walking on my own, see if I can get my sea legs back," she said, then walked around the small room carefully. She smiled and said, "I should be good." The trouble was, she didn't have a jacket, and she was still cold. As if reading her thoughts, Colton said, "My clothes weren't cut off of me, and I was able to get them into a dryer." He took off his jacket and slung it around her shoulders.

She snuggled into the warmth and stopped, closing her eyes. "Wow," she said. "What a difference."

"Remember. You'll feel cold for a while." Snagging her arm, he tucked it in against his elbow. "Come on. Let's go."

She followed him down the ramp and upstairs to the deck of the destroyer. There they stood in the shadows until given clearance. Finally they boarded the helicopter, he behind her, checking on her every move. When she finally sagged into her seat and buckled up, she sighed with relief. "Never would I have thought getting cold like that would have such a debilitating effect for so long."

"Just goes to show you," he said, "how bad it really was."

As soon as the helicopter took off, Kate studied the ocean around them. "Are we still going to the same air base?"

"Yep," he said cheerfully.

Thirty-five minutes later they hovered over the airstrip. "I'm not even sure what I'm supposed to do now. I was heading to the last leg of my flight," she said. "I thought I was taking a flight back to Coronado, but now I'm not sure."

"You need a couple days off," Colton said confidently. "So don't let them send you out just yet."

"I know. Maybe that's why I'm supposed to report to the doctor when I land."

"You came out of the medical bay on the ship," he said. "Standard practice."

When they did land, they were greeted by a team. Kate was separated from Colton and led into another medical bay, where she was checked over and told she was on a forty-eight-hour furlough for medical reasons. She nodded and asked, "Where am I staying?"

One of the men smiled and said, "I'll take you over."

She followed him to some barracks, where she was given a small room to herself. She immediately stretched out on the bed and closed her eyes. She should have asked where Colton was but was so damn tired that she couldn't keep her eyes open, so she didn't fight it.

A knock came on her door sometime later and woke her. "Come in," she called out.

Colton stepped in. "Have you debriefed yet?"

She shook her head. "But, of course, I've got that to do too, don't I?" She groaned and sat up.

"The sooner, the better."

She looked up at him. "Have you?"

"I've just come from there."

She nodded and said, "Better to do it now, if I can."

"That's why I came to get you. I wanted to make sure we got it done as soon as possible. Then it's over, and you can rest." He held out a hand.

Smiling, she placed hers in it.

IT WAS HARD for Colton to not feel the electricity every time he touched her. Even though she still felt sick and was obviously weak, something about this woman stirred his senses like no other. He'd left that morning way back when because that was how he thought she'd wanted it. That was how they'd arranged it, an unspoken agreement—two ships in the night and then carry on. He'd lost track of her for a long time after that.

Then he heard stories. Every once in a while he'd hear her name mentioned, which would bring it all back again. He hadn't realized she was piloting the plane he was on until he'd gone up front. He wondered when she hopped on because he didn't think she'd been there in Coronado. He'd have to ask her, but right now they were approaching the investigators.

Colton had been asked what condition she was in, and he'd volunteered to see if she was willing to do this now. It was obviously better for everyone if they could debrief now and get as much information as possible in the hands of the investigators. Colton pulled up a chair for her and helped her sit down. He knew she wasn't that weak, but it wouldn't hurt for the investigators to understand she was still recovering.

With that, the interview got started. She answered all the questions honestly, at least Colton thought so, if he was any good at reading body language. She had no idea what had happened, just that the left engine blew up without warning. She did explain about her ex-boyfriend and about George's legal case.

By the time they were done, Colton hadn't learned anything new, and that was frustrating. He had hoped she would have picked up something. Then the questions started in his direction again. *Had he seen anything before he boarded in Coronado? Had he seen anyone unauthorized around the plane?* He shook his head. He turned to look at her.

"You didn't board at Coronado, did you?"

She shook her head. "No, Halifax. I was on layover and joined George there."

He nodded. "And, no," he said, as he turned to face the others. "I didn't see anything on that layover either."

"We already asked the Canadian government to take a look at their video cameras," one of the investigators said in frustration. "We do have a good rapport with them, and they sent them right over, but, so far we haven't picked up anybody or anything suspicious on them."

"Several other soldiers were there," Colton said. "Two other American planes were at the base."

"Yes. One ran into trouble and was flying with the second, so both landed," he said. "But that was a different story entirely."

"Maybe," Colton said, "but it was opportunity, if someone was looking for one."

"For one of the other soldiers on the other flights?"

"If this was on purpose, then, yeah," Colton said.

"It's not like the passengers on the other flights would have known they were landing at Gander International Airport," he said.

"No, but it's a normal flight path," he said, "so was always a possibility."

"I hope you're not saying the other plane that ran into some trouble was also sabotaged?"

"No," Colton said. "I mean, it's possible obviously, but that would be taking a big risk."

"If you think about it," Kate said, "it expands the suspect

pool."

The men facing them stared at her.

She shrugged. "Well, just think about it. Now you have to consider all those people."

"Do the video cameras cover all the angles all the time?" Colton asked.

The men shook their heads. "No, but their camera system is good, and it would have been similar to ours," one said. "And we all know that, if somebody wanted something to happen, it's not out of the realm of possibility."

"Unfortunately it's all too possible," Colton said. He looked over to see Kate's color fading quickly. "Gentlemen, I think that needs to be all for the day. We can come back tomorrow, if needed."

The men nodded, and Colton reached out a hand to Kate.

She looked at him gratefully, then addressed the investigators. "I'm more than happy to answer more questions," she said, "I just don't know what else I can tell you."

"If we have more questions, we'll get in touch with you tomorrow. You'll be at least two days recovering, and then I understand you're heading back stateside when you can, right?"

"Yes," she said.

"So you're here forty-eight hours anyway and grounded indefinitely, until we get to the bottom of this. It's nothing personal. We just need to have you available for questioning."

KATE TOOK IT like a sock to her gut, but she rallied and smiled at them. "Let's hope we get a fast answer to all this," and, with a salute, she turned, and Colton led her back outside again.

"Wow," she said. "I didn't expect to be grounded."

"I think it's twofold on their part. Not only were you part of the sabotage plot," he said, "but, if you fly again, and somebody is targeting you, then whoever goes on your flight is also potentially in danger."

She stared up at him, her eyes filled with pain. "That's not what I wanted to think about," she snapped. But he just smiled at her, as if waiting for her to come around. She sighed. "Okay, fine, so it makes logical sense. I just don't like it."

"None of us ever do," he said. "Now, before you crash for the night, how about some food?"

"That would be good," she said. "That muffin was tasty, but it wasn't enough."

"It was two muffins," he said, "and I'm pretty sure you ate part of my second one too."

"Who's counting?" she said with an airy wave of her hand. "But, if we can get some food, that would be good." She shrugged and said, "I don't even know what time it is here."

"It's coming on dinner," Colton said, "so let's head there first."

"I need to figure out where my room is," Kate said, turning in confusion. "I'm lost."

"I'll take you back afterward."

She looked at him. "You'll be here for the next few days too, won't you?"

"Yeah, it seems like my plans might have changed."

"You're not heading off again?"

"No," he said just as cheerfully as before, with almost too much enthusiasm. "I'm grounded as well."

"I'm sorry," she murmured. "It's been a shit day all around."

Inside the mess tent they each picked up a tray and walked down the aisle of food. There was lots of it, and it was all hot. Kate didn't recognize many of the dishes, but she was happy to take whatever was offered. She could hear Colton asking for beef and gravy and getting her plate filled so it was heaping. She stared at it and looked at him sideways.

"Remember the muffins?" he said in a low voice. "Sometimes you come out of a trauma like that without any appetite at all, and sometimes you come out of that extreme-cold situation, feeling like you're starving and can't get full."

"Well, as I first looked at this, I was thinking it was way too much," she said, "but now I'm wondering if it's enough."

"We're not done yet either," Colton said and moved her along, where he served her a hot bowl of soup. "Let's go sit over there."

With their trays set down, she sat carefully and took everything off her tray. Colton took it from her and smiled.

"I'll be back in a minute," he said, then disappeared, only to return with water and more coffee.

She smiled at that. "Do you always treat people so nicely?"

"Always," he said. "It doesn't cost anything to be kind."

"True," she said, feeling bad because, of course, she'd been teasing him, but he really was being very helpful in looking after her. When they were both seated, she started in on the soup and stopped to savor the first spoonful. "Wow, this is really good."

"The soup will help warm you up faster than anything," Colton said. "I can see you're still cold."

Kate looked down at her fingers, still on the verge of trembling. "My body still needs a couple days, right?"

"Definitely a couple days," he agreed.

By the time Kate had finished her soup and had started in on her plate, she began to feel a little better, but, when halfway through, she felt her energy waning. She kept eating, but it was more of an effort. When she finally stopped, she just looked at Colton.

"Let's go," he said. "Let's get you back to bed before you can't walk anymore."

"Too late," she said, standing and wavering on her feet. He gripped her arm and wrapped it around his waist and then wrapped an arm around her. Carefully he moved her through the cafeteria, and she knew when a silence fell around them that they were being watched. "I'm sorry. I'm making a spectacle of myself."

"Don't you worry," he said. "They probably all know what we've survived, and those who didn't now will."

"Yeah, but how come I'm so weak and not you?" she grumbled. He chuckled, the sound lovely against her ear.

"It's not that it's you or me," he said. "We're both survivors. Latch on to that and don't forget it. Everybody here isn't thinking about what kind of shape we're in. Every one of them is damn grateful they weren't in our position."

She smiled at that. "If you say so." But she could see that, if she had been here watching someone else in her situation, she would be feeling very sympathetic and also grateful it hadn't been her. Back in her small room, Colton opened the door and helped her so she could collapse on the bed.

"I don't want you sleeping in your clothes like that," he warned.

"What difference does it make? Sleep is sleep," she muttered, collapsing on her back and staying there.

"No," he said. "It isn't. You really need to get restorative sleep. You need to be comfortable, so you can get the best sleep you can."

"I couldn't possibly *not* sleep if I tried," she said. "You have no idea how exhausted I am."

"Actually I do," he said, "and so I still worry. At least let's get those boots off you—and the pants." And, true to his words, he had her boots unbuckled and pulled off in no time.

She said, "I need the socks on though."

"No way, they're wet from the boots."

She managed to sit up again and said, "You'll have to leave."

He grinned and said, "You don't have anything I haven't seen."

"Maybe," she said with a tiny smile, "but it doesn't feel the same."

"No," he said, "it's not at all the same. But you're being

foolish because what you need to be is tucked under that blanket right now, so shuck those pants and get that shirt off. I'll turn my back."

She stripped down quickly, before dashing under the covers.

"Damn it, your lips are turning blue." Swearing, Colton grabbed another blanket from the cupboard and placed it on top of her. "Do you need another one?" he asked, and she could feel the worry in his tone and the waves of concern emanating from him.

She shook her head, trying to stop her teeth from chattering. "I should be good," she said. "I just need to sleep."

"But will you?" he asked.

"I'll be fine," she said. "Go get some rest. I'll be okay."

"I'm only two doors down, if you run into trouble."

"What kind of trouble can I be getting into? I'll just be lying here, sleeping."

"Don't lock the door, please," he said. "I'll come in and check on you."

"Okay, good for you. I'm sure I'll be snoring, so don't wake me up." On that note, she closed her eyes, and, as her body trembled, she sank deeper into the covers. Once she heard the door shut behind him, she let out a deep sigh and let sleep overtake her.

COLTON HATED TO leave her alone like that, but she, at least, had been conscious, eating and moving well—up until now. But it seemed to hit her like a ton of bricks while she ate. He made his way to his room and sat down. He hadn't been here long when a soldier knocked on his door, saying he had an important phone call. Following the man, Colton hoped it was Mason responding to the message he'd left for him earlier.

"What the hell happened?" Mason asked.

It was with a relief of sorts that Colton told him the whole story.

"Holy shit," Mason said. "Are you guys okay?"

"I am. Kate'll be all right, but I don't know about George. I haven't had an update."

"I'll find out," Mason said. "And Kate'll make it?"

"She's shaky, but she was up, moving around, and she ate well at dinnertime but then crashed. She's in bed now."

"That hypothermia is deadly," Mason said, with a note of warning.

"I know. I don't really want to leave her alone, but she didn't want company."

"Is this Kate? As in *Kate*, Kate?"

Colton winced at that, having forgotten Mason had seen him the morning after he'd been with her. "Yeah," he said heavily. "It's her."

At that, Mason whistled. "Wow. Looks like we've done it again."

"Hell, no," Colton said indignantly. "That's your shit, not mine."

"Apparently it affects everybody who is part of my group," Mason said, chuckling. "And make sure you work things out while you're alive and well because, if somebody tried once to kill her, you don't know that they won't try again."

"We have to figure out whether she was the target or George," Colton said.

"Yes, but, from a safety perspective at this point, it doesn't matter which one it was," Mason said. "Because, even if it was George, chances are they'll be afraid she saw something. So watch it, or you'll end up losing her before you ever get her back again. That means, you could be at risk as well. Now are you sure you're feeling okay?"

By the time the phone call ended, Colton was a little more disturbed than he'd wanted to consider. Just because he was here for a training mission didn't mean other people wouldn't be around who couldn't be trusted. It was a small group, and they were doing Arctic training. He didn't even know for sure who was coming in. He wasn't supposed to be here himself originally, but a lecturer had stepped aside on short notice, and the leader had asked for assistance. So, of course, Colton had stepped up.

Besides, Troy had asked for help. Now, if Colton could find the guy who sabotaged the cargo plane, then maybe things could move forward at a regular pace. The courses in the training session weren't supposed to start for another three days, and Colton wasn't sure if the inspectors would have enough time to get to the bottom of what had happened to Kate and George by then. Colton was still hoping for a good update on George too. Thinking about Troy, Colton called Mason back. "Hey, one more thing. Any update on Troy?"

"He's arriving tomorrow," came back the answer. He was already in transit, which would explain why Colton hadn't heard anything.

"So, is there any way you can get me a laptop and a phone?"

"I know one of the guys who's coming for your training. He should have landed already. Let me see if I can get something from the base for you. It would only be basic-level equipment but—"

"I lost everything," Colton said. "I'll have to talk to the insurance adjuster about it, I guess, but there won't likely be anything worth claiming."

"Cell phone, laptop, what else?"

"Personals, gear, toiletries, that's it."

"Let me talk to the base and see what we can do."

And, with that, Colton had to be satisfied. They ended the call, and he returned to the barracks, grabbed the towel he'd been given and walked to the showers, where he stood under the hot water and scrubbed. When he finally dried off, he put on his same clothes again and headed back to his room. He didn't see another soul while he was there. This was normally a fairly isolated place, and he preferred that in most instances. But tonight he would have liked to have a bit of access to the outside world.

In the middle of the night, he woke up but didn't understand why. He lay here, listening for sounds, but he didn't hear anything out of the ordinary. A wind had picked up outside and was definitely howling as it vented around the buildings, trying to bend them to its will. But instead it just left a weird eerie feeling.

Not exactly sure what was going on, he hopped out of bed, threw on his pants, and, barefoot, padded down toward Kate's room. He listened outside her door and heard her whimpering inside. He knocked gently, and, when he got no answer, he opened the door and stepped inside. The room was in darkness, but he didn't need a light to see her pale skin as she tossed on the bed, the sheet barely covering any of her. He grabbed the sheet and blankets and pulled them around her. He sat down beside her, his hand going to her cheek as he gently stroked it and whispered, "You're safe now, Kate. It's okay."

She whimpered again, curling against his hand, while he gently used his other to stroke the side of her face and her hair. "I'm so sorry this happened to you," he said. "It will get better."

<h1 align="center">CHAPTER 5</h1>

K ATE WOKE UP with a start, caught between the arctic chill of her nightmare and the heated warmth of somebody's hand. Somebody she recognized, bringing back a longing from years before. She stared up at Colton's familiar face and gasped. "Oh, my God. How long will the nightmares last?"

"Quite a while probably," he said, and, picking up her hand, he held it against his cheek. "It will get better though. I can promise you that."

She shook her head. "It just seemed like all I could think about was the engine blowing up and the wing falling off and the crash," she said. "The parachuting down wasn't a problem, but, when I slammed into that icy-cold water, everything inside me went numb. I don't know how I stayed afloat as long as I did."

"I'm grateful you did," Colton said, "because it was hard enough to keep George afloat. Once you started to sink too, I knew I couldn't hold both of you up for long."

"I don't know how you did it at all. But I knew George needed to stay up," she said. "He has a family. Those boys need their father."

"That doesn't make your life any less valuable." Colton stroked the sweaty strands of hair off her face. "Can you sleep again now?"

She rolled over, blowing out a long sigh, and stared at the small room. "I guess," she said. She could hear the wind howling around the small building. "It's such a strange location, isn't it?"

"I like it. I didn't realize the actual training I came for wasn't due to start for another couple days though."

"Are you giving or receiving?"

"I wasn't supposed to be here at all, but Troy is doing some of the instruction, and he needed a hand, so I'll be helping him teach as well."

Kate laughed at that. "Me, I'm just spare baggage apparently," and then she started to shiver again. She cried out, "Oh, my God, I'm so damn cold all the time."

Colton grabbed another blanket and piled it on top of her. She curled up underneath, but no way he couldn't feel her shivering underneath. "I need more clothes," she said, struggling to keep her teeth from chattering.

"Do you want me to grab your T-shirt?"

"I already put it back on at some point," she said. "It's amazing how much not having pajamas makes a difference."

"You're used to California. Out there it's not necessary to wear anything to bed."

"No," she said. "Except when I get chilled, when I get *really* chilled." She lay underneath the blankets, shuddering in the darkness. "What time is it anyway?"

"I think it's just around midnight, but maybe it's a little after."

"And, of course, we have no cell phones," she said, then groaned. "I think I still had a year to pay on that contract too. Damn it."

He smiled. "I'm sure there'll be some compensation for this, wouldn't you think?"

"At least I didn't have my laptop," she said. "I stopped packing it when the phones got so advanced. What about you?"

"My laptop, other electronics, my phone, my personal gear," he said cheerfully. "Yep. All gone."

"How can you be so chipper about it?" she muttered, focused on the upcoming hassle of dealing with the phone contract and getting a new phone. "I wonder if we can even get phones up here."

"If we go into town, we can," he said, "but you might want to wait until you get back to the States."

"Yeah," she said, stifling a yawn. "*If* I'm going home in another day anyway, it'll be inconvenient, but I'll survive."

"It really goes to show how much our world has changed," Colton said. "That we can't go anywhere without feeling lost without technology."

"It's a convenience. An instant gratification. I can get my emails. I get chat messages from family and friends. And I can check the weather," she said, with a hand wave to the window. "From the gusty winds out there, it sounds like a hell of a storm."

"I don't think it's a storm at all," he said. "I think it's literally just wind."

"You're kidding? That's depressing," she said, and again another yawn took over.

"But back to our phones. I like always being able to check the time," Colton said with a smile. He straightened, and Kate watched sadly as he walked to the doorway.

"Why did you never call me?" she asked impulsively.

He stopped, looked at her in surprise and turned the tables on her. "Why did you never call me?"

"It felt weird to," she said honestly. "I kept hoping you'd

call me."

His smile flashed in delight. "And maybe I was hoping you'd call me too," he teased.

"I guess I'm not as modern and forward-thinking as I thought," she said. "Because it didn't feel right, you know? I knew you were really busy, and so was I."

"So why don't we leave it as, *It just wasn't the right time.*" He gave her a gentle smile and said, "Now I'll head back to bed. Try to get some sleep." He shut the door softly behind him.

She lay here, listening to the wind howling outside, thinking about his words about it not being the right time.

So when was the right time? Was there a right time? Or had that right time come and gone, and she had failed to pick up the opportunity when it came by? She had wanted to spend a lot more time with him but felt awkward about trying to call him the morning after—as if they had this odd system in place, where it was for one night only and never again.

At the time she hadn't been looking for anything more, but she couldn't stop thinking about him afterward, and it had bothered her that she never got the chance to see him again, that she never heard back from him. He'd been busy off on missions; she'd been busy flying all over the place. And yet, in all those years, they still hadn't reconnected. And now, of all the times for them to connect, she had to admit this was one of the best times for it. After all, he had saved George's life.

He had saved her life too.

As questions ran through her mind, she lay tucked under the blankets, trying desperately to warm up again. She understood it would take time, and sometimes she thought she was doing better, and then, all of a sudden, she wouldn't be so good. This was one of those times. She realized, now that she was wide awake, how she needed to get up and go to the bathroom. And that meant putting more clothes on to get down the hallway. Only to take away some once there.

She grabbed her pants and pulled them on, then slipped the still-damp socks over her bare feet. She opened the door and moved as quickly and as quietly as she could to the communal bathroom. Once inside, she used the facilities, washed up and opened the door to step back out. She almost screamed at the tall figure standing in front of her.

"Easy," Colton said.

"Oh, my gosh," she said, "you scared me."

"Sorry. I didn't mean to, but I heard you running this way and wanted to make sure you were okay."

"So, the problem with being cold and awake," she said, "is that my bladder won't stop calling to me."

"It's to be expected. You'd have the same problem any-time you woke up, but the cold just makes it harder to ignore."

"True enough." Stepping out, she said, "It's empty now, if you need to use it."

"I'll just follow you back to your room."

She looked up at him in surprise. "Any reason for that?"

"The escort? Just being a gentleman," he said smoothly.

She snorted. "Well, the last time we met, and you were escorting me to the bedroom, a gentleman you were not."

"Hey," he said. "Now that was a two-way street."

"It was, indeed. I guess I wasn't much of a lady, at that," she said with a laugh. In truth, the sex had been hot and heavy and hadn't stopped from the time they'd started to the time they had to leave. "It took me days to recover from that night," she said with a laugh.

"Me too," Colton said. "We were a couple rabbits."

"That sounds terrible," she protested.

He burst out laughing. "It didn't sound very classy, did it?"

"Nope," she said. "It sounds disgusting, but it's very honest." At her door she smiled up at him. "Thanks for the escort." She frowned and mumbled, "Wait. I didn't leave a light on."

"What was that?" He turned to face her, a questioning look on his face.

"I didn't turn my light on before I left," she said, "but look. The lamp is on." Colton stepped inside, closed the door behind her and held a finger up to his lips. She nodded, but nobody could have hidden in this tiny space she called her room. There was a closet, but it had no door, and it was open and empty, as far as she could see. There was the bed, and the only option was under it.

Colton dropped to the floor and checked, but it was empty.

"What the devil?" Kate said, turning to look around. "Am I losing my mind?"

"I don't think so. Maybe it wasn't you who I heard running."

She stared at him. "To the bathroom? I wasn't running. I moved fast—as fast as I could, given the circumstances—because I was cold, but I didn't run."

"No," he said. "Now that I think about it, I should have known. Damn it." He ran his hand through his hair, frustrated. "Somebody else was running down the hallway. You wouldn't have been in the bathroom long enough by the time I was standing there." He frowned, then turned and said, "The chances of catching anybody at this point are nonexistent. They are long gone."

"But why would somebody have been in my room anyway?" Kate asked softly. Confusion and fear spiked through her. "How would anybody have known where I was?"

"We are new arrivals," Colton said, "and got here with a fair bit of excitement, I'm sure. So it's not hard to imagine other people know we're here. Remember how it was when we were at dinner in the mess hall?"

"I get that." Kate looked around and sighed. "It doesn't make me feel any better though."

"My room has bunks," he said, "so you're welcome to grab one, if you want."

She thought about it and then nodded. "You know what? Maybe I should. I don't think I'd sleep another wink knowing somebody was in here. Particularly as I don't know why."

Colton looked around and said, "Do you have anything in here to move?"

She shook her head. "I'm wearing it, except my boots."

"Good. Maybe that also confused him, except that the blankets were turned back, so it's obvious somebody had been sleeping there. Come on. Let's go."

He left the light on, then shut the door. He also set a hair in such a way that, if somebody opened the door, it would fall. She watched him but didn't question it. He just smiled and led her to his room. There, he said, "I'm in the bottom bunk. Are you okay with the top?"

She nodded, shivering still, and said, "At this point"—her teeth chattering again—"I just want to get warm."

"Up you go," he said, "and maybe I'll return to your room and grab those blankets."

"Unless you have some here," she said. He checked the closet and pulled out two. He tossed them over her and tucked her in as much as he could from where he stood. She rolled over against the wall and muttered, "Good night." She waited until he settled back into his own bunk before she relaxed.

A part of her wondered about taking their relationship back to the same level it had been. Only she didn't want to go backward because she didn't want what they'd had, since that had been based solely on sex. She wanted to go forward to something better; she just didn't know how to get there. She wasn't very good at relationships. She'd had plenty of them, but they never lasted more than a few months.

She thought she was a giving, caring person and didn't understand why her relationships kept breaking down. One man had said she didn't seem to care enough, and another had said she cared too much. She figured she couldn't win. Her mother always told her that she just hadn't met the right man and that he'd come along eventually. She didn't know about that either because she'd dated a lot, and there certainly wasn't any sign of the right man for her coming around.

Her mom also hadn't really liked any of the men she'd brought home either. And Kate never introduced someone to her parents unless she had been seeing them for several months. She had tried living with one guy, thinking it was a step in the right direction, but she couldn't handle it. He had been such a messy person to live with, expecting her to be his maid, that she'd found herself screaming at him. He had finally packed up and walked out on her.

She knew she'd overreacted, but, when his hair was everywhere from his shaving—all over the mirror, the sink and the faucets, and he hadn't cleaned up any of it, clearly expecting her to—she'd come undone. She had already had the pick-up-after-yourself conversation with him. Yet his socks and clothes remained on the floor. Until he left. For once he had picked up after himself.

After that, she muted her responses a lot and often checked out the guy's bathroom to see how bad it was. She figured, just out of respect and common courtesy for others, plus a sense of self-responsibility, that people would clean up their own messes, but apparently that wasn't a theory held by all. It was such a dumb thing to have lost it over, but it had been an accumulation of his other aspects. He had just looked at her, like she was being so picky. He had said, if she didn't like it, why wasn't she cleaning it up?

On that note, she stopped wondering about the vagaries of relationships and the problems within them. Then she closed her eyes and let sleep snag her up and take her under again.

COLTON WOKE UP the next morning and froze. Something was different. Then he realized the breathing he heard was Kate above him. He slid out of bed and checked on her. She slept heavily. He picked up his blanket and tossed it over her, so she'd have yet another layer of warmth and headed to the bathroom. He used the facilities, scrubbed his teeth, and washed his face and hair. Realizing it had to be at least sevenish from the light outside, he headed to her assigned room.

At the door, he squatted to see the hair was still in place, so nobody had entered the room since. He stepped back into his room and finished dressing, then made up his bunk without the blanket and slipped out again. If he could find coffee, he'd bring a cup back for her. As he headed toward the mess tent, the base commander stepped out of a building and called him over.

Colton saluted and was told, "At ease, son. Come in and take a seat." As Colton sat down, the commander said, "You want to tell me what happened yesterday?"

He raised his eyebrows. "Yesterday?"

The commander waved his hand. "You guys crashed in the ocean and were picked up, correct?"

Colton nodded.

"Can you give me any details on the flight?"

Colton gave him a rundown, adding, "We lost everything, from our cell phones, my laptop and our personal gear and bags."

"Good thing you weren't taking off on a big holiday," the commander said with a half smirk. "You could have lost a lot more."

"So true. We do need to roust up some cell phones though, as soon as possible."

"I hear you. I have a laptop you can probably use. I was talking to a couple men at the Coronado base."

Colton frowned. "Was it Mason?"

"Yes, Mason. Smart man. He's asked for you to have a laptop for your use while you're here, and he's airlifting a cell phone for you."

"Good," Colton said. "That would be helpful. And the laptop would be appreciated."

"Mind telling me what it is you plan on doing with it?"

Colton lowered his voice and said, "Looking into the sabotage issue, sir."

The commander nodded. "We do have MPs too, you

know? Now, son, I can't have you going around half-cocked, thinking you're James Bond."

"More like Sherlock, sir," Colton said with a smile.

"Same diff as far as I'm concerned. You can work with my MPs, who will be assigned to this investigation. How long are you supposed to be here?"

"I was tagged to help Troy on an upcoming training session."

"That may have to get pushed back a few days," the commander said. "We've got a really ugly weather front coming in, and, when I say *ugly*, I mean ugly. Nobody is going outside if it remains like that."

"Wow," Colton said. "I hadn't expected that."

"Nope, I don't imagine you did. We've got a bunch of guys coming in early for the training too. But nobody will be training outside if that weather doesn't lighten up. We'll put them up for a few days, but, if need be, we'll cancel the whole thing."

Colton nodded. "I guess the supplies don't last long if you're multiplying your numbers and keeping the men inside."

"We're well supplied, and I don't give a rat's ass about the cost, but keeping you all out of trouble when you're bored stiff is not my cup of tea," he said. "I expect good behavior from everybody visiting my base."

"Absolutely, sir."

The commander stood and asked, "And what about her? What kind of trouble will she be?"

Colton jumped to his feet. "None, I believe, sir."

"She already is," the commander said with a grimace. "She's young. She's attractive, and she's a pilot. My boys have already noticed. Believe me."

"Speaking of which," Colton said and then frowned, wondering if he should mention it.

The commander dropped back into his seat and said, "Speak up, son."

"She had a visitor last night. And it wasn't an invited visitor." When he explained what happened, the commander's brows drew together, thick and angry. "I sure hope you're not accusing anybody of anything," he said, his gaze slowly searching Colton's.

"Not accusing anybody of anything, sir," Colton said. "Only that somebody went into her room during the middle of the night and then took off running."

"Interesting," the commander said, staring around the room, his fingers thrumming on the table. "We're a small base here. I run a tight ship and don't tolerate anybody causing trouble."

Colton knew the commander was referring to him. He nodded slowly. "Just thought I'd mention it, sir."

"The only reason I'm even paying attention," he said, "is because Mason spoke so highly of you."

"Thank you, sir," Colton said, realizing he would have to build trust with this man, and fast.

"If you hear of anything else happening, you let me know," he said, "but don't go talking to anybody."

"Anybody?"

"No investigative work without my MPs involved."

"Agreed," Colton said. It was standard practice anywhere. The MPs had to be involved.

The commander gave him a hard look. But Colton stared back easily, comfortable with authority. You didn't get anywhere in life if you didn't get along with it somewhat. They had to know they could count on you. And, if there was one thing Colton prided himself on, it was being counted on.

The commander cleared his throat and asked, "Where is she?"

"Still sleeping," Colton admitted. "She didn't have a good night."

"After a trauma like you three survived, I highly doubt anybody would. She probably needs to visit with our resident shrink."

"I'll tell her that when she wakes up."

The commander snorted. "No. Have her come to me when she's awake and had some breakfast. I'd like to see her condition for myself, and it won't be optional. Make that an order."

Colton understood. It was up to the base commander to keep the base and everyone on it safe. If she was traumatized, she would need help, and the sooner she received it, the better, for everyone's sake.

He walked back to the mess hall. Breakfast was available, but he was more interested in coffee. He grabbed a cup for himself and walked over to the window and sat down. The day was still gray with lots of wind. He could see how the weather was heading for an ugly squall but didn't know how long that would last. When somebody sat down at his table, he was surprised to be addressed personally.

"About time you got here, Colton," a familiar voice said.

He turned, his eyes wide as he smiled and reached across, and the two men gripped forearms. "Damn, it's good to see you, Troy," he said. "I thought you weren't in this early."

"That's my line," Troy said with a chuckle. "When you come in for a hard landing, you come in for a hard landing."

"Didn't plan on the hard landing until that plane cracked apart, and we ended up in the Arctic Ocean," Colton said.

"Yeah, so how are you doing?"

"I'm okay, just haven't had much sleep. The copilot's still sleeping, but she had nightmares throughout the night, and I just couldn't sleep."

"It's pretty traumatizing," Troy said. "Any idea what happened?"

"I think we're leaning toward sabotage," Colton said, "but it'll be hard to do much about it from up here."

"Not necessarily," Troy said. "I understand you told Mason?"

"What you mean is, you've already talked to Mason," Colton said with a chuckle.

"Well, I might have," Troy said. "I came in early to ensure we had all the gear for the training. And then I asked if you could give me a hand with it. But apparently, according to the commander, as of this morning, it's looking like the training may be pushed off a couple days, due to ugly weather."

"I don't know if that's good or bad," Colton said. "The longer I'm here, the more I'll just think."

"You'll do what you can do from here. I'm sure the Coronado base is doing a full search, as is the Halifax base and the international airport."

"I didn't see anybody around the plane," he said.

"Doesn't mean it wasn't put on in Coronado," Troy said. "You also have to consider a remote detonation."

Colton stared at him. "That's a long way for a remote detonation."

"Not if it was somebody else's cell phone," he said. "What if that phone—say your copilot's—rang while you were up there? And maybe she answered it, and it triggered an alarm to blow up the plane?"

Colton froze. "You know what? I was sitting there, half dozing, and I did hear a phone. I don't know how close to the engine blowing up that was though."

"Everybody else is thinking a timer had to be on it maybe," Troy said. "But I would think it's much more likely that somebody called her number, or George's, and, as soon as that phone rang, it triggered the bomb itself."

"God, I should have thought of that already," Colton said, shaking his head. "It's just been so crazy that it hadn't even crossed my mind."

"That's why I'm here to help," Troy said, smiling broadly. "You know how much I love a good mystery."

"Good thing," Colton said, "because this one is looking a little too convoluted, or we're just making it that way when it's damn obvious."

"I understand George is up as a witness against some of his coworkers."

"Yes, we spoke of it a little, while I was keeping some fight in him in that icy water," Colton said. "Damn, I should have asked the commander for an update on him. He might have an answer faster than Mason."

"We'll see the commander later," Troy said. "We can always ask him then."

Colton nodded. "I hear you. I was planning on taking coffee back to Kate, but the longer she sleeps, the better."

"*Kate*, is it?"

"Yep," Colton confirmed without saying anything. But he knew from the twinkle in Troy's eye that Troy already knew. "Mason?"

Troy gave a casual shrug as he settled back, a smile playing at the corner of his lips. "Maybe," he said. "But it wasn't just the two of you at that big party that night all those years ago."

"Shit," Colton said. "Were you there too?"

"I was. I had my eye on her too, but she only saw you."

"Well, considering that she's tucked up in the top bunk above my bed right now, that night didn't make too much of an impression."

Colton kept to himself their discussion about why he'd never called because he didn't have a good answer, except that some things you just knew were a minefield. As much as he'd wanted to stay and to be with her, it would have changed his life completely, and he just hadn't been ready. He meant it when he had said it wasn't the right time. That didn't necessarily mean it wasn't the right time for her, but it wasn't the right time for him to have a relationship. He wondered if now was the better time.

Yet, when he looked back on it and thought about decisions he had made, sometimes he had to wonder where his head was that he would walk away from someone so gorgeous, kind and caring like her.

"She's a really nice girl," Troy said. "And, if the time is right for you guys now, that's perfect."

"Whoa, whoa, whoa," Colton said. "It's hardly anything that serious."

"You've been through a hell of a bonding experience," Troy said, chuckling. "So, breakfast first or do you want to go wake her?"

"She needs sleep." Colton looked at the food, raised his nose tentatively and said, "Besides, the food is fresh and hot right now." He looked at Troy. "You?"

"Absolutely. Come on. Let's go." And, with that, the two men walked toward the food line.

K ATE WOKE UP in a haze of warmth, immediately aware of the aroma of coffee. Her eyes flew open to see a smiling Colton in front of her, holding a big mug of hot coffee.

"That better be for me," she croaked. She cleared her throat and tried again with a smile this time. "And thank you."

He chuckled. "I don't know if you have a place up there to put this," he said, studying the area and then shaking his head. "Better to have you get up and get dressed, or maybe sit up so you can hold it at least."

"The only clothes I've got, I'm already wearing," she said, but she shifted to lean crosswise against the wall and crossed her legs, pulling her blankets up. Then she reached out a hand for the mug. Colton stood on his bunk so he could hand it to her. As soon as the transfer was made, she sagged back and held it, eyes closed. "Nothing quite like hot coffee first thing in the morning," she murmured, her eyes still closed as she let the warmth of the cup bathe her face.

"An interesting reaction," he said. "First you were almost aggressive, and then, when you realized you were getting coffee," he said, "you're just like a sleepy kitten."

"Unless you try to take it away from me," she said and then laughed. "I do appreciate it, by the way." She looked at him. "Have you eaten already too?"

He nodded. "At least an hour ago."

She wrinkled her nose. "Did I miss breakfast?"

"I don't think you missed it," he said. "I think food should be available for at least another half hour."

"Well, I better get up and moving so I get there in time."

Colton thought about it for a moment and then said, "Maybe I can bring you a plate, if you want."

"If you could, that would be really lovely."

"Let me go see," he said. "Every base has different rules."

Kate nodded. "If you can't, let me know, so I have enough time to get there, okay? But I really am still tired and so damn cold."

"Stay there, and I'll check it out." He disappeared from in front of her, slipping quietly out the door. She waited, aware of the passage of time. She was still sleepy, but getting that warm coffee down was her priority. The fact that she even got to wake up today was something she was incredibly blessed to do, and she could only hope George had woken up too. She didn't want to think about losing him. He was a good pilot and a good man.

He had done what was right, and, although some people wouldn't agree with his choice, he was trying to do the right thing. Because military personnel using military flights for something like drug running wasn't anyone they could ever count on. Those were the selfish users of the world, and every company—whether government, military, or large corporations—knew that was a cancer which had to be removed.

Just when she was nearing the bottom of her cup, the door opened, and Colton entered with a large tray. She stared at the food in delight. "Wow, it must have been okay then. Thanks!" She tossed back the last of her coffee and shifted into a better position. From that viewpoint, she realized Colton hadn't come alone. "Hi, I'm Kate," she said. "Who are you?"

"Troy Landry." He reached out a hand and said, "I'd shake, but you're a little far away."

"Consider it shaken," she said, as she leaned forward to grab the tray from Colton. "This looks absolutely wonderful." She stared down at the food. "So did you pick up all this for the three of us, or have you both eaten?"

"We've both eaten," Troy said, laughing. "So, if you think you can do justice to that, then go for it."

Kate beamed at him. "I can do fair justice to it, and I'm so cold that I figure an extra bit of food wouldn't hurt."

"You need it," Colton said. "So dig in."

She nodded. "Will the coffee shut down too?"

Colton reached up a hand for her cup, and it took a little bit of maneuvering to not spill the tray, but she got the empty cup to him, and the two men disappeared again. She tucked right into the food, starting with sausages, bacon, eggs and toast. Pancakes were underneath as well. By the time the guys returned with a cup of coffee, they were joking back and forth, and her plate was half gone.

Colton looked at it and said, "I'm glad to see you've got an appetite."

"More than I expected," she mumbled, chewing a bite of toast. She stared at the coffee with longing. "If you can just find a place to put that for the moment, I'll get to it soon." He nodded, put it down and then held up two big cookies. Her eyes widened. "I can't eat those."

"I was thinking of later," he said.

She smiled. "That sounds good. At least they won't

starve us up here."

"No," Colton said, "but the base commander does want to speak with you."

Her stomach clenched tight at that, but she nodded. "To be expected. I do need to offer my appreciation for the assistance and care I've been shown."

"That would be the prudent thing. By the way, he's also a little touchy about any talk of sabotage."

"But it wouldn't have been done here," she said, studying the two men.

"That brings up a question," Colton said. "Just before the explosion, did either of you receive a phone call?"

Kate frowned, then thought back and nodded. "I'm not exactly sure of the timing, but I did get a call. Why?"

"Did you look at the Caller ID or answer the call?"

"Nobody was there. I think it was a private caller, but no one answered when I clicked on it."

Troy looked at Colton and nodded.

"What does that mean?" she asked suspiciously.

"It means, the bomb could have been installed earlier," Colton said, "but we think it was triggered by the phone call to you."

She frowned. "What? Meaning, if I hadn't answered, it wouldn't have blown up?"

"No. It probably would have blown up regardless, maybe after a certain number of rings or even when voicemail kicked in, but the fact that you did pick it up meant it triggered the detonation when it did."

Her mind churned on the possibilities. She swallowed hard. "Well, that sucks."

"When people want to do something like this," Troy said, "they do it and don't leave much to chance."

She nodded.

"There wasn't much left to chance on this," Colton said. "And there's not much left out there to find."

"Will they do any recovery?" she asked.

"I doubt it because it was a small plane, and there won't be much left," Colton said, "but we can't be sure about that. Still, it's out of our hands."

"It's not like my cell phone is of any value now," Kate said.

"I don't even think that's the issue as much as the fact that it's debris they don't want to leave everywhere."

"That makes sense too," she said. "It's still sad though to hear it was a preset bomb."

"It is," Colton said. "But it could be much worse if, say, George's body was out there too. Then they might consider a recovery operation."

"Right," she said.

"I would guess the commander also wants to get your first-hand impression of what happened."

"Including the phone call?" she asked cautiously.

Troy frowned. And then he gave a clipped nod. "I would tell him. He's not stupid. And, if it was sabotage, he'll suspect a remote detonator as well."

"How many people would have your number?" Colton asked.

Kate winced. "Dozens, if not hundreds," she admitted. "I've had this number for a really long time."

"It could get difficult then," Colton said, "because I'm sure an investigation will involve everybody on your contact list."

"Why?" she asked in confusion. "It said Unknown Number or Private Number of the like."

"Which means it was probably a burner phone, but how many people could possibly know your number and not be on your contact list?"

"I don't know," she said. "Anybody I work with and anybody my friends may have passed my number on to, although I'm fairly strict about that," she admitted.

"That's good to know," Troy said. "The thing is, somebody had it, and somebody may have used it to blow up the plane."

"What about George's phone?" she asked, desperately trying to deflect interest from her phone. "There was no need for someone after George to use my phone."

"What about your ex-boyfriend?" Colton asked. "George mentioned he'd made threats."

"Yes," she said, getting angry, her tone sharp and to the point. "I was lonely and hooked up when I shouldn't have. When I tried to break it off, he became very possessive. Very stalkerish," she added. And then she shook her head. "I'm not mad at you guys. I'm just mad at the situation with my ex. The relationship developed so quickly that I didn't have any warning he was some sort of psycho."

"Would he have had anything to do with something like this?"

"I have no idea," she said. "I think George was afraid he might have, but it doesn't make any sense to me."

"Nothing does on a deal like this," Troy said. "These scenarios are just plain ugly, and there is no real way to know who and what might be involved yet."

"No, but you're already targeting my phone," she said, "and, because my phone is on the bottom of the Arctic Ocean, we'll never know all the contacts on it."

"Did you ever transfer or download your contact list?"

"No," she said slowly, "but my old phone is at home."

"Good," Troy said. "That's a place to start."

"I really don't like the way you're thinking," she mumbled, and she picked up another chunk of sausage and chewed on it as she glared at him. "My friends wouldn't do this."

"Of course not," he said in surprise. "No true *friend* would. The thing is, lots of people on your contact list are probably more like acquaintances or work associates, not friends. And you don't know if someone else's phone was compromised to get your number."

She preferred that thought.

"We also need to know more about your boyfriend," Colton said.

Something was off in his tone. She shot him a glance. "That's *ex*-boyfriend, please," she said, "and, for the record, if I'd had any understanding of just what a psycho he was, I'd have never gone out with him."

"How long were you with him?"

"That's just it. I wasn't 'with him'—not in the way you think. We dated, maybe five or six times over the course of two weeks," she admitted. "Everything was fine until we were at a restaurant one night, and my dinner was a little cold. He got all angry and uppity about it and wanted both of our meals for free because of it and raised a hell of a scene. I was really embarrassed and told him that wasn't the kind of behavior I was interested in being around. He ended up turning on me, saying he was just the kind of person who did what everybody else wanted to do but didn't have the balls for and that I should never criticize him, especially not in front of anyone."

Colton stared at her in surprise.

"The whole thing was really shocking, and he said a lot more, but you can get the gist. When I got home that night, I was pretty shaken over the whole thing and sent him a text saying I didn't want to see him again." She held up a hand. "I know. I know. Not cool. I should have done it in person."

"Maybe not in this case," Colton said. "Doing it in person would likely have triggered him to be violent."

"I have to admit that's exactly what I was thinking and why I did it that way," she said. "The trouble is, by the time I figured out how dangerous he was, he was already well and truly pissed at me."

"Did he respond to the text?"

"Yeah," she said with a wry smile. "He sure did. It was like, 'No one breaks up with me, bitch' or something very close to that." She watched the looks crossing the faces of both men. "Right? Talk about warning signs. Just a little too late," she said sadly.

"How bad did it get after that?"

"Pretty ugly. He kept calling and texting me, and then he left notes at my apartment building and then signs on my door. He slipped nasty threatening letters under my door, and he came to my work once. Of course I travel a lot anyway, and—"

"What does he do?" Colton asked.

"He's another navy pilot," she said, slowly meeting his gaze. "It's one of the reasons I thought maybe it would work out. Someone who would understand my work and my travel schedule. We had some things in common, and honestly, well, I was lonely."

Colton nodded but didn't say anything.

She could still feel something coming off him. It wasn't judgment exactly, but it was almost as if he was unhappy about it. But it wasn't like he'd been around to keep her company, so whatever. She just shrugged and kept eating. "I was taking every job I could just to stay away from him. Then this flight came up, and I was like, perfect, but as you can see, *perfect* didn't work out so well."

"I don't think perfect worked out at all," Colton said quietly. "Sounds like it was a pretty raw deal."

"Feels like it too," she said. She put the tray down beside her, even though she hadn't finished.

Troy looked at it and said, "If you can eat more, you should."

She shrugged, but her mind and heart weren't on the food anymore.

"Do you think he would have attacked you at home?" Colton asked.

"Yes," she said, "I was at the point of talking to the MPs about him."

"So did you?"

"I made the appointment, but this flight came up, so I had to cancel it." She stared at Colton moodily. "And now I'm left to wonder what would have happened if I had stayed and kept that appointment."

"Probably nothing different," he said. "If he was behind this, something else would have triggered it."

"Or not," she said. "Because, in a rash move, I told him that I'd made an appointment and would make a complaint."

Both men stared at her.

She shrugged. "Like I said, I haven't done anything right in this whole deal since it started. All I can tell you is that I needed to do something to send him away, and I had hoped the threat of reporting him would do it."

"Well, it did something," Colton said harshly, "but I don't think it was what you were hoping for."

Troy and Colton shared a long look, silently communicating.

"I know," Kate said. "You both think I should file a complaint as soon as we're back at Coronado." She sighed heavily. "So do I."

"Good," Colton said, a note of finality in his tone. "I'll be notifying Mason of your stalker and his threats when I report in next. Your witness statement is critical supporting evidence."

COLTON COULDN'T UNDERSTAND the jealousy boiling inside him. He understood the need to have companionship because someone was lonely. Hell, he'd done the same thing himself. It just bothered him that she'd been so lonely to turn to some lousy guy like that. But, then again, as she said, he'd seemed perfect on the surface, and then the shadows had shown up.

And, once the decline had happened, it happened fast. Colton got the guy's name, Ned Bertram, and wrote it down. "We'll have to get some of this onto the MPs desk," he said. He looked at Kate's tray and said, "Troy's right. If you can eat a little more, you should. Then let's get you to the base commander and afterward to the MPs."

She nodded. "Presumably all of them will connect from base to base?"

"I doubt it," Troy said cheerfully. "That sounds like way too much communication for them. But we can make sure it gets to the bases we need to contact."

She smiled and snagged up the last half of her toast and

then handed over the tray, munching on her toast while she clambered down the ladder. "I need to make a pit stop first," she said, then looked at her boots and managed to get into them without too much difficulty and headed to the bathroom. When she was done, the guys were standing outside the door, waiting for her.

"Are you guys like my security detail?" she asked. "Because that won't be fun."

"Let's call it a friendly escort instead," Colton said.

She laughed and tucked her arm into the crook of his elbow, and he pulled her close against it. As they walked down the hallways, he told her about the training being delayed because of the weather.

She frowned. "But wouldn't that make for a better training session?"

Troy laughed. "*Oooh!* She'd like to see you suffer, wouldn't she?"

"Not really," Kate said. "I just wondered because, if it's supposed to be for arctic conditions, wouldn't rough outdoor conditions be perfect?"

"The base commander gets to make that decision," Colton said. "What they can't have are fatalities."

An officer approached them up ahead. Smiling, he introduced himself as Petty Officer John Parsons. "How are you doing?" he asked Kate.

"I'm doing fine. Thank you," Kate said with a smile.

"The base commander would like to see you."

She nodded. "I would be happy to see him as well."

Parsons led the way through the building out to several offshoot buildings. Finally they ended up at a large office. The officer knocked on the door, and they were invited to enter. They stepped inside, saluting as required. The commander looked up, and, seeing who it was, stood and walked around the desk to greet Kate.

"Glad to see you looking so well. Please, everyone, have a seat. When I heard the first reports, I wasn't sure what we had."

"I wasn't so sure myself, sir." Kate hesitated and asked, "Have you had any update on how George is doing?"

"He's still holding his own, though a chance still remains that he'll lose fingers and toes."

She winced at that. "I'm sure he won't appreciate that. He's a fine man and an excellent pilot. I would hate to see his career ended prematurely."

"The doctors are working on it. You seem to have come out of it rather well."

"I'm certainly better after getting some sleep," she said, "but I am fully aware I wouldn't be here today if it wasn't for Colton being on board."

The commander looked at Colton and nodded. "Funny, he said something similar about you earlier today."

She laughed. "George and I did what we could to issue a Mayday call and to bring down the plane in an unpopulated area, but Colton was the one handing out parachutes and kicking us out of the plane. Literally. And then, when we were in the air, he obviously navigated himself to ensure he would land as close to both of us as possible.

"He saved George, holding him up nearly the whole time we were in the water and encouraging him to soldier on and to fight to live. I fared better initially, but eventually I was going under too, so he dragged my butt back to the surface and held on to me also," she said with a smile. "But honestly, sir? It's you to whom all three of us owe our lives. Sending the cruiser out to grab us, that was huge. We couldn't hold on much longer."

He gave her a deferential nod, acknowledging her thanks. "Glad you all made it. You'll be here for a few more days, what with the bad weather rolling in," he said, "and it's coming in even faster than expected. I don't think we'll get the flights in that we expected, and I doubt we'll be getting any out either. So get comfortable because you'll be here for a bit."

Her eyebrows raised. "I heard the heavy winds in the night, and I had to wonder how bad the weather would get."

"Bad enough," he said cheerfully. "But, as soon as we can, we'll fly you out."

She smiled and nodded. "I'll accept the rest and the food gratefully, sir. Actually I just finished a big breakfast and coffee."

"Good," he said. "One of the things I do want you to do is write down exactly what you remember, in as much detail as you can." He walked back to his desk, picked up a pad of paper and a pen, and handed both to her. "Return it to me when you're done, please."

She nodded and smiled. Dismissed, they moved back out of the office, and Petty Officer Parsons said, "Let's get you down to the MPs office now."

Once again they fell into step behind him as he led the way back and around. Finally they came to another office. He rapped on the open door and stepped inside, with the three of them following. Only one man was in the office. He stood and motioned at the seats in front of his desk. "So you must be our unexpected guest."

"Yes," Kate said, sounding hesitant. She sat down and said, "The commander just asked me to write down everything I remember from the accident."

He nodded. "That would be a good place to start." Looking at Colton and Troy, he asked, "Which one of you is Colton?"

"That would be me," Colton said. "And, yes, I do believe this was sabotage."

"Your basis for that?"

Colton took a moment to gather his thoughts and then gave the most clear and concise accounting he could. When he added in the phone call just before the engine exploded, the officer shook his head.

"That could be coincidence."

"Yes, it could be," Colton said. "In many ways, it's the perfect crime because it's not like anyone can retrieve the evidence out there."

The MP looked off into the distance and then shook his head. "Not likely. No. If it were a big passenger jet or something, then potentially we could, but, as it is, we don't have any proof of sabotage either."

"And we won't get any," Kate said, "because of the fact that you aren't going after that line of inquiry."

"No," he said. "That's not my call."

She sagged. "So we just wait until somebody tries to kill us again?"

"Who is it you think might have been behind this?"

"It's hard to say." Colton once again stepped in. "George, the pilot, who is still in critical condition, is testifying as a material witness against two men facing court-martial for using military flights to transport illicit drugs."

"Interesting," the MP said, then made a note of it. "I don't know anything about the case."

"No," Colton said. "It's from Coronado."

"*Ah.*" The officer smiled. "That seems like a big-city

problem. It's not really something we have issues with here."

"Potentially," Kate said bluntly. "But you know how it starts, and that's with just two people."

He smiled at her. "I get it. And I also understand you'll be here for a little longer than you expected."

"Yes," she said. "Until the weather clears."

"It's hard to say when that will be. I'll contact Coronado and see what I can do to be of assistance." And, with that, they were dismissed.

When they walked out, the petty officer was long gone. Colton looked at Troy. "Looks like we're on our own."

"Sounds about right," he said cryptically.

Colton could see the confusion on Kate's face. But he just smiled, tucked her arm into his and said, "How about a cup of tea?"

"That sounds like a good idea. I know I had two cups of coffee with breakfast, but it seems like a long time ago."

"It's been a few hours, so it'll be lunch soon."

At that, she raised her head. She smiled and said, "You know what? I am almost hungry again."

Beside her, Troy let out a big guffaw. "Wow," he said. "She eats like you do."

"Not quite," Colton said cheerfully. "Besides, you need energy for writing down that statement of yours."

"How come I have to, and you don't?" she protested.

He gave her a fat smile. "I already told the commander my story."

"And yet you don't have to write it down?"

"Apparently not," he said. "I was just a passenger though. You were the copilot."

She groaned. "Thanks for reminding me. I'll definitely need something to drink then. Maybe food too." When they entered the cafeteria, Colton picked out a table by the window and parked her there.

"I'll get you something to drink," he said. "You get started on your statement. It might take you a few attempts." She nodded and picked up her pen.

Colton and Troy went for drinks and learned lunch would start in twenty minutes. Colton made a pot of tea and grabbed coffee for himself. With Troy grabbing the teapot, the three of them settled in back at the table. "You might as well get as much done as you can," Colton said, "because the lunch crowd will be in here soon enough."

Just then, the same petty officer they'd met earlier walked up to Colton, handed him a laptop and said, "Compliments of the commander for your use while you are here. The form on top is for you to sign it out." Colton signed the form, acknowledging he would be using the laptop, then he sat down and plugged it in, unsure if the battery was charged or not.

Troy looked at him and said, "That's a good idea. You don't have a cell phone either, do you?"

"Nope," he said, "the only communication I've had is on the base phone."

"Did you call Mason?"

"Well, yeah. I left a message, and he called back, and they tracked me down. Not exactly convenient but now I can communicate directly through chat at least." As soon as he checked his email, he brought up the chat window and contacted Mason, who responded almost immediately. Colton gave him an update, including the fact he now had a laptop but no cell phone yet.

Mason responded that it was in the works, though the weather might delay delivery. With a glance at Kate, Colton added that Kate's old phone was in her apartment, and that it had a contact list on it. Wouldn't have the newest contacts but was still viable as a starting point.

Need her permission to get it.

Colton leaned toward Kate and said, "Mason is asking permission to get into your apartment to get your old cell phone."

Her face blanched, but she nodded. "Top dresser drawer in the right hand corner."

"How does he get in?" he asked.

"What?" she asked mockingly. "Won't they pull some of your ninja stunts and just break in?"

"He could," Colton said, "but it would probably be better if he didn't have to."

She groaned and nodded, then told him the manager had a key, but her girlfriend had one as well. She gave him the names of both. "We'll have to contact my girlfriend and let her know what happened though."

"Right," he said. "I'll get Mason to make that call and see if he can convince her that we need to get in." With that information parlayed, Colton passed on a message with an update of their discussions with the base commander and the MPs. **They'll be cooperative but won't necessarily instigate or open an investigation,** Colton typed.

No, that will probably have to come from Coronado, Mason replied.

Troy also suggested it could have been a remote detonator using a phone call onto Kate's phone.

Makes sense, Mason typed.

Next Colton provided the details of Kate's ex-boyfriend, along with a brief overview of the stalking and threats. **So he is suspect number two. Suspect number one is actually**

two persons, the pair court-martialed, who would be based on George's court case.

And that's already being looked into, Mason wrote. **I'll let you know if there are any updates.**

It would be nice if we got a copy of any reports too, Colton typed, **but I know that won't happen.** He looked at Troy, who was watching but had moved and was sitting where he couldn't read the chat window. **Any help would be appreciated,** he added. **We'll be delayed here for a few days due to the weather, and then I'm supposed to stay and do the training, and they'll ship her back home again.**

We need to make sure that whatever flight leaves is safe, Mason replied.

On that note, Colton signed off, closed the laptop and asked Troy, "Did you bring one?"

"Laptop and cell phone," he said cheerfully.

"I miss my cell phone," Kate said suddenly.

"I do too," Colton said, "but the laptop is a good place to start."

"For you," she said, staring at it.

"Do you want to use it?" And he slid it toward her. She moved the pad of paper off to the side and said, "You know what would be easier? If I told my girlfriend that Mason would be calling."

"Have at it," Colton said with a smile. While they watched, she opened up a webpage and her email program and logged in. Then she contacted her girlfriend via email.

"Perfect," he said. "We obviously need to find a way to get some answers, and, at least, this is a start."

"Yeah, that whole 'we' thing is a stretch. The MPs don't seem that interested in helping around here."

"But, like they said, they don't believe it was sabotage."

"Which is kind of hard to understand," she said, "because seriously it's not that big a jump."

"Maybe," Colton said, "but look where we're at now. It's not like anybody is too worried."

Kate groaned and nodded, then returned the laptop and picked up her pen again. "This is starting to sound like, because they don't believe us, it'll take a second attack to get them to consider anything premeditated is really going on."

"Exactly," Colton said, "which is why you need to be safe."

"I'm worried about George," she said.

"George is safe, already under close watch at the hospital, with its own security," he said. "This is about you. We've got to keep you safe."

"But why me over George? I don't get it."

Troy supplied the answer. "It was your phone that rang."

CHAPTER 7

"I CAN'T BELIEVE that the only connection to the plane blowing up is my phone," Kate said in a low whisper. "It could just as easily have been George's phone."

"But it wasn't. It was yours."

"But I'm the copilot," she said. "It doesn't make any sense."

"What does being the copilot have to do with it?" Colton asked.

"Obviously nothing," she snapped, raising both hands in frustration. Just then people started to file in for lunch. She groaned. "Oh, crud, now it'll get busy and noisy in here." She turned back to her task, trying to write down what she needed to say but found that Colton was right. She would have to rewrite this a couple times. It was a matter of a brain dump. She knew the tidbits. Just getting them all down on paper and then putting them in logical order which was the challenge.

"I was a last-minute change to the schedule, so it would be interesting to know why the original copilot didn't show up." She tapped the paper, trying to dredge from her mind who was supposed to be there and then shook her head. "We'll have to contact George and ask him."

"I can do that," Troy said, as he pulled out his phone and sent off a text.

"You have contact with the hospital?"

"And I have his commander's number," Troy said. Almost immediately a response came; then he answered back and forth. She waited until finally she couldn't stand it and asked, "Don't you ever share?"

He looked at her in surprise. "Share what?"

"Whatever is going on with your phone right now," she said. "It's obviously got something to do with me."

He gave her a warm smile. "Not really. George is apparently sleeping at the moment, so we won't hear anything back for a while."

She nodded, feeling stupid, went back to her pad of paper and wrote down several more points. Finally she ripped off those two sheets and started again. The men left her alone, which she was grateful for. She looked up a couple times to see the room slowly filling up as everybody came to grab food. Colton and Troy had disappeared. She looked around, shocked, only to see them in the food line. She rolled her eyes when Colton caught sight of her and, grinning, gave her a thumbs-up.

She didn't know if he was planning on picking her up some food and bringing it over so she would keep working or what. Or maybe they would just grab the first round. Her stomach started to growl again, so she'd be happy to have food, but she wanted to get this written statement done first. She quickly finished writing down her notes, crumpled up the extra pages she'd ripped off and tucked them into her pocket, not seeing a trash can nearby. Setting the pad of paper and the pen off to the side, she stood and walked over to join the guys.

"Maybe I'd like to pick out something for myself," she said, peering around their shoulders.

They made room for her in the middle, handed her a tray and a plate, and very quickly she loaded up on hot steamed veggies and ribs. She carried it to her table and took the dishes off her tray and put it to the side. She hated trays. They always made her think of cafeteria or fast food instead of real home-cooked meals. She walked back over to grab water and another pot of tea. While she was there, she eyed the desserts, not sure if she needed to take what she wanted now or if something would still be left when she came back. Colton walked up beside her with a plate that already had three or four desserts on it.

"Do you want more than this?"

She stared at it, her eyes huge. "Is that just for me?"

He shook his head. "For both of us."

She added a piece of pecan pie to it, and they traipsed back to the table. Everybody else ignored them and just let the three of them sit alone at their table, which could easily hold more. "Are people unfriendly here?"

Troy shook his head. "No, I think they're all busy dealing with stuff. Plus we're the outsiders."

She nodded. "That's how I feel too. Like an outsider."

"Don't let it get to you," Colton said.

She shrugged. "It doesn't matter. I just want to get home."

"I can see that," Troy said. "Any fear about flying again?"

It was a subject she had briefly wondered about and hadn't really given too much thought to. "No," she answered slowly. "I don't think so. I might like to do some more parachuting though, so I'm much less scared about the process."

"I'm sure you've done your training."

"Sure," she said with a half smile. "But it was years ago, and I haven't really maintained it."

"Training is only so good," Colton said. "It doesn't replace the real thing."

"No, it doesn't," she said. "It's trying to keep the emotions, the shock and the fear under control. That's what was so hard. When I saw that water rushing up, I knew I would hit and hit hard, but I was so afraid of drowning with the chute."

"Understood," Colton said. "It's one of the reasons I tried to get there as soon as I could."

"But then George was sinking."

"And his chute filled and sank on me too," he said. "They were too big to try to fill with air and use for floatation. If it wasn't for the temperature of the water, I might have been able to pull that off."

Kate shook her head, getting cold all over again. "It was all so shocking," she murmured, then looked down at her plate of hot veggies and attacked it. "And this is why I'm hungry," she muttered. Picking up a big piece of steaming broccoli, she started munching. "This is really good," she said a moment later.

"Smaller bases tend to have better food," Troy said in a low voice. "They don't have to cook for so many, so it's generally hotter and fresher."

"I don't know," she said. "I've been in all kinds of little bases all over the world, and it seems to me that there's a certain type of food, no matter what."

Colton just laughed at her.

"It's all good," she said with a smile. "I'm just happy to be here and able to eat."

"Good point," he said. "Keep it that way."

"What I would like to do is get answers though. Not knowing is hard."

"Not too sure we can do much about that," he said. "I'm afraid we'll get kicked out of the investigation."

"Maybe," she said, "but what about my ex, Ned? Maybe he had something to do with it."

"Maybe and then what?" he challenged her. "You go back to California and what?"

"I don't know," she said. "Try to avoid him, I guess."

"What if he did go so far as to bring down that plane? Do you think he is capable of that?"

"Can you ever know someone else and their thoughts?" she admitted with a sigh. "Yet, from what I saw, yes, I think so."

AFTER LUNCH, COLTON worked on his loaned-out laptop, digging into Kate's ex-boyfriend's life and calling in favors to get some of the military background he needed. Mason contacted him on a chat window and said that her ex-boyfriend had been picked up for questioning.

Claims he knows nothing about it.

Of course not, Colton replied. **Did he have opportunity?**

We do have him at the airport at the same time she was there, but then he's a pilot, so that's where he belongs.

What about the mechanics? Did anybody see him around there? Colton pushed for more.

Not that anybody is talking about.

Any best friends or family in the mechanics line?

Not that we've been able to find.

Damn.

Plus, the two men being court-martialed over the drug thing are both still detained.

Friends or relatives? Anybody like that close by?

Both have a brother, but neither of them were in the military, nor were they recorded on base.

Somebody would need military clearance or at least contractor credentials to get on or off the base.

Yes, Mason replied. But we both have seen cases where they could get in and out a little easier than actually having clearance.

Yeah, that's true. Colton stared off in the distance. What about Halifax? Why did they fuel up there? That seems weird.

Problem with the gas line.

Another attempt at sabotage?

It's hard to say. Did Kate mention it?

No, but another plane was down for a problem too. Both of them at Halifax. Plus a plane traveling with it landed too.

Interesting. But that's what planes do.

It does all seem awfully hit or miss. I'm probably just grasping at straws here, Colton said.

Maybe so, but the thing you may not realize is that this was the same plane George and Kate flew regularly. Just not always to this base.

How regularly?

Several days a week, Mason replied.

Is that common?

Because of the type of trips they did, this is the long-range plane that they took most of the time.

So really, anybody who wanted to set up something like that could have had it established a while ago and just needed the right timing to execute the plan, Colton proposed.

In theory, yes, Mason wrote. **But don't forget. Maintenance on these planes is pretty specific and thorough. A bomb or any kind of incendiary device should have been noted.**

Potentially, unless somebody there knew about it and was covering for Ned.

But there's not just one mechanic involved, Mason warned. **These planes are gone over by teams.**

Colton knew he was reaching, but there had to be an explanation. **Any chance the ex-boyfriend was on that plane downed in Halifax?**

I can check. Is there a potential Halifax angle for the other suspects?

Yeah.

So that's possible, and they could have been at Halifax too, right?

Possibly, but that was kind of a one-off. How do you set up something like that?

You don't always, but that doesn't mean it's not possible.

Again this sabotage seems like it was preplanned and very coldly thought out, Colton wrote. **Hardly an off-the-cuff thing.**

But it's not that impossible. How hard would it be to put something inside or outside of the wing? It doesn't have to be very big these days.

No, I guess not. Colton thought about that, wondering just what it would take to blow up an aircraft's engine under a wing. And what was the smallest thing that could set off a fire there. He started a Google search on that, when a shadow fell over his shoulders. He looked up to see the commander staring at his laptop.

"Interesting topic," he said. He sat down beside them at the table, waving off their movements to salute. Turning to Kate, he asked, "How is the statement coming along?"

She smiled. "I think I'm done, sir." She handed him two sheets of paper, fully covered in writing. He took a moment to read it, asking her some questions about her statement, then finally nodded, turned to the second page and said, "Sign it and date it, please."

She did just that.

"Perfect," he said. "I'll get it scanned in."

"Thanks," she said with a smile. "I guess I could have put it into a Word document or an email for you."

"This is fine," he said and looked back at Colton. "Any luck?"

"Not yet," he said, "and I'm a little frustrated by it."

"Of course you are. The trouble with sabotage is that it's pretty damn easy—once you figure it out."

"I know, but figuring it out is the hard part. Where was the opportunity? How long ago was something like this planned, and how did they manage to pull it off?"

He nodded. "I hear you, son. Keep digging. Just keep my men in the loop." Then he got up and left.

Colton looked at Kate and then back at Troy, one eyebrow up. "What was that all about?" he asked after the commander had disappeared out the door toward the hallway.

"I don't think the commander likes anything happening on his base without him knowing about it," she said. "So I'm thinking he wanted to see what you were up to."

Colton nodded. "Still, it was a little odd."

"Small base, very involved commander," she said. "Large base, more layers between the commander and the people."

And that was so true. He went back to his research, but his mind was caught up with *opportunity* now. He switched his research to looking up the smallest amount of C-4 required to blow up a plane's engine. He was shocked to see how little it was. Particularly if it was placed strategically.

What was even more bothersome was the fact that the instructions on how to blow up a plane were included. Or a car or anything else. As he kept going down the rabbit hole, he also learned it was easy to cover with something like duct tape to make it blend into the color of the engine. And, as long as it was relatively flat and had a small computer chip for remote detonation, it wouldn't have to be where someone could easily get to it. It wouldn't take long to attach, and, if so disguised and applied underneath, nobody would have seen it.

Which was probably what was done here. It would be impossible to prove at this point, but somebody had taken C-4 or another plastic explosive and had placed it under the wing or at least on the inside where it wasn't easily seen. It could have been attached with just a simple slap, something that could happen as two guys talked and wandered past. Of course, nobody was close to the planes except the people who needed to be, unless something odd was going on.

Colton frowned, then opened up the chat to Mason again, asking him to make sure there wasn't any media event or anything that would have brought strangers into the hangar where the planes are.

Already on it, Mason wrote. **I'm tracking the video feed from that whole area.**

I hadn't realized what a small amount of C-4 would have done the job, or how easily it could be applied and hidden.

And cover it in duct tape, right? We probably read the same article, Mason said. **As these crooks are getting smarter, we have to be that much smarter ourselves.**

Yeah, especially with the directions sitting on the internet. We don't need a suspect with special training now, just an asshole who can read.

CHAPTER 8

KATE STOOD AND said, "As much as I've enjoyed this, that big meal has made me very sleepy. I'll head back and have another nap. I'll talk to you two later."

With that, she headed out. She knew she'd surprised them, and both men were probably figuring out if they should follow her or not. She didn't care either way; she just wanted to go to bed and rest. Something about a big meal when she was already tired was enough to finish her off. She didn't want to screw up a potentially good night's sleep tonight, but she was too tired to keep her eyes open.

She also got lost twice but finally found her way back to her original bedroom and got into her room, noting that the hair Colton had placed was still there. With a sigh of relief she stepped inside and found the privacy absolutely wonderful. Kicking off her boots, she slipped under the covers, fully dressed once again. It wasn't long before her head hit the pillow, and her eyes closed.

The trouble was, she couldn't sleep. It was the same old, same old—realizing the engine was gone, the flames tearing off the back of the plane as it tilted and plummeted downward. In a death spin, they could do so little about it. It was hard to get up off that seat and get to the back, only to be caught by Colton and clipped into a harness and sent out the door.

She recognized that George had been treated the exact same way, and, for that, she realized they definitely owed Colton's SEAL training for their lives. But it was more than that; it was just Colton's cold sense of purpose. He didn't ask questions; he didn't worry about anything. He simply grabbed them, buckled them into their chutes and made sure they got out of the future wreckage heading toward the ocean.

It was her first major plane crash, and, even now, it hadn't really settled in. It was just too devastating. Too emotionally soul-destroying to walk away from. It didn't change the fact that she was a pilot and a damn good one, but she had to wonder if this would impact how she flew. She wanted to get back up in the air and get back down again safely several more times immediately, so she didn't have to deal with stage fright or whatever it's called when you didn't want to go back up in the air.

Flying was her whole life. She'd been wondering about settling down a little bit in the future and taking fewer shifts, but she had never wanted to give up the skies completely. It was a huge part of who she was. Yet sitting where she was now, it didn't seem to make any difference. She was curled up in bed, lost and caught in nightmares just so impossible to figure out.

What about all the equipment and cargo they were carrying? What were the chances that anything from the cargo bay could have been involved? Anything was possible. A timer could have been set inside the cargo that would have set off the engine as well. The bottom line was that either she or George had been targeted. It was also possible that it was all one and the same. Maybe the saboteur wanted both of them done for.

As shocking as that sounded, it wasn't out of the realm of possibility. All they had to do was find a connection between Ned and the guys doing the drug running. Ned had been volatile. He could be very up and then very down too. She now wondered if he took drugs. It would explain the mood swings. As she lay here, she tried to figure out some commonsense rationality about any of it, but it eluded her. Finally she got frustrated and sat back up in bed and groaned.

No point in resting here, if I'm not resting. But, if I can't rest, no point in letting my mind bend upside down and backward. But she had none of her gear, not even a laptop. She should have asked Colton if she could have taken his with her for a bit. Maybe it would have helped—if for no other reason than giving her something to do. Just as she got up and put her boots back on, a light knock came at the door. "Come in?"

Petty Officer Parsons stepped in, smiled at her and said, "I wondered if you were napping."

"No," she said. "I tried, but I've got too many thoughts going around in my head."

He nodded, then said, "The commander would like to have you check in at sick bay, please."

She stilled and then nodded. "I guess that makes sense, but I can't say that I want to." She finished lacing up her boots, then stood, walking toward him and asked, "Any chance you can show me the way?"

"I'd be happy to," he said. "The commander is just looking after your health."

"Maybe so," she said, "but it still feels very much like more poking and prodding that I don't want done."

"You have a fair bit of bruising, according to your file,

but no broken bones. That in itself is amazing."

She nodded grimly. "You can thank Colton for that."

"No, not just him, I don't think so," he said. "Maybe because you got out of the plane so fast, and he kept you alive in the water, but, all in all, the three of you did a great job."

"Maybe."

Suddenly they were in front of the medical center. With a smile she stepped inside, and he faded away. As she walked forward, a woman looked up and smiled, then asked, "Can I help you?"

"The commander sent me to report here for a checkup," she said.

"And you are?"

"I'm the one who just arrived from the crashed plane," she said. "It's Kate. Kate Winnows."

"Good to have you," the woman said. "Take a seat. The doctor will look after you in a moment."

That was the best she could do. She sat down but, of course, no magazines were here, like those found in most civilian waiting rooms. Nothing but windows surrounded her. She stared, realizing just what a unique country this was. When she started to get bored and looked for something to occupy herself, a big burly male stepped in and called her name. She hopped to her feet, then smiled and said, "That's me."

He looked at her, then said, "Well, the fact that you're walking, talking and appear to be quite sane already qualifies you as a miracle. Come in and tell me your secret."

She laughed at his humor, liking him already, and followed him into a small room. He did a very thorough checkup, asked her about all kinds of things she hadn't even considered but were obviously pointed toward the possibility of internal injuries.

When he declared her fit and sound, she smiled and said, "That's what I said, but the commander wanted me to come anyway."

"Doesn't matter," he said. "It's always better to get you checked over, just in case."

He tapped his tablet. "What I do want is for you to see a colleague of mine."

"Why?" she wailed, the smile falling off her face. "I don't see any point."

"Of course you don't. That's because you're not interested in dealing with it right now. But the fact of the matter is, I think you should talk to somebody about it. The point is to make sure that you don't end up with recurring nightmares and that the stress doesn't leave you with PTSD long-term."

Enough common sense was behind his request that she could see his point. "How about I see somebody when I get back home again?"

"How about you see somebody now?" he said firmly. "And I mean like *now*, now."

With that, he handed her a note and said, "Talk to my receptionist out front. With any luck you can go straight from here to your next stop."

Kate nodded glumly and said, "You know that's almost worse than getting blood taken. And I hate needles."

He gave a big laugh. "For anybody who survived what you did, talking about it should be a piece of cake."

"It wouldn't be bad," she said, "if they wanted to know something straightforward. But it's always those tricky questions where they're trying to read between the lines. That's the hard part."

"So then, say you just want to talk straight and don't want your brain analyzed while you're at it."

She looked at him in surprise.

He shrugged. "Why not? That's what I do. I have to go for mental health visits too, whether I like it or not. And like you, I don't like the double-talk stuff. I want, *This is where I'm at. This is what I'm doing. This is how I'm doing,*" he said. "You might try that."

The trouble with that strategy was, when it came to put it in practice, it was easier said than done.

She was surprised when she arrived at the shrink's office. Still a military office and plainer than she would have expected for a psychiatrist's office, but the beaming smile on the woman's face was the biggest surprise.

"I suppose he told you to ask for the no-frills plan," she said warmly.

Kate laughed out loud. "Only after telling him that I hated how you guys always look for answers inside the answers."

The doctor laughed. "I love it," she said. "But seriously, my only interest is ensuring that you are coping okay with the terrible experience you had."

"I'm okay," Kate said boldly. "As much as I want and need to sleep, the nightmares keep me up. I still see myself crashing but drowning instead of being rescued. I presume with time that will ease up."

"Yes," the doctor said. "You weren't hurt physically?"

"No. It was just a bad accident. I avoided the plane crash via parachute, followed by very nearly drowning, and then the hypothermia set in," Kate said with a laugh. "And thankfully I survived it all."

"Thankfully, indeed," the doctor said. "And I heard

from others that you've credited the man flying with you for the survival of you and the other pilot?"

"Yes, Colton," Kate said with a gentle smile. "No doubt about it. No way George or I would have made it without Colton."

"The two of you have a history?"

"A one-night stand four years ago," she said, clear-cut and concise. "I would love to explore the idea of a relationship, but I don't know that he's up for it."

"If he is," she said, "I can tell you an intense experience like this can make for a great bond. Nobody else will understand what you've gone through but him."

"But is that a fair basis for a relationship?"

"Is a one-night stand?" the woman countered, then followed with a big smile. "It's a great basis. It's like a sympathetic understanding with a lot of realism attached to it. Makes for reality and a relationship that is grounded instead of one built on fantasy. Fantasy is great, until you pull back the curtains and see what's really inside. In this case you already know the core of the man. You can create a beautiful world from that without any fantasy required."

COLTON SAT AT an empty table in one of the office buildings, doing his best to figure out exactly what the hell was going on. What he had were all kinds of details and various opportunities to sort out, but absolutely no information that would do them any good. And that was really irritating. He needed answers, but, so far, everything was coming up blank. Troy joined him a few moments later. Colton raised his eyebrows.

"I thought you'd be with Kate."

"She's napping," he explained. "I figured I could do better here, trying to get some answers in the meantime."

"There are definitely answers that need to be found, but I sure as hell haven't had any luck finding them."

"We have to track whoever was on the plane or in the area and compare them against our three suspects," Colton said. "At the moment, all three look good for this, but we haven't gotten anybody verified in position at the scene, so really there's no case."

"All have motive," Troy said, "but motive isn't enough."

"I know," he said with a groan. "Wish it was."

"No you don't, not really," Troy said. "The world would go crazy, pinning all kinds of crimes on the wrong people. Look at what a mess the world is in already. Can you imagine how much worse it would get without due process?"

"I know," Colton said grimly. "Okay, so I've got a passenger list from the other flight that had a mechanical problem and ended up at Halifax. Let's check all the passengers against our three known suspects."

"Give me half," Troy said, and, between the two of them, they broke it up and started covering all the names on the list.

By the time Colton got through his section of the list, he was frustrated to the point of swearing. "Damn it. Not only is nothing here, nobody even looks remotely connected."

"Nobody with any history of assaults or a criminal record flagged for anything at all?" Troy asked, looking up from his part of the list.

"Nothing," Colton said. "It's so freaking irritating."

"It is," Troy said. "There has to be some connection to somebody though. That plane didn't blow up on its own."

"I guess that's one of the things we have to consider—

the possibility of mechanical failure."

"It's possible, but, Colton, given the motives we've got here, it sure doesn't look all that probable."

"Right. In most investigations, you spend considerable time trying to find a plausible motive, but here we've got motive up the—"

"Exactly."

But with Troy's half of the passenger list now completed too, Colton couldn't do much more until he got a couple things from Mason. First, he was still waiting on Kate's contact list from her old phone. So he reminded Mason, who was waiting on the girlfriend's email containing snapshots of said contacts. He'd send that on upon receipt.

Now Colton had a second request, a new one, asking for the list of mechanics working on the base around the planes in the twenty-four hours before their flight took off, as well as verifying what kind of a visual check would have been possible in order to determine how long that bomb could have been sitting there, waiting to be triggered.

When he explained that, Mason had said he'd get back with it in a few minutes. Colton hoped he wasn't putting Mason on the spot over all this purported sabotage—which could have occurred at two other bases—but obviously something was going on. Having been caught by surprise once, Colton sure as hell didn't want to get caught a second time.

Minutes later, Mason came back on the chat window.

Ex-boyfriend is in the clear over Halifax. Confirmed he was in Colorado. Colton, did you ever consider you were the target?

Sitting up a little straighter, he looked at Troy. "Mason just asked if I might have been the target."

Troy's eyebrows rose. "Ooh, I hadn't considered that."

"But it is a possibility, I suppose. But how though? It's not like anybody knew I was on that plane."

"I did," Troy said. "And, if I did, you know a bunch of other people on base, *both* bases, did as well."

Colton frowned. "I wouldn't have thought I had that many enemies."

"You don't need many. All you need is one, one with the right skill set to do this."

"The trouble is, because we don't have the plane to investigate, we don't have a signature on the bomb or anything else for that matter," Colton said.

"In a way, it was a perfect crime," Troy said. "Except for one part."

"What's that?" Colton asked.

"You survived," Troy said. "If this was a murder-for-hire, the guy failed to complete the job, and he'll be coming around, looking for another opportunity."

"Oh, good. Just when this wasn't complicated enough."

"I'm thinking you better spend a few minutes and figure out who might have wanted to kill you."

Colton looked at him. "You know full well, because of the work I do, anything is possible, but I just don't think it's a likely answer."

"Maybe not but it's something we do need to mark off as having been looked at."

"Fine, I just don't like it," Colton said with a scowl.

"Like it or not," Troy said with a chuckle, "it's something that has to be considered and then either discarded or brought up for a further look."

Grumbling about that, Colton faced his borrowed laptop and sat here with a serious look, figuring out just who in his life might have wanted to kill him. And who he had told about his plans. "I told a couple of the guys," he said. "When I was sitting there, waiting for the flight out of Coronado, I was talking to somebody."

"You told him what you were doing?"

"To a certain extent but not with any detail."

"Did you know him?" Troy asked.

"I know *of* him, but I don't *know him*, know him," he said. "As in, he's not a friend, and I've never done a mission with him. At least I don't think so." He tried to recall the man's features, and then he shrugged. "I can't remember very much about him. It was just a casual conversation about how I was heading up to Greenland and that this was the flight I was put on."

"And where did you talk to him?" Troy asked.

"At the plane," he said. Looking at Troy, he repeated, "*At the plane.* That's the thing."

"Were they loading up supplies? Anybody who was involved in the loading there would have had access to the plane. If a bomb was attached to the outside, they could have just walked past casually and done all kinds of things."

"He was there alone," Colton said, quietly pissed at himself now for not having noticed.

Troy said, "Listen. The thing is, because he was right there where you expected to see somebody, it didn't seem like it was out of the ordinary."

"Not to mention it was on the base, where you assume everybody is okay." But, of course, Colton already knew from previous experience you couldn't assume anything. Shit happened no matter where, and sometimes it was worse on the base because everybody assumed it was all clear.

"He had to have been there with the group doing the

loading," Troy said. "At least he was somebody nobody had a problem with."

"True, and, since everybody else was calm about it, so was I. … Then again maybe it looked like he was there with me."

"That's possible too."

Colton sat there a little longer and then sent a message to Mason, explaining that he had spoken to somebody at the Coronado airport himself. And he now needed a list of all the ground crew who might have loaded the gear onto the plane. "I suppose there also could have been triggers inside the plane. Like in the cargo as well," he mentioned to Troy as he worked.

"Instead of a phone call?" asked Troy.

"Yeah," he said. "It's possible. Anything's possible at this point."

"As usual there are too many possibilities. We'll narrow them down, and then, when we figure it out," Troy said, "whatever doesn't make sense and is still left standing, no matter how impossible, that will be the one lead we have to pursue."

Colton looked at him and smiled. "I've been spending more of my time doing training lately than investigations, you know?"

"Yep," Troy said. "Doesn't matter now though because, when it comes home like this one has, you'll do whatever you need to do to make sure you're clear and Kate stays safe," he said.

"We need to put a military guard on George too. Or a civilian one if we can't confirm the guards are clean."

"I wonder if anybody has considered that. You know it won't be well-received if we tell the commander he needs to consider a second attack."

"God, no, it sure won't," Colton said, "but we need to find out and deal with it."

Just then they looked up to see Petty Officer Parsons walking toward the cafeteria area, probably looking for a coffee. They hailed him over to the little office they were in, and he approached with a smile on his face.

"What are you two up to?"

"Just trying to figure out who might have been involved in this," Troy said.

"Right. Like the rest of us, you're trying to figure out if a crime actually occurred," he said with a laugh.

That gave Colton an idea just how much their word was doubted. "Well, there is a downed plane," he said quietly. "If nothing else, that should be cause for concern."

"To the number-crunchers and the supply guys, yes," Parsons said, "and obviously you guys. Plus, whoever's delivery was dumped in the ocean."

Colton hadn't really considered that angle. Somebody wanted that load shipped. Had crashing it benefited some-body else on a budgetary level? He hated to even think along that line, but, now that he had, it was one more thing to look into. When shit happened, it wasn't always easy to sort out who did the shitting. Again, there were no immediate answers. He faced the petty officer and asked, "Does George have base and civilian security on him?"

"I don't know, but I believe his condition is such that you could visit him at the hospital."

"Now that would be good," Colton said. "I know Kate really wants to check in on him."

"Let me know, and I'll arrange it." Then he headed over to get the coffee he'd come for.

"Something about him seems so nonchalant, as if he doesn't care," Troy said.

"I imagine a lot of them don't," Colton said. "When you think about it, the only ones who really care are those directly affected by it. To these guys, planes go down all the time, and, in this case, it was just a cargo plane with no loss of life. So it's an equipment headache. I was working my way through that angle in my mind, but I'm not really getting much of a hit on it being viable."

"Maybe it didn't have as much to do with killing George and/or Kate," Troy said thoughtfully. "Maybe it was as much to make it look like George was a shitty-ass pilot who shouldn't be flying or something. More to discredit him than anything else."

"But it's not like his preflight check would have shown up with something wrong in the engine or anything, not unless the computer revealed something."

"I suggest we talk to George," Troy said, "because you know that he's the one who would have the most answers."

"He also did the preflight before Kate was even there," Colton said thoughtfully.

"Are we thinking suicide?"

"That's a rough way to go," he said.

"It is, but we've seen it before."

"Well, I haven't," Colton said. "Wouldn't want to either. It's one thing if you take your own life but another thing to take others down with you. Besides, why would he want to do that when he has a wife and kids?"

"We don't know that everything's okay in the marriage," Troy said. "What if they were on the verge of a divorce or something?"

"Right, and a pilot may want to go down with his flight,

but would he want to take Kate too? Some people probably wouldn't want to fly with him because of the deal with turning in his coworkers."

"Although," Troy said, "since he'd gone that far into it and had taken all the heat he likely has, you'd think he'd want to stick around to see it through. Unless somehow he has left evidence behind and just doesn't want to be part of the zoo."

"Again, more thoughts I don't really want to consider," Colton said with a wry smile, "because it will be a zoo, going up against his own coworkers like that. And who knows what kind of crap George's been through because of it already."

"Exactly. That won't be fun for anybody. Including his wife and kids potentially. Maybe he thought this would be an easy answer."

"Well, it's time for me to find Kate. Then take a trip to the hospital and find out for sure."

CHAPTER 9

WHEN KATE STEPPED into the waiting room, she saw Colton walking in to greet her. She smiled up at him. "You don't have to follow me around, you know?" she said gently. "You saved my life, but—"

"And you saved mine. We've already been over that old ground," he said. "I came to tell you that we can see George, if that's something you want to do."

"Absolutely it is," she said with excitement. "He's that much better?"

"Apparently," Colton said. "We just have to tell the petty officer, and he'll arrange for us to get to the hospital."

"Can we go now?" she asked hopefully. He looked at her strangely. She frowned. "What?"

"Are you okay after all that? Do you need to rest or eat or something?"

"No," she said. "No more sitting around. I'd like to do something active. And definitely no more talking about my health or mental state, please!" she said.

"As long as all the talking needed has been done, and you're good to go," he said with a smile.

As they went to leave, the receptionist called back, "The doctor wants to see you in a couple days."

Kate froze, then looked at her and said, "I should be going home in a couple days."

"There's a good chance all flights will be canceled due to weather," the woman said. "In that case, she wants to see you again."

Resigned, Kate nodded and waited while the appointment was booked and thanked her. Then, with a smile, she walked out of the office.

"You don't sound so impressed. Was it terrible?"

"No, not at all," she said.

"Did she want you to relive the accident?"

"No, not really. I think she is just wondering how stable I am, mentally, in terms of returning to work. And, of course, any suggestion of me not being stable or not capable to return to work amplifies my own fears in that regard. That's just not something I want to deal with right now, thank you very much." She caught the surprised look on his face, and she nodded. "Of course I'm worried. It was a hell of a crash. I haven't been up since, and I wanted to go up right away, but apparently that isn't allowed."

"I think that's probably standard," he said. "You'll go back up when scheduled, the same as you always have, and you'll carry on just like the professional you are."

Her tone was lighter as she said, "Thanks for the vote of confidence."

"No problem. I'd fly with you anytime."

"You might be the only one," she said. "A certain aura attaches to pilots after you crash."

"Interesting," he said. "Meaning people don't want to fly with you?"

"Well, a crash doesn't exactly garner confidence, does it?" she said with a chuckle.

"I don't know," he said. "You survived. That should boost everybody's confidence."

"It doesn't work that way. But it's fine. I'll deal with it."

"Was this your first crash?"

"Yes," she said.

"Everybody has one bad experience," he said cheerfully.

At that, she burst out laughing. "Often you only get one."

"Point taken, but we made it out, so it's all good."

She loved his blasé, not quite careless, but almost, attitude. And really, the *It happened. It's over. Let's move on* way of thinking was not a bad way to go. Colton really was a good guy.

With great joy that they hooked up with Petty Officer Parsons, who arranged a ride for them and access into the hospital. It took a good twenty minutes to go from the base to where they needed to go, but very quickly they were inside the hospital and directed toward George's bed. He was sleeping. Kate hesitated, not wanting to wake him up. She looked at Colton to see his frown. "What's the matter?

"He was supposed to be awake," he said by way of explanation, but it wasn't enough.

"He's been through a lot," she said. "I'd be asleep too, if I could be."

At that, he nodded. "Right. Good point. And he was way worse off than you."

"Exactly," she said. "We can go get a coffee or something and come back."

"That sounds like a plan." Colton looked around and noted where the cafeteria was. "Come on. Let's go. We can always return and sit outside his room and hope he wakes up again."

She didn't like the way he said that. "You don't mean he might die, right?" she said, as soon as they were moving toward the cafeteria.

He looked at her in surprise. "No! No, that's not what I meant at all, but I have to admit to being disturbed at the fact there's no security on him."

"That's because nobody really believes it was sabotage. Accidents happen, fuel lines break, sometimes engines fail, and things overheat."

"Did you have any problems with the plane before that?"

"You asked that once before," she said. "I told you then it was a no."

"Were you awake the whole time?"

"No," she said, "I wasn't. I took a few minutes of shut-eye, and so did he. But nothing was unusual about that either."

"I know. Relax. I'm just looking into every angle I can," he said. "What is George's mental state like normally?"

She frowned. "Since the whole drug case, he's been a little morose, like he's almost sorry for what he started. He got involved and knew it was the right thing to do, but I don't think it's been easy. Not for him or his family."

Colton took a deep slow breath, and she watched curiously, realizing he was about to drop a verbal bomb on her. "Go ahead. Just tell me what's going on. Trust me. It'll be much better than not knowing what's going through your head because, honestly, you're kind of freaking me out."

"Okay, sorry. So you know we have to look at every angle, right? So one of the questions we have to consider is whether this could have been a suicide attempt."

Kate stared at him. "Oh, my God," she said. "Are you kidding? That is definitely not something I want to consider. I don't want to consider that at all."

"Maybe not but you know everybody else has to consider it. George got himself into a spot, and I'm sure his life hasn't been easy lately. Do you know if he and his wife were doing okay?"

"No, I don't know," she said, speaking slowly. "I know they had a temporary separation not all that long ago, but I can't imagine he would choose something like this. He loves those boys."

"What if he was sorry for dragging them into this mess? What if he regretted his actions and didn't see any way out?"

"But why would there be no way out?" she asked.

"I don't know. I guess that's something we have to look into." They walked into the cafeteria, and Kate picked up muffins and coffee. At least she thought they were muffins; they were a very unique-looking treat anyway. Colton paid for them, and they returned to George's room.

"Listen, Colton. I really don't like that suggestion. I don't like it at all."

"I know, but we've got to keep digging until we find something, somewhere," he said, as if trying to toss the idea back under the rock where he'd dragged it from.

"Do you have a way to check his email?" she asked slowly.

"Why?" Colton asked. At his sharp look, she clarified her question.

"I've spent quite a bit of time with George, and the only way he would do something like that was if his family was in danger. Like if he was being blackmailed into it."

"Oh, that's an interesting angle. I hadn't considered that." Colton pulled out the phone Petty Officer Parsons had turned up with at the request of the commander and contacted Mason. She could hear the conversation and heard Colton say, "I know it's a long shot, but—"

At that moment, she glanced at George, who didn't look very well. His face was turning red. She raced to his side and then hit the panic button. Alarms rang out; Colton jumped to her side. Almost immediately medical staff came running. Kate and Colton were ushered out of the room as medical staff worked on George.

Kate paced up and down the hallway. Colton looked at her and asked, "What happened?"

"He didn't look good," she whispered. From the doorway he joined her to look over her shoulder, trying to see. "I wondered if he was dying. I don't know. I just reacted."

"Yeah, especially if somebody was trying to help him along."

"I would go along with the murder and/or blackmail line," she said, "and both would be shitty options."

"True, but at least it would be him, not you and him," he murmured, his breath drifting across her cheek. Instinctively she leaned back into him, his arms coming around to hold her close.

They watched the medical staff fighting to save George's life.

He said against her ear, "I'll be right back. Stay here." And, with that, he dropped his arms from around her and headed off down the hallway at a rapid clip.

She called after him, "Where are you going?"

"To check the video cameras."

She stared after him in surprise and then realized how right he was. She didn't know what kind of credentials he needed to see them, but she was pretty sure he could pull whatever strings he needed to get the job done. With nothing else to do, she sat down and waited. With relief, she heard the atmosphere and the mood change inside George's room. She stepped up to take a look, and one of the nurses gave her a thumbs-up sign, a big smile on her face.

She crossed her hands against her chest and beamed. George had been saved. She didn't know what the hell was going on, but wow. "That was real shitty, whatever it was," she whispered quietly to herself. Two doctors walked out past her, and she asked the nurse, "Is he okay now?"

"For the moment," the nurse said.

"Do you know what happened?"

She shrugged. "His heart stopped. But he's back again."

Kate nodded and said, "Can I go in and see him?"

The nurse shook her head. "No, no visitors right now."

Kate looked at her and asked, "But what about monitoring him?"

"We've got him on the monitor at the nurses' station, and somebody will check on him every fifteen minutes."

Kate didn't like that one bit. "I'll just sit here for a bit." She sat down, picking up one of the coffees. She slowly sipped it, wondering how long Colton would be. Sure enough, the nurse came back, checked on George and gave her another thumbs-up as she left. That meant it had already been fifteen minutes. She waited and waited, and finally ate one muffin.

Still hungry, she ate the second one. She also drank Colton's coffee. By the time she saw him walking toward her, the nurse had come and gone once more. She bolted to her feet and ran toward him and threw herself against him. His arms closed around her, and he held her close. "It's okay," he said. "It's all right."

"It doesn't feel all right," she whispered against his chest. "Did you find anything?"

"It's what we didn't find. It took us a few minutes to get

clearance, but then, when they checked the security footage, they saw the system for this entire hallway was down for the twenty minutes we were in the cafeteria."

Kate stared up at him.

He nodded. "I know. Very suspicious."

"No," she said, "*deadly* suspicious."

"Exactly." He wrapped his arms around her and held her close.

IT HAD TAKEN a fair bit to get anybody to let him access the security cameras, but, when they realized what they had seen, orders were barked all over the place, and people had jumped in to try and figure out what was going on. Colton had stayed while they searched other hallways, looking for anybody who might have had anything to do with it, but, not finding anything, he decided it was time to go back. He sent Mason an update and then headed toward Kate.

The fact that there had potentially been an attack on George would hopefully bring the case up to a higher priority on base now that people had confirmation George was in danger. And that meant Kate was in danger too, only he'd left her alone. His footsteps rapidly increased until he almost ran down the hall. When he caught sight of her waiting for him, his heart slammed against his chest in relief. He shouldn't have left her alone. He never gave it a thought because she was surrounded by hospital staff.

When she'd seen him, she had raced toward him. It was natural for him to open his arms, and he was grateful she had jumped into them. He didn't know why the hell he hadn't tried to call her in all these years. He should have. Part of it may have been out of fear. That one night had been so good, and maybe it wouldn't be so good again. Foolish, he knew, but it was like one of those high spots in his life, and he didn't want to ruin it. And now his mind was completely overwhelmed with the fact somebody had managed to get into the hospital and to attack George—and could have attacked her too.

That meant it wasn't safe to leave him here. Colton hoped somebody was working on setting up proper security for George. Colton had passed on his own request, hoping it wasn't needed and that people were already working on it. But it was hard to know. His phone vibrated. Reaching for it, he looked down and frowned, then said, "Hello, Commander."

"Where are you?" the commander asked, his tone brisk.

"Standing outside George's hospital room."

"Good. Stay there," the commander ordered. "I have two men coming to stand guard."

With that, Colton let out a heavy sigh of relief. "I'm very glad to hear that, sir."

"The plane was one thing, but a second attack is another, although I don't know that I would have recognized it as such except for that damn security camera."

"Exactly," Colton said with a nod. "We'll stay here until the security arrives."

"When you get back," he said, "I want you in my office immediately." And, with that, he hung up.

Colton wrinkled his face. "Did you hear that?"

Kate nodded. "He doesn't sound happy."

"Doesn't mean he's unhappy with us. But the bearer of bad news has never been looked upon lightly," he said with a smile.

"Got it." Kate motioned at the empty cups and the paper bag beside it. "Your coffee was getting cold," she said, "so I drank it just in time." Enough laughter was in her voice for him to realize she hoped he wasn't upset with her.

"We can get more coffee and muffins," he said. "I'm glad we got as much as we did then. Obviously you needed it."

"I did," she said, moving back to sit down outside George's door. Just then a nurse came and entered George's room.

"We can't go in?" he asked Kate. "I was really hoping to talk to him."

Kate shook her head. "Every fifteen minutes they're doing checks, and apparently he's on a monitor at the nurses' station."

"Good," Colton said, "because the last thing we want is to have any other attempts made on his life."

"Or mine."

He slid his fingers through hers. Gripping her hand warmly, he said, "We'll make sure that doesn't happen either."

"Doesn't this prove it was just George they were after though?"

"Possibly, except they may be worried about what he or you saw."

Her gaze went wide. "I'd rather fly in the worst weather, in a damaged plane, over the worst enemy territory, rather than even *think* about people like that," she announced, shaking her head. "My mind doesn't work that way."

"No," he said, "but mine does, and the security team's does as well, so we'll do everything we can to keep you safe."

"That means you'll have to be with me all the time," she teased.

He gave her a special smile and said in a low whisper, "I plan to. Twenty-four hours a day."

"I'm supposed to be heading home tomorrow or the day after. Remember?"

"I hear you," he said, "but you're not getting on any plane without me and not before it's been checked thoroughly from top to bottom."

As her face paled, she nodded. "I appreciate that. I doubt I'll be the pilot."

"I doubt it too," he said calmly. "Not until you debrief back at Coronado. I don't know what kind of checks and balances they have to ensure you're fit to fly, but you can bet nobody will let you take the controls until it's cleared that you're as healthy as can be and that nobody is out to kill you."

"Somehow I feel like it's more likely about how I'm healthy and ready to fly than anybody is worried about me dying," she said drily. "Truth be known, the brass is probably more concerned about me keeping it together than anything else."

He laughed at that. "There are always jobs that nobody wants to do. That doesn't mean you have to suck it up and do it all the time."

"Maybe not," she said, "but George and I got along well."

"So George would have known you would be there this time too, right?"

She nodded. "Yep, he knew it."

"So any attempt to commit suicide would have been set up knowing he was taking you with him, right?"

"Yes," she said, her gaze curious as she watched him.

"So then most likely he wouldn't have been trying to

commit suicide."

"Except that he was really sad. Depressed even as we took off. So, I don't know, maybe that was part of it."

"It's possible," he said, "but let's hope not."

"What about his emails? Or any other way to check into his life to make sure he wasn't being blackmailed or something?" she asked curiously.

"There'll be a full investigation now," he said. "Whoever attacked him may have thought he would end things. But all he's done has expanded the inquiry, making sure it really does open up into a full investigation. So, this was likely the best thing that could have happened to George."

"A sad way to look at life." Kate's gaze turned to two uniformed men coming down the hallway toward them. "Looks like the security detail has arrived."

"Yes," Colton said. "Now we can catch a ride back."

"Is Parsons in town?"

"Or he'll come back to get us. I don't know."

As the two men approached, they said, "Your ride is waiting out front." Then they took up positions on either side of George's door. Kate wished she could see George one more time or at least let him know she was here, cheering him on, but it was obvious she wouldn't get close to George today.

With a smile she said to the guards, "Thank you for coming. Please keep him safe."

One of the men cracked a smile and said, "We will, ma'am. We will."

She didn't pull rank on them or mention anything other than the fact that it was important to her that George stayed alive. Colton appreciated that. At Colton's urging, she moved down the hall with him. She sighed as they took the stairs and headed out to the front door. "It's really sad," she said.

"What?" he asked.

"George doesn't know how much people are doing for him. I don't even know if his family has been told."

"That is up to other people. Remember? That part of the deal isn't something we can change," he said. "Unless you're good friends with George's wife?"

"I am friends with her. I used to talk to her every once in a while on the phone when George couldn't answer."

"Has that happened lately?"

"No," she said, sadness deepening her tone. "It hasn't."

CHAPTER 10

WHEN KATE AND Colton got back to the base, Kate thanked the petty officer for giving them a lift, and the three of them headed straight to the commander's office. Petty Officer Parsons stayed with her, smiling and saying, "He just wants me to keep an eye on you."

She shot him a sideways look. "For my protection or to make sure I don't run away?"

That had him laughing. "And why would you think that?" he asked.

"It hasn't escaped my notice I was there on the spot too," she said. The smile fell from his face, and he gave her a hard look. "Did you have anything to do with your copilot's attack?"

"Of course not," she cried out.

"Then you have nothing to worry about," he said. With a hard rap on the commander's door, they stepped in. The commander stood and motioned at the two chairs across from him. "Please, from the top."

Kate was grateful Colton did all the talking. When the commander looked to her, she nodded. "What he said."

He gave a clipped nod. "I want the two of you confined to the base, preferably to the cafeteria and your barracks."

Her smile fell off. "Why, sir?"

He shrugged. "For your own safety."

She wanted to kick up a fuss, but going against a commander on his own base was something likely to get her court-martialed. "For how long, sir?" she asked, desperately keeping her tone neutral, though she was heating up.

He grinned. "That cost you, didn't it?"

She gave a solemn nod. "You have no idea how much."

"Well, I'm glad you appreciate authority. Our forecasts shows some ugly fronts moving in. So, you won't be flying out for at least another two days."

She sighed. "Then you better add sick bay to your list of places that I'm allowed to visit. Your shrink wants to see me if I'm still here in a couple days."

"Good, I'll add that to the list," he said, then sat down and wrote a note. "I'll tell her that you'll be here for two more days anyway."

"Great," Kate muttered under her breath. He shot her a hard look, and she quickly added, "Thank you, sir." As soon as they were dismissed, her shoulders sagged.

Colton was at her side and said, "Come on. Let's go to the cafeteria."

"I'm still swimming in coffee," she declared.

"You are," he said with forced cheerfulness, "but I'm not."

She couldn't argue with that, so she nodded and headed that way. They'd missed dinner too. She stared at the staff already starting to clean up. She looked over at Colton and said, "I'm not *that* full."

He laughed. "Let's grab what we can."

They stepped smartly into the cafeteria. The chef looked at them and said, "Uh-oh, did you guys miss out?"

"Yeah," Colton said, "we were asked to stay over at the hospital until a security detail could arrive and relieve us."

"Tell me what you want," he said, motioning at the big serving platters, still sitting on the counter. "And we'll get you fixed up right now."

Kate opted for fried chicken and a huge platter of steamed veggies. With that, she headed for the desserts, even as they were yanked off the counter. She snagged two pieces of pie. With her tray full, she went to an empty table and set it all down, then went back for some milk, water and, as an afterthought, coffee. She knew Colton was making a quick round the same as she was. By the time they sat down, she could see most of the kitchen food had been removed. "Good timing."

"Right," Colton said with a big grin. "We could have been starving all night."

"Not a good thing for me right now," she said with a half laugh.

"How are you doing with the cold?" he asked worriedly.

She shrugged. "It was good timing for the coffee. Let's put it that way."

"Right. Well, let's hope you don't need to worry again for the rest of the evening."

Outside of the banging and clanging of the dishes and the conversation of the staff, they were alone in the big cafeteria, and Kate didn't mind in the least. She leaned forward and said, "Such a weird feeling being on a base like this and isolated in a way."

"But not deliberately," he muttered. His mouth was still half full, and he was plowing into his food at a faster rate than she was, but then she'd already had two muffins and two coffees recently. She picked up a piece of chicken and bit into it, then moaned. "I think fried chicken has got to be my favorite food."

"It would be a toss-up between fried chicken, steak, or lasagna for me," Colton said. Then he looked at her sideways and added, "And crawfish. Well, prawns of any kind."

"You mean, seafood of any kind," she said with a laugh.

"But prawns especially."

She really enjoyed spending the next however long it took for them to eat. They didn't race through the food, even though she knew the kitchen crew awaited their plates. She figured it could be the last load in the dishwasher, and, if two plates had to be done by hand, well, that was hardly a big deal. As they finished up, she pushed her plate to the side and moaned. "I want more, but I'm stuffed full."

"Good thing," he said, "because no more is to be had."

She smiled. "Do they eat all that's left themselves?"

"Possibly," he said, "or it could also be lunch tomorrow."

She brightened at that. "Okay, I'm down for that too." They sat here together, sipping their coffee and staring at the apple pie.

"So, you picked up two pieces," he said in a conversational tone.

She reached for both and tucked them closer to her. Then she grinned. "Were you fast enough to get any dessert?"

"No, apparently not."

"Oh, fine." She handed him one of the pieces. "I did think of you when I was picking this up."

"Sure you did," he said, but he snagged it anyway and drew it out of her own reach to his side.

She just laughed, really enjoying the kibitzing and joking back and forth. "It's hard to imagine," she said, "how much it feels like we haven't been apart for the last four years."

He nodded. "I was thinking that earlier today."

"It's like we're friends who just haven't seen each other."

He nodded again.

"Which," she said, "I would say we are."

"That works for me too," he said with a smile.

"I guess we just crossed into the friends-with-benefits thing back then."

"Considering we'd known each other for a couple years already," he said, "that would make sense too."

"And now we're not quite strangers, but we're not quite friends."

"We're definitely friends," he said in a much stronger tone than she expected. "The question is whether we're still friends with benefits." And then he waggled his eyebrows at her in such a comical move that she burst out laughing.

"Probably not a cool idea," she said, "given the current scenario."

"The scenario has absolutely nothing to do with it."

"You already said you're supposed to stay with me twenty-four hours a day. I don't want you to think that comes with benefits."

"Obviously it does not come with benefits," he said, his tone firm but friendly. "That has to be a mutual decision at the right time."

She was sorry she'd brought it up because it was obvious her comment bothered him. "I didn't mean to insult you. I know you would never take advantage and would never expect something like that."

"Good," he said, "because I would never want you to think that."

"No," she said. She looked down at her plate. She was done. "Did you make the connection that George being attacked in the hospital means that person is here on location?"

He picked up his coffee cup and nodded. "I was wondering if you had."

"I'm a little slow, but I did get it eventually." She looked around. "Does that mean it's somebody on the base?"

"I don't know," he said in a low tone. "But that's a line of inquiry somebody else will likely pick up, so we're probably better off to stay out of it."

"But you know we can't, right?"

He nodded. "And again, I was thinking that maybe it wouldn't need to involve you."

"You can't protect *the little woman* all the time," she said. "In my job I've taken an awful lot of shit just to earn enough respect from a lot of men to do my job."

"Not from me," he said.

"So don't treat me that way now," she said in a firm voice.

He sighed. "Is it wrong to try and keep you safe?"

"How is that keeping me safe?"

"If you start getting involved in this, you're putting your name and your face out front. That'll make you a target again."

"But, according to you, I'm already a target," she said slowly. "So the best answer really is solving this thing, so it won't matter who the target is. We've got to get to whoever is responsible."

"Yes," he said, "in theory. But that doesn't save your ass if it's on the line in the meantime."

"So ... what then? *You'll* investigate, and *you'll* keep me safe?"

"All while keeping you in the loop. How's that?"

She smiled. "That works. But you can't do too much investigating if you're stuck on a twenty-four-hour detail with me."

"Don't forget Troy."

She looked around. "Where is he anyway?"

"Pursuing the line of inquiry you just brought up."

She stopped and stared at him, her eyes widening. "Seriously?"

"Yes," he said. "We figured it was better that I keep you close, and that left him free to wander."

"What we have to know is who was not on base today."

"We know," he said in a soothing voice.

She glared at him, but he just grinned and said, "No, I'm not patronizing you, but I do want you to keep your voice down."

She winced as she realized her voice had, indeed, been rising. She sighed. "Put it down to hormones and emotions."

"How about just plain old stress?" he said.

She figured either he was avoiding any comment about hormones because she might have jumped up and bit his head off or he really did believe it was stress. As she thought about it, she had plenty to be stressed about. She just nodded and smiled. "I hear you. So now what?"

"Now," he said, "how about we go back to the barracks?"

"And?"

"My laptop is there."

She nodded. "Right and that's important too." She walked over to the counter with their dirty dishes and called out her thanks. One of the men poked his head out from the back and gave her a wave.

Following Colton, she headed back to the barracks. One

thing she could guarantee right now was that she was seriously tired. However, she also knew sleep couldn't be further from her head.

IT WAS HARD to walk a fine line between keeping Kate in the loop and keeping her out of things that Colton didn't want her to know. Mostly because he didn't want her to show any reaction to things he said to other people. And her face was so damn expressive. Hell, all of her was. One of the things he really remembered from their night together four years ago was every time they had made love—and it had been several times that night—she'd been so honest and open with her feelings and her response. He'd been completely enthralled, and he couldn't stop trying to make her enjoy herself even more.

And now that he knew for a fact just how expressive that face of hers was, she could never play poker because everybody else would know what she had for cards. That was why he had to play his cards close to the vest, but it was also a fine line. He didn't want to piss her off. Yes, keeping her safe was a priority, but she probably wouldn't hold it very high in her mind.

Her priorities were all about keeping George safe, which was admirable. And she also wanted to know who was doing this so they would be caught. She was right in the sense that it was the only way she could walk away from this and not look over her shoulder for the rest of her life.

As they headed toward the barracks, he looked at her and asked, "My room or yours?"

"It has to be your room. I've got a single bed. You've got bunks."

He nodded and didn't say anything. "Do you have anything in your room?"

"No, we moved it all last night, such as it is," she said. "I went to my old room today for a nap, and that's where Parsons found me." Colton opened the room and let her in. As soon as he got in, he sent Troy a text.

On my way, Troy replied. Colton motioned to the top bunk. "Troy is coming."

"Good," she said, as she stretched out on the bed. "If I fall asleep, don't wake me."

"Do you need a trip to the bathroom first?"

She could feel the heaviness washing over her. She groaned. "Yes, dammit." She made her way down off the bunk and headed to the bathroom. Since it was only a couple doors away, Colton stood in his doorway and watched. At a distance he could see Troy coming down the hall toward him. They stood close enough to have a private conversation in the hallway, the two of them talking as Troy brought him up to date. "I have a list of everybody who was off the base today."

"Was it hard to get?"

"I went straight to the commander and explained why we needed it."

"I bet that pissed him off."

"He was more pissed at the idea that somebody on his base, under his command, might have done something like this. He still doesn't believe it, and he is also interested in proving his men and women were solid and honest."

"That's an angle that works too," he said. "If all his people are clear, then it's not his fault."

"And it doesn't necessarily have to be anybody here either," Troy said. "There are way too many options."

"Not that many, surely," Colton said.

"I have about thirty-four names here, plus he added four names of men who used to work on the base but no longer do."

"No longer military?"

"One is on medical leave. Two are on dishonorable discharge. Another is off pending the outcome of an investigation."

"But not on the base?"

"No. Looks like they live in town."

"Interesting," Colton said. "I guess we have some work to do tonight."

Just then the bathroom door opened, and Kate walked out. She had scrubbed her face, the tendrils of hair around her forehead had curled with the damp water.

He motioned at her and said, "Come on. Time for you to get some sleep."

She smiled at Troy. "You missed the fun in town."

"Nope," he said, "I was having my own bit of fun."

She rolled her eyes at that. "Can't wait to hear."

"Unfortunately I didn't find anything," he said.

"What about people who were off base?" she asked.

"Yes," he said, "I've just brought a list. We'll split it up and start investigating."

"Perfect," she said. "You guys do that and let me know what you find."

At that, Colton chuckled. "As long as we keep you in the loop, right?"

"Absolutely," she said with a smile. "And, if I fall asleep, you can tell me when I wake up."

"Done deal," he said. Colton sat down, and he and Troy divvied up the work. Above, Colton could hear Kate's steady breathing settle out.

Troy stood and checked on her, then sat back down again and nodded, indicating she was asleep.

"Good," Colton said. "It's the best thing for her."

"Let's make good use of the next couple hours," Troy said.

"Seems like all we're doing is running down names," Colton said, after he accepted a sheath of papers from Troy.

"Yeah, in this instance, the commander also wants us to keep it very quiet."

"Of course he does," Colton said, and he opened up his laptop and started with the first name.

CHAPTER 11

WHEN KATE WOKE, it was bright in the bedroom. She rolled over to see Colton lying on the bunk below her, his laptop at his side, with sheets of paper beside him with scratches and notes all over it. His eyes were closed, and his chest rose and fell in a deep relaxed rhythm. She saw no sign of Troy. She slid off her bunk to the floor and opened the door.

"Where are you going?" came his sleepy voice.

"Bathroom," she whispered. "Just sleep."

"No way," he said. "Twenty-four-hour watch is twenty-four-hour watch."

She groaned. "I'll just go to the bathroom real quick." She stepped out, closing the door behind her. She made her way to the bathroom, used the facilities and then gave her face a good scrub. Oh, what she wouldn't do for some face cream and a good brush for her hair, not to mention her own favorite shampoo. As she made her way back, she saw Colton leaning against the doorjamb. She gave him a quick frown. "You didn't have to get up."

"Of course I did," he said with a smile. "Are you okay?"

"Yes," she said, "but I could really use a shower."

"That's easy enough to do," he said. "We do have a couple towels here."

Taking one, she headed back to the shower, not bothering to tell him not to wait for her because obviously he would anyway. He was such a sweetheart. She understood it was also his sense of duty, but she also really did appreciate it. When she was done, she came back out and could feel her body trembling.

"You don't realize," she said, "just how much effort it takes to shower until your body is knocked down with hypothermia."

"Pretty typical when you're exhausted," he said with a nod. He led her back into the bedroom, where she crawled up onto the top bunk. "Any chance of a change of clothes?"

"A bag should be coming in for you, with any luck."

"How can flights come in," she said, "if we can't get out?"

"I believe they landed in another city where the weather had already passed," he said, "then are driving it here."

"So, in theory, I could leave the same way."

He shook his head. "Not until you're given permission."

Cross, because he was right, she said, "Well, that flight better not be just for some of my clothing."

"No, it also brought some of the replacement supplies for those that got deep-sixed into the ocean."

She winced at that. "I don't even know what was on that load."

"It's kind of an interesting topic."

"Why?" She rolled over to look down at him. He was sitting up and leaned his back against the wall with the laptop on his lap.

"Just wondering if those supplies were part of this deal."

"I don't know what you mean," she said.

"What if he was trying to take them somewhere else?"

"George?"

Colton nodded.

"You're back to that him-being-blackmailed thing."

"Maybe," he said. "Grasping at straws, I know. But one theory has to work. There is an answer behind all this. It's up to us to find it."

"Maybe," she said. "Talking to George would be the easiest."

"Maybe we can do that today too," he said.

"What time is it?"

"It's 0730."

"Breakfast?" she asked hopefully.

He let out a barking laugh. "All you're doing is eating."

"I know," she said. "I wonder if I should see the doctor about it."

"No. It's stress, boredom, and you're still cold," he said. "I have to go to the bathroom myself, so I'll lock the door behind me."

"I think I'll be fine," she called out.

"It doesn't matter what you think." He closed the door behind him, and she heard a hard *click*. She groaned and hopped down. Loose papers were everywhere. She picked them up, studying the notes. Most of the men's names had been crossed off, but Colton had circled three with question marks. When he came back, she held up the papers and asked, "Did you find anything?"

"Hopefully today we will talk to two of the men who no longer work here. And we still have to talk to every one of these guys and get their whereabouts at the time the hospital security cameras went down."

She nodded. "I guess you couldn't do that overnight, could you?"

"Nope," he said cheerfully. "We were able to do background checks to see if anything suspicious turned up or if any connection was found to you or George."

"And was there?"

"No, nothing at all," he said. "But that doesn't mean they weren't paid to sabotage the plane for money, not caring who ended up hurt."

"Money does talk, doesn't it?" she said sadly.

"It does, but so does food." He looked at her smile and said, "Let's go and get you tanked up again."

She followed him down the hallway and said, "Where's Troy?"

"He'll meet us at the cafeteria." As they walked into the mess hall, Troy was already sitting in the far corner at a table, and he raised a hand in greeting. Kate smiled at him and grabbed a tray and a plate and looked at the selection. Everything from carbs in the form of waffles, pancakes and potatoes to eggs and all kinds of breakfast sausages were here. She looked at it and said, "Very American, huh?"

"A few traditional items from are also offered," Colton said, "but I definitely want an American breakfast this morning." He proceeded to load up on potatoes, sausages and eggs. Then he added hot buttered toast and walked toward Troy. She followed suit and then went back and got orange juice and coffee. Troy looked at their plates in approval. "Particularly when you're shut in for the weather," he said, "everybody eats so much more."

"I feel like, as soon as I eat," Kate said, "I'm hungry again."

"It just means your body is burning it up, and that's a good thing, from a healing standpoint."

Kate took a quick bite, then said, "I'd love to go back into town and see about visiting with George today."

"It's on the agenda," Troy said. "As soon as we're done eating, we're going in with Petty Officer Parsons. He'll drive us around as we need it."

"Good," she said. "That would be nice. The idea of being confined to the barracks, the cafeteria and sick bay was kind of freaking me out." As they went through breakfast, the conversation remained quiet and neutral. Enough noise surrounded them; they couldn't really talk without shouting to be heard. Kate just wanted to leave. When they were finally ready, they headed toward the front parking lot of the base, where they waited for Petty Officer Parsons to arrive.

When he arrived, he smiled, held up his briefcase and said, "I have a few errands myself, if that's okay with you guys."

"It's fine," Colton said. "Even better would be if we could have our own set of wheels."

"No can do," Parsons said. "The commander wants to know where you guys are every step of the way."

"Of course he does," Kate said with a smile.

Parsons looked at her with a questioning expression.

She just smiled and said, "It's only natural because he's responsible for everything that happens on the base."

"Exactly," he said. "There is good news in that a shipment with some of your stuff is coming in tonight."

"That would be great. What are the plans for today?"

"I'll drop you guys off at the corner by the park," Parsons said. "After my errands are finished, I'll pick you back up. These guys have all your stops for interviews mapped out."

Hearing that, she looked at Colton in surprise. "No MPs to follow us?"

He just shrugged.

"It's not a very big area. Can we just wander around and talk to people?"

"Yep, pretty much," Colton said. He didn't explain how they got clearance to walk around alone though.

"And attract all kinds of attention?"

"We would be in a military vehicle otherwise, so what's the difference?" he said.

At that, she acknowledged the point. "Fine," she said, and, sure enough, they were dropped off at a small park. She looked around and smiled. The weather was crappy, and it would obviously only get worse, but she could still appreciate being outside and being in the location they were in and how very unique it was. The place wasn't so much desolated as it had been a hard-fought battle to establish a civilization here. But once that battle was won, the people were a hearty lot. Parsons drove away, and she looked at the two men. "Where do we start?"

Troy pointed at Colton, who pointed at the closest house. "This one."

He walked up and opened a conversation, saying they were involved in an investigation on the base. Where had so-and-so been at such-and-such time. Did they know or have any connection to George and/or Kate. But never did they refer to her as being Kate. She found that interesting, as was their technique. The questioned men inevitably shook their heads, said they knew nothing, had been home or shopping or otherwise had alibis. The alibis were written down to be checked later.

Colton and Troy looked from one to the other and then at her, but, as nobody volunteered any information, there wasn't a whole lot they could say. When the questioning was done, Colton looked each man hard in the eye and said,

"Any discussion regarding this matter will require an immediate visit to the commander. You are to tell no one we were here."

Each man investigated nodded. "Understood." Each man saluted, and Colton nudged Kate down the stairs again.

"Do you really expect them to say anything different?" she asked, after they were heading down several more blocks.

"No, but if we catch someone in a lie," Troy said, "it's a completely different story."

She wondered about that and said, "You mean, after you check the alibis?"

"Yes," he said, "and I've been checking as we walk along." She'd heard him on the phone a lot but hadn't realized what he was doing.

"Do you think they've contacted their alibis already?"

"Checking their phone records afterward will be the next thing," he said.

"Ah," she said, "right. And, if they have disobeyed an order, not to let anybody know about our visit—"

"Exactly, and the commander will be very interested to have a personal talk with them. It doesn't mean they're involved in any of this, but it does mean their behavior is questionable." Colton smiled at her. "See? You're getting the hang of this."

She shook her head and said, "You're certainly wearing off my breakfast. So, where to next?"

"To see one of the men who lives in town who no longer works at the base."

"Why not?"

"He's pending an inquiry, and he married a local girl."

"Interesting," she said. When they got to the house though, nobody was there. As in nobody. No wife, no one.

They went around to the back of the house, and no sign of life was there either. When they came back around to the front, a neighbor stood glaring at them. "Who are you, and what are you doing snooping around Andy's place?"

"We're from the base," Colton said, his voice hard and authoritative. "When did you last see him?"

The man stepped back, flustered. "Um, not yesterday." He shook his head. "I'm not exactly sure. A couple days ago maybe."

"Do you look after his place when he goes away?"

"He hasn't been going away," he said.

"So do you have any idea where he is now?"

"No," he said, bewildered. "What's this got to do with anyway?"

"An official military investigation," Troy said, not allowing for any further talk or argument. He picked up the phone and made a call, while Colton thanked the neighbor and said, "Now please, go inside and close the door."

But instead the man turned belligerent. "If something is wrong in this town, I want to know about it."

"Interesting," Colton said, pulling out his pad of paper. "What is your name and phone number? And where do you work?"

The man hesitated but finally answered the questions.

"Thank you," Colton said. "We'll be in touch." He turned and looked at Troy, who nodded, and they walked back up to Andy's front door. Opening the screen door, they checked the front door. Finding it unlocked, they stepped inside. Immediately Colton stepped back out and turned toward Kate. "I want you to stay right here."

"Why?" she asked. He just gave her a hard look. She nodded. Seeing a chair on the front porch, she sat down.

"I'll be just inside the door," he said.

She nodded, the neighbor still standing there, his arms across his chest, now more curious than anything. She sat and waited. It took them ten minutes, though they did come to check on her several times. She didn't imagine anybody would be there. But before the men came back outside, the local police pulled up front. They got out and headed up the stairs. Kate opened the door to notify Colton, and her nose was assailed by a smell. She called out, "Colton, the police are here."

The neighbor took one look at the police and backed up to his property. The police shot him a look and made a motion for him to back up even farther. At that, he went up to his property and sat on the porch to watch. When the police came up the steps to Andy's house, Kate smiled at them and said, "Hi."

"And you are?"

She identified herself and then said, "Troy and Colton are inside."

"They better not be," the second officer said.

The wooden door opened, and Colton said, "Of course we are, but we haven't left this room."

"You reported a body?"

"Yes."

The cops stepped inside.

"You'll need something to cover your feet if you're walking through here," he warned them. Colton held out an arm, and she ducked under it to take a better look and gasped. He looked at her, nodded and said, "Please, just go sit back down."

She complied. The whole floor was covered in blood. She figured they'd found the man they were looking for, or his wife, she wasn't sure.

When they finally stepped back outside, she looked up at him. "Was it Andy or Andy's wife?"

"It was Andy," he said, "and he was shot in the head."

"Ouch," she said. "That was a lot of blood."

"Yes, it wasn't a very good shot. He didn't die immediately."

"That's even more awful," she said, gasping.

"It is," he said sadly.

"Are we connecting this to the base?"

"It's definitely something we have to look at."

"What about his wife?"

"According to his cell phone, his wife was visiting her mother on the other side of town."

"Interesting," she said, "so she hasn't been home yet."

"No," he said. "We'll go there next."

"No," the officer said behind him. "This is our case, and we'll take it from here."

COLTON NODDED. THEY had crossed into a different jurisdiction here, but, as soon as he had a chance, he'd contact the base and see what the commander wanted to do. As they stepped down to the sidewalk, he already had his phone in hand. When the commander answered, he explained the problem.

"Shit," he said. "I'll contact the police chief." And he hung up on him.

"Well, he's efficient," Colton said to Troy. "But not so good with explanations. He didn't say if he wants us to stay and work this or if it would just revert to a police investigation."

"I suggest that, before we run out of time," Troy said, "at least one of us heads off to the last three names."

"Let's stick together," Colton said. "And then we'll hear what the commander has to say." With that, they quickly and efficiently went through the last few names. But no surprises were had, and, of course, nothing but more alibis came. As they returned to the house with Andy's dead body inside, they saw a forensic van and more cops. Just as they approached, Colton's phone rang.

"You can go to the hospital now to visit George," the commander said, his voice sounding tired. "The police chief has taken over the investigation, but he'll keep us in the loop."

"Good enough," Colton said, "I would like to know if the wife has been found alive and safe."

"That I can confirm," he said. "Did you get a look at the bullet wound?"

"Yes," Colton said. "And, yes, it could easily have been army-issued."

"Of course." And the commander hung up on him.

On that note they headed toward the hospital. Colton pulled up his GPS and said, "It's about a mile to walk there." He looked over at Kate. "Are you up to walking, or do you want me to call for a ride?"

She shook her head. "A walk would be good. Something to shake off some of that heavy emotion."

"I get it," he said. "Let's go."

He exchanged hard glances with Troy. All this did was bring up more questions. What they needed to do was find a link back to either George or Kate. As they walked toward the hospital, they compared notes. "Absolutely nothing is here," Troy said in frustration.

"It could be a website or something, like a murder for hire?"

Both men turned to look at her. She shrugged. "I don't know. Maybe the best answers will come from George himself."

"Maybe." Colton had his doubts though. Too much was going on that they didn't know about. He knew the answer would be simple, and they just had to dig deep enough to find it.

"Did you guys get into George's emails?"

"Coronado is checking that," Colton said. "So far I haven't had any answers."

"Poke Mason again," Troy said.

Colton nodded and pulled out his phone and sent a text.

"What did we ever do without a cell phone?" Kate said, watching him.

He smiled and said, "I'm sorry that we don't have one for you."

"I presume the commander gave you one?"

He nodded. "It's a burner phone."

She nodded. "I hope somebody told my family that I'm alive and well."

"I believe Mason took care of that," he said. "He contacted your girlfriend anyway. She would have done the rest, I presume."

Kate nodded. "Not that they would have known there was a problem. I doubt the plane crash even made headlines."

"Do you ever look at the manifest or check over the cargo?"

"No, only if there's a problem," she said. "The manifest is checked over by the ground crew, then loaded and secured, and we just fly it from point A to point B."

"You don't get to know what's in it?"

"Don't get to know, don't get to argue, don't get to re-fuse," she said.

"Right, so military."

She laughed at that. "Isn't it always?"

"Minions are supposed to do as told, to not question, ours is not to know the reason why," Colton misquoted badly.

She nodded. "Are you really thinking maybe it was sup-posed to go somewhere else?"

"Maybe. And when George passed the point where they realized he wasn't following the new route, they blew it up. It's a theory." Colton shrugged. He wasn't sure it was the right one, but this was a process that wouldn't end until they found the proof to take them in the right direction.

"Well, somebody needs to get out there and start diving for that then."

"If we get proof that's what was going on, they will," he said. "But, until that point, it's an expensive recovery operation to avoid if at all possible."

She nodded and didn't say anything.

Up ahead Colton saw the large hospital. "Still a few blocks, but that looks like it up there." And he pointed.

She nodded. "Sounds good," she said, wrapping her arms around herself. "There's a definite chill to the air."

"I'll go past saying there's a chill to saying there's a real bite."

She glanced around. "Doesn't it feel like we're being watched?"

"I imagine everybody in town is watching," he said. "We're strangers, and now they've heard about the murder."

"Surely not," she asked, horrified.

"Oh, I'm pretty certain their great friends are well and truly on to this one by now. Andy's neighbor was mighty interested."

"True," she said sadly. "Everybody likes a good story, don't they?"

"Wonder if Andy had anything to say?" Troy asked.

"We'll never know now," Colton replied.

She nodded.

Finally they came to the hospital. Colton opened the front door, and they all walked in. At the reception the woman looked at him, smiled, nodded in recognition and said, "Last I heard he was awake."

They nodded, and Kate asked, "Do you know an Andy? Used to be at the base?"

She nodded. "I heard about something happening at his house." She lowered her voice. "Is it true he's dead?'

Kate nodded and whispered, "Do you have any idea who might want to kill him?"

She shook her head. "No. He hung around with a rough crowd some of the time. You know what I mean? A little bit of recreational drugs and stuff, but I don't think it was anything major."

"Any idea who we could ask to find out more?"

The receptionist looked down the hallway both ways, then grabbed a little scratchpad and wrote down a number. She slipped it over. "Don't tell him where you got it."

"I won't," Kate said with a beaming smile and turned to join the men.

"That was smooth," Troy congratulated her.

She handed over the number. "Figured we might as well figure out what kind of a person Andy was."

"True." As they walked forward, Colton dialed the number. When a voice answered at the other end, he said, "Hi, I'm a friend of Andy's."

"What about it? Are you looking to score too?"

"Maybe," Colton said. "I just don't know the town very well. I wouldn't know where to meet up."

"Where are you now?"

"Just around the hospital."

"Meet you out in the parking lot in five." Then he hung up.

"Shit," Colton said. "This guy wants to meet in five out in the parking lot." He glanced at her and then over at Troy.

"Take Troy," Kate said. "There's one dead guy already. I'll go sit with George."

From where Colton stood, he could see George sitting up in bed with a cup of tea. He nodded. "Don't leave this room."

She smiled. "Go before you miss your appointment." She walked in toward George and smiled at him. The two men turned and headed for the elevator.

CHAPTER 12

A s Kate walked in, she smiled at George, who looked so much better than when she'd seen him last. "There's a sight for sore eyes."

George's beaming smile flashed. "Didn't think I would pull through. Looks like I'll keep most of my fingers too." He held up his hands. Two fingers were bandaged and looking pretty rough, but the others were fine.

"Toes?"

"I'll lose most of them," George admitted. "But I'm alive, thanks to you guys."

"It was pretty touch-and-go," she said with a smile. "Honestly I wasn't sure I would make it either."

"That ocean," he said. "Man, was it ever cold."

"A full-scale investigation is going on into what happened."

George rolled his eyes at that. "Good luck."

"Meaning?"

"Meaning, nothing." But something cagey was in his voice.

"Will their investigation do no good?"

"No idea." But his gaze slid to the windows.

"Did you have anything to do with it?" Kate asked quietly.

He turned and looked at her, startled. "What do you

mean?"

"I'm asking if you were trying to commit suicide."

His eyebrows shot up. "No," he said. But his voice broke. He glanced at the doorway, where a nurse was coming in. She checked his temperature and his blood pressure, then clucked like a mother hen and disappeared.

"Are they still coming in every fifteen minutes?"

"They're coming in too damn often as far as I'm concerned," George muttered.

Kate walked closer until she stood right beside him. "What's going on, George? We can't tell if you've been blackmailed, if you were following orders or had ditched orders, or you were trying to take us all out with you."

He shook his head. "I don't want to say. Enough people are in trouble over this already."

"Someone's dead now," she said and filled him in on Andy.

"It's related?"

"I don't know," she said, "but it seems too coincidental not to be." Then she stopped, looked at him with a smile and said, "You don't know you were attacked here, do you?"

His eyebrows shot up as she explained about their last hospital visit.

"Holy crap," he said, reaching over and grabbing her hand. "What about my wife? My boys!" His voice was suddenly demanding and hard.

"I don't know. I would presume that somebody—"

George abruptly let go of her and sank back, but she could see he wasn't in any way at peace.

"I need to get out of here," he snapped, trying to sit back up again. "I have to find my family."

"Is your family in danger, George?" she asked, pulling

his hand back.

He stared at her with anguish in his eyes.

"Tell me," she cried out. "We can't fix it if we don't know what we're supposed to fix."

"I should never have done it," he said. "If I hadn't turned in my coworkers, my life would be normal, and I'd be happily looking toward retirement." So much pain was in his voice, as if this was tearing him apart.

"So what happened? Was somebody pressuring you?"

"They wanted me to stop," he said. "They threatened my sons. Said they wouldn't make it home from school one day, and I'd never know when."

"And what were you supposed to do? Withdraw your accusations?"

"I tried to recant. I did try," he said, "but the military wouldn't let me."

"And then what?"

"The blackmailers said I had to bring this shipment in here—drugs for Greenland. But I didn't dare. Because, once I did, then I would be just as guilty as they were," he cried out in agony. "How can people be like that?"

"Did you ditch us into the ocean?"

"Kind of. But I wasn't trying to kill us. I was hoping to come in for a crash-landing, and that would get us out of it and would burn up the cargo," he explained. "But it went badly."

"What did you do?"

"It's pretty easy. I just put some C4 inside the engine and triggered it from the cockpit. Only I used a bit too much. I'd hoped to bring the plane down, not have it blow up mid-air. I had a burner phone set to call yours to trigger the blast. It was in my pocket, all I had to do was push the talk button."

"Oh, my God," she said, staring at him. "You could have killed all of us."

"I wouldn't have done it if I wasn't desperate, and if I didn't think I could crash land close to the base," he said quietly, "and if I wasn't terrified for my sons and my wife."

"So, if they couldn't make the runs, then you were going to?"

"Yes," George said. "Didn't you ever wonder how I ended up taking over this run?"

"Since we were both new on the run at the same time, I wasn't really thinking about it. But I guess it was after you turned them in, wasn't it? What happened to the guy who I replaced on that fateful flight?"

"No clue. He called in sick. And yes," he said. "The thing you don't understand is that somebody here on the base is involved."

"Well, somebody local," she said, "was having a heyday attacking you. They actually took out the security cameras in the hospital so we'd have no idea who it was."

George fretted in bed. "That means I'm not safe," he said. "And, if I'm not safe, my family isn't safe either."

"We'll make sure your family is safe, and then we'll make sure you are too." Kate sat back for a moment. "Did you realize you were tearing apart my life? Colton keeps wondering if it was somebody I knew."

"That ex-boyfriend of yours is a piece of shit," George said, "but nothing like these guys."

"The two being charged aren't even on active duty, and I was told they're in custody and have been for weeks," she said. "So who else are they working with? And how are they communicating?"

"They used emails and mail and text, all kinds of ways," he said with a wave of his hand. "They could be working with anyone and everyone. It's likely a big operation and easy enough to cut ties with a few to keep everyone else safe."

"Like you?"

"Yeah, like me," he said. "I just couldn't do it though. I kept thinking about my sons and all the young men like them here on the island."

"Why Greenland, I wonder?"

"They were trying to stay under the radar, so to speak," he said. "Then they moved the drugs from here."

"Jesus. You'd think they'd fly into Germany."

"Sure, but the base here is much easier to get things in and out of. It's a small island. Nobody would ever think of it as a major drug center."

"Of course not," she said, "we don't even know how *major* is major here."

"All that cargo," he said. "I'd bet at least 50 percent of it was hard drugs."

Kate sat back with a *thunk*. "That's not good. And chances are, if they are doing that here in Greenland, they're doing it other places too."

"That was the impression I got. I don't know where it goes from Greenland, but it goes. A big population isn't here, so I highly doubt too much of it gets sold here. But all they have to do is get it to one of the major centers, and then, of course, the whole world is their oyster."

"Unbelievable." Kate sat there, not sure what to say. "The blackmailers would check your emails too, I bet. Trying to make sure you were toeing the line."

"Good," he said. "The emails will back up what I'm saying."

"But we still have to keep you safe." She looked around and said, "You don't even have any clothes here, do you?"

He snorted. "No. Not likely. I think they cut everything off me on the navy cruiser."

"Yes," she said, and then she thought about the other ships that called this base home. "They could have even moved drugs in through them and other ships."

"Anything is possible," he said. "Even small planes fly out from here. I mean, it's pretty easy to start moving it in different locations, once you break it down. The hard part is getting in a big shipment, and we just delivered it."

"Yeah, but we delivered it to the ocean," she said. "Hopefully it'll be thoroughly ruined, and nobody can salvage it."

"I'm not sure it's safe to leave underwater though," he said. "It probably poisoned the ocean."

So much bitterness remained in his voice that Kate reached out and stroked the back of his hand. "Remember why you did this," she said. "Keep your boys in your mind."

"I get it," he said. "But I'm not out of danger, and neither are you."

Kate sat back and said, "And here I was thinking I wasn't in danger now."

"No," he said. "Because you were with that shipment. If I go down for transporting drugs, it'll mean you go down too."

She wrinkled her face up at that. "I didn't know anything about it."

"Where's Colton?" George asked, suddenly frowning. "He survived, didn't he?"

"Yeah, he's fine. That cold water didn't seem to faze him. He's here at the hospital with me."

"Thank heavens for that. I thought I heard him onboard the cruiser, but I don't even know that I asked about him."

Such shame filled his voice that she just smiled. "Hey, George. You need to look after yourself now. It's a mess."

"It's a bigger mess than you know. This is a military mess …"

"One who was military but more recently a civilian was just shot."

"Right, Andy," George said. "And I doubt he'll be the last one before this is cleared up."

"The commander will sure be pissed when he finds out what's been going on under his nose. He'll get to the bottom of it."

"That would be good. Somebody sure needs to."

Kate looked around, wondering where Colton was.

"Are you waiting for Colton?"

"Yeah. They went to meet a friend of Andy's, somebody who is dealing drugs." She slid George a sideways look. "Sound familiar?"

George winced. "Let's hope they do more than just meet him because somebody needs to get to the bottom of all of this, and fast."

"Yeah, you're right there." Kate got up and walked to the hallway, looking up and down, but she saw no sign of Colton yet. She turned back to George. "Are they feeding you?"

"Yes, I don't want for anything. I'm fine. I'm healthy. I'll make it," he said firmly.

"I'm glad to hear that," Kate said with a big smile. "Now I need you to survive." She opened up all the cupboards in the room, but she found no clothing for George. Frowning, she said, "We'll have to get you some clothing from the base."

"That would be good," George said. "I mean, if I'm under attack again, I'll come out buck naked if need be, but I'd feel more comfortable if my Johnson was covered."

At that, Kate burst out laughing. He grinned at her. "Let's see if I can find anything here. Maybe in the lost and found."

"Okay," he said, "maybe ask at the nurses' station."

Kate headed down the hallway to the nurses' station. She found a receptionist or maybe a head nurse. She didn't know; she didn't understand the uniforms here. She asked if there was any clothing for George. When the woman understood the question, she frowned, shook her head and said, "Only what he came in with."

"Which was nothing unfortunately," Kate said.

"Let me check the lost and found." She came right back with a large black bag, saying, "This is all we have."

"May I take it to his room?" Kate asked. "That way we can see if anything will work for him."

She nodded. "Bring back what's left when you're done."

Kate took the bag to George, still lying in bed. "We've got this to work with," she said, holding out the bag. Carefully she dumped it on top of him. And, between the two of them, they managed to find a T-shirt and a pair of shorts. They found no underwear and no socks for him.

"Well," he said, as he looked at his toes, "I won't have much to cover soon anyway."

"You won't be running for a while, but this will give you something to wear, just in case." Kate piled everything back into the black bag. "If you're good with the T-shirt and shorts, I'll take the rest back."

"That's fine. I don't know what happened to my underwear. You'd think they would have left those on."

"I know, right? We'll get you some from the base. This is only in the case of emergency."

"Let's hope it doesn't come to that," he said with a heavy sigh. "But you're right, it gives me something. Not very much but enough that I could make a run for it, if I have to."

"You need to try walking first," she said with a nod to his damaged feet. "You may very well find you can't run for your life."

COLTON AND TROY ran down the stairs, choosing that over the elevator, and bolted out the back door to the parking lot. As soon as they hit the lot, they separated, with Troy going to the shadows to keep an eye on Colton and his meeting. Colton, not knowing who he was looking for or where he would find him, headed toward the far end of the lot, figuring anybody looking at a drug deal would stick to the shadows. But he couldn't guarantee that.

As he'd come to learn, many people working in the world of drugs were fine upstanding citizens with reputations that kept them front and center. But they weren't always the most forthcoming about their drug habits. And they always had dealers in the background. As he walked all the way to the back, he saw no sign of anyone. He leaned against the cement wall and crossed his arms, keeping himself visible, just in case. He could see Troy moving between the vehicles up ahead. When a sound came from his left, he glanced casually over to see a male of around fifty, standing with his hands on his hips, his eyebrows raised.

Colton raised his eyebrows and looked directly at the

man. "Hey."

"No fucking *hey* with me," the dealer sneered. "How did you get my number?"

"Off the phone," he said. "You want to talk drugs or no?"

The guy looked around hurriedly. "What the hell are you, suicidal? None of this is brought out in the open."

"Andy was pretty verbal about it."

"Andy was a fucking idiot," the man snapped. "And, if you're thinking I haven't heard he's dead by now, you're wrong."

"Good," Colton said. "Then we're on the same ground."

"And what ground is that?" the dealer asked suspiciously. "And why the hell did you contact me? You don't look like a user."

"No, but I might be a supplier."

An odd stillness came over his face. "Shit," he said, glancing around. "The plane went down, I heard."

"It did," Colton said quietly. "And, yes, the cargo was lost."

"It was a dummy run anyway," he muttered.

He spoke just barely loud enough for Colton to hear. His eyebrows rose. "Interesting," he said. "Three people almost died on that flight."

"Yeah, I heard," he said.

"Interesting gateway."

"Coming in from the north, nobody else expects it, but an awful lot of the population lives within just a few hundred miles. Much less regulation and a lot fewer eyes."

"All the good points," Colton admitted. "Interesting," he repeated.

"Hey, you got to do what you got to do."

When Colton looked back again he saw a small snub-nose revolver pointed at him. "Is that the gun you killed Andy with?"

"I didn't kill Andy," the dealer said, taking several steps back. "But you are not a user, and I don't think you're a supplier either. You didn't come with any goods."

"Of course not," Colton said, laughing. "I don't know you from anyone, and I do know Andy is dead. So why would I bring anything here to a meeting with you?"

The guy sneered. "I don't like anything about this. You turn around and walk away, and you forget you ever saw me."

"If I turn around and walk away," Colton said calmly, staring him down, "you'll put a bullet in my back."

"Hell, no, but I might just put one between your eyes."

And, with that, Troy, who had slipped down the vehicles after seeing the gun, came up behind the man. And just as the gunman lifted his weapon and pointed it right at Colton's head, Troy took him down. With him on the ground, the handgun now tossed off to the side, Troy sitting on the guy's back, pinning his arms underneath him, Colton said, "Now we want to have a talk with you." He pulled out his temporary burner phone and contacted the commander. "You want to bring in the local police on this one?"

"I don't want to, no," he said. "But that is a citizen and not one of my men, so, yes, stay where you are and keep him there. I'll have the cops to you in just a few minutes."

"Will do," Colton said. "Keep in mind we don't know if the cops are clean."

There was a hesitation in the commander's voice as he said, "No, but I have to follow proper chains of authority, and I hope the people I'm calling understand that too.

Generally they don't have a drug problem here."

"Well, one has been uncovered. I can tell you, this one is a dealer, Andy was one of the dealers, and supplies have been coming through the base, so it will be a little hard to keep this hush-hush once this guy starts talking."

"If he starts talking."

Colton hung up and motioned at the man and said, "The cops are on the way."

The guy just laughed. "Like that'll make a fucking difference."

"Why is that?" Troy asked. Jerking him up to his feet, they secured his arms behind his back while Colton picked up the handgun. He studied it and nodded.

"Same model that put that bullet in Andy's head."

"I didn't do it," he said. "A few of those are around town. A guy was selling them about four years ago, and a bunch of us bought him out."

"Interesting," Colton said. "Who else would have one?"

At that, the dealer fell silent.

"And why is it we won't get any satisfaction out of the police?"

The look on the guy's face wasn't what Colton expected though. All the bravado was gone, and instead there was only fear. "I won't make it that far," he said. "I'll be taken out."

"Maybe you better start talking now then," Colton said. "Just to make sure you have a voice in what happens to your future."

"No," he said. "Once you take me into the station, I'm done for."

"Bad cops?" Troy asked from behind him.

The guy shook his head. "No, the goddamn cops here are too damn squeaky clean. You don't understand what it's like here, how many people don't own their own land. They just kind of live and borrow as needed."

"So why would you want to mess with a nice system like that?" Colton asked.

"Because they're all so innocent," he said. "We can move a lot of drugs through here."

"But through here is still through nowhere," Troy said. "You could have taken them to England and had a distribution network all through Europe."

"They get to England, but we can also hit all the Nordic countries and Russia. And we're coming down from Europe on the topside. It might take a little longer, but it's safer, with fewer roadblocks and fewer people in the know. You generally find the country folks are a little more naive when it comes to drugs. Hit any major port, and it's a damn puzzle to get stuff moving."

"And yet you say you'll be taken out if we get you to the police station."

"Once they figure out I'm being taken in, they'll assume I'll talk," he said.

"But who is *they*?" Colton asked.

"Those above me," he said, his shoulders sagging in defeat. "I'm already a dead man. You can bet somebody is watching us."

In the distance Colton could hear emergency vehicles coming. "That might be the cops now. Who killed Andy?"

"Not me." He looked up, smiled and said, "You still haven't figured it out, have you?"

"Not all of it," Colton said slowly. He needed more answers and desperately needed this guy to talk but wasn't sure what the magic was to get him to loosen up that tongue.

"That's because it's right in front of you," he said. "You

can't see it, and you're looking right at it."

"We know a couple pilots were involved, and they are in the custody of the military and have been since they were turned in," Troy said.

"Sure, but more will replace them."

"More military personnel?"

He shrugged. "It's a huge population to tap. A lot of users among the military—and a lot of dealers too. But the minute you get a network like that, you always get a couple who rise to the top."

"Right, the ones doing the drug running," Colton said.

His suspect nodded. "That's one way to look at it."

"And, of course, it has to be somebody at the Greenland base."

The man nodded again. "You're getting warmer."

Colton and Troy exchanged hard glances. "Who set up the pilot for this last run?"

"*Them*," he said with a hard emphasis.

"And that's because they were afraid George would do something and you'd lose the product?"

"Yeah," he said, "but more's coming in soon."

"Except for the bad weather."

"There's always bad weather here. It's one of the reasons the base isn't overrun with military resources, and that works really well."

"Does it move from one military branch to the other?" Troy asked.

"It's pretty easy to do that too. The military network is vast and is already in place."

"But it has to start somewhere. Any idea where it's coming from?"

He raised his gaze. "You got to be kidding me? The volume of drugs coming out of the US is massive."

"Sure," Colton said, "but how are they getting into the US?"

"That supply train has been moving steadily for decades. You'll never stop that one. It's a matter of getting it from one place to the next. The military provides a lovely global network."

Colton and Troy exchanged more glances. The guy was right. United States military bases were all over the world, and they did Joint Task Force operations with military units from multiple other countries as well. It was probably pretty simple to piggyback on that. "Did you guys have anything to do with blowing up the plane?"

The dealer shook his head. "I didn't know anything about that."

"Was it sabotage? Or was it the pilot?"

"I suspect both," he said. "If they didn't trust him, if he argued with them or told them what he might do, or maybe he sabotaged the plane on his own to get out of it. Or maybe it was a suicide mission. I don't know. He wouldn't be the first."

"Wouldn't be the first what?"

"To take his own life to get out of this hell. Once they get their claws into you, they learn everything they can about you and your family, and it's either follow their path or not."

As Colton went to ask something else, cop cars pulled into the parking lot toward them.

"Well, it's trouble now." The guy stared glumly. "I might yet get out of this," he said, "but I can't get out of it without blowing this wide open to get protection from the cops, then it hitting the news too."

"The media isn't likely to pick up your arrest, is it? Are

you wanted?"

He shook his head. "No, but gossips are everywhere. And the network on this island is unbelievable. Within five minutes of being booked into the police station, my head will be numbered."

With misgivings, Colton watched the cops load up their man. As one of the cops walked over to talk to him, Colton said, "I need an ID on who he is."

"That's Eric Strange," the cop said. "What's your business with him?" His suspicion was obvious, but as Colton and Troy explained what was going on, he relaxed and said, "I have instructions to move the information up the chain as it happens. I believe the commander will contact you as needed."

"I can only hope so," Colton said. He and Troy watched as the vehicle took off with Eric Strange in the back seat.

"Do you think Strange is right?" Troy asked.

"Unfortunately I think he probably is. He might not be marked right now, but tomorrow or the next day, yeah, it's possible. If this is as big of an operation or jumping point as he makes it sound, an awful lot is at risk."

"An awful lot is at risk, but it also means a pretty big deal if we can get it stopped," Troy said.

"What do you think he meant," Colton said, as they walked back toward the hospital, "about not seeing what's in front of us?"

"I'm afraid he means the base. Like whoever is masterminding this is somebody we've already spoken to."

"*Great*. The good news is," Colton said, "the shipment wasn't full of drugs, so there's no point in going through a recovery operation. And another plane is coming in soon with more."

"Right," Troy said. "Something else we'll have to brief the commander on."

"Let's collect Kate and head back," Colton said. "She'll need food, and it's been a long day already."

"Productive in many ways though," Troy said. "One dead man, one captured man, and George is awake."

As they wandered back up toward his room, they could hear George and Kate inside. When they walked in, she looked up, and a big smile crossed her face. Colton felt his heart warm in response. He held out his hand, and she slipped under his arm and gave him a big hug. "There you are," she exclaimed. "I was starting to wonder if you were okay."

"Not to worry," he said. "It's all good." He looked over at George and smiled. "You're looking better than the last time I saw you," he said with a little emotion in his voice.

George reached out a bandaged hand and said, "I want to thank you for saving my life."

"I'm not exactly sure what happened," Colton said. "So I'm not sure if you're responsible for the plane being ditched or not."

"I was partly responsible," George said. "The end result was not at all what I had planned, so I'm not sure if it was my actions that did it or not, but I definitely didn't want to bring that plane into the base."

"If it makes you feel any better," Colton said, "we just spoke to one of the men involved in this mess, and he said your plane didn't have any drugs on it. It was a test to see if you were trustworthy."

"I guess I failed that then, didn't I?"

"Exactly," Colton said with a smile. "On the other hand, I'm sure the military is happy to hear that."

"They aren't, however, happy about something else," Troy said, leaning against the doorway. "Apparently the base is being used as a jumping off point for distribution on the northern network."

"Crap," George said. "That's really disturbing."

"The fact that we even know this much," Colton said, "will help us track it down."

"But the bad weather will stop the next plane coming in, won't it?"

"Yes, but …" Troy said, turning to look at Colton. "Did he actually say it was coming into the base?"

Colton thought about it for a long moment, then shook his head. "You know something? I don't think he did."

He looked over at George. "Sorry about the toes."

"Hey, I'll trade my toes and a couple fingers for my life any day. Maybe it's time to take an early retirement and go spend time with the boys who I'm fighting so hard to get back home to." He looked over at Kate. "Kate here can keep up the runs."

"Hey, you know me," Kate said. "I was wondering about changing up my schedule too."

Colton looked at her in surprise.

She shrugged. "I wouldn't mind more time at home," she confessed. "Especially once the Ned issue is handled."

"Do you have enough seniority to change your routes?" he asked. "Or do you want to go private?"

"Both are things I'll consider over the next few weeks and months," she said. Looking back at George, she smiled. "The bottom line is to get you healthy."

"And keep you safe," Colton said, as he stepped out and looked at the doorway. "When did the guards leave?"

George's eyebrows rose. "I didn't see any guards today."

The three exchanged hard glances. Troy said, "Wait here. I'll go find out." Then he disappeared down the hallway.

"You didn't mention anything about guards," George said to Kate.

"I forgot all about them," she exclaimed. "After what happened yesterday, a security detail was assigned. We waited here for them to arrive. They took up their posts outside your room, and we headed back to the base."

"So, who pulled them off the guard duty detail?" Colton said slowly. He grabbed his phone and dialed the commander. When he answered, Colton said, "We're checking in on George, but the security detail is gone."

"It shouldn't be. They were supposed to be standing on a twenty-four-hour watch." The commander's voice rose in anger. "I'll get back to you."

Colton pocketed his phone. "Heads will roll." His voice was cheerful though because he liked to see people follow orders, and to see something like this happen meant that either somebody had changed the orders or somebody was trying to get out of following orders. In either case, somebody was about to get their ass handed to them. He said, "I guess that means we'll sit here and wait until we get this sorted out again."

George shook his head. "Go on. I'm fine."

"No, you're not," Kate said, walking over to the bedside chair and sitting down. "You weren't fine yesterday, and you won't be fine today, should someone come in here, intending harm."

"It's almost dinnertime already," he said. "I don't know how long you guys have been here, but you look exhausted and cold."

"I don't know about you," Kate said, motioning at him in the bed, "but I'm always cold now."

He nodded. "Yeah, I've got a few more blankets than a person should need. But I'm hoping that'll ease up over time."

"It will," she said. "Over time."

They stayed and visited with casual small talk until Troy came back. "They were released early this morning."

"Released or replaced?"

"The nursing staff thought they were supposed to be replaced, but nobody else showed up."

"The commander is on it now too," Colton said. Just then his phone rang.

"Stay where you are," the commander said, "I have two more men coming."

"Apparently they were released this morning," Colton said.

"They were to be replaced, but the order didn't go through as issued. Don't worry. I'll find out why." And, from the tone of his voice, Colton realized he was beyond furious.

"Understood." Colton hung up and said, "We're to wait until the new detail arrives."

George shrugged. "An awful lot of fuss over nothing."

"Not nothing," Kate said. "Keeping you safe is the difference between having a witness and evidence to the blackmail and not. If we want to stop this, we have to stop it, not just slow it down."

George nodded. "I was kind of hoping I could go home to my family and put this behind me."

"You'll never put it behind you," Colton said, "until it's over. And you're at risk until it is."

CHAPTER 13

KATE HATED TO think Colton was serious, but it was pretty obvious he was. She was tired and hungry and was more than ready for an early night again. She couldn't believe just how exhausting this day had been, but the shock of finding that poor dead man and then waiting for the cops and walking around the houses to question the locals and all had made for a very long and tiring day. Not to mention her long and emotionally taxing reunion with George. Her energy reserves were already thin, and now they had been maxed out completely. It was a relief to see Colton and Troy step out into the hallway to greet two new soldiers. And then Colton looked at her and said, "We should get going now."

She smiled and, leaning over, gave George a kiss on the cheek and said, "You stay safe." She walked out to meet Colton and wrapped an arm around his waist, his arm instinctively coming around her shoulder. "So how are we getting back to the base?"

"Parsons is coming to get us again," Troy said.

She smiled, then nodded and said, "Perfect." Outside, they waited for a vehicle to come. Finally a military vehicle did pull up. It was Parsons.

"Sorry," he said, "I didn't get the orders until I was back at base again."

"It's been a long day for everyone," Kate said, sliding

into the front seat, while Troy and Colton took the back. By now darkness was settling in, but it wasn't the darkness of night; it was the storm and the cloud cover taking over. She looked up and groaned. "It looks like a crappy day weatherwise too."

"It is a crappy day," Parsons said. And it probably was for him because of the news and whatever the commander had told him or possibly even reamed him out about. He didn't look terribly impressed either. As they drove back to the base, Kate could hear the men in the back seat talking. She twisted a couple times, but their voices were low as they compared notes and showed each other texts. She didn't understand what was going on, and she knew Parsons himself was curious too. Finally she looked around to face forward again and realized they'd taken a different route this time. "Where are we?"

Parsons yawned. "It's faster this way," he said, "particularly if the weather is getting bad."

She settled back and said, "I'm so damn tired."

"Did you eat?" Parsons asked. "I have a flask of coffee down there, if you want."

She was tempted, and then she shook her head. "No, it's all right. I'll just close my eyes. Wake me up when we get there."

He gave a bark of laughter. "No problem. I can do that."

She dozed a little. Finally she looked up to see headlights coming toward them. "Are we almost there?"

"We are," Parsons said.

She looked out to see an almost empty wasteland of a road. "It's very different country here."

"Very," he said.

Just then a vehicle came up behind them and another

one ahead. Kate looked from one vehicle to the other, and then checked on the guys to see that they were both aware. She frowned at Colton, but he lifted a finger to his lips. She sagged back, but her nerves were shot as she realized something was going on that she didn't understand. She could tell from Parsons' reactions as he looked from window to window that he wasn't happy either.

"A lot of traffic," she murmured.

"Too much," he said. "It's unusual."

Just then, the vehicle ahead hit its brakes and started to slow down.

"What's up ahead?" she asked Parsons. "Is that the base?" The ugly weather was dark enough with clouds churning all around them that it was hard to see much.

"It could be an obstruction on the road," he said. As they went to drive past the vehicle, it turned at an angle, blocking the road. "It happens when there's a road slide or some other problem. There could be an accident I don't know about or something." He pulled off to the side and said, "Stay here."

He hopped out and went to talk to the men in the truck up ahead, around to the driver's side and then carried on around to the front of the engine, the vehicle now blocking view of Parsons.

Troy and Colton both said, "We want you to stay inside." They opened the doors and slipped out. And then she saw the guns.

And the gunmen were US military personnel, all in fatigues.

Somebody was coming up behind Colton, holding a handgun against him. And the same for Troy. And she realized that whether Parsons was a part of it or not, this was a trap. And they were well and truly caught. She slipped out of the vehicle, wondering if she should head cross-country. She looked over at Colton, and he yelled, "Run."

Swearing, she raced ahead to the front vehicle, looking for any place to hide and to get away from here. Just when she was ready to bolt, she heard gunfire. She was out of sight of both Troy and Colton and decided on a more dangerous move than she'd expected. She threw herself under the big rig in front of them.

And, from here, she checked out where all the legs were. Two in front and four on the left. So three men were nearby, and then one collapsed to the ground. It was Parsons. He held his shoulder, which oozed blood, but he was facing away from her. She didn't know if she could help him or not, and yelling came from the two men still standing.

Then Colton and Troy were brought over, which meant a total of six men that she could see, plus Parsons on the ground. She was completely outnumbered, and it wouldn't take long for somebody to figure out she'd either taken off cross-country, or she'd hidden somewhere. And the chances and options to hide were slim. She was only minutes away from being found.

But, as long as all the men were on one side of the vehicle, she could head somewhere else. She rolled out to the other side and headed back to the military jeep which Parsons had been driving. She climbed into the open passenger door, slipped over to the driver's seat, then turned on the engine.

Instead of backing up and turning around, she yanked the wheels hard and drove off-road until she'd circled around, then drove back onto the pavement. And she hit the gas as hard as she could. Shots were fired in her direction, but nothing hit the vehicle. She didn't know where she was going or how far, but she needed to get the hell away.

Another vehicle came up in front of her, but she had no way of knowing if it held good guys or bad guys, and she didn't dare take a chance of choosing wrong, so she slowed. When they pulled out and crossed the road in front of her, she realized exactly who they were. The men were out and holding guns on her within seconds. She lifted her hands slowly, and they ordered her from the vehicle. She stepped out and saw they were from the base too. At gunpoint she was marched back up the road a good mile to where she'd left the men.

When Colton saw her, the muscle at the corner of his jaw started twitching. She ran to him, and he wrapped his arms around her and held her close.

"Isn't that cute," one of the men said.

"Not really," Colton growled. "What the hell is this all about?"

"Drugs of course."

"So you're part of this?"

Troy asked, "How the hell can you do that? You're supposed to be serving your country."

"What the hell has my country done for me?" he said. "Good thing we had our last truck coming up behind us. He was supposed to get in early, but he didn't make it."

So now there were even more men to deal with. She looked over at Troy to see he had a handgun hidden at his back. Had he brought it with him? Or taken it off someone? Troy stepped slightly closer to her, gave her a hug and whispered, "When things blow, get under the truck."

And, with that, he stepped forward, grabbed the gun arm of the man closest to him, then turned it and shot the man who'd been speaking. Kate dropped to the ground and rolled under the truck as chaos broke loose. Shots were fired in all directions. She slipped up to where Parsons lay very still and took his revolver from his holster and waited for things to calm down.

As she peered out, she could see two men now holding their guns on Troy. She rose up on her elbows and fired, taking one man out with a headshot. Troy grabbed the other, knocked him to the ground and subdued him. Kate wasn't sure if that was everybody, but Colton dropped to his knees to find her. "Is it safe to come out now?"

He helped her roll out from underneath and back onto her feet. He looked at the gun, and she nodded.

"I got it off Parsons." Parsons was on the ground, softly moaning.

"We've got a lot of men down now," Colton said, already dialing his phone.

Kate walked over to Troy. "Are you okay?"

He nodded grimly. "A couple of burns but nothing major. It's Colton who's been shot."

She spun around to look at him. Colton just shrugged, and she could see blood welling up on his leg. She ran back to the truck, looking for a first-aid kit. Not finding any, she went to the guy she'd shot in the head and ripped his T-shirt off. With Troy's help, they cut off a big strip. While Colton was still talking to the commander, she bound up his leg.

When she was done, he looked down and smiled. "It wasn't that bad, you know?"

"You're tracking blood everywhere," Kate said, as if cleanliness were the most important thing here. Then she laughed and sat back on her haunches. Looking up at him, she said, "You know what? We're damn lucky to have survived this."

"Damn lucky," Troy said. "And I owe you my life."

She shook her head. "I think we're all past that at this point. It seems like we've done nothing but save each other."

She looked down at Parsons and said, "How bad is he?"

"Not," Troy said. "But the commander is sending in the troops."

At that, Parsons managed to sit up. "Wow," he said. "Talk about an ambush."

She nodded. "Do I need to work on your shoulder?"

"No," he said. "I'll just sit here and wait until the rescue comes." He smiled up at her. "Can I get my gun back please?"

She handed it to him without a thought. Immediately he reached up and fired a shot. She took the bullet in her shoulder and stared at him in shock. The gun went off a second time, but she was already on her way to the ground when the burn slashed into the same damn shoulder.

COLTON BOLTED TOWARD Parsons, only to be facing the handgun.

Parsons smiled up at him. "Fooled you, huh?"

Colton just glared at him, the muscle in his jaw working. It was sure death to take a step forward. But Kate was lying beside him unconscious, and he didn't know how badly hurt she was.

"I didn't kill her," Parsons said, "if that means anything to you."

"Not much," Colton said, his voice deadly soft.

"Of course not. You're one of those big macho guys. Got to do everything right."

"Not necessarily," Colton said. "But we're also in a relationship, and I really don't appreciate you shooting her."

"And I really don't appreciate you guys getting in my face," Parsons said.

"Is this all your deal?" Troy asked, taking a step forward.

"One more step," Parsons said, "and I'll blow your friend's brains out."

Troy stopped moving. But even Colton could feel the assessment in his hard gaze.

"How do you plan to get out of this now?" Colton asked.

"I need a moment to figure that out," Parsons said. "Somehow you guys managed to wipe everybody out. I mean, I've seen a lot of guys who were damn good, but I wasn't expecting this. You guys are a cut above." He looked at the men on the ground around him. "Like, what the hell?"

"If you'd stayed quiet," Troy said at Colton's side, "nobody would have known."

"You don't know anything now. But it wouldn't take long I'm sure before it would come out."

"All you had to do though was stay quiet. Pack up on leave and never bother coming back," Colton said persuasively. "You can still do that."

"You think I'll get off Greenland safely?"

"Do you really think, after all this, you'll still salvage this somehow?"

"If I kill you three," he said, "then nobody will know."

"The commander has already been brought in on this," Colton said.

Parsons stared at him. "You've already reported in?"

"I could show you my phone to see it for yourself. Some of it was telephone, and some of it was text."

At that, Parsons started swearing. "Goddammit. He could have another half dozen vehicles on the way."

"If we don't check in soon, he certainly will." Colton glanced around. "Exactly where are we anyway?"

"It's a back way to the base," Parsons said. "But it's not exactly the easiest way to go."

"So why did you go this way?"

"Because they do a lot of practice out here, and I knew some of the guys could come and give me a hand without being noticed."

"So you arranged this lovely little ambush?"

"If that's what you want to call it, yes. Rescue is the other answer."

Troy just shook his head.

Colton agreed because none of it made any sense. "I still don't understand why you blew your cover. You were set up to walk away as an injured good guy. With that injury you might very well have just gotten a discharge and stepped out."

"Maybe," he said. "But I figured, with you guys in the middle of this headache, and George still alive, there wasn't any way to walk away free and clear."

"Are you the one who attacked George?"

Parsons waved his gun at him. "Just shut the fuck up right now," he said. "I have to think."

Colton went quiet, but he watched the sweat on the man's face. Not only was the pain making it hard for Parsons to think clearly, but he was in a pickle.

"The easiest thing would be to say you were pressured into doing this," Colton said in a conversational tone.

The gun was immediately pointed at him again.

"I said shut the hell up," Parsons snapped. Using the

truck, he slowly stood, keeping the gun leveled on Colton and Troy. When Troy stepped forward, Parsons smiled and said, "I don't really care if I kill both of you or not, but you know for sure your buddy will be dead because I can't miss at this range."

Colton said, "But you're not likely to kill both of us. And that'll still leave you with one death on your record. At the moment I don't see any on yours. These guys," he said, waving his arm, "are all on us."

"And I'm still figuring out how you did that," Parsons said. "None of it makes any sense."

"Makes more sense than you think," Troy said cheerfully. "It's kind of what we do."

"Hell, I'm military," Parsons said. "What the hell are you guys?"

"Navy SEALs," Colton said, his voice hard and dry. "If you got your fat ass off the ground and into the water, you might have learned a little more."

"Well, that just means you're sea, air and land. I'm just land, but I should still be better than you."

At that Colton's eyebrows shot up. "Not sure how you figured that," he said, "but whatever."

"The *whatevers* in life count," Parsons said, but it was obvious the pain and maybe the blood loss was starting to get to him. "I can't handle two of you, so I'll have to kill one. The other one will drive me out of here."

"Maybe," Troy said. "What will you do about her?"

"I'll shoot her," he said.

"Wow," Colton said. "So you've got absolutely no problem shooting a defenseless unconscious woman on the ground. That's like shooting one of us in the back. Absolutely no honor in that."

"Honor? There is no honor in this job. I've been trying to get off this goddamn base for four years, and I haven't been able to. At first I thought, if I was good as gold, I'd get a transfer. Instead, they just kept me on because I was so damn good at my job. At some point my dissatisfaction turned to hatred. And that hatred turned to revenge and trying to find any way I could to screw this place. When I finally figured it out and hooked up with the drug-running, life became interesting. I'm not even too bothered about leaving now, except for the fact that you busted my position here wide open. Who the hell needs that?"

"That won't stop now, no matter what you do to us," Troy said. "The commander is already running a full investigation. Plus we already know the next plane that comes in will have the real drugs. The one George flew in with Kate was supposed to have drugs, but they were running it as a test, and it literally was just cargo."

"So I heard. Figures I wouldn't hear about it until afterward. All I could think about was all that money sitting in the Arctic Ocean."

"You can always try to recoup some of it," Colton said cheerfully. "But I highly doubt I would trust anything anybody says in your outfit."

"That's the problem," Parsons said. "I can't trust anyone. I can't trust the people who told me it was full of drugs, and I can't trust you guys telling me it was a trick. The trouble is, I can see them doing the trick thing to test out members in the chain to see if we're loyal."

"If you're making money on this," Colton said, "then that's a smart way to be. Nobody is loyal long-term. They're only loyal as long as it benefits them."

"By the way, did you kill Andy?" Troy asked, studying

Parsons like he was a bug he'd never seen before.

"Forget about Andy," Parsons said.

"Why is that?"

"Andy already botched his situation at the base, and getting him out of there without getting court-martialed was a trick, but I managed it. I figured he could be useful from town, but then he stopped being useful."

"Wow," Colton said. "And what about the plane? Did you guys sabotage it?"

"No, it was all part of the trick to keep George honest. But instead he ditched the plane."

"I'm not so sure about that," Colton said, "because the engine did blow up."

"I wondered about that too. It's possible that, when the bosses realized George wouldn't do what they told him, they blew it up to get rid of him anyway. I don't know. They don't tell me anything."

"How will we deal with them?"

"You won't," Parsons said. "Some are at Coronado base. Some are on the German base. They're all over the place. They infiltrate even the big military groups. Once you're in, you're caught, and you follow orders."

"Like ordering you to take others out, like Andy."

"Didn't have a choice with Andy. And look at the guys you've just taken out now." Parsons's gaze cast around to the dead men on the ground, and he shook his head. "A bloody massacre."

"They pulled guns on us," Troy said softly.

Colton just gave Parsons a fat grin. "And you do see the relevance of what you're holding on us now, right?"

"It's not as if you guys will stop me," Parsons said, "at this distance nobody could miss."

"Sorry to say," Colton said, "we're willing to take our chances."

Parsons stared at that. "You're willing to take certain death for one of you in order to make sure you stop me?"

"For what you did to Kate, absolutely," Colton said.

"And what you did to Andy and George and possibly a half-dozen others," Troy said.

"How is that sensible? Why don't you just decide between you which guy will die, and the other one get in the damn vehicle and drive me back into town. I need medical attention."

"You'll take the gun into the hospital and force them to treat you too?"

"Sure," he said and smiled. "Actually, you know something? I think we'll put her inside the vehicle too. We'll keep her as collateral, to make sure you behave. And, if you don't, I'll blow you all apart."

"You won't get far," Colton said.

"You keep giving me that bullshit," Parsons said, looking around at the vehicles, "but I don't want one of these big rigs."

"What do you want?" Troy asked helpfully.

"I want the one she took in the first place."

"I can go get it," Troy said.

"And take off on me?" Parsons said derisively. "I wasn't born yesterday."

"No, but you have her and Colton captive," Troy said. "Of course I'll come back."

"I don't know. I don't feel like I can trust you."

"I'll do anything to stop you from shooting these two," Troy said quietly. "Hasn't there been enough death already?"

"Go get it and bring it back because you can bet that, if

you don't, I'll have people waiting for you at the other end."

"Why don't you bring some people in here to grab your guys so they're all taken care of?"

"No, we'll figure out how to blame this all on you."

Just then the wind picked up, and Colton's hair whipped back tight around his head. He brushed it back, turning his face into the wind. He looked over at Troy, and they could see how black and dark the clouds were. He yelled over the wind, "We have to do something soon, or we won't be going anywhere." He could see the vehicles rocking in the wind. "Come on. We have to get you somewhere to get treatment."

Parsons took several deep breaths. "It's not that easy," he said.

"It's not that hard."

Troy made a decision and said, "I'll go get the jeep," and he took off at a run. From his position, Parsons couldn't even move to stop him. He just held the gun on Colton.

"You're not going anywhere," he said.

"What will you do if he takes off?"

"I don't know," he said, but his breath was gaspy and choppy. "It's not how I wanted to go out."

"Then don't make this a case of going out," Colton said. "You can do this. Let me give you some help. You don't have to die from this."

"If I don't get help soon though, I will. I don't have any choice. I'm losing too much blood."

Colton studied the man, seeing the pale waxy look to his skin, the sweat on his forehead and the odd fevered look to his eyes. "How badly are you hurt?"

"Bad enough," he said, then he started to swear. "God damn it, this is not what I wanted."

"Then let me help you," Colton snapped. "Even if you do a few years, you'll still be alive."

"It won't be a few years, and, just like Andy, I'll be taken out. And the dealer you sent off to jail today? He'll get taken out too."

"If he hasn't already," Colton said with a nod. "That's what he said would happen."

"Exactly, and it'll happen to me too."

"I doubt it," Colton said. "Let me help you. We'll get you back to the base, and the doctors can help you."

"No," he said. "Not the base. They'll shoot me for sure."

"Tell us who else is involved in the drugs."

"I don't know—somebody, but I don't know who."

"Above you?"

Parsons nodded. "Yeah, definitely above me."

"No idea, no hints?"

"None," he said, and slowly he sagged to the ground. Colton took the gun from his hand, then tucked it into the back of his jeans and said, "Damn it, man, you don't have to die from this."

"I think it's too late," Parsons whispered.

Colton ripped Parsons's shirt apart and studied his shoulder. He grabbed more of the T-shirt that had been used to tie up his leg. It was sitting on the ground, already dirty and getting rained on, but it was something. He folded it with the cleanest side out, then pressed it against the shoulder and said, "Here. Hold this." And, while Parsons held it tight, Colton checked Parsons's vitals and said, "Were you shot anywhere else?"

"No, but I think it must have nicked something major."

Colton stepped back and walked to where Kate lay and checked her shoulder.

In her case both bullet holes were generally superficial wounds, so it must have been the shock that dropped her. She opened her eyes slowly and looked up at him. "Did you stop him?"

"I did," he said. He helped her into a sitting position. "You took two hits, but one of them was more of a burn."

"It just seemed like a huge stab wound," she said. "I didn't know how bad it was, then everything went blank."

"Yeah, that second shot put you down like a ton of bricks."

"That's a good description," she said, "because that's how I feel." He helped her back to where Parsons sat, then helped her inside a vehicle, out of the rain that was starting to pick up.

"Let's get you inside, both of you." He could hear a vehicle coming toward them.

Parsons smiled. "I guess your buddy meant it."

"Yeah, he meant it," Colton said. "He also knew I'd have no trouble taking you out."

"Damn," Parsons said. "I was only fooling myself, wasn't I?"

"Yeah," Colton said, "you were."

The vehicle pulled up and parked beside them. Troy hopped out, and, seeing Kate sitting on the driver's side, helped her to the other vehicle. He buckled her in, then came back, picked up Parsons and loaded him in the back. Then Colton and Troy checked on all the men on the ground. But nobody was left alive, so they hopped in the military jeep, with Troy driving and Colton in the back to keep an eye on Parsons. Troy turned around and headed back toward town.

"You could keep going the other way," Parsons said. "It

would be faster."

"Is it though? What's the road like?" Troy asked, turning to look at him.

"It's not bad. You've got about another fifteen miles to go. It would be faster. By the time you head back to town in this storm, you won't get back to the base."

"I'm not sure I care to go back to the base anyway," Troy said. "We need to pick up these men."

"Why don't we do that?" Colton asked. "Let's load them up into the back of the bigger truck, and we'll drive them into the base." So, with that, Troy turned around, and he and Colton carefully loaded up all the men into the back of the first truck. Then Colton returned to the jeep and looked at Kate. "Are you okay to stay there while Troy drives?"

She nodded slowly. "Yeah," she said. "As long as we're getting out of this storm." By now the thunder was crackling and the lightning flashing, and the wind was terrible. Her words were picked up and swept away every time she opened her mouth. Colton nodded, raced back to the big truck, started it up and drove off. Through the rearview mirror, he could see them following him, so he stepped on the gas and kept going.

CHAPTER 14

TALK ABOUT FEELING like shit. Kate turned to look at Parsons, who was leaning on the back seat, his eyes closed. "Why the hell did you have to shoot me not once but twice?" she growled.

"Sorry," he said, "at least I shot high."

"Yeah, but you also could have killed me," she said. "Instead, my shoulder is killing me."

"I probably won't make it through the storm anyway," he muttered. "So, whatever."

She had to admit that was a hell of an argument. She looked over at Troy. "The storm is really picking up, isn't it?"

He nodded grimly. "There's a reason why we were all supposed to stay on base."

"Or in town," she said.

"True enough." Just then a heavy blast of wind hit the jeep sideways. It didn't dislodge it off the road, but it buffeted them heavily.

"Should we have gone in the big truck too?" Kate cried out.

"If it gets too bad," Troy said, "we'll move to Colton's truck."

"Right," Kate said. They were staying close behind where at least they could still see the faint glow of the rear taillights. But that was about it. It was all shadows with no sign of the road anywhere. "I hope his visibility is better than ours."

"I doubt it," Troy said. "It's all I can do to see him. What's he following?"

She stayed silent at that. "So how will we know if we're even still on the road?"

"We are," Troy said, pointing to the edges of the shoulder. "I'm keeping an eye on that too."

"It's just nasty out here. I've seen a lot of storms, but not like this."

"The storms they get up here," Parsons said faintly from the back seat, "they're brutal."

"So it's a good night for murder and mayhem then, isn't it?" she snapped.

He didn't say anything. She turned. "Who above you is involved?"

"Don't know."

"What about those below you?"

"Don't know," he said. "Andy and Strange were the ones who handled that."

"Strange is in custody," Kate said, "so hopefully the cops can get answers from him. But we're heading into the base, which means going to whoever is still controlling this. So any answers you have that will help keep us alive would be appreciated."

"It won't keep me alive," Parsons said.

"So, if it won't do you any good, you don't want to help anybody else?" Kate asked. She waited a moment and then prodded him again. "Don't you have any siblings? Don't you want people to know you lived a life of honor instead of shame?"

He just glared at her.

She nodded. "Either you can help or you can go down as a traitor. What do you want your family to hear?"

"Of course I don't want them to know about this shit," he said. "They were never supposed to hear about it."

"And yet," she said, "that's not what'll happen. You'll go down as part of a drug-running group the military cleaned out. I have no idea what they'll do for a pension if you have a wife," she said. "I imagine you'll be dishonorably discharged, with no benefits, but I don't know."

"I don't know either," Parsons said. "When you get involved in shit like this, you don't think about the consequences on that end. And, to a certain extent, I still don't. I don't have a wife. I don't have any kids, and my mother is gone. There's my father and my brother, and I would just as soon they didn't know about this, but I don't know who it is working above me."

"So how did it work?" Kate asked. "The drugs come in, so who loads them onto the vehicles?"

"The dead guys," Parsons said faintly.

"And you?"

"I check the manifests and keep the product moving," he said.

"How do you know somebody is above you?"

"Because the planes have to come in and be approved, and all the cargo has to be moved. People have to sign that."

"What does it come in as?"

"Medical supplies usually," he said. "Or basic supplies for the base."

Kate nodded and sat back, wondering. "Do you think the commander is involved?"

"No," he said. "The commander has always been good

to me. And I'm sorry he'll find out about this."

"Not as sorry as he'll be," she muttered. "He put his trust in you, and look how you repaid him."

"Guilt really doesn't matter much now," Parsons said, gasping.

"But it makes me feel better," she snapped. "All of this is just bullshit. I almost died several times now because of it, and all I was doing was bringing a plane load of supplies into the base."

"You delivered drugs before too," he said with a sneer. "You get a manifest, and, as far as you're concerned, all of the cargo has been loaded up, and you fly it. You don't know what's being flown. There is no doubt drugs have made it onto your loads many times."

"Great," she said in a whisper. "That's not what I want to hear."

"No, maybe not," he said. "But again somebody has to be signing this paperwork."

"What about in purchasing?"

"Maybe," he said, "but somebody higher up has to okay the orders."

"That takes us back to the commander," she said. "Aren't you his right-hand man?"

"Yep," he said, "and I did sign a lot of the paperwork. But a lot of the stuff I didn't."

"So you signed on his behalf?"

He nodded. "I knew that wouldn't last too long either. Just think about it. Not everybody will believe that the commander was bringing in forty pallets of toilet paper."

"Actually pallets of toilet paper make a lot of sense," she said.

"If one of those pallets is drugs, nobody checks."

"Shit," Troy said from the driver's side. "I can see that. For a base like this, you need a ton of supplies."

"And easy enough to hide drugs in the shipments to move as needed," he said. "It just gets moved into the back of another truck, so we had men at every level."

"Great," she said. "That doesn't sound good."

"It doesn't matter. It happens in every big organization. Company theft or moving things through the company is a common problem."

"Never where I worked," she said. "Or no one I ever worked with anyway."

"Which is why you wouldn't have been included," Parsons said, "but, trust me, every corporation has a group like that."

Troy nodded. "Unfortunately he's right."

Kate stared. "That's pretty sad."

"It's realistic," Troy said shortly. Another heavy gust of wind slammed into the jeep, jolting her sideways. "Damn," she said, "I feel like we won't make it to the base."

"We'll have to sit in the vehicles, if that's the case," Troy said.

She looked ahead and could see Colton still driving steadily. "I guess as long as he's moving forward, we are too."

"Yep."

She looked back at Parsons. "How much farther?"

"Shouldn't be too much longer," he said. "It's hard to say though."

Then Troy pointed and said, "Look."

Up ahead through the heavy storm were lights. "Is that the base?"

Parsons nodded.

COLTON HATED TO admit it, but he was damned relieved to see the base. A part of him had been worried Parsons had sent him into another ambush. But as he entered and opened his window to the man at the gate, he explained who he was and what he was doing. He said, "Call the commander and have him meet us down here too."

With that, the gate opened, and he drove through, and he could see Troy had been stopped as well, but he was eventually let through too. The gates closed heavily behind them. There shouldn't be anybody else coming and going, but somebody needed to stand watch just in case.

Colton drove up to the warehouse on the left. He wasn't sure where the hell to go, but this one had a door partially open, and he figured he could get inside and unload their cargo. Although he might have been better off going into town and taking them right to the hospital and to the morgue. As he drove in, his phone went off. He answered it. "Commander, I'm just pulling into a warehouse. I've got eight men dead in the back."

"Jesus Christ! I'm on my way," he said. "What the hell is this about Parsons?"

"You better come down here, sir. It's pretty bad."

As Colton pocketed his phone, he hopped out and opened up the big warehouse door farther so he could get in under it. Hanging onto the vehicle every step of the way in order to not get thrown sideways, he hopped back into the truck and drove it in. Immediately the heavy sound of the wind stopped, muffled by the structure. He pulled over to one side so Troy could pull up beside him. As soon as he shut off the engine, he opened the truck door, hopped down and opened the door for Kate. He looked at her, seeing the fatigue and the exhaustion in her face. "How you holding up?"

"I'm okay," she said. "But I guess we missed another meal, didn't we?"

He just grinned and helped her out. Just then half-a-dozen men swarmed into the warehouse. At the orders to halt and raise their hands, he lifted his. Kate lifted hers as much as she could, but her shoulder was killing her.

The commander stepped forward. "Colton?"

"Here, sir," he said. He lowered his hands and moved Kate forward. "She has been shot twice, compliments of Parsons."

The commander's eyebrows shot up. "Jesus. Where is he?"

Troy stepped forward. "He's in the back of this vehicle, sir."

The commander strode forward, fury, frustration and maybe a little grief on his face as he opened the door, and there was Parsons, lying flat out now. The commander checked for a pulse.

Parsons whispered, "Sorry, sir."

"Damn it, man."

"Got in over my head, sir. Couldn't see my way out. It'd be nice if you wouldn't tell my father and brother." He looked up the commander and said, "Yeah, I messed up big time." And, with that, he closed his eyes, and, in front of everybody present, he took his last breath and expired. After that, it was chaos.

Colton opened up the back of the big truck and brought the commander around to take a look. When he saw the dead men were from his own base, and Colton told him about the ambush, the commander swore up and down. But he issued orders quickly. As the men started removing the bodies from the back of the truck, Colton pulled the commander aside and told him that Parsons had said this involved US bases all over the world. But here, at Thule, somebody was upwind of Parsons, but he said he didn't know who.

The commander glared at Colton, shaking his head, his mouth a grim taut line.

"He did clear you, sir," he said, a tiny grin at the corner of his mouth. He knew he was insulting the commander, but at least he would also know he'd been cleared.

"This is unbelievable. So he was signing my signature to smuggle drugs into *my* base?"

Troy stepped up beside him. "Yes, sir," and he related the last little bit that Parsons had shared. "He said he really didn't know who it was, but he did mention medical supplies."

At that, the commander's jaw worked. "Then I guess we better deal with the corpses first. Hell, I don't even know if we have room for them all." He headed out after the last one was taken away, and all headed to the sick bay.

Although nobody was technically on duty, two doctors raced toward him. When they saw the line of dead soldiers, their faces showed anger and grief.

"What happened?" one of them snapped.

"Good question," said the commander, his voice powerful and brooking no argument. "I'd like to see all the medical personnel who are here, including the nurses, please."

It took about ten minutes before there was a full assembly.

The commander looked them over. "We highly suspect at least one of you has been helping this group of dead men run a drug operation through this base. I don't have time to deal with finding out which one of you it is, so step forward now, and it'll go slightly easier on you. Make me do a full investigation, and I'll make sure all of you, including your families, pay for this," he roared.

There was dead silence, as everybody processed his words.

Colton stepped forward and said, "We understand a ton of medical supplies have been ordered, but what's been coming also are drugs. Somebody has been signing those forms."

Kate was at his side, and she addressed the doctor she had seen earlier. "Please tell me that it wasn't you."

He looked at her in surprise. "Why do you care?"

"Because Parsons shot me, *twice*," she said bitterly. "And I came here to get medical treatment. The three of us are the only ones who got shot and survived today," she said. "Another man in town was murdered, and a second is likely to be taken out, even though he's in prison. Parsons didn't make it, and, as you can see from the rest gathered here, nobody else made it either. I don't understand how anybody in the profession of saving lives could be dealing in drugs that are killing people."

Several of the doctors said, "I didn't have anything to do with it."

However, Colton watched Kate as she studied the doctor she'd seen, her gaze steady, as if she knew something he didn't. Casually Colton walked over and around, behind the doctors, as if going to the cabinet. And, just as he went past, he took a look at the doctor whose hand was in his pocket. Something was there. Colton pulled out the handgun he'd taken off Parsons and held it against the doctor's ribs. "Pull your hand out gently," he ordered. "Now."

He pulled his hand out, and, sure enough, he had a

handgun. "Of course I needed the handgun," the doctor snapped. "You just brought a mess of dead men into my medical clinic. I have to be prepared for anything."

"I wonder if that's what you were protecting or if you were just waiting for an opportunity to get out of this. Even maybe shoot your way out," Kate said quietly.

He continued to glare at her.

The commander addressed him now. "Brody?"

Brody and the commander glared at each other. And then the commander's shoulders sagged. "Jesus, Brody. Why?"

Brody shrugged. "I needed the money."

"But why?" the commander asked, lifting his shoulders. It was obvious from the interplay that they were friends and that this was a betrayal the commander hadn't seen coming.

"Cheryl left me," he said. "She took everything. The bank accounts, the house, the kids, the vehicles, literally everything. And since I'm the one with the paycheck, I'll get stuck paying alimony to boot. The last time you told me to take a leave," he said, "I didn't have anywhere to go. I ended up staying in town and was approached by this group. They offered me a path to retirement that she couldn't touch and enough spending money so I could go someplace on my days off without losing everything."

"Instead you'll lose it all anyway," Kate said.

"Maybe so, but I want to make sure she doesn't get more."

"What about your kids?" Kate asked.

As if understanding something more was going on, Colton watched the interplay suspiciously.. "Just to be clear," Colton said, "is anybody else in this department working with you?"

Brody shook his head. "No, nobody is."

"Then go sit down," the commander said. "We'll do a full search and wait for the MPs to come and take you to the stockade."

Brody smiled, looked at the commander and said, "You know me. That won't do me for very long."

"But you shouldn't have done this," the commander said. "I don't have any damn choice in the matter."

Brody nodded, then quick as a flash, he lifted his hand and sliced his throat. Blood spurted as he took an instinctive step back. Within seconds he was on his knees, a pool of blood forming around him. "Don't try to stop it," he said. "There's no life for me after this. There was no life for me after Cheryl left anyway." And he collapsed face-first.

The other doctors rushed forward, but the arterial bleeding was too much, too fast and the cut just too deep.

And they couldn't save him.

When Colton stood back up, he walked over to Kate, opened his arms and just held her. "It's all over with now," he said. "It's over—at least here."

"Says you," she said and turned to the commander. "Can I at least count on you to clean house?"

"Yes," he said, "that you can count on. And, while this is all being dealt with," he added, "let's get your shoulder taken care of and get you back to your room. You too, Colton. Looks like that leg needs some attention."

"And here I was hoping for at least a hot bowl of soup," Kate said. "That storm is brutal out there."

"I can handle that too." The commander gave her a smile and patted her gently on her good shoulder. "The next time you come this way," he said, "it will be a whole different story."

"I can't imagine it being much worse," she whispered.

CHAPTER 15

I T SEEMED LIKE forever, but, in less than two hours, Kate was back at Colton's room, after declining the doctor's recommendation for her to stay in the sick bay. The damage to her shoulder had been cleaned up and repaired as much as possible.

"Is it finally bedtime?" she asked with a yawn. Outside she could hear the wind howling and banging against the windows.

"Yes," Colton said, "and hopefully this time you'll sleep for a long time."

"Until the storm is over?"

"It can last for a couple days apparently," he said, "and it doesn't look to me like it'll end anytime soon."

"I guess, if we get to stay and veg out for a day or two, that's okay."

"And the commander did call the hospital, by the way, and George is fine. And so is his family."

"Good," she said. "What about the drug dealer guy?"

"He is still alive, and the police have extra security on him."

"Good enough," she said. She sagged down on Colton's bed and looked up at the top bunk, which looked very difficult to access with a bum shoulder. "Tonight do you mind if I sleep down here?"

"Nope," he said. "Let's get that shirt off you. She had her outer shirt slung over her shoulders. "Did I hear someone say my bag had come in?" Then she noted it on the floor beside her. "Oh, good. Maybe a loose T-shirt is in there that I can wear for the night."

"Or whatever makes you comfortable. But you should decide soon because that painkiller they gave you may hit you at any moment."

With his help, she was completely stripped down, slipped under the covers and tucked up against the wall. "If you want to join me," she said, "I won't argue."

"You need to rest. Besides, I might bump you and hurt your shoulder in the night."

"Maybe," she said, her voice drowsy and sleepy already. "Or I might bump your leg in the night. Or I might not even know you're there."

"I don't know if my ego can handle that," he said jokingly. "And my leg is fine. Besides, we're both on painkillers."

She smiled. "Your ego doesn't need any stroking. It's just fine."

"It's definitely healthy," he said, "but I thought that after we were together last time. Then I just couldn't forget about you. I kept trying, but it didn't work."

"Ditto," she said, yawning. "Maybe we'll have to try again."

"I'm up for it." Pulling the blanket up to her chin, he kissed her gently on the cheek and said, "Go to sleep. We'll talk in the morning." She closed her eyes and sank into a deep sleep. The trouble was, she didn't stay asleep. She surfaced, went under, rolled over, moaned and went under again. Finally she lay here, shaking. "I don't feel so good," she whispered.

"I know," he said, right beside her. She looked up to see Colton lying as far away on the bunk as he could.

"That can't be comfortable," she said, when she realized he was trying to give her space. "Your leg has to be aching, and this sleeping arrangement can't help."

"No," he said, "but watching you toss and turn wasn't good either."

She rolled over and said, "Switch places with me," and then, with her good shoulder down, she tucked up close to him. "This is much better." He chuckled, and the rumble of laughter rolling up his chest made her smile. She stroked his chest and said, "I had just enough sleep that I'm awake now."

"But not enough sleep to keep you awake for long," he said gently, tapping the tip of her nose. "Go back to sleep."

"Maybe I don't want to," she said, sliding her hand across his chest, around his ribs and down onto his belly. His core muscles tightened, and she could feel the ridges of his abs. "You guys are all so damn fit," she muttered.

"You're looking pretty fine yourself."

She smiled. "Not like you guys."

"You don't have to be though," he said, as her hand strayed lower and lower. He grabbed it and said, "Don't go starting something you can't finish."

"I'm just not sure how the logistics would work with our injuries," she said. "I'm not in the greatest of shape right now, but I'm game if you can figure it out."

He murmured, "Maybe you should wait until you're feeling better."

"And yet ..." she said, her voice drifting dreamily. Her hand slid out from under his to glide across his hip to his muscled thighs. "I know just what would make me feel better."

"How do you figure?" he asked, his voice catching in the back of his throat.

"Because some hurts are physical, and some hurts are emotional, and then there are those that are spiritual. Today was a really rough day. And although the physical part of me can't heal as easily, you could do a lot to heal the other two."

He tilted her head and whispered, "Are you sure?"

"Yes," she said, "my soul needs this—and my heart. My body does too. It's just a little more cautious since we're both injured."

"So we'll take it slow," he whispered. And he started by shifting so she lay flat on her back. "I don't want you to move."

"Not happening," she said. "You've got too much of this gorgeous body for me not to touch it."

He lowered his head, his lips leaving a moist trail across her skin as he moved from one breast to lick the nipple before suckling it deeply and then crossing to the next. She twisted beneath him, moaning gently, but he wouldn't let her move much. He held her tight against him as he kissed and stroked, tasting and testing every inch of her until he came to the curve of her ribs, gently caressing, stroking and exploring, making up for the last four years they'd been apart.

She whispered, "I forgot how good you were at this."

"It's not a case of me being good," he said. "It's a case of us being good together."

She moaned as his fingers drifted lower, sliding into the curls at the apex of her thighs. She opened her thighs and whispered, "You know even just this much, to be back in your arms and to know we have this time together is—"

"It's not just tonight," Colton vowed. "I missed you all these years. I kept putting it off, saying it wasn't the right time."

"What makes you think this is the right time?" she asked, but she knew in her heart of hearts she wanted it to be.

"My theory is that fate had a hand in it," he said. "It threw us back together so I could see if I really wanted what I'd lost so long ago."

"And?"

"And the answer is yes," he whispered, as he gently kissed her hip bone. When he shifted to taste the heart of her, his tongue doing crazy magical things, her hips lifted as she moaned, her body twisting under his caress. But he held her hips firm as he deepened the kiss and used his tongue as she'd never known before. When she came apart in his arms, she realized that had been his solution to avoid hurting her. She dragged him up close to her and whispered, "Now your turn."

He shook his head. "You're too injured."

But she wasn't taking no for an answer. She reached up with her thighs wrapped tight around his hips and started to ride the outside of his shaft. He shuddered and shifted so he was in a better position and then slowly entered her.

"Yes, … that's exactly what I want," she said.

"You might get hurt," he said as he gently, ever-so-slowly entered her until he was seated deep inside her. She could feel him holding back. She reached up with her good arm, gently caressing his chest, his neck and his shoulders, her thumb stroking across his lips, and she whispered, "I want this all over again. I want everything you have to give me, so forget about my injury. Give it to me now."

As he lost control, she wrapped her good arm around him to hold herself steady as he drove into her again and again, and unbelievably she could feel her body reacting with the same emotions and passion twisting deeper within her. Arching her body up against him, she cried out yet again. And with great joy and satisfaction she heard him roar above her as he reached his own climax before he slowly collapsed on her good side. When he lay there, gasping for breath, she whispered, "I knew you could figure it out."

He chuckled. "It took a bit, but, yeah, we got it." He kissed her and whispered, "Thank you."

"For what?" she asked.

"For being you and for accepting me being me."

She opened her eyes, wondering where that came from.

"We both needed time apart," he said, "but now that we've had it, we both seem to have rekindled what we want, and, for that, I'm grateful."

She kissed him gently. "Me too," she said. "Now let's not lose the opportunity to work together to have exactly what we both want for tomorrow, not just for tonight."

"No, this isn't just for tonight," he said. "As far as I'm concerned, this is forever." He lay down beside her, gently tucked her up into his arms and held her close.

With a smile and her heart full and her soul so much happier, she closed her eyes and fell back asleep. But this time she knew she'd sleep easy and rest well. Not only did she have everything to make her soul happy and her emotions full but her heart was smiling too.

Her body? Well, that would heal in good time. But it didn't have to heal on its own. Now she could be with Colton and would know they were both reaching for something together.

Forever.

Dale Mayer

BOOK-24

PROLOGUE

A FTER TWO WEEKS in Greenland along with Colton, Troy Landry had finished up the training they had been trying to get done. Once the weather had cleared, their progress had improved rapidly, and now he was on his way back home again. First to Coronado base and then onto a US destroyer. And he was okay with that. He liked to spend as much time out on the water as he could. It was very different being a Navy SEAL on shore versus out on one of the big destroyers. He wasn't sure what the mission was this time, but he was happy to be a part of it, no matter what was happening. He liked excitement; he liked the action. But some downtime would be nice too.

If any was coming his way.

Back in Coronado, he unpacked, then repacked his gear to be ready when the call came. Just as he moved his bag to the front door before heading to the pier, he got a phone call.

"Change of orders," Mason said in a clipped tone.

"Okay," Troy said, quite used to having his schedule spin on a dime. "What are we doing instead?"

"Heading up to the coast of Alaska. An oil rig's in trouble. Quite a few workers being rescued right now. A programmer called in with an SOS on a suspected sabotage," he said. "She's still on board, as are a few others. Bad storms are coming in."

"So, why are we still talking?" Troy said. "I figured you'd be out front already."

"I am," Mason said, his laugh dark. "I was hoping you're on your way to the pier."

With the phone still in his hand, Troy took one last look around, shut off the lights, grabbed his bag, and opened his front door. Locking it, he said, "I'm coming down the hallway toward you."

"Good thing," Mason said. "This one looks bad."

"How many teams?"

"One six-man team," Mason said.

Before they were done talking, Troy was out front, storing his duffel bag into the rear of the navy jeep, before taking the last vacant spot in the back seat. Lots of faces he knew, and a couple he didn't. He just smiled and said, "Good to go." He slammed the door shut even as Mason pulled away from the curb. "Are we going incognito, or is this with full military backing?"

"Always military backing," Axel said from the front of the vehicle. "Just, in this case, we're also talking a little bit of stealth."

"Great," Troy said. "And what's our cover?"

"Two of us are part of the oil company, heading onto the rig itself," Mason said, "and two will be on a nearby destroyer and will secretly come in from the ocean. We'll let them onto the rig, and they will be our eyes and ears in the shadows."

"Oh, now that's an interesting way to handle it," Troy said. "And the other two?"

Mason shot him a look through the rearview mirror. "You and Axel will go on as deckhands."

"Why are we new deckhands, if they're getting every-body off because the oil rig is in danger?"

"Because they still need somebody to stay on board and hopefully stabilize it."

"Surely they're not taking off the entire crew, are they?"

"They're trying to," Mason said. "Nelson here and I will go in as part of the company. Unfortunately one of the actual company board members is coming with us."

"Unfortunately?"

"It's never a good idea to have civilians involved," he said.

Troy sat back and nodded, agreeing fully. This started to sound like an interesting mission. "Loss of life?"

"They're still checking. Four people are missing."

"But not confirmed dead?"

Axel shook his head, as he twisted around to look at him. "No, none confirmed yet. Several were fished out of the arctic water already."

"What's it take? About twelve minutes for hypothermia up there?"

"If you're lucky," he said. "An arctic front is heading down, so the weather'll get vicious."

"My favorite kind of mission then," Troy said with a laugh. "Maximum danger, potential for betrayal, chances of not coming home—all good." He grinned, and the others laughed. Because, just like him, they'd all been there before. And, just like him, so far they'd been lucky and made it home. But, just like him, they all knew many who hadn't. Being part of the oil rig crew suited Troy just fine. He'd done a stint up on the oil rigs himself when he was eighteen, which may be why he'd been tagged for this. He looked at Axel. "You ever been on a rig before?"

"Yeah," Axel said. "A couple times."

Troy wasn't at all surprised at that. The men on this team had a wide and varied set of experiences. When they pulled into the base airport, without talking they headed for the plane that was already refueling.

One of the pilots stood there, glaring at them. "You're late," he said.

Troy lifted an eyebrow.

By the time they made the switch to a connecting flight to head to Alaska and then eventually landed on the destroyer, Troy would be tired and ready for either action or a break. This hurry-up-and-wait scenario was driving him crazy. They'd done as much research as they could, but, so far, it looked like it could be an accident, sabotage, or somebody making it look like sabotage to hide something else. He'd seen way too much betrayal in his life to not consider that as an option.

After several hours on the destroyer, they were called up on deck to climb into the helicopter heading to the oil rig platform. He and Axel were in oil-rig uniforms but were fully armed inside their coveralls and heavy jackets. Mason was there in a heavy parka, but he wore a suit, as was the stranger standing with them, looking uncomfortable. Presumably the board member.

Mason introduced them. "This is Gregor Stanovich, one of the board members, and the one who looks after this particular rig." Mason motioned everybody toward the chopper.

Troy studied Gregor carefully and concluded he definitely looked like the paper-pushing kind. But Troy had been deceived before. He glanced at Axel to see him eyeing the stranger with the same harsh eye.

Not everybody was as quick to do this kind of work as they were. And Gregor shouldn't be doing this. Everybody had a place in this world to do their own thing, but it was also important to know what capabilities somebody had.

By insisting on going into this nightmare, Gregor was putting himself in the line of fire. And that just meant Troy and his team would have to keep an eye on Gregor, in case things went south.

Civilians tended not to listen; they tended to underestimate the danger, and they just didn't see the traps as they headed toward them. Troy could only hope this was a case of a simple oil rig accident, but there was a reason his team had been called in. And it was rarely for a simple accident. Too often a "simple accident" ended up being something far worse.

From the helicopter, Troy watched the ocean dance below them. There was no sign of the oil rig in the distance. Which meant they still had quite a distance to go. He looked at Axel. "I wonder how close the destroyer is planning on getting."

Axel nodded. "Nobody can handle the frigid water, no matter what kind of protective gear they've got."

"Do we have a submersible down there?"

Axel shot him half a glance and said, "What do you think?"

The two spent the rest of the flight watching for the oil rig to come into view, while surreptitiously eyeing Gregor.

"Do we know if it's safe to land?" They both kept their voices low, looking out the window at the oil rig. There might have been an accident, but Troy wasn't seeing anything to indicate just what that had been. "They said something about an explosion, some part of the rig collapsing, and a fire." He motioned down below. "I'm not seeing evidence of that."

"It was inside, I believe," Axel said, but his look was hard as he studied the rig they approached. "Stay alive," he muttered.

Troy's reaction was instinctive. "Always."

CHAPTER 1

STAY ALIVE WAS a twist on *stay alert,* and both meant the same thing. Watch out for the knife in your back in order to make it home again. Something Troy always kept in mind.

They landed easily, the pilot having done the trip many times. The weather was just starting to brew outside. It promised to be a full-blown gale soon. Perfect. A damaged rig out in the middle of the Arctic nowhere with a storm coming on. Sounded like his kind of deal.

He hopped off with Axel, grabbed his bag, the same kit that anybody else on board would have, only his was fully loaded with weapons. They headed into the main part of the rig. One man stood, waiting for them. He looked at the two deckhand guys in surprise.

"What the hell? No crew is supposed to be arriving. We're a skeleton crew as it is."

"Beats me. We were told to get on board," Axel said easily. "If it wasn't for the board member on the flight with us, we probably would have begged off, but he said that we were needed." Axel shrugged.

The guy looked over the two men. "We just busted our humps to get everybody off this place," he complained. Then he turned and saw the board member walking toward him and frowned. "Of course the suits are here."

"Right," Troy said in agreement. He leaned forward

slightly. "A real namby-pamby sort."

"Aren't they all?" he said. "Well, you're here now. I'll talk to this guy, and maybe you can leave with him too."

"Appreciate it," Axel said cheerfully. "I'm Axel. This is Troy."

The guy nodded, then shook his head and said, "I can't say I know you two."

"We transferred in from another rig," Troy said smoothly. "Again, board members are moving people around."

"They should stick to what they do and leave us alone," the guy ahead of him snapped. The ID tag on his overalls read Daniel.

"I agree," Axel said. "Instead of moving people, they should stick to moving paper."

At that, the three of them sniggered, a bond already forming. It was always that way in the world. Nobody liked the brass; nobody liked the board members; nobody liked anybody moving in and stepping on their toes. Daniel was obviously of a position here where he felt quite comfortable being the last one on board, then giving new crew shit for showing up. But he wasn't so high up that he didn't immediately smile and have a complete change of attitude when the board members arrived.

Mason, true to form, stared at him with a haughty look on his face. "Daniel," he said, by way of acknowledgment.

Daniel stumbled a bit, then immediately put out a hand and said, "Glad to have you here." He looked down at his clipboard. "I was only expecting one of you though, and I wasn't expecting new crew at all."

"Change of plans," Mason said casually. He looked around. "I do want a full report though, as of five minutes ago."

"It was sent around," Daniel said apologetically, "but I guess our internet facilities took a hit." He looked at the two new crewmen, Troy and Axel. "Head down the hall, take the first left, then follow the signs to your bunks. Grab any that are free. The place is empty. But don't get comfortable." His tone turned icy. "You'll be leaving on the helicopter with these guys."

"Will they?" Mason asked, one eyebrow raised. "My understanding was that you needed crew here."

"Hell no," Daniel's words slammed out. "We're trying to get everybody off. It's not safe anymore."

"Well, who'll do the repairs if you don't have any crew?" Nelson asked.

Daniel stared at him in frustration.

Nelson returned the stare. "I do know how to handle myself on a rig," he said. "And the longer we stand here, the longer it'll take. But, if you need a repair crew, why aren't they here?"

"I have a six-man repair crew on board, plus my cook and an IT contractor," he said. "I don't need these two. Particularly when they're new."

"What difference does that make?" the real board member asked.

"You're Gregor, aren't you?" Daniel asked.

Gregor nodded slowly. "I am, indeed. How is it you don't know Mason and Nelson here?" he asked with that air of arrogance that always made others uncomfortable.

"I heard some shuffling was happening at the top end," Daniel said. "Sorry, we don't always get the memos out here." His tone was just barely above polite, and it was obvious that Mason in his role recognized the slight.

"Then I suggest you stop wasting everybody's time and

lead the way." Mason turned to look back at the helicopter and raised his hand. The pilot lifted his hand and settled down to wait. With any luck, they would all be leaving within a few hours.

It was up to Axel and Troy to get the other two crew members on board without anybody seeing them. And then it would be a clear-cut case of finding out what the heck was going on.

But, for the moment, they needed to separate themselves from Mason and the others. Troy picked up his duffel bag, and, with a nod to Axel, the two of them walked down the hall, following the instructions they'd been given.

As soon as they were out of sight, Troy pulled out his sat phone, which was needed out here with the wet and cold weather and the lack of usual internet connections, and brought up a map of the oil rig. "I figure we should probably grab our bunks, nice and central," he said, as he tapped one of the rooms that appeared to be midway in the rig. "It's got two sets of stairs, so we've got easy access from both sides of the rig."

"Good enough," Axel said, but his jaw was clenched with tension. He glanced around. "Definitely something fishy here."

"I smell it too," he said. "A six-man repair crew, huh?"

Axel gave him a sideways glance. "Is that not enough?"

"Absolutely, depending on who and what," he said. "But you and I both know, if you get the right guy, they can do the business of five or six other men. You get the wrong one, and you'll still need a dozen, because all of them are too damn stupid to do anything."

"Nobody stupid should be hired on these rigs," Axel said.

"True, but look at how we got on," he muttered.

At that, Axel gave a clipped nod and led the way to the bunks.

As soon as they got into the room, Troy tapped the wall behind the bunks gently. Satisfied, he nodded and said, "On the other side of this," he said, "is one of the big storage units."

"Meaning?"

"Meaning," Troy said, "I think we should stash some of our weapons."

"And how do you want to get in and out of there?"

From his duffel bag, Troy pulled out a small saw. "Something along this line," he said.

Axel's eyebrows shot up. "And you'll hide that new opening how?"

"You'd be surprised," he said. "I brought some duct tape. If nothing else, we can close it up that way and just hang a blanket on the downward side."

Axel studied it for a moment, then nodded. "That just might work," he said. "But how will you check the studs for a space you can get into?"

"Don't worry about me," Troy said. He gently tapped at the far corner. Nodding, he picked up the saw and cut through the wall, noting that it was not drywall but more like fiberglass. He quickly slid the saw all the way down and cut the top and the bottom. Then he pried it apart so he could look behind it. "A decent space is back here," he said. "Let's hide some of the weapons now."

They stashed several of their machine guns, some of the ammo, a bunch of C-4, and a spare set of handguns. With that done, he grabbed one of the blankets off the top bunk and arranged it so it, more or less, hid the cuts in the walls.

"You know something? That's actually a damn good job," Axel said, studying it. "A damn good job."

"I don't like to be without weapons," Troy said, "and, if we're ever caught with any, you know they'll start looking for more."

"That's the truth," Axel agreed. He grabbed a couple pillows, threw them at the far end by the cuts in the wall, covering up one of the cut corners still visible. He said, "The cut edge is even the same color as the damn wall." And, with that done, they threw their duffel bags onto their bunks and headed out.

"Where to?" Troy asked.

"I want to see this crew," Axel said.

"Yeah? Do you know something about them that I don't know?"

"Maybe," he said.

"And what's that?" Troy asked, intrigued.

"One of the communications specialists here is a friend of Tesla's."

At that, Troy sucked in his breath, as multiple things fell into place. "Which is why Mason is here," he said, with a nod.

"It's why a lot of us are here," Axel said.

"Sure, a crew is needed. But who's the friend?"

"Berkley Milford," he said.

Troy stopped and turned to stare. "Berkley's here? Why the hell is Berkley here?"

"Not because she's part of the crew. She works for the company doing an overhaul and an update of the IT system on the rig. A global company and she's a contractor for them. Similar to what Tesla was doing for the national defense system. Berkley sent out an SOS and gave us a heads-up that everything wasn't what it seems. And that's when the last of the tumblers fell into place."

"So, we already know this is a FUBAR mission then," he stated.

Axel nodded. "We sure do. Bottom line is, get her off here, along with anybody else who's innocent. The rest of them? We really don't care. Seal food maybe."

BERKLEY MILFORD LIFTED her gaze from the monitors. She studied the data as it scrolled on her second and third monitors.

One of the men, Phil, stood beside her and swore. "How the hell you can even look at any of that shit is beyond me." He sneered.

"Doesn't matter if it's beyond you or not," she said firmly. "This is my deal, so get the hell away."

He reached down as if to tap her keyboard.

She snapped out her hand and grabbed him by the wrist, applying pressure on the inside joint. She stood up slowly. "I don't know what your problem is," she snarled, glaring at him eye to eye, "but don't you ever touch my fucking equipment." He glared at her, and she could see the *I'll kill you* threat in his eyes.

But then, glancing around at the others, with half a laugh, Phil shook off her hand. "Just kidding," he said. "Don't be so touchy." He rolled his eyes, playing it off as if dealing with an overly hormonal woman.

She was all about hormones. Particularly the ones that raged the minute she realized she was in a shitty situation, and that millions, if not billions, of dollars of damage had been done, putting a couple hundred lives at risk too. Not to mention the profits of the company she was contracted for.

The facts worried her. Eight men were left behind with her, and she was here only because she'd fought to stay to work on the electronics and to keep communications open, and she was the one monitoring the oil pressure via the main computers. Bruce, one of the other guys, was a programmer as well, and Jonesy had several degrees in handling these kinds of engineering databases, whereas her expertise was in a completely different kind of database.

But she'd learned fast not to trust these guys. Jonesy had been friendly and open and, in many instances, had stood up for her. But she didn't know how long that would last, since she was an outsider, not one of the regular crew.

He leaned toward her side of the consoles. "You okay?"

"I'm fine," she said, brushing the hair off her forehead. "Phil's an asshole."

"That he is," Jonesy said, as he patted her hand. "We'll keep him in check."

She doubted that. But she wouldn't start any other issues right now. She'd sent out an SOS, and she trusted the men she'd contacted. Not that she'd made the contact, but she had a friendship with Tesla going back to their time together at MIT. If anybody would come and sort out this mess, it would be Mason's group. She didn't know who it would be or when they'd get here, but she sure as hell hoped it would be soon.

Two of the other men, Chucky and Winslow, walked in, dropping their bags.

"We're screwed," Chucky said. "One of the sets of drills and all the computer equipment on it are damaged."

"What about the other three?" she asked.

"Ooh, you think you're something funny," Phil said,

from behind her.

She shot Phil a hard look and turned to Chucky and Winslow. "The other three?"

"One is operational," Chucky said, "but we've shut it down. One appears to need some new collars and potentially new drills. We're not sure about the tanks though."

"And the third one?"

He shook his head. "That'll need several engineers to go over it first," he said. "I'm not starting up that sucker. It looks buckled."

"So the structural integrity is compromised on all of them?"

"On two for sure," Winslow added. He walked over and sat down. "Jonesy needs to start running some diagnostics on the pumps and drills themselves."

"That's what I've been doing," Jonesy said, "but I can't run any tests on the structural integrity."

"Why not?" Berkley asked, looking at him with a frown. "Don't you have the ability to measure the steel chambers?"

"We measured the pressure inside and out," he said, "but it's hard to say what a blast like that might have done to the tanks themselves."

She stared off in the distance as she thought about it, then shrugged. "That really is out of my league."

Immediately Phil jumped all over her words. "Wow, look at that. Little Miss Brainiac here admitted she doesn't know something."

She ignored him, but it was getting downright hard to. She took a deep breath, trying to keep her cool, so she could keep an eye on the others. The atmosphere was generally negative and depressing.

"The helicopter also landed," Winslow said.

She studied them closely. "What helicopter?"

"Board members," he said. "Company men." His tone turned, and he seemed to spit out the words.

She'd never spent much time on any rig, mostly popping in and out of several of them, troubleshooting various programs. But one thing they all had in common. The men working on the rigs couldn't stand the men in the offices. She nodded slowly. "I guess that makes sense. Somebody has to come look at the damage."

"Only if they brought some engineers with them," Winslow said in disgust.

She kept her gaze on the monitor in front of her.

"How many men came then?" Jonesy asked beside her.

"According to Herman, three company men are on board."

"That's a lot," she said.

Jonesy snorted. "One is too many. Three is a damn crowd."

She shifted from one screen to the next, working to decipher what was going on; she ran split-screen testing, searching for malicious software in the system. On another one, she ran diagnostics on the software. Two different things but both related. On her center screen, she worked away on the electronics that ran the actual rig here. Just enough damage had been done on some of the computerized sections that she was rewriting code and creating patches to connect to the older systems. She sat back and said, "One day they'll have to buy a new system."

"If it makes our lives easier," Chucky said with a half groan, "you know they won't."

She nodded. "That's always the way, isn't it? Save a few pennies, then blow a massive amount later to fix what they could have fixed now."

"I'm sure there is a saying like that," someone said.

"But it sure as hell ain't that one," Phil added.

She shrugged.

Jonesy clicked on some of the security footage around the place and whistled. "Why do we still have two guys outside on the rig?"

She glanced over his shoulder, and her heart stopped because no way could she not see Axel. That man was massive. She'd met him and Troy a couple times at Mason's well-attended backyard parties. With her heart slamming against her chest, she said, "Maybe they came in with the helicopter."

"It'd be typical of the company to do that," Jonesy said, swearing. "Somebody better go roust them. They'll be lost, looking all over this place."

She wanted to go herself, but she knew that she had to stay where she was, and, even if she went, one of the guys would likely come with her anyway.

Just then the door to command central opened and in popped their foreman, Daniel.

She gave him a half smile. He looked a little rattled and, behind him, in came three men in suits. Daniel closed the door behind the men and disappeared from sight. Her gaze shifted to the suits that had walked in and froze when she caught sight of Nelson and Mason.

CHAPTER 2

BERKLEY'S BREATH CAUGHT in the back of her throat. She'd been in the act of standing, but she slowly sank back down again.

"Heads up," the foreman said. "The company men are here, and we need reports as soon as possible. Two crewmen came on board with them, and everybody is looking to leave within a couple hours."

"Good thing," Chucky said. "We probably don't have grub for longer than that."

"Unless you came in with a new supply," the foreman said, turning to the suits.

The only true company man she recognized—because she knew the other two were faking it—shook his head. "No," he said, "I didn't bring food supplies. Pretty hard to carry on a helicopter."

Something about his tone she couldn't register. Meanwhile Mason was looking around. He noted her, but his gaze bounced off her and went over her head. She was grateful for that. Nobody knew that she'd put out the word. It figured that Mason would come in person. Tesla wouldn't have accepted very much else. Berkley would remember to thank her friend for that. What Berkley really wanted was to get off this rig, safe and sound, and to ensure none of the other men were in danger.

"We'll break you up into threes," the foreman said. "Actually no." He stopped and frowned. "Maybe we'll do this one at a time." He walked to his office. "Chucky, you're up first."

Chucky bounced to his feet. "Up for what?"

"We want to hear from you just what happened," he said, "but we'll do it over here in the office."

"Why? You're separating us to get our stories straight?" Winslow asked, his tone disbelieving, yet a note of anxiety was in it.

Berkley kept her head down while she kept on working. She listened as the men grumbled among themselves.

Chucky had no option but to head into the one office on this rig, connected to the bullpen, where the rest of them worked—right where they could see him, sitting slouched before the suits, who sat off to the side and out of sight.

Jonesy leaned over and said, "That's not cool."

She leaned back and asked, "Why not?"

He studied her face. "Really?"

She flashed him a quick frown. "Where I come from, all meetings are done one-on-one. What's different here?"

He settled back and said, "Yeah, I guess you're more of an office worker anyway, aren't you?"

It was a slight, but it was more than that. It separated her from them. She shrugged. "I've been here long enough to understand these nuances that I'll never get because I'm deemed as different," she said, "but I don't understand what's wrong about this."

"They're looking for somebody to blame," Jonesy said, his voice short and tight.

At that, Phil walked over. "Well, they're not fucking blaming me," he sneered. "I'm lucky to be alive as it is."

She'd heard his story. Apparently he'd been on his way back from checking one of the drills when the explosion happened. He'd been flung a good ten feet in the air to land on one of the poles. His ribs were badly bruised, and he had a slight concussion. She herself had been inside when it had all gone to hell. She didn't have a clue what had gone on. It depended on what was the root cause of it all.

Winslow caught her attention. He was pacing back and forth. She glanced at Jonesy and nodded toward Winslow. Jonesy studied him. His gaze narrowed, and he nodded. "Well, he's upset about something."

She bent her head again to her monitors and kept working away. When the office door opened, and Chucky came out, a thunderous expression on his face, the suits motioned at Winslow to join them. As the two men crossed paths, they said something to each other, but she didn't hear what it was because she was too far away. Something was going on. And they had everyone's attention. Even Bruce, who tended to stay by himself, watched the proceedings.

Chucky glared at the wall as he threw himself into the closest chair and said, "Well, that went well."

Phil walked over and asked, "What's going on?"

Chucky turned and looked back at the men gathered in the office. Just as he went to open his mouth and say something, the foreman glared at him. Chucky shrugged, settled back. "You'll find out." He slapped the top of the desk and said, "I'll roust up Denny and see if there's any grub." And, with that, he took off.

Denny was the only cook left on the place. He was the eighth man of the regular group—the six-man crew; the foreman, Daniel; and Denny, the cook. Eight men and Berkley—not the best odds.

Most of them were decent; just Phil worried her. He was the kind of guy who couldn't stand to feel threatened by a woman. And his only way of feeling powerful was to subdue. She'd bet that he was the wife-beater type. But the last thing he would do was get a chance to beat on her. Still, knowing that Mason, Nelson, Troy, and Axel were here made her feel a hell of a lot better.

They needed to know that they were on camera.

That little inkling might not have been something they had heard about. She grabbed her purse and headed to the women's washroom. She knew as soon as she left that the bullpen conversation would turn to something that she wasn't privy to hearing. And that was okay because she wouldn't let them know what was going on in her world either. And she had to warn Mason and his men.

TROY, WITH AXEL at his side, headed out, getting the lay of the land in his head. When he looked up, he saw the foreman glaring at him. He raised an eyebrow. "Hey."

"What the fuck are you doing here? I sent you to your rooms."

"Company orders," he said. That pretty well covered everything. There were always those *with* and those *without*, and those *with* had permission. If you could pull the company's name on your side, you were good.

"Where's the kitchen?" Troy asked. "We haven't eaten, and, if we're shipping right back out again, now's as good a time as any." It was almost like a note of relief crossed Daniel's face. Troy canted his gaze slightly as he walked toward him. Something shifty was going on, and he didn't know who this guy was, other than his name tag read Daniel.

"Kitchen?"

"The mess is around the corner," he said. "I'm heading there myself. Denny is the only guy we got left who cooks."

"Good," he said. "We've been traveling for hours."

Daniel nodded. "I guess if you guys are heading back out again soon, it makes sense."

"How come you guys are here?"

"Skeleton crew," Daniel said calmly.

Troy looked at Axel, but his partner was studying the hallways, the layouts, the size of the rooms. You could almost see his analytical mind working in the background.

"Come this way," Daniel said, his tone a little more on the friendlier side.

But not close enough to call it friendly.

Keeping an eye on him, they walked into the dining area, where a cook worked away behind a big stove in the kitchen.

Daniel said, "This is Denny, our cook."

The cook looked up and frowned when he saw the two new men. "Is a crew coming back in? Why wasn't I told?"

Troy immediately put up his hands. "Just the two of us," he said. "It sounds to me like the company got their wires crossed somehow."

Denny snorted. "What else is new? I've been asking for supplies."

"Were they due to come in today?" Troy asked curiously.

"They were due in two days ago," he said, "but, with the rough seas, they said we wouldn't get them for another forty-eight hours. And then this mess happened. But, if you guys got in, my supplies should have made it in too," he said, glaring at Troy and Axel, as if they were personally responsible.

Axel nodded. "Pretty hard to keep track of what you're supposed to supply if you don't know how many men are coming and going, isn't it?"

Denny nodded as he sized up Axel. No way to treat Axel as anything other than what he was, which was one huge hulking man who looked like he could beat the crap out of everyone around him, all at the same time. Denny appeared to back down slightly. "Fresh coffee and some cinnamon buns are on the table behind you, if you're interested."

"We're definitely interested," Troy said with relief, only a little bit of it fake. "We haven't eaten all day."

"Of course not," Denny said, with a shake of his head. "And yet you were expected to do a full day's work. Figures that they don't even give you a chance to grab a meal."

"Well, a cinnamon bun is a great way to start," Troy said, as he reached for a big one and slathered it with fresh butter. He poured himself a cup of coffee and sat back, thinking that maybe life wasn't too bad right now. Now, if only he could figure out exactly what was going on here. "If a meal is coming our way, then we'll accept that gratefully too."

"You aren't likely to be here that long," Daniel said briskly. "You're going back with the company men."

"What company men?" Denny asked, in a thunderous voice.

Daniel looked at him. "Three of them came with these two."

Denny stared at him in horror. "Three company men and you didn't tell me?"

"Hey, I didn't get a memo either," he said. "I just saw them when they arrived."

Denny looked around his kitchen in a frantic motion; then his eyes lit on the cinnamon buns. He walked over and snagged up the rest of them, taking them back.

Axel reached out and grabbed one before they got too far, but Denny didn't even appear to notice. As soon as he put them on the counter closer to his side of the kitchen, Daniel walked over and snagged one too.

Denny glared at him. "I have to have something for the company men," he roared.

"Then make something," Daniel said. "If you're lucky, they won't even come in here."

"I'm supposed to know whenever they come," he said. "If I don't have any notice, I can't produce any food."

"Well, I don't know if they'll be here for dinner or not," Daniel said, "but you might want to start considering that."

At that, Denny turned and muttered as he opened his fridge, studying the contents.

"I'm sure they'll be easy to get along with," Troy said. "It's not like you guys got any warning."

"Like they'll give a damn about that," Denny said. He waved him off. "Take that somewhere else," he said. "I want my kitchen to myself."

Daniel gave a snort, grabbed his cinnamon bun and a coffee, and said, "Wait 'til the other guys see my cinnamon bun."

"Tell them you got the last one," Denny said smoothly. "Otherwise there won't be any dinner for you either."

Daniel shot him a look and took off down the hallway.

Troy looked at Axel. "I guess we can go explore this place."

Axel gave a half shrug and started toward the doorway.

"I wouldn't be going too far," Denny said. "As soon as

they're ready, you'll be leaving with them."

"Everybody is real friendly here," Troy said. "It's almost like nobody wanted any new crew in."

"Damn right," Denny said. "Everybody wants the crew out. It's dangerous right now, and a skeleton crew is all we need."

"Maybe," Troy said, "but we're here, so you may as well make the best of it." With that, he turned and left.

Axel and Denny eyed each other carefully for a long moment, until Denny turned his back on Axel.

Hearing the big man come up behind him, Troy turned toward Axel, only to see Daniel leaning against one of the hallway walls. He was polishing off the cinnamon bun. "Well, that's one way to stop a fight," Troy remarked.

"It's a shitstorm around here right now," he said. "If a cinnamon bun makes me feel better for one moment in time, then I'll take it."

"Sounds personal."

Daniel nodded. "My brother is one of the four who went missing."

Troy winced. "I'm really sorry. That sucks, man."

Daniel shot him a hard look. "It sure does." And he took off down the hallway.

As they stood here, looking at the crossroads of the hallways, wondering which direction to go, Troy heard a sound to the left. He turned to see a tall, lean brunette with her hair stuck in a clip at the top of her head, motioning at him. He walked toward her quietly, Axel pushing him faster. She motioned inside a room and disappeared ahead of them. As soon as they stepped inside, she shut the door behind him.

"Berkley?"

She smiled up at Axel. "Hey, am I ever glad to see you."

He reached out and gave her a gentle hug, which she seemed more than happy to accept.

Troy was struck by the moment, wondering, and then realized that it wasn't anything. But because Berkley was a close friend of Tesla's, she likely knew all of them. Except for him. "And I'm Troy," he said quietly. "I think we've met, but it's been a while."

She smiled. "Well, we've been at the same parties," she said, "but I don't think we met."

"I'm sorry then," he said in surprise. "But, if it was at Mason's, sometimes it can get to be quite a crush."

"It was, indeed, at Mason's," she said, chuckling. "So listen. Things here are ugly."

"Can you tell us what happened?" Axel said.

"First off, you have to understand that you were picked up on cameras," she said. "That's the only reason I know you are here. Jonesy has been monitoring the cameras on the rig and caught sight of you. He got pretty agitated and upset about it."

"Why?"

"New crew," she said. "Everybody is on edge. Nobody knows what the deal is, what happened, whether it was sabotage or not. Although they're not talking either."

"And yet you seem to think it was sabotage?"

"Definitely it was," she said. She pulled something from her pocket and held it out to Axel.

He looked at it and frowned. "Part of a C-4 package," he said, and his gaze hardened as he looked at her. "Where did you find it?"

"Heading to the number one drill that blew up," she said. "It was tucked at the bottom of the ramp."

"Nobody else saw it?"

"I don't think so," she said. "There was so much chaos, and everybody was racing back and forth. Only later, when I went to take a quiet look, did I see it jammed down on the corner."

"But how did it get there?"

Berkley shrugged.

Troy studied the paper inside and out. "But any sign of C-4 on a rig like this, especially in one of those drill locations—"

"Exactly," she said. "And maybe they do keep it around. I don't know. But there was no need for it to be an open package at the site where we had an explosion."

"Anything else?" Axel asked, tucking the piece into his pocket.

"I saw in my data," she said, "that a hacker's been going through some of the emails. I'm running scans right now to see what files he's been after. So far it seems innocuous, which makes me very worried."

"Wondering if it's a cover for a Trojan or something more devious?"

"Yes," she said. "I'm not the only one working on electronics here. We have a programmer, Bruce, who's been tracking the electronics controlling the pumps and doing analyses on those. And then we have Jonesy, who's not necessarily a programmer, but he's been doing a lot of the same work I was doing, prior to me arriving. So he's kind of stuck himself to me as my friend, but I think he's sticking close to see what I know."

"In order to take your job? Or to see what you might find and whether or not he's in trouble?"

"No real way to know," she said. "There are six crewmen total, plus Daniel, the foreman, and Denny, who does the cooking, and I'm the ninth on the rig."

"I'm surprised you were allowed to stay."

"I'm the one who needed to stay," she said. "I definitely found hacking throughout the system."

"What could a hacker do on a rig like this?" Troy asked, puzzled.

"Cause the chaos he already did," she said.

"And yet C-4 could easily have caused the chaos anyway."

"Exactly," she said. "So, no, I don't have any answers. What I do know is that somebody has been into the computer files, and somebody blew up one of the drills on this rig."

"Okay, do you have any suspects?" Axel asked.

"There's one guy. I call him Idiot but not to his face. His name is Phil. He's one of the guys here who gives me a lot of trouble," she said.

"What kind of trouble?" Axel asked.

She took a deep breath. "He's, … well, he's the female-beating kind," she said, "but he's also one of those power-mad people, who thinks that nobody else can do a job but him. He feels that my job is useless, and, since I've been here and haven't found anything regarding the explosion, I should just take myself off the rig."

"Outside of personal feelings," Troy interrupted, "does he have access to do any of the hacking stuff?"

"Anybody with a laptop could gain access," she said mildly. She glared at him. "And it's not personal. This guy is one freaky dude."

"Big, mean, tough?"

"Slimy, skinny, sleazy. But something's dead in his gaze."

At that, Troy stopped and slowly nodded. "I've known guys like that," he said quietly.

"I don't want to know any more," she said. "Honestly, the worst thought in my mind is that they're *all* part of it somehow."

Troy let out a slow whistle. "That would be a pretty major conspiracy theory."

"Maybe," she said, "and I get that it's probably not fair to everybody here, but Chucky and Winslow are both oddballs. They've been working the rigs for fifty years, I swear to God. Probably only forty, I guess. But, listening to them, it's been at least seventy."

Axel cracked a grin at that. "And we all know guys like that too," he said, "but what benefit does anybody get out of blowing up the rig?"

She took a deep breath. "The company was bringing in a new management control team. They would get rid of a lot of people here who were troublemakers."

"What kind of troublemakers?"

She winced.

"Come on. Fess up. Let's hear it all," Troy said impatiently.

She glared at him. "You forget," she said, "that I'm an outsider. I'm not one of the crew and a part of things."

"And you're female," he said.

She gave a clipped nod. "Exactly. Three other women were on board, but they're all gone now."

"Why did they leave?"

Her glare upped in wattage. "Sexual harassment and—well—rape." Her words landed into a heavy silence in the small room.

CHAPTER 3

BERKLEY TOOK A deep breath. "One of them was my friend," she said. "And I know for a fact that she was assaulted in the shower."

"Is she okay?"

"No! Of course she's not okay!" She glared at Troy. "Will she eventually come out of this okay? Yes. At least I hope so. Was she physically damaged? No. And she wasn't murdered afterward. Although I fear she wishes she had been. Getting her off the rig seemed like the least I could do."

"Did she go to management?"

Berkley nodded. "Yes, she did. And that's part of the reason behind this change of this whole male-only culture."

"So, a lot of the old guys would get the sack?"

"Well, let's just say, they would all get investigated. All three women claimed rape. All three women have been shipped off, and all the men say it was the women's fault. All the men say it's not an atmosphere where women are welcome. The men say it had nothing to do with them, that this should have been a male-only culture, not a mixed culture."

"A lot of oil rigs have great success with coed cultures."

"Maybe so," she said. "This one is full of old rednecks who grump a lot about it and say it has nothing to do with them and that the entire crew was being treated as guilty."

"But wait, couldn't the women ID the men?"

"I'm not sure about the others, but my girlfriend said she was blindfolded, but she does know it wasn't just one guy."

Troy sucked in his breath at that. "Oh, God, I'm sorry," he said gently. "That's difficult for everybody."

"It's particularly difficult being the only female left behind," she said boldly. "Not only is there a large group of the men who resent me for being female—because it reminds them of the change of management coming in and the investigation happening—but also another large group of men were protective, but all those protective men are gone," she said.

"Are you in danger now?" Axel's tone was harsh and raspy. Even as Troy watched, his partner's big hands clenched into fists.

She smiled up at him. "Well, now that you're here, I expect you to pound them all into the ground as needed," she said with a laugh.

"Just point him out to me," he said. His words were a promise.

"So far I've been fine," she said, with a shake of her head. "I've never had any trouble any of the times I've been here. And the fact that eight men are on board with me, well, it makes the odds not that great in my favor, but it'd be a lot easier to pinpoint who was causing the trouble now than to have a full crew on this rig."

"So, back to the other two women, you don't know if they could identify their attackers?"

She shook her head. "I don't know. One left almost immediately, and a lot of secrecy surrounded her exit. I presume she went straight to the top of the line and said she needed to get off. Her accusations came afterward, so I think she just ran first."

"So, of course, no rape kits or anything like that for the medical team were here to process either, right?"

"No," she said. "The doctor said he didn't have any. It wasn't something that he's expected to stock."

"But he could have done something in the meantime," Axel said. "Just because he didn't have an actual rape kit doesn't mean he couldn't take semen samples and photographs."

"I took photographs," she said quietly. "And, with my girlfriend's help, we did swab for semen."

"Good," he said, "and did they get to a lab?"

"I pulled some strings, and they've gone to a private lab, yes."

"Does anybody know you did that?"

"I hope not," she said cheerfully, "because I'm pretty sure I'm in more danger if they do."

"Yes," he said, "I can see that. Well, this is not exactly what we expected to hear."

"Of course not," she said, "nobody does. You come here, and it's all about a rig blowing up and potential sabotage."

"Maybe," Axel said. "But, at the same time, it's not necessarily what's going on."

"Would somebody blow up a rig in order to stop an investigation into the rapes?" Berkley asked.

"Well, it got them out of being part of the investigation, so quite potentially, yes," Axel said.

"So hang on," Berkley said. "These guys rape three women, know that they'll get in trouble over it all, so they blow up a drilling rig, and manage to get off when all the crew is taken away? Now they just aren't available to come back for work and don't answer their phones when the investigators call them?"

"Quite possibly, yes," Axel said.

"But didn't four men die while this rig got blown up? Or went missing?" Troy asked.

"If so, those rape charges just escalated to murder," Berkley stated.

"And the only reason for that to happen is if somebody really didn't want to get caught, as in somebody with a powerful position or somebody who already has a rap sheet and knew he would have the book thrown at him, like a third-strike thing or something?" Troy frowned.

"All of which is possible," Axel said. "And unfortunately so are half a dozen other options we have yet to think about."

"Really sucks," she said. "But, first off, we have to take out those cameras."

"What will that do?" Troy asked curiously.

"You can search the place," she said.

"I can search it anyway," he said. "I just hack into the system and get to the security cameras to choose which ones we need on, which to turn off."

She stared at him, feeling a sense of disquiet. "Are you that good?"

"We both are," he said with a smile. "Remember. You called us for help. We're not here to make your life more difficult. We're here to make sure you get off this rig safely and that this doesn't happen again."

"I hear you," she said, looking worried. "I was planning on disabling the cameras, but you're telling me that I shouldn't?"

"It will make things a whole lot more suspicious if you

did it," he said.

"Maybe not," she said. "We've got so many electrical issues now, stuff is going offline all the time."

"They should be coming back online, if you've got a repair crew."

"I'm not sure how much of a repair crew these guys are," she said. "Honestly I think they're just sitting around, eating and drinking, watching what's going on."

"Interesting," Axel said. "A full analysis should be going on here. Tell us who is doing what roles here so that, when we get hooked up with the company men, we'll know more of what's going on."

At that, she cracked a smile. "Mason looks good in the suit."

Axel gave a tilt of his head. "So, who is what?"

"Chucky and Winslow are drillers. Between them, they've got at least a century of experience," she said with an eye roll. "They were supposed to see what work was needed for the repairs. Jonesy is part IT, but he's one of the machinists. So he's supposed to be reporting on what machinery needs to be fixed and what's involved. And then there's Idiot—Phil. He's, … well, he's one of the engineers," she said with a shrug, "but, along with the foreman, they were supposed to be doing studies to check the status on the other drills' pressure and do an overall security system analysis."

"And Denny is just the cook?"

"Cook and first aid," she said, with a nod.

"Okay, so we need to find out where these supposed reports are."

"I can tell you that I haven't seen any one of them typing a report yet."

"Do they not care?"

"I think they expect the new management will come in and will put their asses out anyway, so why bother."

"Why bother? Because they need to," Troy said. "They were told to do a job, and they damn well better do it. That right there tells us a lot about them."

AS SOON AS they slipped away from Berkley, they headed to the lower levels. Troy wanted to see the accident site for himself. The weather was building up to an ugly nightmare outside. As soon as they went outside—which they had to do each time they went from one level to the next—they lost the ability to speak to each other.

By hanging on to the railings of the rig, they made their way through to where the damage was. The fact that the two other drills were compromised, but one was still operational but shut down, was an interesting tactic, if it was intentional. Now the company had to decide if they would pour millions into fixing this or if they would completely walk away from it. But that would be almost impossible. These weren't million-dollar rigs; billions were involved.

Would somebody do that just to avoid a rape charge? Mind you, anybody who was up for rape wasn't too worried about anybody else's feelings or actions. It was all about the violence of the sex act or for the sense of power. Bullies of the worst sort. So, in a situation like this? Then, hell yeah, the criminals were protecting themselves.

As Troy and Axel walked through the rig, it was sobering to see that the entire side of the station listed to one side. The anchors in some of the steel had been jolted apart, making walking treacherous on this damaged side.

Axel grabbed one of Troy's shoulders to get his attention. The winds had picked up, splashing sea spray over them. Waves pounded up against the steel girders of the rig. Troy twisted around to look and saw his partner pointing. On the side of the drilling rig itself were signs of buckling from the inside. He didn't understand what that was all about.

Axel bent forward and yelled, "Looks like the C-4 went inside the casing."

"The housing around the anchors?"

He nodded. "Part of the support structures. Just enough to cause some damage."

"But this here," Troy yelled back, motioning at the whole area where the walkways were damaged, "was a separate blow."

Axel nodded, his face grim. "This was definitely sabotage," he hollered. "How anybody could say it isn't is beyond me."

"And that's another consideration," Troy called out. "Why would anybody try to make this look like anything other than what it was?"

"It's a question of who they'll blame." After taking a good look and managing to get as many photos as they could, they made their way back inside.

As soon as the door shut, the pounding from their eardrums came to a complete stop. Troy took several deep breaths, letting his ears adapt to the relative silence of being inside again. "Pretty ugly out there," he commented. He opened his coat, shaking off some of the ocean spray.

"Yeah," Axel said. "I want to do a full search down here."

"What are we looking for?" he asked. "Do we care about the cameras?"

Axel hesitated at that. He looked down at him and asked, "Can you shut them off?"

"Yeah, I can." He pulled out his phone and accessed the system. As soon as he got into the spot he wanted, he immediately shut them down. "Okay," he said, "we've got about eight minutes before the emergency override kicks it back up again."

"Let's go."

They quickly raced through the lower section but found absolutely nothing to see. Rooms for equipment, yes. Rooms for storage of food and parts and basic medical supplies, yes. And a whole lot of industrial storage rooms, but not a whole lot else. And yet no signs of damage here or any equipment here that might have led to some damage like this.

At that point Troy said, "Okay, the cameras are back on."

"Let's grab a coffee," Axel said, "and then check the other side at this level."

Making their way back to the dining area, Denny still muttered over his stoves. He shot Troy and Axel an absent-minded look and then glared when he realized who they were.

"Just after a hot coffee," Troy said. "We made the mistake of venturing outside."

"That's your fault," Denny said.

They grabbed coffee and immediately disappeared.

"Friendly sort, isn't he?" Axel said.

"Not very often, I don't think," he said. "Typical. Nobody works on these rigs if they have a preference to work anywhere else." And that was so true about a lot of it. But they paid well, so guys were usually here for the short term not the long term. Except for ... "So what's the story on

Chucky and Winslow?"

Axel shrugged.

"Probably two bros who never could make it in the real world," Troy said, having seen guys like that before too. They didn't fit the norms; they didn't deal with the modern digital world. This place here had completely stepped out of whatever the universe was like around the big cities. Those two old-timers would be stuck here until they died.

"I guess," Axel nodded. As they headed to the bottom level to search the other half, he whispered, "We'll need the cameras off."

As they stepped forward, one of the regular guys stepped out of a hallway and glared at them. "What are you two doing down here?"

"Any reason we can't be here?" Troy asked.

"It's off-limits."

"We're repair crew too," Axel said, crossing his arms over his chest.

"I don't give a shit who you are," the guy said.

The name embroidered on his shirt pocket read Phil. This was the one pressuring Berkley. The one she called Idiot. "So, what is it that you're hiding?" Troy asked cautiously.

"I ain't hiding nothing," he said, as he turned and spat on the ground, "but you're not fucking coming in here."

"Actually we are," Troy said. "So, it's the easy way or the hard way. You choose."

At that, Phil's eyes lit with a hot fire. Just a stage short of madness. But it was better than the dead look that Berkley had described so well.

"I wouldn't do that if I were you," said a man behind Phil.

Daniel stood there, leaning against the wall, coffee in his hand.

"Finished your cinnamon bun, huh?" Troy asked.

Daniel sent him a sour look.

But Phil spun to look at Daniel and said, "What the hell? Did you eat a cinnamon bun? I was up there, and Denny wouldn't let me have one."

"I got it before he took them away," Daniel said.

Swearing fluently, Phil stared at Daniel and then disappeared.

"Interesting character," Troy said.

"You get used to him after a while but don't rile him. Something's wrong with him on the inside."

"Yeah? What was your first inkling?" Axel asked. At that, Troy cracked a bit of a smile.

"He might not seem like much," Daniel said, "but he does his job."

"Does he though?" Troy asked.

"Yeah, he does," Daniel said, "and nobody is supposed to be down here."

"Why is that?" Axel said.

"It's off-limits. When there's no crew, we keep this area closed."

"And yet you're here, and Phil's here," Axel said, once again in that same mild tone.

"Maybe," Daniel said, "but that doesn't mean it's not the way it's done. If you want to get along, follow the rules," he said, "and don't start by being one of those guys who says, *Rules are for fools.*"

"It's not like we're causing any trouble," Axel said. "Just getting the lay of the land. Seeing the damage, so repairs can be done."

"Maybe so," Daniel said, straightening up, "but go find the lay of some other land to look at."

"Will do," Troy said, turning around to leave. "It'll be interesting to see if the company guys want to come look at this place." He heard the strangled sound coming from Daniel's throat and pivoted toward him. "Unless you're hiding something too," he said, in a smooth tone.

Daniel narrowed his gaze at him. "You look like you're nothing but fat-ass trouble," he said, his face turning a florid red.

"Can't say I've ever liked being told what I can and cannot do," Troy said. "So I suggest you get out of my face."

With that, Daniel went for Troy. One second before it had gone completely quiet, and, in the next, Daniel's hands reached for Troy's throat. Except Troy no longer stood there. He had stepped to the side and tripped Daniel and he went down.

As soon as he hit the ground, Daniel let out a weird sound.

Axel picked him up and, as if he were a little kid, dusted him off and said, "Looks like you tripped there, bud."

Daniel stumbled back several feet and glared at the two men with hate in his eyes; then he turned and disappeared.

"Interesting," Axel said. "You know how to make friends, don't you?"

"Yeah," Troy said, with a smile. "I'm really good at that." At another odd sound, he turned to see Berkley standing there. "You do get around," he said.

"You mean, *you* do," she said. "I've never seen Daniel move so fast."

"Well, he and Phil both told us that we couldn't come into this area," Axel said. "Do you know why?"

"It's always been an off-limits area," she said. "I've never been allowed in there either."

"I suggest we take a look then," Troy said. When he turned, they immediately headed into the area they supposedly weren't allowed access to.

"Life raft, life preservers, emergency vehicles, emergency kits," Berkley noted. "So why would nobody be allowed in here?"

"Maybe to avoid anybody tampering," Axel suggested.

Berkley shot him a hard look. "Then you'd think that one of the first things they would be doing is checking down here."

"Not Phil. Maybe that's what Daniel was doing," Troy said. "Just because he seems and comes off like he's guilty and an asshole, like Phil is, doesn't mean Daniel is one. Maybe he was looking to see if his brother was still alive out there."

"It's possible," she said. "Let's check the inventory." She brought up a tablet in her hand. She clicked away for a minute. "According to the database there should be four of those emergency submersible life rafts. The ones that can handle the ocean conditions here. Are there?"

It didn't take Axel but five minutes to confirm that.

"Life jackets?"

"How many crew on board normally?"

"All staff and crew, 180 at a time," she said.

"So, at least two hundred life jackets, you'd think." Axel walked up and down, checking. "I'd say that they're all here. Who knows what their stocking level is, but at least 180 are here."

"Also some extra oxygen tanks for the medical facilities." She walked forward and opened a door. "Right, this is where the medical clinic is." She frowned. "I wonder why Daniel doesn't want anybody in here."

Troy stepped inside and looked around. His heart slammed against his chest. "Probably because two body bags are in here on the floor. And they are full."

Axel stepped in to confirm and said, "Body bags. So they're probably from the accident itself." He looked at her. "Why has nobody come to collect them?"

She looked at them in surprise. "I had no idea they were even here."

"Does the company not know?" Axel asked. "I understood no fatalities were declared, but four remain missing."

"Looks like two missing and two fatalities. Or potentially not even two missing," Troy said, nodding toward the very large cooler in front of them. "If that's a temporary morgue, I suggest we check it out."

Axel was already there. "It's got a lock," he said.

"I'll take care of that in two seconds," Troy said, and he had it open almost that fast. From behind him, he heard Berkley sucking in her breath. He looked at her, smiled, and said, "It's all right. Standard skills in this line of work."

She nodded once and said, "Great. Now open up that thing."

He opened it, and they all stood there, stunned.

CHAPTER 4

"SIX MORE BODIES?" Berkley said softly. "Plus the first two we found?"

"Exactly, so what the hell?" Troy asked. "How come we have eight dead bodies, yet we were told only four were missing?"

She walked over to the original two body bags on the floor, took a deep breath, and slowly zipped open the top of one of the body bags.

"This is Daniel's brother," she said. "This is Lionel." She took a picture of his face, then closed it up, and walked over to the next one.

She took a photo of his face. "Why are they hiding the fact that they have eight dead bodies? Or does no one know because the communication here is such a mess? Or do we have eight fatalities *and* four missing?"

"Because they most likely didn't die in the same accident," Troy said quietly. "It's starting to sound like a whole lot more is going on here, and none of it makes any sense."

"I hear you," she said. "I hate to ask, but can we pull these bodies out of the cooler so that I can take photos and try to confirm ID?"

One by one they pulled out the trays, until she had photos of all six men's faces. She looked at the bodies inside the cooler, then at the two body bags on the floor, and turned to

Troy and Axel. "Any way we can combine two to a shelf, so we can get these two guys off the floor and in there too?"

Axel nodded. "Yeah, these two are pretty small." They quickly shuffled bodies. It was a tight squeeze, but they managed to close that drawer with two inside, and then he reached for the next drawer.

As he did so, Troy stopped, dropped to the floor, opened one of the body bags then the other. "Who are these two guys?"

"That's Charlie, I think," she said. "The other is Lionel. Why?"

Troy looked over at Axel and said, "Check for a pulse."

Axel frowned but knelt over Charlie, placed two fingers at his neck, then shook his head. He repeated the actions on Lionel and immediately looked back at Troy. "There's no pulse, but his body is warm."

"What does that mean?" she asked. "Of course it's warm. It isn't in the cooler with the others."

"No. Warm, as in, he hasn't been dead very long." He slowly straightened, looked at her, and said, "This guy died today. He didn't die two days ago in the accident. He died today." On that note, he turned and looked down at the body bag that belonged to Daniel's brother and slowly reopened it.

"What about him?" she asked, her voice breaking.

Axel looked at her and asked, "Is he special to you?"

"No," she whispered. "Not necessarily. But he was the gentlest of the group."

Axel reached over, checked him, and said, "Without any equipment, I can't be real specific," he said. "But I can tell you that he didn't die two days ago because he is still warm now too."

"And what we need to know is," Troy said quietly, "how did they die."

She stepped back, her hand going to her mouth as she stared down at Lionel. "There was a confrontation a week or so ago," she said. "I wasn't here, but it happened just before I arrived. They found out that Lionel was gay."

"Oh, shit," Troy said, shaking his head. He stared down at Lionel and saw a young man, clean-shaven, with an almost feminine look about him. "That may not have gone over so well here."

"There was no *may not* about it," she said. "A lot of people really hassled him."

"Not very progressive here, is it?" Troy said.

"No, and it goes right along with the rape climate," she said. "The men are the men—or are supposed to be—and nobody else counts."

"So we have what? Another motive?" Axel asked in disbelief.

"But that outing happened several days ago," she said, wide-eyed, as she looked at them. "If these two men died today, that means they died before you guys arrived. So I was here."

"Yes," Troy said, "and what happened this morning?"

She shook her head. "I don't know," she said. "I slept like a log. I wasn't expecting to sleep, but I did."

"Did you have anything with the guys last night?"

"What do you mean?" she asked.

"Hot chocolate, coffee, whiskey?"

"Yeah. We had rum. I just had the one though. Still, it seemed to have done the trick."

"Yeah. So where is the glass? Do you happen to have it?" Troy asked, his tone neutral.

She stared at him suspiciously. "I don't have it anymore. It's likely gone through the dishwasher as well, since I brought it to Denny this morning."

"Too bad."

She glared at him, but he could see fear taking root within her. "Why?"

"Because," he said, as if that was an answer.

She looked at Axel, and he just stared back at her with that same patient look he always had, but now something indomitable had been added. She would do whatever they asked in order to stay safe. She groaned. "Are you done down here?"

"We can't fit this other body in," they said, "but he needs to go somewhere."

She nodded. "Especially since it's Lionel," she said. And then she stopped, looked at them, and said, "Daniel was here, right?"

They both nodded. "So does he know his brother is here?"

"He told me earlier that his brother was missing," Troy said, "so I'm not sure."

"Interesting," she muttered. "What are the chances the killer or killers were planning on deep-sixing the bodies?"

At that, Troy stopped, nodded at Axel, and said, "You know what? That's not a bad idea. They could easily get them out of here that way, and nobody would know."

"But there are eight bodies. That's a lot to dispose of."

"You think?" he said. "Looks like all we're getting so far is lies. But I can tell you that Lionel and Charlie didn't die in that explosion."

"We need to keep their bodies for the sake of that alone," Axel said, looking around, as if wondering what the options were. He turned toward her. "What does the cook have, four freezers upstairs?"

"Some freezer space is down here too, I heard," she said. "Let's take a look."

They headed over to the side and, on the back side of where the cooler was, sure enough, was a meat freezer. They came back, picked up Lionel, still in his body bag, and moved him into the freezer.

"He'll freeze solid, won't he?"

"Yeah," he said. "He will. But he's dead, and nothing we can do for him now. But it would be nice if we can keep him for the lab and get him home with the helicopter today."

"If you say so," she said. "At the moment, I really want to go back on that helicopter with you myself."

"Of course you're coming," Troy said quietly. "It's not safe here anymore."

"I don't think it was safe to begin with," she said, her voice a little raspy.

"You could be right, but it's definitely bad news now."

She nodded slowly, took a deep breath, and said, "So, what's next?"

"Let's finish searching this area and then go up a level."

It took absolutely no time to finish that search, and, when they went up a level, they headed back into the dining area. Almost everybody was gathered there. The three company men were here too, and the one real company man talked to the group of crewmen. Mason stood to the side, looking bored. But his gaze narrowed when the three of them arrived.

The company man, Gregor, looked at them, nodded, and said with a little relief, "There you are. I was wondering. We need to have a talk," and he pointed at Berkley. "You missed your one-on-one meeting."

"Sorry about that," she said. "I wasn't feeling very well."

Daniel just rolled his eyes at that. And even Jonesy snickered.

TROY WATCHED THE climate around him and saw that the atmosphere was strictly a male-dominant one. He didn't think any female would have it easy on this rig. He'd been on several rigs with plenty of women, and it was no problem. But, if this kind of climate were allowed to fester, all hell would break loose eventually. Apparently it already had. He crossed his arms over his chest and stood protectively at her side. Jonesy appeared to catch his movement and glared at him.

Troy just stared back. But Phil had him worried. Because he was openly glaring at Berkley.

"Women are bad luck," Phil said.

"What? So you're blaming me for everything that's gone wrong?" she said in outrage.

Troy reached out, gently grabbing her hand with his. She looked at him almost glaringly too, and, when he gave a tiny shake of his head, she subsided.

Good thing, because this wasn't the time for an all-out war. He understood her feelings on the matter, but it didn't change the scenario they were in right now. Their subtle movements and silent communications were caught by everyone in the room.

Some of the men hid snickers, and the others just glared at Troy. He stared calmly back, daring anybody to say anything.

Gregor turned to her and said, "I want to speak with you

next."

She nodded. "Absolutely." As she headed forward, she went to loosen her hand, but Troy didn't let go. She frowned at him.

He smiled, leaned over, and gave her a quick kiss. He whispered, "Just setting the scene."

She growled under her breath at him.

He chuckled and said quietly, "Worth it, if it keeps you safe."

She stopped at that and then gave a grudging nod. "Okay," she muttered, "but I still don't like it."

"Of course not," he said. "Nobody does. But, the fact of the matter is, something is very wrong here."

"Yeah, you think?" Her tone was caustic, but there was enough fight there to keep a smile on her face.

He glanced at Axel and said, "I'll go with her to the meeting."

"You do that," he said, "and I'll stick around here with the guys."

Troy almost laughed at that because Axel was anything but *one of the guys*. Still, he was somebody to keep an eye on things, whether these guys liked it or not.

As soon as Troy got into the hallway, he looked behind him to see the three company men were still standing, talking business. But Mason watched them. His hands behind his back, he gave a thumbs-up sign.

"Let's go," Troy said.

"Was that really necessary?" she asked him.

"Maybe not," he said, "but, as long as they think something's between us, they'll think twice about coming after you to run into me."

"Will they though?" she said. "I've turned them all

down."

"Of course you have," he said. "It's the only safe thing to do in this environment."

She laughed at that. "Yeah? But that's what got my girlfriend in trouble," she said, and this time her cry was broken, and her tears were close to the surface.

"I'm sorry," he said quietly.

"We couldn't believe it," she said. "Who'd have thought that would be a problem here in the twenty-first century? In America—well, technically working with Americans, but we're in international waters. Still, where we're supposed to be a first-world country, the greatest place to live, *blah-blah*."

"It shouldn't have been. That's on management," he said.

"*Right*," she said, with a snap of her fingers. "That's who's in the cooler."

"Who?"

"I think those could be three of the management guys who are in charge of different divisions on the rig."

He stared at her in shock and quickly pulled her off to the side. "Are you serious?"

She nodded.

"Were they known to be missing?"

She nodded again.

"Who's the fourth one?"

She shrugged. "I'm not sure. He looked familiar, but just one of many faces that I've seen. A lot of men were on this rig. And remember. I'm not here full-time, and my focus is pretty narrow."

He nodded. "Got it. But you know how this looks, don't you?"

"Well, I wasn't thinking it looked like anything, until we

saw Lionel there," she said, "but now I don't know what to think."

"Well, I do," he said, "and none of it's good." Troy understood exactly what she meant. It was a shock to find out the world around you was happening when you weren't paying attention.

Obviously there'd been so much chaos in the last forty-eight hours that something had gone on, and yet nobody knew anything. It was also obvious that the newcomers' arrival was something nobody had expected. As such, whether the skeleton crew was trying to move the bodies now, to store them, or just hoped to keep everybody away from that section, the fact was, more bodies were there than should have been under any situation. And that was an issue of concern.

Finally the three company men stepped into the hallway to follow Troy and Berkley.

With her close at his side, Troy headed toward the office in command central. She walked through the command post, heading to her computer, checked her log, then nodded, and carried on. He raised an eyebrow. Under her breath, she whispered, "Just making sure nobody touched it."

He nodded, and the three company men stepped inside the office, closed the door, and then drew the curtain, so that nobody outside could see them.

In a low voice she said, "Just in case you think this is private, it's not. Anybody standing outside right now can hear us."

At that, Mason sucked in his breath, then looked at her and said, "Where is a quiet place then?"

She shook her head. "There really isn't one anywhere.

Between cameras and nosy people, almost everywhere is suspect." She motioned toward the room behind them. "But that storeroom is probably the best of them."

They headed into the back storeroom, which was a tight squeeze for all five of them. Good thing Axel had stayed with the crew.

As soon as they stepped inside, Mason asked Troy, "Have you found anything?"

"Bodies," he said, "eight of them."

Gregor sucked back a breath. "Seriously? I thought four were missing."

"Well, I'll say four aren't missing now, because eight are dead here. But, for whatever reason, it's quite possible they want you to believe that four of those bodies won't be here if you were to come looking."

"What do you mean?" Mason demanded.

Nelson leaned against the back wall and studied the two of them together. But he didn't say a word.

Troy gave him a half nod, then explained what they'd found.

"So Lionel didn't die in the accident?" Gregor asked.

Troy shook his head. "Both Lionel's and Charlie's bodies were warm. Obviously they're cooling now. But I'd say they haven't been gone for long. This morning I'd say."

"And nobody expected us to be here at all," Nelson said. "So are you thinking those two would get deep-sixed first?"

"Exactly," Troy said. "We've moved Lionel's body into the freezer section. We'd really like you to take him back with you for an autopsy."

"Consider it done," Gregor said in a harsh tone. "Jesus Christ, what's been going on here?"

"Potentially a lot, though some you may know," Berkley

said, speaking up. "And a lot you've probably ignored."

He raised his eyebrows and stared at her.

She identified herself and said, "I'm sure you heard about the three women who were gang-raped during their stay here."

Gregor's face paled. "We heard rumors of a sexual assault," he said cautiously.

She immediately shook her head. "No. Not rumors, and don't soft-sell it as sexual assault. Take that directly as gang rape. One of them was my friend. I saw her and photographed her injuries afterward. I also got her off this rig as soon as I could."

Nelson straightened up and came over, fury lining his body. "In a climate like this," he said, "that is bad news."

"It's bad news anytime," she said, her tone gaining a bit of temper.

"Could she identify her attackers?" Mason asked.

"My friend was blindfolded."

Mason spoke up. "You told us about Tabitha. Is that who you're talking about?"

She nodded. "Tabitha won't talk about it much. She's too traumatized by it all. We have spoken, and I've told her that I'd look into it, but she was terrified I'd be next. She didn't, doesn't," Berkeley corrected herself hastily, "know about the other rapes. My priority was getting her away, and I pulled every favor I had to get her on the next flight out."

"So then how will we prove what happened to her?"

"Well, I sent semen swabs off to a private lab," she said, "with my own money. And I have the photographs. She also needs to see a shrink. I'm trying to get her to do that, but, while I'm here, she's not being very cooperative."

"Of course not," Mason said, running a hand through

his hair. "She wants to put it off, not think about it at all."

"Well, she won't be able to as soon as I can land and be with her," Berkley said. "I'd really like to leave with you today, if I could."

"The weather has taken a downturn," Gregor said. "According to the pilot, we might not be leaving at all."

"In that case," Troy said to Mason and Nelson, "you better be armed."

"That bad?" Mason asked, but already he knew.

"Something's definitely wrong here," Troy said. "And that's in addition to the dead bodies and the three women who were raped. So, Lionel is the brother of Daniel, the foreman, who's having a hard time right now. He flat-out told me that his brother is missing, and instead his brother is in the cooler. Lionel didn't die in that explosion two days ago but sometime within the past twelve hours. According to Berkley, Lionel was gay. Something that he tried hard to keep quiet but—" Then he stopped, looked at Berkley, and said, "Wait. Berkley, any chance that Charlie, the man in the body bag beside Lionel, was his lover?"

"It's quite possible," she said steadily. "I don't know. Again I come and go from this place, and I kept a schedule that didn't match up with all the staff."

"Can you leave?" Gregor asked. "How much value are you adding by being here?"

"I can work via remote access," she said, "but you also need to know a hacker's going through your files."

"What?" he said in outrage. "Did you cut him out?"

"No," she said. "But I'm tracing every spot he touches, trying to figure out what he's after."

"You have to get him out of there," Gregor said, moving a couple steps forward, pacing, but the storeroom was way too damn small. He ended up slumped against the far wall. "Jesus, what a nightmare."

"Another thing you need to know is," Troy said, "several of the bodies in the cooler are likely managers from this rig."

"I assumed," Gregor said. "It's one of the reasons chaos ensued immediately. Once the top guys went down, nobody else knew how to handle themselves."

"But that's not normal, is it?" Nelson said quietly. "Three of your top managers?"

"Who are the others?" Gregor asked.

"I don't know," Troy said and turned to look at her. "Can you bring up your photos?"

She quickly brought out her phone and flipped through them—past Lionel, his friend Charlie, then stopped as she got to the photos of the six in the cooler. Three she suspected were managers. "Who are they?"

"Don't know that one, but that's Stedman … and this guy must be a crewman … but this one is Doug … and Pete," Gregor said, stopping. "Three managers among the dead here. In fact, Pete was here early, as part of the takeover that was happening. We were doing a complete sweep of the staff, breaking up the group here. We had heard a lot of problems originated here, then after the sexual assault rumors," he said, holding up a hand to stop Berkley's hot response, "we decided to break them up and to move them around different rigs."

"Moving them elsewhere doesn't solve the problem. The men here are trouble and would be anywhere else," Berkley said. "Not all of them. Some are damn good guys. But then you get the bad apples, and they're just ugly."

"Which is what we were trying to avoid," he said quietly.

"Too little, too late," she snapped.

Troy reached out a hand for hers and squeezed it. "I understand how much this hurts you," he said, "but right now we have to make sure that everything stays calm, quiet, and under control. We have eight other crewmen on this rig beyond us, and all eight could have had something to do with those bodies in that cooler."

"It's not even a matter of extra bodies," Mason said. "We were told flat-out four were missing." He turned to look at Gregor. "Did you know anything about deaths being reported?"

Gregor shook his head. "No. I didn't know anything about it."

"I knew about four missing, and these management guys were three of them," Mason said.

"However, none of you are really putting together something here though," Troy said, trying to keep the conversation under control. He gripped Berkley's fingers, and she subsided. He looked at Gregor. "The thing is, if those managers died in the explosion, I'd eat my hat."

Gregor stared at him in shock. "What are you saying?"

"No signs of violence, like from a blast, appear on any of the men in that cooler down there that we could determine," he said. "So, however those men died, it wasn't from an explosion."

CHAPTER 5

B ERKLEY LOOKED AT the three company men, seeing the shock in their faces. "With the caveat," she added hurriedly, "that we couldn't see their whole bodies. But, no, none had massive burns or blackened faces or obvious bloody wounds, nothing like that. Now were they shot or stabbed in the back or poisoned or something else? We don't know."

All three men slowly nodded.

"Interesting point," Mason said, studying her. "And, of course, that's the reason for getting the bodies off here sooner rather than later."

"Yes," she said, "and Daniel's brother in particular."

"And why him again?" asked Gregor. "Why him?"

"Because, based on one of our current theories, he was targeted for being gay," she said.

"And we know for a fact he and the other guy near him didn't die two days ago," Troy added. "They died much later. Like today."

"Well, the pilot says we're not going anywhere today," Nelson said, relaxing against the other side of the storeroom, his arms across his chest. "But, if we've got murderers on our hands here, that's an entirely different story."

She nodded grimly. "It's been such chaos here. I can't confirm that any of these remaining men are responsible. Tons of other crewmen have been coming and going over the last two days."

"Of course there have been," Gregor said. "We had to get everybody off."

"Exactly. And, just because these are the men who are here now," Troy said beside her, "they make for great suspects."

"Meaning that the last person off-loaded could have been the murderer, and nobody would know," Berkley stated.

Troy nodded. "Exactly."

"Is anybody here someone you suspect?" Mason asked her.

Now all eyes turned to Berkley. She shrugged. "A suspect? Not necessarily, no. Are there some I don't like? Yes, absolutely. Are they all women haters? No, not necessarily, but women don't belong here. This group is homophobic, sexist, and probably racist. Although I'm not sure about that last part." She tilted her head to the side. "In this world, black men still rate above white women."

"Not an uncommon thing in these areas, where it's mostly a man's world," Mason murmured.

She gave a clipped nod. "Still, it's not something I'm particularly used to seeing all that often. Only on the rigs."

"Glad to hear that," Troy said. He looked over at the other three. "What do you want us to do?"

"I want to get our other two men onto the rig safely and without being seen," Mason said. "That's the priority right now for you and Axel. We'll keep Berkley with us, and we want her to keep working on her computers."

Troy hesitated.

Mason raised an eyebrow. "Is there a problem?"

"A lot of cameras are on the rig," he said. "We could use

her help shutting them down as we go, or we need to take the entire system offline," he said. "Just long enough so that we get our crew on board and get them stashed somewhere."

"I don't quite understand why you felt you needed two extra men here," Gregor said curiously.

"We've potentially got a far uglier situation than we thought," Troy said. "And, if *we* have two men the skeleton crew don't know about, it's surely possible that other crewmen are here we also don't know about."

At that, Berkley gasped. "I guess that's possible, isn't it?"

"Of course it is," Troy said. "Think about all the places on a rig where somebody could hide."

"But what would be the point?" she asked.

"It depends whether Daniel's kid brother was targeted," Troy explained, "or whether somebody stayed behind to take care of business or whether it was an accident because somebody was involved in more sabotage. We really have no answers. All we have are more questions."

"Now that is par for the course," Nelson said, straightening up. "And the longer we sit in here, the more problems we'll have."

"Exactly." Berkley walked out of the storeroom, stepped into the outer office, and opened the curtained door, where all the crewmen, including Axel, stared at her from the bullpen adjacent to the office. Every last one of them. She tilted her head high and tried to make it look like she'd taken a verbal beating from the bosses as she headed to her computer and sat down. Without a word, she logged on and resumed working.

An uncomfortable silence ensued as everybody studied her.

She let her hair fall over her face as she quickly scanned

through the systems. Nobody had logged on to her area since she had been in her meeting, which she was grateful for. She was always worried that the hacker was after something that she didn't understand. The fact that he was even in her system bothered her.

Could she kick him out? Potentially, yes. But then he'd just get more devious to get back in. At least this way she could track where he was moving.

Jonesy, sitting beside her, leaned over and asked, "You okay?"

She gave him a slight head nod. But she wouldn't look at him.

"They rip into you?"

She gave another little shrug. "They have every right," she muttered. "All kinds of hell is going on here."

"Isn't that the truth," he said with a heavy sigh. And then he eased back into his chair and started to work on his computers.

That they were both in the computer field was just part of a bond that they had. He was also the one who had stuck up for her when that idiot Phil, or one of the others, got a little too over-the-top.

The other four in the storeroom filed out and stood, staring at the outer room. Mason talked to Gregor in such a quiet voice that nobody could hear anything.

She didn't even look up when Axel and Troy left. But she immediately watched them on the tracking system. She looked over at Jonesy. "What are you working on?"

"Pulling the data from that drill," he said. "We need to save as much as we can."

"What about the backup?"

"It's still there," he said. "Yet I'm sure the bosses want

cameras and everything that we can pull from around that area. Even now. And the storm is getting worse out there, so you know that means doing extra backups."

"Right," she said. "In case you hadn't heard, the helicopter won't be leaving today." She heard him suck in his breath, and she gave a slight nod again. Then returned to her work. On the monitor he couldn't see, she brought up the camera system, and, watching where Troy and Axel traveled, she quickly shut down cameras ahead of them, so that nobody would know what exact pathway they took. She roughly understood where they were going and where they would need the cameras off.

Then, just as she thought she had it under control, all the lights in the command central area went down. Groans came from all around.

"What the hell was that?" she asked. Inside, worry gnawed at her.

"I don't know," Chucky said. "It's a shitty night to be out there."

"Every night out here is like that," she said in a calm voice. "So tonight it's no worse, right?"

"Feels like it," he retorted, then slammed out of the room. Winslow, as always, went with him.

She thought of them as the Bobbsey Twins. Something was off about them. Maybe it was the closeness of their relationship. She didn't know anyone who had bonded quite like those two. And she wasn't even sure that Chucky was the leader because it seemed like Winslow was more the silent one, but, when he did speak, Chucky listened.

It gave her a good excuse for all the cameras to be down. She wished she had a way to contact Troy and to let him know what was going on. And then, once she thought about it, she realized that she did. She quickly sent Mason a message—under the pretext of typing as usual at her computer—and, when he looked down and pulled his phone from his pocket, she knew he got it. He didn't look up at all but sent a message back to her, saying he'd handle it. She closed every program she had running on the side and worked on the backup because, as soon as the power went off, all kinds of systems started going off too.

"Wait until somebody visits Denny," she said, her voice at a normal pitch.

Idiot stood off to the side. "He'll be livid," he said, with glee in his voice. "You just shut down his ovens."

"I didn't shut anything down," she snapped.

"Yeah, says you," Idiot said, laughing. "You're the IT person. If you didn't shut it down, who did?"

"How about Mother Nature?" she said. All the while, she kept checking on the power system, looking for the source of the problem, thankful for the generator power for essential operations. She found nothing on this level, but power was supplied to the levels below as well.

"One level down is fine," she said. "Something tripped the breaker for up here. And the kitchen is fine," she said, "so maybe Mother Nature wants us to have dinner after all."

Everybody laughed and joked at that. The power did go off enough times in the main housing areas, and, as long as it wasn't affecting the power sent to the drills, they didn't think much about it. Two other men got up and left to go check.

That left her here with the three men in suits, plus Jonesy at his station next to hers, and Idiot, who sidled a little bit closer to the suits. She looked over to see the company man, Gregor, with Mason and Nelson, heads together. She looked over at Jonesy. "What do you think the company men are discussing?"

He shot them a hard look. "Whether we keep our jobs or not, most likely," he muttered.

"Wow, is that even on the table?"

"A place like this? It's always on the table," he said. "We heard about a lot of heavy shuffles going on from the top all the way down."

"Well, something like this makes everybody do a reevaluation too," she said, "so I hope not for your sake."

He looked at her in surprise and then realized. "Of course that's not your issue is it?"

"Meaning?"

"Meaning that you're on contract. Your job isn't dependent on this."

"Well, it's not like I'll have a job if, everywhere I go, disaster strikes," she said.

"Good point," he said, with a grin. "Has it ever happened before?"

"Has what ever happened before?" she asked, distracted by the data scrolling on her screen. She narrowed her gaze as she watched her hacker move through the system. If he was moving right now, was he on the rig? Or had he hacked in remotely?

"Have you ever been on a rig that basically self-destructed like this?"

"No," she said in surprise. "Have you?"

He shook his head. "No, never."

"Besides, it's only one of the drills that's permanently damaged," she said. "We haven't got further reports on the two others, have we?"

"Nope, not yet," he said, "but it won't be long before we know how bad this really is."

TROY AND AXEL were on the bottom level, working their way closer to the rendezvous spot, when the power went out. They both froze, then turned to look around, and Troy said, "Man-made or …"

"It's hard to say. Like they said, they're still getting issues from the original damage."

"She was taking out the cameras, but now she doesn't have any control over the cameras," he said smoothly.

"You think somebody shut down the power in order to stop her from helping us?"

"I wouldn't be surprised about anything at this point in time," Troy said. "Absolutely nothing is what it seems around here."

"Isn't that the truth," Axel said. "Including us."

They made their way along the far side. There was no way to know if the power would come back on, but Troy could see that the level above them was dark, yet the next level up had electricity; those lights reflected outward. "So we're on the water level," he said. "We have no power, but at least some of the levels above us do."

"It could be random," Axel said.

Troy shook his head. "I don't believe it."

Keeping a close eye and their weapons handy, they headed to the rendezvous position. There they found the second SEAL team. They smiled, helped the two men on board, and quickly secured their vessel in a nearby storage room.

"Rough trip?" Troy asked Dane, who'd headed the underwater trip.

"Just slightly," Dane said. "Rough waters and it'll only get worse." He studied Troy. "You guys got any intel for us?"

"Yeah, but good luck figuring it out. All we've got is a

lot of questions and mass confusion." Troy quickly filled them in on it all. "Now nobody is to know you guys are here. Currently this level has no power, but the next level up does. We're not sure if that was deliberate or a random outage."

"We've got the blueprints," Dane said.

Troy nodded. "Then you know what to do. We've got a lot of dead bodies right now."

"Good to know," he said. "What we want to do first is take a look at the accident site and see what we can come up with."

"Go for it," Troy said. "Particularly right now while we've got power issues. Should the power come back on, we can shut down the cameras on the side where we'll be," he said.

Very quickly the four of them were at the accident scene. Dane had brought France, a heavy-duty mechanic with Red SEALs credentials, someone who'd trained on oil rigs, so he knew his stuff.

France studied the area, bending to inspect the explosion site and the damage to the various metals, spending at least an hour. Troy looked at his watch and turned to Axel, who just shrugged. When France was done, they gathered to hear his assessment.

"These explosions were definitely man-made," he said. "It wasn't weakness in the steel. It wasn't pressure from the inside of that drill," he said. "This was man-made, and that's a real shitter."

"Billions of dollars of damage and all these lives lost," Dane said.

"I know," Troy said. "Keep up covert security on this level for now. We'll run food and coffee down as we can."

"We brought supplies," France said. "You guys better go back before you're missed."

"Will do." Troy headed up to the level above. With Axel at his side, he said, "I want to make a thorough inspection of every room. No power is on here, so, in theory, nobody should be here."

"What are you looking for?"

"I don't know," Troy said. "I can only hope I recognize it when I see it."

Moving slowly and methodically, they went through every locker and every bunk room, looking for something. When they came back around to where all the spare life jackets and boats were, he realized that the crew had set up a simple system. They could hook up to the outside hoist and slip personnel and boats off to the side and out into the water without any problem.

He looked at that and nodded. "That's a really easy way to get these out there."

"This setup can't even be one level lower—where we came in," Axel said. "Too much Mother Nature battering it up down there."

"Exactly. And those hoists allow you to move heavy weights."

"That they do." He walked closer to one with a big winch on it. "I wonder if that's what they were planning for the bodies."

"I don't think anybody needs to do anything. They can just drop them overboard at various places, no winch required."

"But they don't want any of them coming back," he said. "That's a consideration too."

The two men looked at each other. Troy took several

photographs in the dark, trying hard to get something that would give them clarity, but, even with Axel using a flashlight, it wasn't that easy. And they continued to search.

By the time they were done, Troy still had that sense of looking for something and not finding it. He shrugged. "I don't know what's still bugging me, Axel," he said, "but something is."

"Well, we're not quite done here," he said.

"I know. I just feel like something's wrong."

"You want to check another place?"

"Yeah," he said. "I want to go to the bodies."

"Let's go then. We should probably check on them anyway."

They headed back to the medical bay and into the cooler in the morgue. There were the seven bodies they had left.

"For some reason," he said, "I was half expecting them not to be here."

"Where were you thinking they would be?"

"I don't know. I can't explain it."

They walked around to one of the freezers here to confirm Lionel's body remained there as well. As they opened it up, Chucky came bolting out from inside, his body white and the look on his face sheer panic. Troy grabbed him and shook him hard. "What the hell were you doing in there?"

He shook his head and tried to talk, but his teeth chattered too badly to speak at first.

"Where's Winslow?" Axel asked. He stepped inside the freezer, using his flashlight, but found no Winslow.

"I don't ... know," Chucky said. "I don't even know ... what I was doing in there," he said, looking around. "Denny asked me to get something."

"From down here?"

"Well, I thought so," Chucky said, looking puzzled. "He said four freezers were here. But they're all at different temperatures, so one's used more as a cooler." Chucky was barely making sense, and it was obvious that he was rattled.

"So how did you get locked in there?"

"I don't know," he said. "I had to go in with my flashlight because it's so dark, but the door shut behind me. My phone's battery is almost dead, so I couldn't even see. I was pounding on the door, pounding and pounding." He held up his hands, where the pads looked like hamburger meat. He wrapped his hands under his armpits.

"Weren't you supposed to be checking on why the power is out?" Axel asked suspiciously.

"I was, yes. Then Winslow and I went to check with Denny. He's got power, but he was worried about the power being off here."

"It's so cold that I don't think the freezers will be an issue," Troy said.

"That's what I told him, but he wouldn't listen. When Denny gets on a roll like that, you can't even talk to him."

"So then you came down here?"

"Yes," he said. "I came down here, and, next thing I know, I'm locked inside."

"Interesting. And what about Winslow? Did he come with you?"

"No," he said. "He was drinking coffee and visiting."

"Interesting," Troy said again.

"In what way?" he asked aggressively. "It's not like Winslow doesn't deserve to have a break."

"Absolutely," Troy replied. "But, at the same time, you two never seem to be apart."

"We are a lot," he said, defending his relationship.

"However, we've been buddies for a lifetime."

"Yeah, I see that," he said. "Now, will you be okay? Do you need medical treatment?"

"I'll be fine," he said, wrapping his arms around himself.

"Do we need to check for whatever it is that Denny was worried about?" Axel asked.

Chucky shook his head. "No," he said. "I'm pretty sure it's all okay. Jesus, it's cold in there."

"Of course it is," he said, "with or without the power."

"But something is wrong in this place right now," Chucky said. "I don't know if it's just bad voodoo or what. But I can't wait to get the hell off this rig."

Troy looked at Axel. The thing is, he almost agreed with Chucky. Something was seriously wrong here.

But he doubted the supernatural had anything to do with it.

CHAPTER 6

BACK AT HER desk, Berkley struggled to work her way through the power issues. When the door burst open, she looked up, and Chucky came in. She frowned. "Are you okay? You look like you've seen a ghost."

He shot her an ugly look. "You could say that," he said. "I was checking on the freezers downstairs for Denny," he announced.

She caught her breath in the back of her throat because, of course, that's where Lionel was.

He stared all around the room, his eyes still wild. "Then the door shut, locking me in the damn freezer."

Jonesy bolted to his feet. "What?"

Chucky nodded slowly. "That's what I thought. I damn-near busted my hands, yelling and pounding on it, to get myself out of there," he said. "The two new guys heard me."

"What were they doing down there?" Idiot asked in a snide tone.

"You know what? I didn't even give a shit about asking. I was too damn glad to get out." Chucky stopped and looked at him, then shrugged. "I'll go see if there's any food yet or at least some hot coffee. I ain't coming back to this godforsaken place. At this rate," he said, "I'll ask for a transfer out of here permanently." And, with that, he turned, and he left again.

She slowly sank back down into her chair, studying the

other men. Idiot was laughing like a loon. She wondered if he really was losing it or if he cared so little about somebody else's fate that he enjoyed the idea of Chucky getting locked up in a freezer. But she couldn't imagine what that had been like. No wonder he was freezing. She looked over at Jonesy. "That's not good," she said.

"No, it's not," he said. "How many of us are there again?"

"I thought just nine of us were here. You and me, Chucky and Winslow, Daniel and Denny, and the idiot over there," she said, with a nod to Phil. "Oh, yeah, and Herman and Bruce. That's nine. Now we have Gregor, plus the other two company men and the two new guys, so fourteen total." She nodded. "So originally the eight crew and me," she said.

"Right," he said, "but now we have five more today. Six counting the helicopter pilot, I guess."

She nodded again. Fifteen total. Fourteen men now. "Hope Denny has got hot food for us." Her stomach growled on cue.

Jonesy laughed. "We could shut this down, if you want."

"Well, the power seems to be back up again," she said. "I did a reset on all the different breakers."

"That's often all it is," he said. "Sorry, I should have done that. It's hardly your job."

"I was in all the systems anyway," she said, with a shrug.

He stopped and looked at her. "Were you? Why?"

"Checking to make sure everything was running smoothly," she said, as she stood up. "Part of my job." She smiled and motioned to the door. "Are you gonna check out if there's food or no?"

"Yeah, we should." He looked over at Idiot. "You coming?"

Phil nodded. "I am."

But when he didn't move, Jonesy sauntered toward him. "Hey, Phil, get off your goddamn program and come on."

Phil looked at them, frowned, and said, "Is it dinner-time?"

"We'll check to see if there will be dinner," she explained.

He looked at her in horror.

She shrugged. "Well, we don't really know," she said. "Plus, with that power off, Denny may not make very much."

"Well, he better," Phil said, as he stood. "If I've got to work my ass off, so does he. And I don't care if that means he's out there with a fishing rod."

She started at that but grinned. "I hear you."

Together the group walked toward the dining area. She turned and looked back at the offices. The board members were still sitting in the one office. They'd retreated there early on and had stuck it out. She wondered exactly what they were doing, but Mason was on a laptop and so was Nelson. She wished she could talk to him, but it really wouldn't do any good for her cover. She suspected they had enough work running down all the crew members to take up a dozen men's time. She could help, if they'd give her a heads-up on it, but, chances were, they wouldn't take a chance on her getting found out either.

As they all trooped into the dining area, Denny looked up and frowned. "Did I call you for dinner? No. So get the hell out of here."

Her eyebrows shot up. It never ceased to amaze her how much the cook always ruled the kitchens and how much the kitchens always ruled the rigs.

She walked over to the coffeepot, lifted it, and sighed. "Why is there never any coffee?" She set about putting on a new pot. Denny completely ignored her. She looked over to see Chucky, hugging a big cup in his hand. It explained why there was no coffee; he'd taken the last cup and was hardly in any shape to put on a new one.

What bothered her was there was no Winslow. After she put on the coffee, instead of sitting with the group that she had walked in with, she walked over to Chucky and sat down. "Where's Winslow?" she asked.

"Gone to check the freezer," he said quietly. "To see if, in any way, it could shut without my knowing it."

"I thought they all had to be so that you could open them from inside or out."

"Yeah, I thought so too." His tone was morose, and his shoulders were stiff.

"Do you think somebody did it on purpose?"

He shot her a hard look and then glanced around the room. "How many were in the control room with you?"

She said, "All these guys, plus the company guys are still in the office."

"That doesn't leave very many then, does it?"

"Not if Winslow was with you, when the two new guys found you," she said. She looked over at the others, then lowered her voice and said, "Chucky, is there any chance somebody else is still on the rig here?"

His eyes widened in surprise. "I don't know why there would be."

"I don't know either," she said, "but I'd have to presume not for a good reason."

He snorted at that. "You know what? I've made a lot of enemies in my life, but facing down that cold storage door was not the way I wanted to end it."

"Nope," she said, sitting sideways in the booth. "I figured, in my sleep, after partying all night long on a beach in Tahiti, would be about right."

He looked at her in shock, and then he started to laugh and said, "Isn't that the truth. I can get behind that totally."

Just then the door opened, letting in the two new guys. Chucky immediately lifted a hand. "She just put on fresh coffee."

Troy looked at him and nodded, then headed to the coffeepot. It had almost finished dripping. He looked at her, lifted an empty cup, and she nodded.

"Yes, please."

With three cups, the two men came over and sat down at the table with Chucky and Berkley. "Man, I didn't thank you at the time," Chucky shook his head, "but I so don't ever want to revisit that freezer."

"Well, while you were in there," Troy joked, "did you at least check that the meat was okay?"

"No way it couldn't be," he said. "It was freezing in there. My flashlight battery was damn near gone. So I couldn't see jack shit."

Well, that answered one question, she thought, because he hadn't seen the body bag, given his response just now.

"The generators are still working," she said quietly. "The freezers are all on thermostats, so it shouldn't have been an issue."

"Tell Denny that. Even when everything is moving smoothly, he always sends somebody down to check on the freezers all the time."

"Makes sense," Troy said, easing back in the chair. "Just think about it though. He's got to face you guys if the meat spoils, and he's got nothing to feed you."

Chucky snorted. "Yeah, that's true enough."

"Where the hell is Winslow?" Axel asked.

"Down checking out the freezers," Chucky said. "I told him to go ahead if he wanted, but I wouldn't bother. I'm okay to never go back down there again."

"And you didn't see anybody else? You didn't hear anyone?"

Chucky shook his head. "No, I didn't. I didn't hear anything that made me suspicious at all. Just that damn door shutting." He shook his head. "And it's not exactly an easy door to move, so it wasn't just the wind. And it wasn't anything heaving in the ocean. It wasn't a big jarring that might have unhooked it or anything. You guys can go check," he said, "but I got to tell you. Nothing would have moved that door except for somebody pushing it closed."

"So that begs the next question," she said, her voice quiet. "Who the hell would do that?"

He shot her a hard look. "I ain't got no idea," he said. "Everybody is gone. I don't have a beef with any of these guys."

They looked around, and she asked, "Where's Daniel?"

"Which one's Daniel again?" Troy asked, feigning ignorance.

Chucky shrugged. "The foreman. And I ain't seen him in a while."

She looked over at the other two, who both shook their heads. "Well, maybe we should find him," she said. "Maybe he's got some idea of what happened."

"The only way that'll work out," Chucky said, "is if he was there, and I can tell you that nobody was down there with me."

"The ghost of the rig?"

"Or maybe the ghost of the missing men," Chucky said morosely. He stared down at his coffee cup, and it was obvious from the look on his face that he was thinking about death and ghosts and all manner of things unnatural.

"It'll be fine," she said quietly. "After a good night's sleep, you'll feel better."

He looked at her with a shaking head. "I doubt it." He got up from the table, refilled his coffee, and turned, saying, "I'll go lie down. Denny, let me know when food is ready." Not giving Denny a chance to say anything, Chucky slammed the door shut and left.

She looked at Troy and, in a low voice, said, "So, where the hell is the foreman?"

He slowly shook his head. "We didn't see anybody."

"Why were you at the freezers?"

"Because I was wondering if somebody else had been left behind or maybe one of the dead was gone," he spoke under his breath, just loud enough for her to hear. "We did a complete sweep of that level. And that's when we came across the freezers."

She leaned forward. "Was the body bag still there?"

He looked at her and slowly shook his head.

THAT WAS THE one thing he wanted to bring up with her but hadn't been able to. They had no clue where that body bag had gone. Lionel's body was missing, and Troy would like to know why and how. It was the one they especially wanted to go out by helicopter.

"We need to search the other levels," she announced.

He didn't bother telling her that they'd already contacted the rest of their special crew, who had just arrived, and they were doing a full sweep too.

"And what about Winslow?" Axel said. "We didn't see him either."

"Unless he went down while we came up," she said. "According to Chucky, Winslow went to check out the freezer door."

Troy didn't like the idea of anybody getting locked in. But he was even more aggravated at the thought that somebody had deliberately tried to lock Chucky in.

"The other question was, who knew that Chucky was going down to the freezers? Just Denny? Or had somebody else heard the request?"

"Maybe we ought to go look for Winslow," Axel said suddenly.

Troy looked at him. "Gut instinct?"

"Yeah," he said, "and it's not feeling very good right now."

The two men hopped up, refilled their coffees, and headed out. Troy knew that she wanted to go with them. But that was the last thing he wanted. At least she was surrounded by people. And, maybe at the end of the day, that would be what saved her. Yet he couldn't count on any of them who were sitting here. But what he did know was that something else was going on outside. And they had to get to the bottom of it and fast.

He followed Axel downstairs to where the freezers were. They found no sign of anybody, but power had been restored, and, with the lights on, they quickly took a solid look into each of the three freezers. Not only was the body not there but neither was Winslow. They moved back around to the medical side and checked the morgue refrigerator trays. Still the same number of bodies, so they were just missing the one. Troy turned to Axel. "Of course it's the one we really wanted to see, right?"

"Of course it is," Axel said, his hard gaze glancing around. "Why are no cameras in here?"

"There should be, shouldn't there?" He pointed up to where a camera had been because the mounting was still there. "Somebody took it down."

"What kind of a place is this?" Axel murmured.

"I'll say a murderous one," he said.

"Maybe we should take a closer look at some of these bodies." Axel walked over, closed the door to the medic room, and locked it. "Maybe now we'll have a bit of privacy."

With a final search around to make sure they had no cameras on them now, they pulled out the first body and checked it. His head was at an odd angle, and he was fully dressed, but they found no bullet holes, and nothing else appeared to be different. "I suppose he could have broken his neck falling down the stairs or from the blast," Axel said, as he studied him.

Troy nodded. "That one will be inconclusive. Not without X-rays to see what other damage there is. We don't know, but a hard blast could have turned his guts to jelly."

On the second one, his face was beaten. His nose was broken, but his hands were clean, and nothing else appeared to be damaged. "I would think a fight," Axel suggested, "but look at his hands."

"Or again, maybe something battering him in the face, but I don't know what," Troy said, as he shook his head, and they zipped the body back up again. By the time they'd gone through all seven bodies, they still had no clue.

"No burn marks on any and I don't see a ton of blood with open wounds, so I'll say it wasn't the blast on the last five for sure."

"Well, the blast and the fire, both got shut down fairly quickly," Axel said. He turned to look around. "I'm surprised the medic didn't stay."

"Maybe he needed to get off too. Or maybe he's one of these dead we haven't ID'd yet."

"Often there's more than one medic. So there should have been a first aid medic, like Denny, a doctor, like our missing one, and a third somebody to relieve both of them. Especially when the rig's manned by almost two hundred individuals on a normal week."

"Depends on the crew," he said. "You and I have both been places where anybody who was a paramedic or an EMT could have had enough training for what they needed here. A helicopter would have taken off with anybody who had a serious injury, as soon as he was stabilized enough to survive the flight anyway. It's not like they would be doing surgeries here."

After a thorough check of the place, and still none the wiser, they unlocked the door and stepped out. Only to come face-to-face with Winslow.

He glared at them, his hands on his hips. "What the hell are you two skulking around here for?"

"We were looking to see who locked your friend in the freezer," Troy said immediately.

He fell back a step. "You're the ones who let him out. Maybe you're the ones who locked him in?"

"Well, maybe," Axel said. "But, if I were you, I wouldn't go down that pathway though because you're wrong. We opened it up."

His face fell a little bit. "Something strange is going on here," he said. "I don't know what the hell it is, but it's getting dangerous."

"It sure is," Troy said. "For a start, seven bodies are in that cooler."

He looked at him, looked at the cooler, and said, "What are you talking about?"

"In the morgue, a temporary morgue," he said, "are seven dead bodies."

"No, there should be two," Winslow said. "Just the two. One of the guys was blasted off the side. His face was slammed into the column of the steel walls there, and that killed him. The other one, his neck was broken from the fall."

"Well, I get that," Troy said. "Except we were told that you had no fatalities and that four were missing. Still your version accounts for two of the dead, but what about the other six?"

"What six?" He looked at Troy in horror and rushed past them toward the morgue room. As they watched, he opened it up and cried out when he saw the body bags. He looked back at them. "Help me open these up," he said. "I want to see who these people are."

With his assistance, all seven body bags were opened. He confirmed the two killed in the blast two days ago, Roger and Clarence; and then he stopped and tapped the next one. "This is our doc," he said. "Jesus Christ, what the hell's going on here?" After he ID'd each of the three managers, he then opened the last one, and he shook his head. "This one's just a kid. He was Daniel's brother's buddy."

"Yeah," he said, "and where is the brother?"

"He's missing." Winslow looked at him. "Remember?

Four are missing." And then he stopped and shook his head. "Wait. But three of the dead are some of those missing. And Lionel was the fourth person missing too."

"Who is this guy? The brother's friend, right?"

"This is Charlie. Him and Daniel's brother, Lionel, they were really good friends."

"How good of a friend?"

Winslow looked at him and glared. "I don't give a shit what the kid's sexuality was," he said. "As long as he did his job, that was good enough for me."

"I get that and commend you for it," Troy said. "But, the fact of the matter is, not everybody might have had that attitude."

He slowly stepped back, looked at him, and said, "Are you saying somebody killed these men?"

"Are you telling us that they died in the blast?"

He looked down and shook his head. "No, there's no way."

"So, how can you possibly not think that somebody killed these men?"

He leaned back against the side, his face pale. He was clearly shaken. "Two of these I knew about, Roger and Clarence, from the blast a couple days ago, although I don't know if a report was sent in on them yet. You've got to realize we have little communication here now, and that's hardly been our priority," he said. "But Doc and Charlie? When did that happen? Now the three managers—Stedman and Doug and Pete—were reported as missing, yet they are part of the dead here too. The only one still missing then is Lionel, Daniel's brother."

"He's in the last body bag we found. So is anyone truly missing then?" Axel asked. "Because it sounds to me like all are dead, and something really fishy is going on."

"You think?" he said. "Jesus, we have to get security in on this."

"You're kidding, right? No security is here anymore. The cameras are down throughout half the place, and the whole place is collapsing in on itself. Remember?"

"I remember," he said. "And I remember that you guys were brought in after the fact. And you're the ones who are involved in all this shit now. For all I know, you're the ones who killed these men."

"Right, so we arrived late—*after* you had four missing people and two killed in the blast—*but* we killed three of them somehow, finding them in the dark during this storm and killed them and stuck them into the refrigerator?" Troy stared at him in disbelief. "Get your head on straight, man. Somebody here on this damn rig has gone rogue. Or was rogue already and got the hell off before anybody found out what he'd done."

Almost pathetically grateful, Winslow grabbed at that straw. "That must have been what happened," he said. "Maybe he found these people and then heard one more spot was left on the last flight out, and he grabbed it."

"And didn't say anything to anybody?"

"Hell, I wouldn't," Winslow said. "People would probably misconstrue everything. Look at you guys."

"What do you mean, 'look at you guys?'" Troy snapped. "It's not like you didn't immediately turn and blame us."

"True," he said. "Jesus, I wish Lionel was here though. It would make Daniel feel a lot better."

"His brother?"

"Yeah, his brother."

"We haven't seen Daniel in the last hour or so. Have

you?"

He looked at him in surprise, then frowned and shook his head. "He's with the company men, isn't he?"

"I don't think so," Troy said, "but I'm not exactly sure."

"Well, he better be," Winslow said. "Otherwise, that's just even more that's messed up."

"Apparently this whole place is a mess. Chucky needs you too," Axel said quietly.

Winslow pulled away from the morgue drawers and said, "Yes, he does. That's what I'll focus on."

"So, just because we don't know what the hell's going on here, don't mention anything about the extra bodies."

He frowned at that. "I don't keep secrets from my buddy."

"I hear you, but what if he had something to do with this?"

"I doubt it," he said. "I've known Chucky for fifty-odd years. He's no murderer."

"Who knew about him coming down to the freezers?"

Winslow shook his head. "I didn't even know," he said. "I didn't know anything was up until he told me what happened."

"So what are the chances that somebody was checking up on the bodies, and Chucky disturbed him?"

"No, he was at the freezers on the other side," he said, "but I hear what you're saying. You think he might have interrupted somebody doing something else?"

"We're looking for answers," Axel said. "If you've got ideas, we could really use them."

"If I had any, I would," Winslow said. "I just want off this rig and will never come back. This has been a piece of shit trip right from the beginning."

"Meaning?"

"Meaning, the women," he said. "Not just one but three of them. Now we'll be turned into an all-male rig because they can't trust the guys with women around."

"Was an investigation ever done?"

"Sure, but it got washed under the carpet, like everything else does around here. That was the problem with Lionel too. Like I said, I didn't have a problem with his sexuality, but some of the other guys did in a big way."

"No surprise there," Troy said. "What about the explosion two days ago?"

"I have no idea," Winslow said.

"Any other stuff? Anything else going on?"

"Just the usual bullying. This life is rough," he said. "You know Chucky and I have lived it for a long time, but we've both been talking though, thinking this is our last trip. We want to retire. We've got houses close to each other, so we can pick up a six-pack of cold beer and sit out by the barbecue and cook some steaks. We're done with this rig living. We're done with this whole attitude."

"Did you have anything to do with those three women?"

He shook his head. "Not us," he said. "We both had wives. We've buried them both unfortunately. One died in a car accident and the other from cancer," he said, "but we've got daughters. We'd never treat anybody like that. But the guys, the younger guys, really don't give a shit. As far as they're concerned, women don't belong here, and, if they're here, it's because they want one thing. It was a bad deal, not just the first time but the third time too. Nothing ever got better."

"I'm sorry to hear that," Troy said. "That makes for a shitty atmosphere."

"It sure does," he said. "We wanted to get out then, but we had contracts. They're up in another ten days. At this point in time, it'll be all we can do to make it to the end."

"At this point in time," Axel said, "it may well take all you've got to make it to the end. There's a damn good chance that somebody didn't expect Chucky to survive being frozen."

Winslow stared at him in horror and then bolted.

"Too much?" Axel asked, his hands on his hips as he stared at the empty doorway.

"It doesn't matter if it was or not," Troy said. "It had to be said. He needs to keep an eye out for him and his buddy."

CHAPTER 7

B ERKLEY LOOKED UP, relief crossing her face when she saw Troy, Winslow, and Axel all walking toward her in the dining area. As soon as Troy and Axel sat down beside her, she watched Winslow at the coffeepot, pour himself a cup, and walk back out again. "At least you found him," she said, in a low voice.

Troy nodded, leaning over slightly. "But we still didn't see Daniel."

"Did you look for him though?"

"Not seriously, no," he said. "Have you seen him?"

She shook her head. "No, I haven't. But he could be in his room. He could be anywhere, really."

"Exactly. Winslow knew two of our dead had died from the explosion but didn't know about the extra bodies," he said. "He was shocked and angry. Now he's wondering what the hell happened."

"Interesting," she murmured.

With him leaning even closer, he whispered in a lower voice yet again. "But he did mention the rapes and said that the atmosphere on board sucked and that he and Chucky were leaving. They have ten days left on their contract, and they will go home, put the steaks on the barbie, and chill some beer. They're done with this lifestyle. This trip was the final straw."

"Interesting," she murmured again.

Just something was so intimate about having him beside her. And what an idiot she was for even thinking that. It's not that she felt she was in any personal danger now, particularly not with Mason and his crew here, but Troy was different. She knew so many in Mason's group, but something about this guy sparked a connection somehow that she didn't have with Axel or the others.

He slowly rotated the mug of coffee on the table with his hands. Long lean muscled fingers, capable hands, a man who exuded power. That's what put off the others. Something was just so self-confident about these men. It wasn't so much even a can-do attitude, as having already done it. And knowing they could do it again.

She leaned over slightly, so that their shoulders touched. "So, you don't think Winslow had anything to do with it?"

Troy shook his head. "No, I don't."

Just then Idiot got up from a nearby table, walked toward them, and said, "Didn't take you long to jump him." He sneered at Berkley.

She raised her eyebrows. "I don't know what in the hell you're talking about," she said, "but it seems to me that we're just sitting here, having coffee."

"Yeah, but you won't be sleeping alone tonight. You could have had all kinds of opportunities for all the time you've been here," he said. "And you turned us all down. This guy walks in, and you're just like a slut, lying down and spreading your legs."

Very slowly, almost in slow motion, Troy stood, towering over Idiot. She reached out to grab his hand. He looked down at her, and she could see the tic from the muscle of his jaw twitching. She shook her head. "He's not worth it."

He didn't shake her hand off his arm but turned to look at Idiot. Immediately silence took over the rest of the dining area.

Idiot sneered. "Big guy, you think you're something?" he said. "You think I haven't gone rounds with a bunch of these guys here?"

"I don't care if you have or not," Troy said, his voice low and hard. "But nobody talks to a woman like that when I'm around."

He sneered again. "Or what?"

Troy's hand shot out lightning fast, grabbing Idiot around the neck. Troy squeezed.

Idiot struggled to get away, gasping and choking. Troy just kept squeezing, with a single hand.

She could see the bicep bulging on the arm that was squeezing, growing incredibly huge. "Stop," she said, reaching out. "Don't let him get you in this mood."

He looked at her casually and said, "Hey, I'm in total control." Then he lifted—absolutely lifted—Idiot off his feet, just by the one-handed hold he had on his neck. A spluttering noise came from Idiot as his feet kicked free and as he tried to kick Troy. But he didn't seem to have that much control, and ever-so-slowly Troy lowered him to the ground. Then he removed his hand from around his neck.

Idiot grabbed a chair to keep him upright, still gasping for breath.

"Listen to me, Idiot. I stopped this time," he said, "but, if you ever speak to her like that again, next time I won't. Now get your shitty ass away from us. You're spoiling my view."

Idiot was bent over double, coughing and choking, his hands around his neck. "I'll have you charged for that," he roared, when he could. The trouble was that his voice came out like a squeaky little mouse.

"Good," Troy said. "Let's have a full investigation into things on this rig, and we'll see if you had anything to do with the three women who were raped."

Idiot took a step back. "Just because she won't sleep with anybody doesn't mean the others didn't," he sneered. "All three of them spread their legs for anybody and everybody, and I think one of them was even taking money for it." His expression held more anger than fear.

As Troy took a step forward, Idiot backed up hurriedly and then took one last look at her, hating her with his gaze, before he turned and bolted away.

Jonesy walked over. "I get that you probably felt you needed to do that, but there *is* something wrong with Phil. You know that, right?"

"That's obvious," Axel said. "Not too many people are stupid enough to cross us."

"No," Jonesy said. "They have the smarts not to. But that's what I mean. Phil's not quite right in the head."

"So you tolerate that behavior, using his mental state as an excuse?" Troy asked, a curious tone in his voice.

"We tolerate all kinds of shit around here. For peace," Jonesy said.

"We shouldn't have to though," she said. "This place has gone to hell."

"Well, I won't argue with you there," Jonesy said. "Just watch your back. Phil is not somebody you can trust."

"I know that already," she said. "It just really sucks that I can't be safe at my workplace."

"It's not just your workplace though," Troy said. "It's also where you sleep and have almost no time on your own, because you can't trust—"

"I know," she said. "He's been crossing the line further and further all the time."

Jonesy looked at her in surprise. "You haven't said anything?"

"You've seen him," she said. "You've stuck up for me a couple times."

"Well, I did," he said, "but obviously I'm not needed anymore. I sure hope you know who this guy really is," he said with a motion to Troy. "Because all of us noticed how quickly you fell into his lap."

She glared at him. "You don't know anything about us," she said, her tone biting. "For all you know, he's an ex-boyfriend and an old friend," she said.

"No," Jonesy said. "He isn't. But we can all see the attraction. The two of you were zinging right off the bat. I get it. We'll back away, but watch out for Phil. His attitude obviously is a little off-center." With that, he turned and walked off.

"Shit, shit, shit," she whispered under her breath. Axel looked at her with interest, and she shrugged. "I don't need this."

"Do you want me to leave?" Troy asked.

She shook her head. "No, you've appointed yourself my guardian," she said. "And, as much as I would prefer not to need anybody in that role, now it'll be worse if we change it."

"Well, hopefully none of us will be here long enough for it to be an issue," he said.

She nodded. "Speaking of which, where the hell is the pilot who brought you in?"

"Hopefully with Mason," Axel said.

"I left the three of them in the office," she said. "I didn't see any pilot with Mason. I haven't seen a pilot at all."

"Well, it's not his first trip onto the rig, so maybe he's holed up somewhere," Troy said.

"Most of the time they're holed up here in the dining area," she said, motioning toward Denny, still muttering to himself as he banged around large pots.

"Good point." Troy got up and walked over to talk to Denny.

She couldn't hear the conversation, but she studied Axel. "Is Troy a good guy?"

"The best," Axel said. He turned to look at her, his lips quirked as he added, "And your buddy there was correct. It's obvious something is zinging between the two of you."

She shrugged self-consciously. "Not so you'd notice on my part," she said.

"Oh, you're interested," he said. "And you can bet that Troy will never be the kind of guy who will let somebody abuse or even disrespect a woman in his presence."

"And that is much appreciated," she said, "but I wish he hadn't pulled that macho tactic here. It won't go down so well with the crew."

"He's worked on oil rigs before," Axel said, surprising her. "He knows perfectly well that dominance needs to be slammed home before it becomes a bigger problem."

"Right," she said with a sigh. "Top dog and all that. What am I? The spoils of war?"

"Tell me," Axel said, leaning forward across the table, his gaze intent. "Have you gone out with or hooked up with anybody here?"

She shook her head. "No, that would be suicide."

"Exactly," he said. "And so, if somebody is pushing the

line, what will you do about it?"

"Push back," she said with a shrug. "I'm not completely helpless."

"Except three women were raped by multiple men. And now you're the only woman around. That will sit in the back of their minds."

She stared at him, feeling the color bleach from her face. "So you're saying that Troy really had no choice but to do this?"

"To keep you safe, yes," he said. "Unless you want to sit here and fight them all off." And he added, "I can tell you that your idiot buddy there *is* mentally unstable and will go off half-cocked on you. At some point in time that's coming up. So keep Troy or me close, just for your own protection. At *all* times."

"If he's got a weapon," she said, "you or Troy could do nothing about it."

"We're hardly unarmed," he said with a half smile.

She looked at him in shock. "You brought weapons here?"

He shrugged and gave her a wink.

She took that to mean yes, and somehow that made her feel better. "Make sure you keep them well secured, because, if any of these guys find them, I don't know what they'll do at this point."

"We'd like to find out who had something to do with all those bodies," he said. "I'd like to keep everybody in tight and up close, so I don't have to worry about where people have disappeared to."

"If that's even possible," she said. "Unless we can call a meeting and get everybody to stay in one area. As far as I'm concerned, everybody should be off this rig now."

"That won't happen," he said. "Too much money has been invested in these rigs. They have to keep a skeleton crew to keep it floating, solid, and safe."

"There should be a repair crew," she said.

"We understood *this* was the repair crew," he said.

"No, Daniel said they weren't coming until after the storm."

"You know what? This company really needs to work on its communication." Axel looked where Troy was still talking with Denny. "This company seems to have some basic problems."

"Every big company is the same," she said, "and the bosses never want to tell the workers what the hell is going on."

"And yet it's the workers who need to be in the know," he said.

Just then Troy walked back over. He sat down with a hard *thump* and said, "Denny hasn't seen the pilot."

"Shit. Let me up," she said. "I'll go back to the company men and see if they've seen him."

"We'll come with you." The three of them got up and headed toward the door.

Denny called out. "Grub is in fifteen minutes. If you're late, you don't get any."

They looked at each other. She nodded and said, "He means it."

"We'll be back," Axel said, and the three walked out.

She knew the rest of the guys were sitting there, watching her. She didn't care. She knew where she was safe, whether she liked it or not, and this had nothing to do with defending herself. This had everything to do with having an inkling how to survive. It would just be ugly from top to bottom.

TROY HADN'T MEANT to go all ballistic on the guy, but something was so off in the man's gaze, and just thinking about those three other women and how helpless they'd been on a rig like this, well, that just made his blood boil. Sure, he'd worked rigs before, and there'd been women. But not with this same nonchalance or casual disregard for their wishes, their health, their sanity. One had a full-time partner, and maybe that guy had been enough of a strong-arm influence to keep everybody else in line. But the other two women he'd known at the other camps, and a couple others as well, they'd all been fine. Treated with respect. Nobody had gotten in their face about it. And certainly not like what he'd just seen this guy do with Berkley.

As the three headed off, he realized he was stalking more than walking. He tried to ease back down, letting some of the stress roll off his back. He rotated his neck and his shoulders so that, by the time they walked into command central, he wasn't quite ready to jump down anybody's throat. The three suits stood in the center of the bullpen area, talking around all the computer systems. They looked up and nodded to the three new arrivals.

"Problems?" Mason asked.

Berkley stepped forward. "Have you talked to your pilot lately?"

He pulled out his phone and said, "Last contact was about an hour and a half ago." He quickly sent a text. He looked up at her. "Why?"

"Nobody has seen him," Troy said.

At that, Gregor, gasped. "He's flown for me for years,"

he said. "I hope he's okay."

"I hope so too," Troy said. Then they filled in the suits on what happened to Chucky and their subsequent talk with Winslow.

Gregor sat back down again. "What the hell is going on?"

"Nothing good," Mason said. "Nelson and I have just done a full rundown on all the crew who works here. Everything from felons with conviction records, to a couple guys on the dodgy side that Interpol might be interested in, and the rest appear to be harmless." At the word *Interpol*, he heard her gasp. He turned to look at her. "Do you know those two?" He pulled up their names and photos.

She shook her head. "No idea, but heavy background checks were done on everybody who's here."

"Sure, but, if you've got a friend of a friend," Mason said, "there are ways to get people *in*, no matter who you are."

"There shouldn't be," Gregor said bitterly. "These rigs are billion-dollar investments. We can't afford to have things go wrong."

"Maybe not," Mason said, "but it looks like you're already past that point."

"And what else have you got to say?" Gregor addressed the trio.

"Lionel's body is missing, Daniel's brother," Axel said. "And no one has seen Daniel the foreman in the last few hours either."

Mason froze and looked at him. "What the hell?"

"Yeah, not exactly sure what that's all about."

"What about the power outage?"

"It's back on again," she said. "I've done a full system

analysis, but it's not coming up with anything."

"Meaning, nothing went wrong?"

"Exactly," she said. "So the only thing I can think is that it was done manually."

"So," Mason asked, "who needed to move something or to get somewhere and needed the cover of darkness for it?"

"Outside of us?" Troy asked with a grin. He caught Berkley looking at him carefully, but he didn't say anything. She had overheard Mason earlier telling Troy to get their two extra men on board. It should make her feel better, but he didn't have clearance to tell her fully about them. If she came across them unexpectedly, that was a different story.

"What do you think is going on?" Nelson asked Troy.

Troy said, "I've taken a look at the blueprints, and a hell of a lot of places exist where people could hide."

"And I think that's exactly what's happening," Axel said. "I think we've got a couple extra bogeys on board who are here deliberately."

"To take out the rest of the crew?" Mason asked. "Or to dispose of the dead who aren't supposed to be here?"

"Dispose of evidence for sure," Troy said, "and maybe clean up their tracks. I don't know if anybody has handed in notice recently or has been fired, but that's someone who we should take a hard look at."

"Two men were just fired," Gregor said. "And both Chucky and Winslow are done in ten days. They've told us they're not renewing their contracts."

"And that coincides with what they said to us too," she said.

"What Winslow said anyway," Troy corrected. "Chucky is pretty shook up. He's not talking much."

"And neither of them knew about the extra bodies in the

cooler," Axel said.

"So potentially those two are in the clear, but we can't be sure of that," Gregor noted.

"Exactly," Axel replied.

"Sounds like we can't be sure of anything," Troy continued, "so we need to start checking things off. I want to do a full sweep in the place, and I want anybody else we find—other than the eight crewmen we expect to be here and us six right here, seven, if we count the pilot—to be brought up to the bullpen here."

"I think you can probably make that happen faster than we can," she said to Mason.

"It's already in progress," Mason said with half a smile.

She frowned at him.

He shrugged and said, "Some things you're better off not knowing about." He looked over at Gregor. "And who were the two just fired?"

"James Baldwin and a buddy of his." He stopped for a moment, frowned, and then said, "Oh, right, Stephanopoulos Canker. They are good friends, but they're feisty, and they get into trouble all the time. They had three warnings each, and we decided that, this time, we were done."

"Could they be behind this damage to the rig or the recent rapes?" Mason asked.

"I don't know," he said. "It's possible, I suppose. The managers who died would have been in conflict with them and could have been blamed for them getting fired. But I don't know if James and his buddy were violent or just troublemakers."

"Got it. And it really is a far stretch for somebody who likes to have a good brawl," Troy said, "to creating this sabotage that would hurt these men."

"Exactly," Gregor said.

"Anybody else on the troublemaker list?" Mason asked.

Gregor shook his head. "Not according to any notes I have. We have multiple rigs that we oversee," he said.

"Winslow ID'd one of the men in the cooler as the medic," Troy added, "which then stopped the others from getting any decent medical aid."

"We always have two medics on-site," Gregor said, "and sometimes we're lucky enough to get doctors. But, of course, all we're trying to do is stabilize the injured or sick and get them shipped out right away."

"Of course," Mason replied.

"But damn, if that's Dr. Ramos in the cooler, that's not good, since he had a lot of military field-surgery experience. We were quite happy to have him come on board."

"I'm sure you were."

"*Dr.* Ramos? *Military?*" Berkley said, as all the men turned to look at her.

Troy watched as she worked away at the question formulating in her mind.

"What if some of this has nothing to do with the rig itself?" Berkley asked. "What if this is old history, like, you know, with the medic? An old enemy from the military days or something."

"It's possible," Troy said with a nod. "But why now?" He turned to look at Gregor. "Do we have any idea whether there was a problem with him? Was there any objection when he came on board? Did anybody have a hard-on—you know, an argument with him? Any complaints about lack of care or his abilities?"

"No," Gregor said. "Nothing on record."

"Where the hell is Daniel anyway?" Mason said. "These

are questions we should be asking him."

"But still, he's a foreman, not a manager," Gregor stated.

"I thought three of the dead were the missing managers," she cried out.

"Yes," Gregor said. "The three missing were found dead. And one of the other dead men is the fourth manager as well."

"So, does Daniel even know about all these dead people? Seems he should because one of them is the medic."

"He was also a manager, our fourth manager," Gregor said. "Sorry, his position was a dual one because of his extensive medical background, but also because he was very good at what he did in managing one of the teams."

"So, by taking him out," Troy noted, "it doubled up the confusion among the crew. Management and medical assistance."

"Possibly, yes," Gregor said. "But I still don't see a motive, if this is a man-made issue."

Still thinking hard on an issue she had yet to bring up, Berkley walked over and pulled up one of the chairs and sat down.

Troy could see the fatigue at the corner of her eyes and the slump of her shoulders. He wanted to give her a hug, but, at the same time, he knew he'd already been a little too overprotective as it was. And, even if there was a zing between them, as Idiot had pointed out, it wasn't necessarily something they would follow up on. As soon as things were wrapped up here, he would be off on another mission assignment, and she would be bouncing around between here and her other contract jobs.

"Uh-oh," she said suddenly. "Denny said, if we want any food, we better not be late. And he means it. Trust me."

"Well, it would be interesting to see him try and *not* feed me," Gregor said, as he strode toward the door. "Denny is a bit of a different case himself," Gregor added.

"In what way?" Mason asked.

"He's a convicted felon," Gregor said. "Two counts of murder."

Everybody froze. He looked back at them, smiled. "Right? Who would have thought? But everybody gets their second chance to be integrated back into society. And often they become camp cooks. In this case he learned to cook in prison."

"And you trust him?" Mason asked Gregor.

"He has worked for us for over twenty-five years," Gregor said. "So, yeah, I do."

"You didn't mention him when we were talking about your staff," Mason said, anger threading through his voice.

Gregor looked back at him and shrugged. "We don't see him as a problem. He's been good to us, and we've been good to him. End of story."

"But what if somebody recognized him from prison or something?" she asked quietly. "Or what if somebody from the families of the people he murdered recognized him?"

Gregor turned and looked at her in surprise. "He's worked for us twenty-five years now, and he did fifteen years hard time before that. So his crime occurred well over forty years ago. Who cares now?"

Troy shook his head. "Everybody cares," he said. "In some cases these people never forget. What if a son or nephew here grew up without a family member because of Denny? And now he's in the same place and that anger just took over?"

"Wait. ... What?" Gregor raised his hands in frustration.

"Blow apart the rig, shut down one of the drills, and blast two of the other drills so they're inoperable? What's that got to do with Denny?"

"It's hard to say," Axel said, stepping up as they walked toward the door. "But just think. Who else is left behind? We've got eight dead, the eight-man skeleton crew working here already, not counting Berkley, excluding those of us who just arrived, plus our pilot, so one of those original eight crew members is Denny."

Gregor stared at him. "You think all this was just to isolate Denny so he could be taken out?" He shook his head. "That's garbage," he said. "Come on. Let's go eat. The one thing I do know is that Denny is one hell of a cook. I'd travel this distance just to have one of his meals." He slammed his way through the doors out to the hallway.

The five of them stopped and looked at each other. Troy shook his head. "I'm really not liking too much about any of this mission at all. What the hell are we even doing here?"

Mason slid a glance toward Berkley.

Troy sighed. "Of course I get that," he said, "but it still has to be official."

"It is official," Mason said. "The C-4 that was used? Remember we have that packaging?"

Troy nodded. "Yeah, sure. What about it?"

"Military supply," he said. "It came from one of our bases."

CHAPTER 8

BACK IN THE dining area, Berkley was surprised, and yet not, when Troy reached out and grabbed her hand, then bent down and whispered, "Stay with me."

She nodded. It amazed her in a way that he *wasn't* acting this way. She was grateful, not to mention the fact that she really liked him, though she didn't really know him. She knew his kind though. Just like Axel and Mason, they were all about doing the right thing. A stark contrast to the guys she worked with here, who appeared to be only after their own needs. It was a little disturbing to look around and to see just how many of them may not see her as she'd hoped and believed they did. Just the thought of the three gang rapes on board was disturbing enough.

More than disturbing, her friend Tabitha deserved a whole lot better than what she'd gotten from everybody here. It wasn't fair that, when she needed support and help, she hadn't been able to get either. The entire mess had been brushed under the carpet. Berkley didn't even know now if she could do something about it for her friend. Berkley wanted to think so, but so much had happened, and most of the men were gone.

It was hard to look at the men still here and wonder if they had participated in those crimes. Unfortunately Tabitha hadn't said anything about who her attackers were as she'd been blindfolded. Thankfully Berkley had been here to help collect evidence and to get her friend out of here. Berkley had never really thought about it or had the same insecurity or fear after what happened to Tabitha, somehow thinking it was specific to her, since she was a full-time crew member. But then Berkley hadn't heard about the other two women until more recently. And now Berkley didn't know what to think on the whole inhumanity of it, unless it was to point fingers at the unholy men who did this and throw them in shackles and dip them into shark-infested waters.

Denny looked up as they stepped into the dining area and frowned immediately. "About time," he scolded them, ushering them to one of the big tables. "You sit at this one."

She raised her eyebrows at that but didn't say anything. Ahead of them Denny had seated the three company men at a smaller table off to one side. They had a tablecloth and silverware. Her table was just a regular cafeteria table, where Jonesy and Idiot were at one end. She took her place quietly at the other end of the table, with Troy on one side and Axel on the other. The other men looked from her to her two guardians but didn't say anything. She wondered what they were thinking but didn't dare ask. She looked over at Denny, wondering if they were supposed to get up, but he brought platters of food to their table. Roast beef, mashed potatoes, Brussels sprouts, and maybe meat loaf. She quickly served herself a normal portion and handed it to Troy.

Axel looked at her and asked, "How come you didn't give it to me first, huh?"

She grinned at him. "I figured Troy here, being a *little guy*, might need some, and, if I gave it to you first, there wouldn't be any left afterward."

He chuckled.

"You guys know each other?" Idiot asked, interrupting their conversation.

She nodded. "I've met them both before several times," she said smoothly. Of course she knew Axel well, better than Troy, but that seemed to settle something in the other men. As if understanding that prior relationship explained why she was sitting with them.

"I guess this isn't the only rig you go to, is it?" Idiot asked.

She shook her head. "Nope. I travel a lot. I work for the company, just like you guys, but I can end up on any number of their rigs, depending on what the issues are." She cut into the meat loaf and took a bite. Her eyebrows shot up. She stopped and looked at it, then took a second bite.

"Is it good?" Axel asked.

She nodded slowly. "Very unique flavor but very tasty."

Before she realized it, she'd finished the meal on her plate. She pushed the plate slightly away and put her knife and fork on it, then settled back. "That was really good."

"Don't you eat here all the time?"

She nodded. "Sure, but this was especially good. Company men, you know?"

"What?" Axel looked at her, confused.

"When the company men are here," Jonesy felt the need to explain, "everybody gets the benefit."

"Ah," Axel said with a nod. "That Denny is a sly one. He was all wound up earlier about not knowing they were coming."

Everybody nodded.

"Well, it was definitely good," she said.

"Good." Jonesy reached out and grabbed another slab of roast beef off the platter.

She contemplated the food for a moment and then shook her head. "I want more," she said, "but I don't dare. I'll just be miserable."

She watched as the other men all appeared to be on their best behavior. Maybe it was because the company men were sitting in as well. A lively conversation was going on at that head table, but it was too far away for her to hear the details. She glanced from Troy's to Axel's plates and realized they would still be here for at least twenty minutes.

Troy looked at her, leaned over, and whispered, "You okay?"

She smiled up at him. "I'm fine. I want more to eat, but I'm too full." She said, "I'd like to go back to work."

"Is there any work you can do?"

She shrugged. "There's always work one can do," she said. She stared out one of the large windows to watch the storm rage outside. "I wish we'd found the pilot."

He nodded. "So far there's been no news."

"What news can there be?" Jonesy asked. "The pilot probably got too close to the edge and fell."

"Is that a normal problem?" Troy asked. "You have warning signs up and around, and he's been here many times."

Jonesy shrugged. "It happens. In bad weather like this, it's fatal. Most of the time somebody's out there with him, and it's okay. We can grab him back in again, but, once they hit the water, you know what it's like. Hypothermia sets in within minutes."

Everybody dug back into their food, not wanting to take the conversation any further.

When Troy's phone buzzed, she heard it, but she didn't think anybody else did. Although she glanced at Axel, a stillness had come over him. Troy fished his phone from his pocket and glanced at the message that came in. He shoved the last bite of food in his mouth, then asked, "Is there any place to make a phone call around here?"

"With that storm, not likely," one of the men said. "You can try the office though."

Troy nodded, shoved his phone back in his pocket, and shot Axel a hard glance. With a gentle nod toward her, he turned and left.

She looked at Axel and raised an eyebrow. He shrugged and reached for another slab of meat loaf. She watched him inhale it and said, "I'll go back to my office and get some work done."

He nodded and stood up with her.

"Finish your meat loaf," she scolded. He looked down and grinned, then cut it and wolfed it down faster than she could have imagined. She walked over to the coffeepot that miraculously seemed to be full right now and poured herself a cup.

Denny came running to her side. "There's dessert," he said. "Don't you want dessert?"

"What are we having?" she asked.

He pulled out trays of puff pastry with some fruit in them.

She looked at it and smiled. "That looks delicious." Reaching toward a tray, she grabbed two bowls of dessert, one for Troy and one for herself. She looked over at Axel, who nodded, so she grabbed a third one as well.

Finally, with three cups of coffee and three desserts now heaping high with whipping cream, she balanced it all on a clean tray and headed back toward the office. She could hear the other men at the tables moving about, getting desserts for themselves.

Back inside the computer bullpen, she put a dessert and coffee down on the main table, and then headed with hers and Troy's over to her computer. She sat down and immediately froze. She looked around, logged on to the computer, then called over to Axel. "Come here, hurry."

He walked toward her. "What's the matter?"

"Somebody logged onto my computer," she said.

"When?"

"In the last hour while we were eating."

"Everybody was in the dining room though, right?"

"Everybody we know of," she said. "Except for the pilot and God-only-knows whoever else may be here."

"I get that," he said, "but we don't know who could have done this, right?"

"No," she said. "I'm trying to check right now."

"Did they hack in? Or did someone use your log in?"

"Good question," she said. "I've been dealing with this one hacker going through the system as it is. But, so far, it's like he's just a troublemaker and not really having any plan that I can make sense of."

"So somebody just starting out maybe, not really understanding what he can do?"

"Maybe. I figured it was an employee getting access, wondering what the company was up to. Or upper management, tracking what we were doing here."

"Sometimes hackers start that way."

"Or it's all a diversion," she said. "It was my log-in access from my computer, somewhere about the time that I was finished with my plate and that you guys were still eating."

He looked at his watch. "So about twenty minutes ago?"

She nodded slowly. "I'll change all my passwords right

now," she said. "Yet, because he went in with my log in, he wouldn't have had a lot of access."

"Do you use the same log in for every area of the system?"

"I don't," she said. "Depending on where I'm going, I have different log ins."

"So that would have curtailed where he could have gone then, correct?"

She nodded. Quickly tapping keys and studying her monitors, she said, "Three attempts were made to get into the electronics controlling the pump system. And the drills."

"And then what?

"Log in failed, and he was locked out," she said with a note of satisfaction. "Which is exactly why I have it set up that way."

"But he knew exactly how to get to that area within the computer software?"

"Yes," she said.

"If your computer test runs say that everything with the drill is fine and dandy, would they go ahead and use it again?"

She frowned. "I would think there would still need to be a manual inspection done. But, if they couldn't find anything, or they're not too bothered and think that the damage is minimal, I'd imagine they would do a trial run, yes. Why?"

"I just wonder if they'll make it look better than it is so that, when they start back up again, another accident happens. Or altering the damage described and, therefore, this is just shutting down the rig and costing the company billions of dollars for nothing."

"There are all kinds of fail-safes," she said. "It's not just a singular system, where one person can do an override, and everything moves forward or shuts down," she said.

"A repair team should have been here," Axel said.

"I understood the team *was* here," she said, "but instead this skeleton crew is here, and they aren't a maintenance crew who could do detailed assessments and make repairs."

"No? So then they've still got to bring in more men, correct?"

"I think so but not while the storm is raging. All I'm seeing so far," she said in frustration, "is that nobody knows anything for sure, and you can hear one thing from one person and something completely different from another."

"Unfortunately, when chaos like this happens, that's quite common."

"For two days," she said, "all we had were alarms going off, people being packed up in the middle of the night, and booted out of here. It was complete chaos. Lots of guys left gear behind, and some were pretty panicked and wanted to leave in the lifeboats."

"But it wasn't that bad, was it?"

"No, but once the rumor started—"

"Got it," he said.

Just then the door opened and in walked Troy. "Good. Glad to see you guys are here."

"What was your phone call about?" she asked.

"It wasn't a phone call," he said. "It was a text from our crew. They found the pilot."

His tone of voice had her gasping. "Dead?"

He shook his head. "He's alive but with a head injury."

"We need to make sure he's okay."

"Our crew has him," he said. "He's awake, but he doesn't want to join us. He's pretty damn sure somebody came up behind him and hit him over the head."

She stared at him in shock. "But why would somebody do that?"

Troy and Axel looked at each other with wry smiles. "So that nobody else could get off. Without a pilot, nobody'll be flying out of here."

"That makes no sense," she said. "We're in the middle of a heavy storm, so nobody's getting off this rig anyway."

"Good point," Troy said cheerfully, "but this way nobody's getting off at all."

TROY HAD SPOKEN to the pilot, who was pretty fervent about being hit over the head. He'd been inside his helicopter, checking to make sure everything was lashed down, given the storm coming. He was heading back into the main part of the rig under cover, when he thought he heard something. He turned, saw a shadow, and then got smacked on the side of the head and knocked out. He didn't want to join anybody else. He was more than happy to stay with Mason's secret crew and was happy they were here.

In his own words, he said, "Something really weird is going on in this place."

As Troy stood in the bullpen, listening to Berkley explain about somebody using her log in to get into the system, he shook his head. "This is all just Mickey Mouse stuff, as if somebody is a complete amateur and doesn't know what he's after."

"And that's a good thing," she said in a joking manner. She got up and walked around, picking up a cup of coffee and a bowl and handed it to him. He looked at her in surprise.

"You left without dessert," she said, "so I brought some

for you."

He smiled and said, "Great service."

"Well, if you look after me," she said lightly, "I'll look after you."

At that, he burst out laughing.

"That was a good move, letting everybody know that you knew us beforehand," Axel said. "That'll help take the pressure off, and it seems like it already has."

"Ever since I found out about *three* women being assaulted," she said, "I look at these guys and wonder if they were one of them. We don't know who the rapists were or even how many of them were involved."

"Did Winslow and Chucky show up for dinner? I didn't notice them."

She nodded. "Yes, but they sat at the end of a table by themselves and were pretty quiet."

"Makes sense. They'd like to get off this rig damn fast too."

"I think everybody would," she said quietly. "Me included."

"Have you had any contact with your company?"

"Everything I do, everything I investigate, is recorded. Once I've added my notations, it's automatically transmitted to my company," she said. Both men stopped and looked at her. "Yes, that's how I knew that somebody had gotten into my computer while we were eating."

"Because that information was transmitted back to you?"

"Because I get a record of everything that happens on my computer," she said. "Every keystroke. It's the only way I can keep track if somebody else is going through my programs."

"Interesting," Axel said. "I don't pretend to understand, but, as long as you do, that's all good for me."

She smiled up at him. "What's the matter? You don't have the brains like Tesla does?"

"I'm not sure anybody has brains like hers," he said, shaking his head. "She's scary smart."

At that, Berkley burst out laughing.

Troy grinned at her. "Obviously you are too," he said. "Particularly if you're friends with Tesla."

"Tesla's in a land all her own," she said. "Any more on where that C-4 came from?"

"Not yet," Troy said with a frown. "Military surplus can be bought all over the place, but C-4 usually isn't on the list of things you can buy just anywhere."

"Do you ever have anybody here from the military bases?" Axel asked her.

She shrugged. "I guess if they left the military, and this was their second career. For all we know, somebody here is purchasing from the base that you're on."

"We've had that happen a time or two," he said. "We also have war games in this area a fair bit. So we can't be sure that something didn't come from there."

"Is there a way to track that specific C-4 back to a navy base?"

"They're on it. But nothing so far," Axel said.

"There were war games not far from here and not very long ago," she said. "I think they lasted about three weeks."

"Really?"

She nodded. "I wasn't here yet, but I think some of the military men came over to the rig on one of their days off to see how the rig operated."

Both men froze and turned to look at her. "Wait. What?" Troy asked.

"No way," Axel said.

She shrugged. "Well, I wasn't here at the time, so I don't know for certain. But you could probably talk to Gregor and see what he has to say."

"Or Denny," Troy said thoughtfully. "He's the one who seems to keep track of numbers."

"He does, pretty carefully actually. He has to justify all the food he goes through on the rig, so he keeps track of how many he's feeding all the time."

"Time for a little talk with Denny," Troy said. He looked over at Axel and asked, "You okay to stay with her?"

"Well, I can, but I'm not sure Denny will talk to you," Axel said. "Either you may need the company men for muscle or you might need her to sweet-talk him."

"You don't need either," she said. "He has to enter everything into the computer." She sat back down again and quickly opened her programs. "Just give me a second," she said.

She went in under a visitor log in, one that she kept for jobs like this, so nobody would know where she was, then headed into the food services department. There she brought up the meal planners and numbers Denny had entered for the month. "Here's how many people he fed on a regular basis."

"When were the games here?" Troy asked.

She brought up his calendar and said, "Looks like a visiting crew came over on the twelfth of last month," she said. "Ten men were here."

"Do we have any images?"

"We certainly should," she said, as she switched to a different monitor and brought up the security system. "Normally they get rid of the security images after thirty days," she said, "but this is just inside that window. It's all uploaded and archived." She quickly brought it up, and, as soon as she caught sight of the day she wanted, she turned the monitor for them to see. "This is when they arrived."

Both men stood to the side and studied the faces as they came through.

"So these aren't SEALs, but definitely US Navy," Axel said quietly. "Two of them were carrying bags, and several men came without gear at all. They all look like they were interested in having a great day trip."

"I don't recognize anybody. Do you?" Troy asked, turning to look at Axel.

Axel shook his head. "No, can't say that I do. Interesting though. We've all done things like that. I've gone to war games, and, whenever it's over, there's a break, and we're doing more training or sightseeing. In this case it was a great opportunity for them to come here, but how would anyone know ahead of time? Unless circumstances just played into their hands. Whoever used the C-4 might have used it because it was there, but that doesn't mean they didn't have an original plan in case the meetup didn't happen."

"It's hard to say," Troy said. "Maybe it was preplanned, but then it would have to be, right? The whole trip itself would have been preplanned."

"Would they have taken the C-4 off the destroyer?" she asked.

"It's possible, yes," he said, scratching his head. "The destroyers are fully loaded for weapons of all kinds because you never know when you'll need something."

She nodded quietly. "So, what are the chances that this was an off-the-cuff deal?"

"I don't know. That leaves a little bit left to be unknown."

Just then as they watched the screen, another helicopter flew in.

"And there's our company man," he said, "the same one who's here today. Gregor."

"Interesting," she said. "He's got a bag too."

"Right, but that's not unusual, is it? He could be here for a day or two occasionally, right?" Axel looked deep in thought.

She nodded. "Yes, I think so. A room's kept ready all the time for anyone from the company."

They kept flicking through the days. The navy crew was only here for the day, and everybody appeared to be having a good time, as far as Troy could see. They tracked them through the place, and they were always with the tour. It appeared they were given a full tour of the rig and then a meal. After looking around a bit more outside, they then got on the Zodiacs, heading back toward the destroyers. "So, that was a pretty interesting day, and both men have their bags still."

"But one's lighter," Axel said, tapping the monitor.

"What?" Troy asked, as he looked to see the second one. "Good eye, Axel. Now we're getting somewhere."

"Berkley, can you give us a freeze-frame on that guy's face?"

She immediately took a screenshot of just the face and sent it to him by email. He sent it to Mason and then sent it to their two-man team secreted downstairs, with a short explanation. When his phone rang, he stepped off to the side. It was Dane from downstairs.

"I know him," he said. "He's been in trouble a lot."

"His bag is noticeably lighter on the way out," Troy said, "as if they came with something, and then he left something behind.”

“You’re thinking the C-4? Well, he’s certainly in a position to do it. He’s a weapons specialist.”

“Let’s cross-reference this guy with everybody who works here.”

“You won’t have to,” Dane announced. “His brother works here. Been here for years.”

“And who is his brother?”

“Jude,” he said. “Jude Lensly.”

Putting down his phone, he turned to look at Berkley, and asked, “Do you know a Jude Lensly?”

“I know of him,” she said. “Why?”

“He’s the brother of the guy with the lighter bag.”

“Well, that makes sense,” she said. “It could be anything then.”

“True enough,” he said, admitting that.

“It’s not indicative that he brought C-4 with him,” Berkley noted.

“No, but he does have a rep in the navy,” Troy told her. “He’s a troublemaker. And a weapons specialist, by the way.”

“Sounds like we need to get an update on him right now,” Axel said, stepping away, his own phone out now.

“Yes,” she said slowly. “But Jude’s not here,” she said. “I don’t know that he was even here when I arrived this trip.”

Troy pointed to the monitors. “Can you check to see when he arrived and when he left?”

She nodded. “Of course. Give me five minutes.”

CHAPTER 9

B ERKLEY CLICKED AWAY through her computer, heading for the administration side in the schedules. As soon as she brought up the last month, she typed in his name. "Well, look at that," she said. "He was here when I arrived, and apparently he was here right through the explosion."

"But he's off now, correct?"

"None of this has been filled out since," she said. "It was such a panic that everybody took off as soon as they could. I don't think anybody's done the checkouts."

"Don't you have tag scanners or something so that, as they leave, they're all counted?"

"In a perfect world, yes," she said simply. "In this case, not so much. We do have a bunch who have been tagged as out but not everyone."

"So then, how is it that Daniel knew four were missing?"

"You'll have to ask Daniel that," she said, shaking her head. "I don't really know. And, of course, his information was wrong anyway, so it's not likely we can count on that."

"Maybe that's something we should go back and ask him."

Only they didn't have to, as they looked up just moments later to see Chucky and Winslow walking in. The two of them had their heads together and their voices low. When they saw the three of them in here, they froze. She smiled at them and asked, "You guys okay?"

"Nothing about this is okay," Chucky said, shoving his hands in his pockets.

"How did you determine the four were missing?" Troy asked them bluntly.

"I had a clipboard," Chucky said. "Once I did the calculations and a roll call check, four were missing." He looked over at Winslow. "But what I didn't know was that three of the managers were already in the cooler downstairs."

"Right," she said in surprise. "That makes sense."

"Never thought to check." And his tone was morose.

"So then how many are missing?"

"No one apparently. They are now all accounted for," he said.

At that, nobody said anything.

Chucky walked farther into the room and sat down at his desk on the far side. "I don't even know what I'm doing here," he said. "The power's flickering all over the place."

"I heard there's talk of several engineering teams coming in to do the repairs," Axel said.

"Can't happen soon enough for me," Winslow said. "Like I said, we've got just ten days to go."

"Well, it's almost bedtime anyway," Berkley said. "I'm tired. All this stress has been pretty rough."

"I hear you there," Chucky said. "I'm just a little worried that I won't get to live out my ten days to even get off here."

"In what way?" Troy asked curiously.

Chucky shrugged. "All kinds of shit is going on." He reached up and tapped his head. "Somebody put me in that freezer," he said, "and I don't know who." He glared at the three of them. "For all I know it was you three."

"Well, for that matter, you don't know that it wasn't

Winslow either," Berkley said in exasperation. "We have no reason for locking you in, and, if we had locked you in, why would we have let you back out again?"

"Unless you wanted to scare me," he said, "or maybe you were hoping I was frozen already by then."

Axel shook his head. "I get why you are probably looking at everybody with an accusing eye," he said, "but don't waste your energy on us. We just got here. We had no reason to do anything to you."

"And the fact that you're even here is bullshit," Winslow blurted out. "I don't get it."

"Just the company, man," Axel said.

"I don't understand why all three of them are here either," he said. "The one is always here. Gregor. He's a pain in the ass too."

"But you've got to admit, the food is better when he's around," she said with a smile. The two men grumbled off in their corner, and finally they stood and said, "We're heading to our bunks."

She nodded. "Good night."

They didn't answer, just went out, and slammed the door hard behind them.

She looked over at the other two. "A part of me wants to go too." She picked up some papers off the printer. "Here's the schedule, and you can see Jude was here at the time of the accident." She picked up a clipboard sitting off to the side. "This could very well be the list as everybody got off," she said, flipping through the pages. Using a pencil, she went down line by line. "Here it says Jude left on the second round."

"How did they all get off?"

"A couple ships nearby came in to help, and some helicopters came and got a bunch. Several went out on some of the lifeboats that were here anyway. Hopefully they were following the ships or being towed by them," she said. "Looks like Jude left the afternoon of the first day."

"And do we know that it was actually Jude? How do we know that somebody didn't just put down all these names?"

"Good point. We don't," she said. "Lionel isn't on here. That's for sure."

"I'd take that list with a grain of salt," Axel said. "All kinds of shit can go wrong at times like that. It's a list, but that doesn't mean it's accurate."

"No," she said, "but it's all we've got."

Axel nodded. "But, if the data isn't complete or if it's corrupt, it's useless. It's worse than useless because it gives you a false sense of security, and then you're stuck believing that list, when it may or may not be valid. Especially on a screwed-up deal like this."

She smiled. "So, what do you want to do then?"

"No idea," he said. He looked over to Troy. "Maybe time for a rendezvous?"

They both looked back at her, and Axel said, "Why don't we walk you to your bunk and lock you in. Then we'll go check in with the rest of the guys."

She hopped to her feet. "Works for me," she said, as she picked up her coffee cup. "We should return these dishes to the kitchen."

They made a detour and dropped off all the dishes for Denny, but the kitchen was dark, and nobody was there. "Is it out of power?" Troy asked.

"Denny always shuts it down," she said. "As soon as the dishes are done and the kitchen is clean, you can't find him again 'til morning."

"That's interesting," Troy said. "Doesn't he socialize with you guys in the evenings at all?"

"If he does, I've never seen him," she said, "but I will admit that I'm not much for socializing at night either. However, I've heard of private poker games and all kinds of shit going on here that I've never been privy to."

"Because you're female?"

"That, and because I'm not regular staff," she said. "I'm an outsider, and they like to keep it that way."

"Any inclination to change that?"

She snorted. "Hell no. I'm happy the way it is. Although the rapists should all be in jail, and I would like to see this inequality and prejudicial shit change."

"Well, it's in for a change as soon as we can get the repair crews in."

"True enough," she said, as she put her dishes in the sink. They turned and walked back out again, her gaze flickering over the tables. "Seems so weird to see it empty like this. At the height of its day, it's a massive group of people, and good luck finding a place to sit. Now it's like a graveyard in here."

"I think that's a common sentiment," Axel said, "with any large group that comes and goes. It's like, all in and all out."

She laughed, then smiled and said, "True enough. I'm more than ready for a hot shower, if there is such a thing to be had. I don't know if the boilers have been working or not."

"Well, you've got massive generators and backup generators," Troy said, "so you might be lucky."

She headed down, showing the guys where she stayed. "I have one of the female rooms," she said with a sneer. "It's a temporary room as well."

"They shouldn't have labeled it as a female room," Troy said. "I get that nobody'll stop anybody from tracking down one of the women if they want to accost them anyway, but this is just like a road map that says, *This is where you guys are.*"

"I never really thought about it," she said. "I'm here so rarely that it never really mattered."

"And now?"

"Now it feels like a target. Like this giant flashing neon sign that says, *Hey, she's in here.*"

"Change your room," Troy said helpfully. "Some 180 are empty now, right?"

She shrugged. "It won't change anything now though," she said. "Besides, the bathroom is right beside me, which is convenient."

He nodded and said, "We'll go do a rendezvous. Are you okay here alone?"

She nodded, pulled out her phone, and said, "But I wouldn't mind getting your numbers." They quickly exchanged contact information. "I'll have a quick shower, and then I'll go to bed."

"Text me when you're out of the shower," Troy said, "and when you're back in your room with the door locked."

At that, she hesitated and looked at him. "Do you really think I'm in danger?"

"IT'S NOT THAT I think you can't take care of yourself under normal circumstances," Troy said cautiously, "but obviously things are not normal here. I would rather that we hung around and waited until you've had your shower and get you locked in before we take off." He watched the indecision on her face.

She nodded and said, "Well, instead of having a shower, can you guys wait here five minutes, while I use the washroom, get ready for bed, and then you can lock me in. How's that?"

Troy gave her a pleased smile. "That sounds much better to me."

She went into her room, grabbed her toiletries, then headed to the bathroom, while they waited outside in the hallway.

Axel looked at him. "She's a nice woman."

"She is," Troy said. "She's a unique mix of anger, frustration, and smarts."

"We've often seen the smarts but not with too much common sense. I like that she's practical."

"Sounds to me like she had a rude awakening when her friend was attacked," Troy said. "All women should be safe in the workplace. So to think that it happened to somebody she was close to and only later find out that it wasn't the first time must have been quite a shock. The fact that this rig has been operating with that kind of underground atmosphere and God-only-knows-what-else is bad news."

"Have we figured out if that company man, Gregor, knows about it?"

"He knows," Troy said. "He showed absolutely no surprise when it came up."

"Then again he's management, so he's probably making light of it all," Axel said.

They waited another few minutes until the bathroom door opened, and Berkley walked out, her face pink from being scrubbed, the hair around her face damp. She walked past them, opened the door to her small bedroom, then turned to face them. "I'll be fine from here," she said. "Thank you."

Troy nodded. "Listen. Don't open the door unless it's one of us."

"Got it," she said. And gently closed the door. They waited until they heard the *click*.

Once she was locked in, Troy turned to Axel and said, "Let's go."

CHAPTER 10

BERKLEY LAY IN bed but couldn't sleep. Of course she couldn't sleep. So much was going on in her world. She waited a good half hour, battling with herself on whether she should contact Troy. Finally unable to sleep within the next half hour, she gave up and sent him a text, asking if he'd found anything.

Nope came back the answer. **You're supposed to be sleeping.**

She smiled at that and tucked the phone up beside her pillow. She had just pulled the blanket up over her head when a light knock came on her door. She froze but didn't answer. When the knock came again, she wished a small peephole was in the door that she could look out.

The third time it was almost a pounding on the door; then she heard a male voice. "Open the door, you bitch."

She froze and pulled out her phone and put it on video. But all she heard were footsteps walking away.

She quickly texted Troy.

Someone was just at the door. Knocked lightly, then not so lightly, and then pounded on the door and called me a bitch.

The response was immediate. **Who was it?**

I don't know, she responded. Now sleep was the furthest thing from her mind.

She had her laptop with her, but, outside of logging in

to work—if and when she could get on the system, given the storm—she couldn't do a whole lot but monitor systems and track the hacker. But needing to do something, she sat cross-legged on her bed, with the blanket wrapped around her shoulders.

She started typing out the little bits and pieces that she knew. She wasn't very good at handling all these multiple threads in her head, and none of them were making sense. She knew the guys would tell her that they would make sense at some point in time, but she'd always been a note-taker and a list-maker. She always needed to put everything down in order to make clarity happen for her. She loved puzzles for that reason, but, at the same time, this wasn't her type of puzzle. And with the guys heading down to look and to meet up with the rest of their team, she just wished she understood what was going on.

Three rapes? Were they connected? How could they not be? But were they connected to the sabotage of the rig?

Lionel's body missing. Seven bodies in the cooler. Sabotage or accident? Were the skeleton-crew guys left here on their own?

Chucky and Winslow—was the freezer an accident or deliberate? The latch was wonky, so it could easily have been an accident but ...

Next she started to plot out who was around when Chucky had gotten locked up. The trouble was, everybody was accounted for. The same as whoever had been hacking into her computer. Everybody had been at dinner. Except for the pilot. The only conclusion that she could come to was the fact that somebody else had to be on board that they didn't know about. And that was one hell of a scary thought.

She sat here, writing down names and wondering if the

connection with the C-4 was really a connection or if it was just another nebulous thread. Would any of these threads weave into a pattern?

It occurred to her to question whether Lionel was dead. What if he'd been in the body bag, and he'd been unconscious but not dead? Had anybody checked?

She pulled out her phone and quickly sent Troy a text asking him.

Not sure anybody specifically checked if Lionel was dead. We knew he wasn't cold like the others, but we didn't check his pulse. Why?

She added, **Wondering if he could still be alive.**

Interesting thought. He left it at that.

But she continued her notes on her random thoughts. Troy and Axel had been the ones who had picked up Lionel and had put him into the freezer because they wanted to take his body back in the helicopter. Would he have woken up in there? Or had Chucky seen him, realized he wasn't dead, woke him up, and maybe an altercation ensued, and somehow Lionel had locked Chucky in? But why wouldn't Chucky have said anything? No, that wasn't making any sense either. She sat here, trying to work her way through all this, when another text came in from Troy.

I'm headed your way.

Fine, but you better identify yourself, or I'm not opening that damn door.

She got a happy face emoji in return. She smiled and grabbed a sweatshirt and put it on atop her pajama top. At least now she was wearing bottoms and a sweatshirt.

When a rap came on her door, and she could hear Troy's voice calling out, she opened it up and let him in. She stepped out in the hallway, looked in both directions.

"Where's Axel?"

She came in and shut the door behind her to find Troy standing in the middle of the room, trying to keep a smile off his face at her outfit. She shrugged. "I didn't exactly feel like sleeping, and I was too cold to sit up and do nothing."

He nodded. "Axel's downstairs meeting with Mason."

"Right. Has anybody found anything?"

"No, not yet," he said. "So far, even after a top-to-bottom search, we haven't found any extra personnel on board."

"And that's just stupid," she said. "It has to be somebody else."

"And why is that?"

"Because there's no other way. Everybody was having dinner at the same time, but somebody was hacking into my system."

He nodded. "That's one of the questions I wanted to ask you," he said. "Could somebody do it remotely?"

She froze and looked up at him. "Oh, my God," she said, collapsing on her bunk. "I didn't consider that."

He sat on the opposite bunk, his hands held loosely together in front of him as he studied her. "A lot of guys had phones at the table."

She nodded slowly. "It's a real problem sometimes," she said. "Hell, I think phones have destroyed the family dinner system."

He cracked a smile at that. "So, is it possible?"

She frowned, thinking about it, and then slowly nodded. "I could do it."

"Right," he said, "but what good would that have done?"

"I don't know," she said. "They didn't get into where they were trying to go."

"But that's because you had extra safeguards in there, correct?"

She nodded slowly. "Yes."

"How would anybody know your log in?"

"I don't know," she said, with a shrug. "It's possible somebody was somehow recording my keystrokes."

"If that was the case, wouldn't they have recorded any keystrokes as you worked to get through the rest of the blockages you had?"

"In theory, no," she said, "because I type it manually, so, unless somebody wants to go through a ton of data to find those particular keystrokes and to see that they were different from the code I was working on, it's not like they would have noticed."

"Right," he said. "Because, if nobody else is on board, we have to consider the fact that everybody was there in the mess hall at the time of the hack in question."

"And, of course, you'll vouch for *all* your guys, correct?"

He gave her a gentle smile. "Absolutely."

"Anyone seen any sign of Daniel yet?" She sighed. "And the pilot? Which side is he on?"

"Well, there's a big question mark over the pilot. That's for sure," he said, "but he's also been injured."

"But so was Chucky," she said. "At least in theory."

"You don't believe him?"

"I don't know what to believe," she said.

"I can tell you that he was locked in, but, beyond that, I'm not sure," he said.

"Could he have gotten free from the inside of the freezer?"

He frowned and shrugged. "I'd have to go check."

"Then let me get dressed," she said. "That way we can at

least knock something off our list."

He grinned at that. "Does that mean you don't want to stay here and try to sleep?"

"I'm not sleeping at all," she said, "particularly after whoever the hell knocked on my door."

Immediately his frown disappeared, and he studied her with an intense gaze that she had already come to recognize.

He wanted answers, and he wanted them now. With whatever little tidbit of information she had to offer. She shook her head. "No, I have no clue who it was."

He nodded. "You didn't recognize the voice? You didn't recognize anything?"

"No. I didn't. But I did recognize the anger in the voice. Not per any one person, just the fact that whoever it was either expected to be let in or hoped to be let in and was angry that he wasn't."

"Which could be all kinds of things."

"In a place like this in this situation? Yes."

"Unfortunately we do find a breakdown in human decency under emergency situations sometimes," he said. "And the fact that you've been friendly with us could have sent somebody over the edge."

"Not surprised if it did," she said quietly. "I've already told you about a couple guys giving me trouble."

"But only one who's here now, correct?"

"Yes," she said. "Most of the other guys are harmless. Go stand facing the door, and I'll get dressed really fast."

He nodded and asked, "Do you want me to step out?"

"You don't need to." She was already pulling on her jeans. She left her sweatshirt on over her pajama top and grabbed her socks and shoes. "I'm ready to go."

He turned and looked at her and smiled. "Okay, let's

go." He led the way out. "I want you to stay with me," he said, as he went down the stairs.

"Don't worry about that," she said. "I have no intention of getting more than an arm's length away."

"So, how about we make sure you're close enough." He held out his hand.

Smiling, she grabbed it. "This is getting to be a habit."

"Safety first." He smiled, barely over a grin.

"Is that all it is?" she said in a teasing voice.

He looked at her in mock outrage. "Of course not. You're too beautiful to ignore. But I obviously won't distract either of us or do anything that could make you feel uncomfortable, while we're in a situation like this."

"Ah," she said, "I wondered."

He shook his head and smiled, tugging her closer. Heading down the hall, he released her hand to send a quick text while she watched; then he reached out, snagged her hand again, and repeated, "Stay close."

"This way I don't have much choice," she murmured.

"We're not turning on any lights," he said, as he led her down a different hallway.

Very quickly they were in the storage area. He walked over to the cold rooms.

"So this is where he was, in this first one?" She walked over, nearly being pulled.

He studied it, using a flashlight, and then pulled open the door.

She studied the door and then stepped inside, using her phone for a flashlight. "Well, no sign of Lionel here."

"I know. We still haven't found him either," Troy said, a dark edge to his tone. He looked at her. "Do you trust me?"

"Meaning, you'll shut the door on me? Yes," she said,

with a smile. And, just like that, the door closed in front of her. She stood there for a long moment, studying the door. No handle was on the inside. She called out, "Why would no handle be here?"

"Check on the side of the door," he said, "There should be a quick-release lock."

She ran her hand up and down the side and found a button. She pushed it and heard an intermittent grinding noise.

He pulled open the door and said, "I heard it try to work," he said, "but obviously it's broken."

She nodded. "But, if he went in here and didn't know that, he might have ended up locked inside, unaware that he couldn't get out."

"But he never mentioned that. And we don't have a motive," he said quietly. He studied the inside, now that the door was wide open, and the two of them were standing in the open doorway, using their flashlights.

"I can't think of any motive, except for the fact that Lionel was in here," she said. "Or at least I think it was this one, wasn't it?"

"Yes, it was this one." They stepped out and checked the other two freezers.

"This is the only one that doesn't have an automatic opener from the inside," she said. "This one's got a lever, but it opened and closed easily."

"So the only way somebody would be caught inside any of them is with that broken one."

"Exactly," she nodded. She stepped out and ran her hands up and down her arms. "Now that I've been inside all three," she complained, "it's damn chilly."

Immediately he wrapped his arms around her and tucked her up close. He wore a jacket, so she took a moment to spread the side of the jacket wide and tucked in close, as he wrapped the jacket around her, so they were both wearing it.

"That helps," she murmured, the shivering starting to rock her body.

"Hey, I didn't realize you were that cold," he muttered and wrapped both arms around her and held her tight.

"I think it may have been the subject matter as much as the cold," she muttered. When she could feel some of the chills settling back, she looked up at him and smiled. "Thank you. I feel better."

He let his arms drop to his side, and she stepped back out again and immediately felt a sense of disappointment. It was a perfect opportunity for him to kiss her, but he hadn't. But then why would he? It's not like they were in that kind of a relationship. Hell, she didn't even know what the hell they had right now. And given the same thing that she had just thought about him, she hadn't taken the opportunity to kiss him either.

She stepped a little farther back, looked around, and said, "Is there anything else down here to look at?"

"Well, we're still missing the one body," he said. "And Daniel hasn't shown up yet."

"And what about the others, are they still there?"

"They were the last time we checked."

"You didn't see a cause of death on Lionel, right?"

"No signs of beating or anything like that. But we didn't check too closely. We saw what appeared to be a dead body and accepted that."

"So, any chance he is still alive?"

"I wouldn't have thought so. His body was warm though, as in recently deceased. You were there. You saw it."

"Could he have just been unconscious? Heavily drugged?"

"I'm starting to wonder myself," he said. "So, if Lionel is alive and is hiding somewhere here and is potentially behind some of the craziness going on here, what would be his motive?"

"Depends on if any of the dead men left here were some of the ones who tormented him," she said.

He gave her a sharp look.

"Lionel was gay. Remember?" she said. "And his partner is one of the bodies in the morgue."

"Right," he said. "So you're wondering if somebody here gave him a hard time, so he pretended to die in order to get back at them?"

"No, he's not capable of that kind of violence," she said. "That sounds foolish, even to me."

"All of it does," he said. He led her around to the far side where there was a locked door. He reached up and knocked.

She looked at him in surprise, and, when a voice answered from inside, he opened it up and guided her in.

She froze. "Wow," she said, recognizing Dane and France easily. "So you do have more than the four of you here. I did wonder." Even Axel was here and Nelson. Mason too. She smiled at them. "So what's this? I get to step into the inner circle?"

"You're the one who called us in," Mason said, "so it seemed like a good idea."

"And still no sign of Lionel's body," Troy said. "That freezer does have a button mechanism to open it up from the inside, but it's broken. The other freezers have an inner release button or lever that's a lot more evident and functioning as well."

The men digested those tidbits of information. Mason studied Berkley's face for a long moment. "Do you have any idea what's going on?"

"No," she said. "To make matters worse, Troy asked me if the hacker in my computer system while I was eating dinner could have done it remotely, since everyone was there in the dining room, and the answer is yes."

"Hell. Remote?" Nelson said, straightening up.

She looked to where he'd been sitting on a bench, one leg on either side, but he now stepped free to stand with his hands on his hips as he looked at her.

"Theoretically he could have been at the same table. Our internet with this storm has been pretty rough, so I don't imagine it was somebody back at the home company," she said. "But then think about everybody who you saw touch his phone during dinner. It could have been nearly any-body."

"Do you know of any of them who would have good enough computer skills?"

"Not as hackers per se," she said. "Obviously Jonesy be-cause he's an IT guy. The engineer, Bruce, he's knows IT to a certain extent and certainly as it applies to his system. Does that mean he can hack into mine? I don't know. And why would he?"

"How far did the hacker get?"

"Only to the next firewall I put in," she said. "It has an additional password attached. He gave it three tries and got locked out."

They all slowly nodded. "What was behind that second password?"

"Controls for the drills," she said. "Everything's comput-erized these days. But the thing is, one of the drills is out of service, and two are damaged and have been taken offline. So the fourth one isn't operating, given everything else that's going on, but it's still mechanically sound and intact. It's just been put in a neutral status at the moment."

"Would that give them anything? What would access to that area do?"

"It's hard to say," she said. "Everything is backed up, but, if they were looking to see if damage had been done, that's possible. I've been trying to figure that out myself, but it's not my area of expertise."

"Could they erase damage that may have been done, if something computer-wise caused this?"

"Delete the data? It's possible," she said. "I'm worried about backups with the weather as it is. They do lose a lot of backups here occasionally."

"Deliberately?"

She stopped, looked at him, and frowned. "That's possible as well."

"Are you the only one who comes here to do maintenance and to troubleshoot?"

She shook her head. "No, there are four of us. We travel around a lot."

"Women or men?"

"I'm the only female."

One of the men asked, "Have you been to this rig before?"

She nodded. "Yeah, several times."

"Any trouble?"

"No. Not like you mean," she said. "Definitely not like my friend had."

"We were talking to Gregor," Mason said. "He did know about the rapes. He said he wasn't terribly impressed with the way the company handled it, and that it was something he'd bring up to the board next time."

"Which means nothing," she said. "There should have been an immediate and full investigation and charges."

"The trouble is, they keep these things quiet," Axel said.

"It shouldn't have happened the second or the third time," Troy added. When the men looked at him, he turned to her.

"I only found out after my friend was attacked," she said. "I had no idea women were at risk on this rig."

"The fact that this isn't just a single rapist changes things considerably. They could be colluding to protect each other—or the opposite, trying to eliminate each other to protect themselves."

The conversation was clearly stirring up these men.

"So how is she doing now, your friend?" France spoke up, looking concerned.

"She's different now," she said. "She doesn't go out. She doesn't date and is generally scared to be alone. Yet scared not to be," Berkley said, feeling bad all over again that she couldn't be spending time with her friend.

"Of course," Dane said. "It's not an easy trauma to get over. It changes everything."

"Exactly." She walked over to one of the benches and sat down. At this point the tension in the room was palpable, so she decided a change of subject was in order. "I still think Lionel could be alive and hiding here on the rig. But, if you guys have already searched everywhere and can't find anybody hidden, what the hell is going on?"

"We don't know."

"We did find a storehouse of C-4 though," Dane said. He leaned against the locker. "The locker belonging to

Jude."

Her eyebrows shot up. "Interesting. So his brother *did* drop off something for him."

"So this Jude, did we find any personnel files on him?" Troy looked around the room, seeking an answer from someone.

She pulled out her phone and quickly tapped into the system. "I can send the company files to you, but there isn't much in them." As soon as she had access, she emailed it to Troy and to Mason. When their phones buzzed, they pulled them out.

Mason spoke up. "You open that one, and I'll open the one we have, so we can compare timelines."

"Got it," Troy replied.

"You won't see it in those company files, no doubt," Mason said, "but apparently he was a bit of an activist early on. His brother is a big activist. When Jude was younger, he actively protested against oil rigs."

"Right, and here he is working on one," Axel said, shaking head.

"But only for six months," Mason said, as they sorted the information between them and discussed it out loud.

"What? So his brother wants him to blow up the place, you think?" Berkley asked.

"Maybe," he said, "or maybe the brother didn't want anything to do with it, and Jude is behind it all. Or maybe the older brother tried to pressure Jude into it, and, when something happened, he got off as soon as they could because he didn't want to get blamed. He might not have wanted anything to do with it."

"And again, tons of speculative thoughts," she said, "and no answers. I deal in data. I need real evidence, real data, in order to sort this out," she said in frustration.

The men stood in a circle, looking at her, and smiled.

She raised both hands. "Is that really so unexpected? What?"

"No," Mason said with a smile. "That's how Tesla talks."

The other men all chuckled.

"Yeah, if she were here, she'd be into all kinds of shit," Berkley said.

"What would she be doing?" Nelson asked.

She thought about it a few moments. "She'd have hacked into God-knows-what and already cross-run everybody's history and cross-matched for connections. And then she would have done the same for everybody in the navy who was here during the recent war games. We already found Jude and his brother's connection, but there's got to be a reason why these eight guys are here now—plus Lionel—and nobody else is."

"I gather you don't believe in coincidences," Troy said.

She snorted at that. "No, I don't."

Just then Mason's phone rang. He answered it and immediately said, "I'll be right there."

He looked at Nelson. "That's the boss man. Apparently one of the men has been found dead."

TROY STARED AT him in shock. "Which guy?"

"The marine engineer, Bruce," he said.

"He was there at dinner," Berkley said. "They all were."

"And they just found him in the hallway outside his room," Mason said.

"Is there a clear cause of death?" Axel asked.

"Don't know for sure, but there's evidence of a blow to the head."

"Of course there is," she said, crying out. "This place is such a nightmare. Why can't we just leave?"

"Everybody will be leaving, and a whole new crew is coming in," Mason asserted. "In a situation like this, it just has to happen and should have been done already. There will be duties to hand off and a full investigation of everybody who's here."

"But now we have another death," she said. "Accidental or not."

"I don't know," he said. "Nelson, get your suit jacket back on, and we'll go get a briefing." He looked at Axel and Troy. "Maybe take her back to her room, and one of you at least come up and hear what the guys have to say."

"I want to hear too," she said, wrapping her arms around her gut. At their silent looks, she added, "I brought you guys in on this. Remember? And if something else even nastier is going on, I want to know."

"I'm not sure that's wise," Troy said.

"It doesn't matter if you think it's wise or not," she said, turning on him. "We need answers, and somebody has to have them. So far it doesn't seem to be us."

"Ouch," Axel muttered.

"Maybe she'd be better off staying with us," Troy said, crossing his arms over his chest. "Better that she understands and knows what's going on."

Mason frowned and then shrugged. "Okay," he said, shaking his head. "I don't like it, but I know I'd have the same damn problem with Tesla, if she were here."

Immediately Berkley smiled, sparks flashing in her eyes. "We are a trial, aren't we?"

Mason grinned. "Worth every moment of it," he said with a laugh.

As they all headed out, she looked back at the other men. "Are they staying here?"

"They're guarding the rest of the drills," he said. "None of us want to end up dead before this scenario is over."

She nodded. "If you say so."

Troy looked at her, surprised.

She shrugged. "It all just seems so odd, this whole scenario. I don't know what is proper or what to think anymore."

"Not sure anything proper is to be done about any of it, but Mason is the one who pulled strings to get us all here, based on your SOS," Troy said quietly. "We're in international waters, and that can cause all kinds of chaos. We don't know who's responsible for the sabotage or the aftermath, all those unrelated deaths."

She thought about it. "Not needing to be said, of course, but it's an American oil company that clearly has military ties."

"That it does," he said grimly. "That it does."

They went back to the dining area, where everybody was gathered. The crew stopped and glared at her as she walked in.

"And here I thought you were going to bed," Jonesy said with a sneer.

She stared at him in surprise, as that wasn't his usual attitude. "Well, I was," she said, "until I heard that Bruce's been hurt."

"If that's what you call it," he said, staring at the men behind her. "For all we know, it's these assholes. We didn't have any trouble until they showed up."

She looked at the two men behind her, realizing he meant Axel and Troy. "These two who arrived this morning? You call the explosion two days ago as *no trouble until they showed up*? I beg to differ about that. Nevertheless I highly doubt these men have anything to do with any of it," she said calmly.

Jonesy glared at her. "If they hadn't shown up," he said, "I doubt any of this would have happened."

"Well, that's possible," she said, "but that's hardly a reason to blame them for somebody else's reaction. They certainly didn't attack Bruce." She sighed in frustration. "Jesus," she said, "this place is a mess. How soon can we get off this rig?" She looked around at the gathered men, realizing they weren't all there. "Where's Denny?" she asked suddenly.

"You know exactly where Denny is. He's right where he always is at this time of night," Jonesy said. "He's in his room."

"Do we know that for sure?" she asked. "If Bruce is dead, how do we know Denny is okay?"

They just stared at her.

"There's no reason for him *not* to be okay," Jonesy said, with the same condescending attitude.

"Then what logical reason is there," she asked, "for Bruce to be dead?"

"I imagine he was digging into things he shouldn't have," Jonesy said. "Did you not know he has a history as a hacker?"

"Jesus," she said, reaching up and rubbing her temples.

"And, of course, you didn't even notice, and you're supposed to be the IT guru," Jonesy said.

"Wow," she said, noting a very drunk Idiot was hanging

on to Jonesy. "Have you guys been drinking all this time?"

"Why not?" Jonesy said. "Nothing else to do here."

"I thought this was mostly a dry camp."

"Under normal circumstances, it probably is," Jonesy said, "but who cares?"

"A lot of people care," she said. "What if we need your help?"

"Cry me a river," he snarled.

Berkley glared at Jonesy. "That's not helpful at all."

"Who gives a shit?" Idiot said, and, with that, he started to laugh like a loon.

She stepped forward. "Did you hurt Bruce?"

Idiot looked at her, and all pretense of being drunk fell away. "Why would I hurt Bruce?"

"Maybe he got into things you didn't want him to," she said, getting into his face.

"I don't have anything to hide," he said, "so don't even bother trying to make it look like I do."

"Good," she said, "but somebody hurt Bruce, and nobody else is on board but us."

"I wonder about that," Troy said, from behind them all. "Just because nobody new has shown up here today in this room doesn't mean that someone else isn't on the rig still."

She turned to look back at him. She knew they'd been doing nothing but searching, but, of course, the rig was a huge place, and it was pretty easy for somebody who knew the layout to hide or to stay one step ahead. She looked back at Jonesy. "Have you seen anybody else?"

He immediately shook his head. "Hell no. Just these new guys."

"Well then, you might as well say the same thing about the company men," she said quietly. "Do you suspect them too?" She waited for an answer but didn't get one. "But we need to check and make sure Bruce's actually dead," she said, out of the blue.

The crewmen looked at her, and Idiot snorted. "What? Now we can't tell if a man's dead or not?"

She stared at them. "I'd like to know for sure that nothing could be done for him."

"I'll take you," Troy said suddenly.

She knew that he understood what she meant, and she nodded. "Where is he?"

"He's in the medical room," Chucky said, suddenly breaking his silence. "I'll come with you."

She looked at him in surprise.

He shrugged. "I haven't seen him either. Bruce was a good person, and he didn't deserve this."

"Any chance it was an accident, Chucky?"

"I don't think having your head smacked makes it an accident," he said. "But, if he managed to fall down the stairs and then stumbled toward his room or something, I guess that's a potential as well."

"I never thought of that," she said, "but you're right. It is a possibility."

He nodded, and the three of them looked at the others.

"Anybody else coming?" Troy asked.

"No," Axel said, "I'll stay here."

He nodded. "Sounds good."

And the three of them headed toward the medical office.

As they stepped outside, she looked at Chucky. "Sure would be nice if the generator would give us the lights back."

"We had to shut down a lot of it," he said. "We've got the one for essential services, but that's it. You got flashlights, use them."

"Got it," she said with a smile.

He looked at her and said, "You're awfully calm, considering the situation."

"No," she said, "I'm not calm at all. I'm just screaming on the inside instead, and I can't wait to get away from here."

He laughed at that. "I'd be screaming too, if I could get away with it," he said. "This whole thing is just such a bizarre situation, and it makes no sense."

"Have you ever seen anything like this before?" Troy asked him.

"Somebody dead? Absolutely. Somebody murdered? Yes, that too." He shook his head. "But not in a really long time. But not on top of all this other nonsense."

"Interesting," Troy said. "Who was it and when?"

"About ten years ago," he said, "we were in a camp up in the north fields," he said. "A couple guys got at it after getting murderously drunk. They had a big dust-up bash out. Both of them lived through it, but, the next day, the one guy died. We found out that, while he'd been passed out, sleeping it off, his drunk buddy, the other guy, had come up and stabbed him. He'd been just drunk enough to think it was a good idea and just sober enough to pull it off."

"Wow," she said. "You've lived an exciting life."

"I'd like to go back to being bored," he said. "Hasn't it occurred to you that one of this group is a murderer?"

She stopped and looked at him, then nodded. "Yes, Chucky, it has. You got any clue which one?"

"Hell no," he said. "I can tell you that it's not me, and it's not Winslow. But everybody else is fair game."

On that dark note they headed downstairs. There were no lights once again in the medical center. With all their flashlights on, they found Bruce laid out on an exam table. Troy walked up and immediately checked for a pulse, but there wasn't one to be found, and the body was still cooling.

"Interesting," he said, as he held up the flashlight to look at his head. "That's a decent head wound," he said. He shifted the man's neck just slightly and then nodded. "He wasn't going anywhere."

"What do you mean?" she asked.

"His neck is broken."

"So, even if he did fall down the stairs," she said, "he couldn't have dragged himself or gotten up and walked to his room, correct?"

"Correct," he said. "So it's very unlikely that he had an accident. This is murder."

Chucky looked at the two of them. "So who the hell are you?" he asked. "And what the hell is going on with this place?"

She looked at Troy, who looked at her, and they both turned to look at Chucky. "What are you talking about?" she asked.

"I'm not a fool," he said, "and you sure as hell aren't any deckhand. You might have been up on one somewhere in the last thirty-odd years of your life," he said, "but it's not what you do. So speak up. Who are you?"

She smiled and faced Troy. "You might as well tell him."

"But then he'll tell Winslow," Troy said, his arms across his chest. "How do we know we can trust him or either of them?"

"We don't," she said, "but he's not capable of some of the stunts we've seen. I suggest that we start by trusting somebody."

He nodded at that. "I'm a Navy SEAL," he said, "and so

is Axel. We currently believe that the explosion was caused by navy-issued C-4."

Chucky's face blanched, and he stared at him in shock. "Seriously?"

Troy nodded. "So maybe it's time for you to start talking. Tell us exactly what you know, before somebody else gets hurt."

Chucky looked at him and shook his head. "That's the trouble. I don't know anything."

CHAPTER 11

"A RE YOU SURE about that, Chucky?" she asked him, her tone gentle and quiet. She'd never seen him be anything other than what he was, a grizzled old grump whose time had come to walk away.

"I haven't seen anything that I can count on," he corrected. "There's been lots of talk, plenty of rumors. You know how guys are. You get twenty of them in a room, and you'll have people who don't get along. You get two hundred of them on a rig like this and leave them here for six months with lots of hard work and no way to really blast off their resentment and energy, and you're bound to have trouble."

"And do you know anything about the rapes?" Troy asked.

Immediately Chucky's face turned rigid. And then slowly he nodded. "I might at that," he said, "but I don't know anything for sure. It's all just rumors."

"Well, we'd really like to hear those rumors," Berkley said. "My friend will never be the same."

He turned and spat on the ground. "There is no way for men to do something like that and keep their humanity," he said, "but, a place like this, it brings out the worst in some of them."

"Have you worked on rigs before where there were women?" Troy asked him.

"Of course," he said, "but this is the only place I've ever had a problem or seen a problem not be quickly corrected."

"And do you know any of the men who were involved?" Berkley asked Chucky.

He shot her a veiled look and then shrugged.

"That's not helpful," Troy said in an exasperated tone. "I get that you don't want to be involved and that you might be afraid of repercussions."

At that, Chucky glared at him. "I ain't afraid of nothing," he said. "Guys talk, but that doesn't mean I know all the ins and outs of the conversation."

"Okay, so what guy do you think is most likely involved in the rapes?"

He shuffled his feet as he stared at them. "That may not even have anything to do with this mess either," he said.

"Are there really likely to be that many psychos in a group of two hundred men?" Troy asked.

"Hell, I don't know," he said. Then, taking a deep breath, he sighed. "One of them was the doctor."

She gasped in horror. "Seriously?"

He nodded. "I know he used to drug some of his patients. It's one of the reasons he was up here."

"And how do you know that?"

"Because I knew him before, from another rig, and he had to leave that company under a cloud. So, when he showed up here, and there started to be some talk," he said, "I wasn't so sure what was going on, but I figured he had to be involved."

She swore and exchanged a hard glance with Troy. But inside she was just wrecked. "Tabitha did go to the doctor a couple times," she said. "She was definitely having some issues."

"Before?"

She nodded. "She did say she was really bothered by something but wouldn't clarify it and said that we could talk next time I got here. But I'd barely arrived when the rape happened, and she was in no shape to talk at all. My goal then was to preserve some evidence and to get her out of here."

"Have you contacted her since she's been gone?" Troy asked.

"I was due to leave next week," she said, "and we would spend some time together. I needed her to physically heal and to see a shrink to begin dealing with the mental issues. The fact that she didn't know who it was made it so much worse. I wondered if she had any inkling, but she seemed to be completely beside herself, and I couldn't really get her to talk."

"And, if the doc is involved," Troy said, looking over at Chucky, "what about the other guys in the cooler? Winslow did fill you in on that, didn't he?"

"He did, yes. Well, it is possible," he said, with a nod. "When you think about it, one of the reasons that maybe nothing was done was because the people that Tabitha reported to were the ones involved."

Berkley gasped. "Jesus, I never thought of that," she said. "I just assumed it would be some of the lower echelon groups, some of the men of the type who were angry all the time." She paused for another moment. "But, if she reported it to the men up above, and it didn't get any higher up, or at least nobody took anything too serious, then it would make sense that somebody was minimizing the damage to her over all these reports," she said.

"Or not even so much minimizing the damage, they

could have reduced or significantly changed the actual report," Troy said. "And that's the three missing division managers and the doc, who served as the fourth division manager, all in the cooler, correct?"

She nodded. "Yes, that's correct, but I don't know about the others." She looked back at Chucky. "Any chance the others could have had something to do with it?"

"I don't know," he said quietly. "I didn't see those bodies, but Winslow did earlier. He told me how the two guys who died in the blast were here. That would account for Roger and Clarence, but that was from two days ago. Add those four remaining managers, one of them being the doc, then that's six bodies right there. The managers are all friends though. Of course not friendly with Lionel and Charlie. So, if those four are involved, I don't know at what point in time the rapes would quit. That's pretty personal shit to share with others, who could tell on you. And it comes with criminal charges and a lot of jail time."

"Only if they get caught, apparently," Troy said. He looked at her. "I think we should take a look at their rooms."

"Oh, I don't know about that," Chucky said.

Troy looked at him, studying him for a long moment. "They're dead now, Chucky."

"It's just that it's their space," Chucky said. "It's creepy, and I ain't going to be a party to it."

"You don't have to be," Troy said. "I doubt they've even left any evidence behind. Surely they weren't that stupid. Even if they lived to be one hundred, they should hide the evidence for each successive decade."

"What could any of it possibly have to do with the Jude theory?" she asked.

"Maybe nothing," Troy said. "We've got a lot of ideas

and pieces of things to consider here that don't appear to be necessarily connected. But what we do know is that we have three rapes, eight dead bodies still on the rig because God himself is the only one who knows what's happened to Lionel, and then we've got C-4 taken from a military base."

"Not to mention the sabotage of the rig itself," Chucky said. "That's the big one."

It really hurt her to think along those lines because those three women would never be the same, yet their shattered psyches and dashed hopes in a just humanity ran second to the damage to the rig—more a case of money out of the shareholders' pockets—though it could have been much worse and there could have been several hundred deaths.

"I'm going back to bed," Chucky said.

"Good idea," she said and headed out toward the hall-way as if heading to hers. Troy grabbed her and tugged her up against him, as they watched Chucky disappear into the darkness. With his arms wrapped around her, he leaned down and whispered in her ear, "Do you know where the dead men's rooms are?"

"No, but I can find out." She pulled up her phone, logged into the system, and checked for the rooms assigned to them. "I have it here," she said, "but chances are they'll be locked."

"No problem," he said smoothly. "Take me to them."

She quickly led him toward the sleeping quarters and stopped to point out the rooms provided to the four now-dead supervisors. "The three guys should be here, and the doctor, as the fourth supervisor, had his own room along here too."

Troy stepped into the first room. It was unlocked, and it had already been cleaned out. He looked at her. "It's completely empty."

She shrugged. "I don't know what to say."

He checked the second one, but it was locked. He popped the lock in seconds and stepped in. "This should be one of the managing supervisor's room," she said.

He tossed the entire room within seconds, checking under the mattresses, through each layer of the sheets, and then went to the closet and pulled out personal gear, looking for anything that might show some evidence that he'd been involved in anything criminal. They should have done that first when they realized who the bodies were.

With her help, they found his cell phone tucked inside his pillow, among the padding there.

"Why would his cell phone be here?" he asked out loud.

"I don't know," she said. "Normally you would think it would be in his pocket."

"But he didn't have it on him, so that meant he was here, maybe in his room, when it happened." He pulled out the cell phone and said, "And it's not locked." He quickly checked through it.

"We can also log in to his online account," she said, "but I highly doubt he would do anything company-wise."

"No, most of the time people save that stuff in the cloud." As he went through the emails, he found a folder and opened it. And then he sucked in his breath. He quickly scrolled the photo up slightly.

"Berkley, do you recognize her?"

Berkley stepped over and nodded. "It's one of the first two women who were raped."

He let her see the rest of the picture, which showed the woman unconscious on the ground, completely nude, obviously beaten, and male hands were on her.

She immediately clamped a hand over her mouth. "Oh, my God," she whispered.

He nodded. "We need to get this to the authorities."

"This makes it look like somebody was getting revenge by sharing these photos," she said. She shook her head. "This guy is a complete asshole, but these women haven't been here for weeks if not months now."

"Well, we'll have to check the timelines to see who was here during the attacks."

"Well, we need to find out what their alibis are for sure," she agreed. As he went through the pictures, she winced to see the women in various positions. "At least in this case, she's unconscious," she said.

He scanned through them and then stopped. "What about this woman?"

She looked at it and said, "That's the second woman."

He nodded and went through them, and finally he said, "I'm not seeing a third woman."

She could feel a sense of relief inside. "I hope not," she said. "I think it would absolutely finish Tabitha to think there were photos of her too. She didn't say anything about being photographed at the time though."

"I doubt if she knew," he said. "Remember? She was blindfolded. And these two weren't, which is interesting."

"That was probably an added development," she said caustically.

He slipped the phone into his pocket and quickly searched the rest of the room. But he didn't find anything. He said, "So one of the managers' possessions have been searched, and one manager's room had been gutted, so what else have you got for me?"

She noted that one of the managers had his room nearby

but that the doc's room was coming up next.

Troy nodded. "Let's check the doc's room next, then the other guy's."

They went to the doctor's personal quarters. It was larger than the others, but, even though they went from top to bottom, there didn't appear to be anything to see.

"What about his phone," she wondered.

"I wonder if it's still on him," he said. "You know what? If you find a body—like me, for instance—you'll find my phone on me," he said.

She groaned. "I really don't want to go back down there."

"What room was the final managing supervisor in?"

She nodded and went back to her database. "I just have his initial assigned room. He had asked for a room reassignment, but it doesn't say what room he was given."

They stepped out into the hallway, and Troy checked the room directly across the hall. It was full of gear. "Do you know whose room this is?"

She checked the roster. "It says it's supposed to be empty."

"What do you want to bet that this was a manager's lair? It's a decent size too." He quickly went through the stuff and found some personal belongings for a Doug Driscoll.

She nodded. "That is his room then."

But nothing incriminating was found.

TROY LED THE way back down to the medical clinic.

"Do you really think we'll find anything here?" she asked, dreading the task ahead.

"Where do you hide stuff if you don't want somebody to

know what it is?"

She looked at him in surprise. "I can't think of anything I've tried to hide."

He burst out laughing. "That's because you've led a blameless life," he said with a snicker.

She punched him lightly in the shoulder. "That sounded almost like a criticism," she said.

"Not at all," he said with a gentle smile. "Greater to have led your best life than to have led a bad one and then fix it now."

"I wonder how many bad people try to fix it," she murmured. She hated the darkness now that it was jet-black outside as well. The angry sea raged outside, with spray coming up every time they had to go outside a door and go back down again.

She stopped and stared at the whitecaps lighting up the world around them. "There's such savagery to Mother Nature at times."

He wrapped an arm around her and tucked her up close as she shivered.

"Maybe it's the water-loving SEAL in me, but I don't see this as savagery," he said calmly. "But she never really gives us a chance to ignore that she is truly all-powerful," he said. "We're such small ponds in her world, and yet we think we're the ones who are so powerful."

"Until there's a hurricane or an earthquake or rough seas like this," she said, motioning out there. "Then, just like that, complete devastation in seconds, if she chooses "

"Unfortunately man doesn't need any help with destruction," he said. "Come on. Let's get you back inside again."

They moved inside down another level to the clinic.

"There's an eerie feeling to this place now," she said. "I

won't be at all sad to leave it."

"Will you come back?"

"Well, it's not like I really have a choice in some cases," she said. "It depends on what ends up happening with the company, I suppose. But again, I'm a contractor, and my company sends me all over the place."

"How much are you gone in a regular week?"

"I usually do a couple trips a month," she said. "Trips that can last from a couple of days and sometimes a week or two. Depends on how big the problem is. Last year we were short-staffed, so I did a fair bit of traveling, but we've hired new staff since. So, with any luck, some of that traveling will calm down now."

"Good," he said. "A little hard to date while you're always out of the country."

She stopped in her tracks just in time to see him turn and flash her a bright grin.

"That is, if you want to go on a date, when we get out of here and back to some normalcy."

She smiled. "I'd love that," she said warmly. "As long as whatever is going on between us isn't a result of this nightmare."

"Not even close." He smiled. "But Mason's group has got such a dating thing going on where I may have been keeping my guard up a little."

She laughed out loud. "You've heard about that, huh?"

"Heard it and seen it in action," he said, again with that big grin. He smiled as he watched her navigate the walkway beside him. "You do seem quite comfortable here though."

"I've been here enough," she admitted. She stepped in front and led the way to the clinic. As he walked, he kept a careful eye on their surroundings. There was an eeriness, an echoing emptiness to the place, but, at the same time, he knew that more people were here than anyone understood. As they stepped into the clinic, they found Mason and Nelson in there.

She gasped. "What's the matter?" she cried out.

"Nothing," Mason assured her. He looked back at Troy. "Why are you guys down here?"

"We just turned over the four dead managers' rooms to see if anything incriminating turned up, indicating why they were killed," Troy said. He pulled out the manager's phone he had found and lifted it up so they could see a couple of the photos.

Nelson whistled. "Now that's pretty ugly." He looked back at the body bags in the cooler. "Are you thinking all four of these men might have had something to do with the rapes? All managing supervisors? Because, if that's the case, that gives us a completely different angle here."

"Yet," Troy said, "what are the chances of several different serious crimes happening on the rig, all completely unrelated? Sabotage and rapes. And then murders," he added.

"And the hacking," she said.

There was silence in the clinic for several moments as everybody contemplated that line of thought, and then Mason gave a decisive shake of his head. "I don't buy it," he said. "Maybe one of these things is unrelated, but, in my book, the chance of them being unrelated is pretty minuscule. I'd say they are all connected."

Troy was glad to hear that. "That's my take on it too," he said, as he looked from Nelson to Mason. "Where's Gregor?"

"He's gone to bed," Mason said. "We would go too, but

I wanted to come down and take a look at the bodies myself."

"And that's why we came down as well, to check their pockets," Troy said, "because we couldn't find any personal information, like phones or wallets in their rooms. Other than this one with the pictures."

At that, the three men turned to the bodies on the drawers in the makeshift morgue and quickly checked. "No phones, no wallets," Nelson straightened.

"So what happened? Somebody collected them?" Troy asked.

"It's possible," replied Nelson.

"Well, they would have taken this one if they could have found it, but it was tucked inside his pillow."

"Inside his pillow? That's different."

Troy nodded.

"So maybe it's a private phone and not the company phone that all these guys should have had here. Especially at this level," Nelson speculated.

"I didn't think of that," Troy said, frowning. "But we do have these crimes on his phone, so he was there at the time."

"But it doesn't have any photos of Tabitha," she said to Mason.

"At least not that we've found yet," Troy corrected her. "It could be those photos are still being processed somewhere else, like maybe somebody else took them and emailed them. Could be that they're being sent a link to look at online, and he hasn't downloaded them yet."

She winced at that. "That's just lovely, isn't it? So that she can be raped over and over and over again."

Mason nodded soberly. "I'm sorry for your friend," he said gently. "Obviously something will need to be done about that. But we also need to know what's going on with the sabotage. You're the one who brought us in here. What exactly did you see that had you thinking something was wrong?"

"Lots of things," she said bluntly. "The explosion for one. It didn't sound like a drill mishap. It sounded like a blast going off."

"Well, the condition of the metal certainly seems consistent with that idea," Troy said. "But you also didn't trust the men you'd been left behind with, is that correct?"

"I didn't trust most of them," she admitted. "But, when I sent out that initial message, we were still all trying to get off. At that point in time, my boss hadn't yet asked me if I was okay to stay behind with the skeleton crew and to monitor the computer systems until the engineers and the repair crew came in."

"Why did you stay?" Nelson asked.

She frowned, then shrugged. "I don't have a good response for that. Except that I felt like I needed to get answers while it was still possible."

"Answers for Tabitha or answers about the sabotage?"

"All of it," she said simply. "I'd put out a call to you guys, so I felt responsible, you know? Like I couldn't just take off and dump the whole thing on you."

"Most people would have," Troy said. He studied her face as she looked up at him, gave him a small quirk of her lips.

"I know, but that's not me."

He smiled, really appreciating who she was. The fact that she had made a bold move and had done something in the face of an emergency, then stuck around to see if she could help, said an awful lot about her character.

She looked around and said, "I still don't understand where Lionel is," she said. "And what about everybody else? Are they all accounted for?"

"Yes, the pilot is staying with our other two guys," Mason said, "and they're covering sentry duty across the whole platform. We're still looking for Daniel."

"Making sure there are no more attempts at sabotage?" she asked. "Daniel's disappearance is disconcerting. I figured he was finally catching up on some sleep or grieving for his brother. It's not like him to disappear like this. But then there's not much he can do and he's got a lot to deal with right now so avoiding us almost makes sense."

He nodded.

"That's a lot of area to cover, with just the two of them, and trying to stay in the shadows too," she noted.

Just then a huge blast sounded, crashing into this area, and they were all picked up off their feet and thrown across the room.

CHAPTER 12

BERKLEY SAT UP, groggy and disoriented, only to see Troy leaning over her, his hands reaching down, helping her to her feet. She gave him a shaken look. "What was that?" she cried out.

"I don't know for sure," he said. "I want you to stay here though."

She glanced around the room and found the dead bodies had been forcefully ejected from their drawers and were now on the floor with her and shook her head. "Oh, hell no."

He gave her a frustrated look and said, "I don't want you coming into the blast zone."

She stared at him. "*Blast* zone?"

He nodded. "We're pretty sure that was probably more C-4 explosions happening."

"Then let's go," she said. He hesitated. She nodded and said, "I get that you want to keep me safe, but that's not the point right now. We need all hands to see if anybody else is injured too."

Nodding, he relented, and they headed off after Mason and Nelson. When they got to the main blast area, part of the platform was damaged, the steel twisted and torn to the side. Mason's team stood in a circle, staring at the area.

"How much damage did it do?" Troy asked Mason.

"France's initial assessment shows structural damage to

the rig and less to the drills and the operational equipment this time. Our skeleton crew is running more analyses on the stability and the safety of the rig as we speak," Mason said. "Two field inspectors for the company are supposed to be coming in ASAP. It's the storm stopping them from being here right now. The initial report says no one has been seriously hurt though, and the blast impact didn't hit the actual operations of two of the main drills on the rig," he said.

Just then one of their men, supposedly in hiding, joined him.

"I found C-4 along the rig earlier," France said, pointing where the wall was still intact. "We'd been through here once, and there was nothing. Once I realized that somebody had gotten in here to plant this C-4, I called Dane to help search this whole area again, and I had just headed back to meet him when it blew." Dane approached from the shadows and stood by France.

"And, if you hadn't headed back to meet him," Mason said, his voice rigid with anger, "you'd have been ripped apart in this."

"Do we know for sure that nobody else has been injured or has been tossed into the ocean?" Troy asked. He walked over to the side, testing the metal as he went. Everything appeared to be solid, from what he could see. Nobody was visible in the waters below.

Axel appeared here suddenly as well. "I don't know how many others saw Dane and France," he said, "but, if they need to be kept hidden, we need to keep our numbers down out here." With that, Dane and France disappeared. Axel stood here, staring at the platform, and swore. "So France did his checks, then somebody came back and planted the C-

4, obviously knowing that France had been here. Then France spots the one C-4, disengages it, and goes to call Dane for somebody else to give him a hand with the full sweep. And that's when another C-4 rips?"

"Exactly," Troy said. "Now we must search the rest of the platform, especially the area around that one working drill. I don't know how much C-4 the saboteur may have, but this is a little ridiculous."

"We found a bunch, right?" Mason asked.

"Yeah, we did. A locker full of it. But we moved that," Troy said, turning to look at Axel.

"That's all still right where we put it," Axel said. "I checked before I came here."

"So, somebody has another stash," Mason said. "Dammit."

"How much was used here?" Troy asked.

"I'm not sure what size the pack was that they found," Mason stated, "but we need to see it."

With that, they headed inside and met up with Dane and France, who showed him the small pack of C-4. "This is the one that I took off the side, with these wires," he said. "I didn't give it another thought. I removed it immediately, but then, like I said, it's a big area, and I couldn't search it all without help."

"Hey, it would have been much worse if that wall had blown too," Mason said. "We might all be swimming in the ocean now. It was the right call." Then he addressed all the men. "I suggest that a full sweep of this floor happen in groups of two," he said. "One starts at the north end and heads south, while the other starts at the south. We'll meet at this latest blast site." Mason turned to his secret team. "Dane and France, take any level that's dark and do your best to scour it without being spotted. Report back to me after you've done each level. Avoid the lit levels. We'll handle those ourselves." The two men left with a nod.

Troy turned to look at Berkley.

She shook her head. "I'll run my tablet and track anything you find," she said calmly. "Don't even think about sending me back to my room."

He planted his hands on his hips and glared at her.

She planted her hands on her hips, shoved her chin toward him, clearly mimicking his actions.

He raised both hands in mock surrender and muttered something about women.

"You love us," she shot back.

He glared at her. "Maybe," he said, "but there are times and places."

"Both times and places are right now," she said. "Remember that dating thing? Deal with it now, or forget it."

"I didn't say I wouldn't deal with it," he groused. "And you're the one who brought up the dating thing."

"Sure, after we already agreed."

When somebody cleared their throat, she turned to find Axel standing there, a huge grin on his face.

Her frown deepened. "Don't you start," she warned.

"I wouldn't start anything, Axel," Mason said with a laugh. "But, while our secret team works in the darkness, it doesn't appear like anybody from our skeleton crew gives a shit about coming down here—which I don't understand. So I suggest we do a full sweep, and let's get at it right now."

With that, they organized into two teams—Mason and Axel as one team, starting at the south end, with Berkley and Troy and Nelson starting on the north end, both teams checking steel girders and such, doors, walls, and corners.

They searched all the way back to the blast area. There they found the rest of the crew, including Denny, frozen in place and staring in horror.

When they joined them, Denny turned to look at him. "What are you guys doing?"

"Searching for more C-4," Mason said grimly. "You don't happen to know where any is, do you?" His flashlight swept across all the faces in front of them.

Chucky stared at them all. "C-4? I thought this was an accident."

"Nope," Troy said. "This was C-4." He held up the one that he had in his hand. "We found this one."

At that, several of the men stepped back.

"Holy shit," one said. "Who's trying to kill us?"

"I don't know," Troy said, "and maybe it's not even a case of *who*, but maybe it should be a question of *why*. In the meantime, we need to keep searching for C-4, so either move out of our way or join us."

Chucky and Winslow immediately joined them, as the others just stood off to the side and watched, as the search parties went step by step, slowly girder by girder, by each steel railing and ramp, and finally across to the opposite side.

When they got there, Troy said, "We're clear on this side."

Axel stepped toward him. "We're clear on this side too." Slowly they moved back down along the center, checking inside the doors, checking the walls, checking as much as they could. When they returned to the blast site again, all the crewmen remained there, waiting for them.

"Did you see anything?" Jonesy asked curiously.

Berkley couldn't tell if anything other than curiosity was in his tone.

Troy shook his head. "No, I don't believe any explosive is here, at the moment. But we need to check the next level up."

"That'll take forever," Jonesy said. "There are so many rooms, and lots of the guys' personal belongings are there. You can't just go through the place."

At that, Gregor stepped forward from the group. "Hell yes, they can. Do you have any idea what kind of money is involved here?"

"Shutting down this rig is probably costing billions." Now Jonesy's voice sounded positively cheerful.

Berkley tucked away that little tidbit of information in the back of her mind. It didn't make any sense to her though, because it affected his paycheck too. What she really needed to know was whether there was any connection between these men, the women, and Jude and his brother. And maybe not even so much a connection to Jude and his brother. Maybe somebody thought these crewmen had participated in the rapes. But, if that were the case, she figured they'd end up in the morgue too.

Slowly they disbanded into groups and went upstairs to conduct the next searches. Gregor ran the group going through all the personal rooms.

By the time all those rooms had been searched, except for the rooms housing the current crew, Mason spoke up. "Now we'll go search your rooms," he said to the group, his hard tone, daring somebody to argue.

They all looked at each other. Chucky and Winslow broke the silence as they both spoke up, with an invitation to start with theirs. They opened the doors, and Troy and Axel, along with Mason and Nelson, went through their rooms, checking for anything potentially lethal or incriminating.

But found nothing.

The four went through each room set aside for the remaining crewmen, and still nothing was found. When it came to her turn, Berkley just shrugged. "Come on in." She walked down to her room and opened it up. Her bed was still disheveled the way it had been, her pajama bottoms thrown off to the side. The four men she trusted above all others here went through her belongings and, of course, didn't find anything.

When they stepped back out, they looked at each other. Wondering what to do next.

Gregor asked, "What are the chances all the C-4 this saboteur has on hand has been used up now?"

"It's possible," Troy said. "I took pictures of it and sent it out for some extra information to be tracked on it."

"What kind of information?"

"It still had its packaging, with barcodes," he said, "so we'll track where it was shipped from."

"Good," Gregor said, "because this is bullshit."

They moved up one level to the kitchen, dining area, and management rooms, and carefully went through everything.

By the time they were done, Denny was beside himself. "Did you really think I've got C-4 in my kitchen?" His tone was incredulous.

"Do you really think that you will be spared from another blast like that last one?" Mason asked quietly. "Somebody hates you. Somebody hates everybody here. Did you ever consider that?"

Immediately Denny fell silent.

She knew about his record. He probably didn't want anybody else to know though.

NOW GATHERED IN the dining area, she looked at the clock. "It's five a.m."

"Well, I'm not going back to sleep," Denny muttered, returning to his kitchen, where he started banging around his pots and pans.

"What will you do?" Berkley asked him, interested in his reaction.

"When I'm upset," he said, "I bake. I'll make breakfast."

"Isn't it a little early for food?"

"*Food*-food, yes," he said, "but I just said, *I would bake.*"

Troy listened to the cook's tone, and Denny really was upset, but Troy didn't necessarily understand what his reason was. Granted, there were lots of reasons to be upset right now. Troy walked over and, on the quiet, asked, "Denny, did you know the three women who had trouble here?"

Denny looked at him with a hard gaze. "Is there a reason you're asking me?"

"Yes," he said, "because we found some very disturbing photos on one of the managers' phones."

Denny's eyebrows popped up. "Disturbing, how?"

"Let's just say, disturbing sexual-exploitation photos."

Denny winced. "That no-good son of a bitch," he said. "That man has been trouble the whole time. And not just with girls."

"Oh?"

"Yeah, ask Daniel about his brother. If anybody did deserve to die, it's that no-good doctor."

"Did you know him any other place than here?"

"No, but people talk," Denny said. "That guy was a rat, and I'm glad he's dead. If I'd known he had something to do with hurting those poor girls, I would have poisoned him myself." At that, he started sifting flour and sugar.

Troy looked over and caught Berkley yawning. He walked toward her. "Come on. Let's get you back to bed," he said. "No reason you can't sleep for a couple hours."

She looked up at him, valiant, yet her eyes were red-rimmed and exhausted.

"Come on," he said, gently grabbing her arms. "Let's go."

And, with that, he led her back to her room. She stared at her door and groaned.

"Feels like I'm quitting," she said.

"There's nothing to quit," he said. "We need some equipment to check for other devices around the rig, and we need everybody in one area. At least if something else goes wrong, we'll have a better idea of who it isn't."

She walked in, kicked off her shoes, and collapsed full length on her bed. "I'm exhausted," she murmured.

"Will you be able to sleep?"

"I don't know," she whispered. "It doesn't feel safe anymore."

He hesitated at the doorway.

She waved him off. "Go. I'll be fine."

He looked around the small space. "I could grab my laptop and work in here, if you want."

She looked at him gratefully. "Would you mind?"

"Hang on," he said. "I'll be right back." With that, he turned and disappeared. While he was gone, she got up, went to the bathroom, came back, and put on her pajamas again. If she could sleep, she wanted to sleep comfortably. She tucked in under the blankets, and, a few minutes later, the door opened, and he stepped inside.

He shut the door behind him, locking it this time, and walked over to the table and set up his laptop. "Go to sleep," he whispered. "It'll be over soon."

"Yeah, maybe for you," she said. "Honestly I would like to catch that helicopter out of here."

"I'm sure everybody feels the same way," he said. "I'm not sure what the capacity is on that one."

"Right." She closed her eyes, yawned again, and started to drift off. But every time she went to sleep, she was jolted awake, hearing a repeat of those large blasts ripping through her dreams, along with the screams and the panic, over and over again.

Finally he got up. "Slide over," he said. "I'll get in with you. That might help."

"You shouldn't have to do this," she murmured, as she scooted over.

"Somebody has blasted holes into this rig, twice so far," he said, against her ear. "You're allowed to be jumpy. But you need to get some sleep," he said, "and this is the best way for you to get it." And he wrapped an arm around her and tucked her up against him.

She took in a deep breath and let it go. Immediately she could feel herself drifting deeper and deeper. As she was just about to go under, she asked, "Do you really think those managers were murdered because of the rapes?"

"I think it's all too possible, yes," he said. "Sleep, remember?"

"So then what's the deal with Lionel?" she asked.

"I don't know," he said softly. "I really don't."

An ugly thought was starting to form in Berkley's mind. "I know you said he was dead, but, what if he took something, so he wasn't dead, but he was just in a really deep coma."

"It's possible," he said. "We haven't found him."

"That's why I was thinking someone might be helping him," she said.

"Who did he have for friends?"

"One of the dead guys."

"Right, but anyone else?"

"I think he knew all the guys, but I don't know if he was especially close to anyone. Other than his brother, of course."

"Sleep," he said. "We'll figure it out later."

She smiled and whispered, "You're a nice man."

"Oh, there's an ego booster," he said with mild affront. "I'm not sure any man likes to be called nice."

She chuckled. "Maybe not," she said. "But it's true. You're just like Mason and Axel."

"Okay," he said, "I'll take that as a compliment."

"And I meant it that way," she said. "Besides, that's the kind of guy I'd want to date."

"Why them?" he asked curiously.

She smiled. "Because they're men of honor. And that's missing in so many of the guys I meet."

"I hear you," he said gently.

The last thing she remembered was him leaning over and his lips brushing her temple. She smiled. "That was nice."

"Then go to sleep, before I'm tempted to do a whole lot more."

She smiled. "Well, you wouldn't, because it's not who you are to take advantage." And, with that, she let out a deep sigh.

WHEN HE THOUGHT she was truly asleep, he gently disengaged himself and struggled off the bed. He sat down at the little table with his laptop and started to research. First, he wanted to know what drug would allow somebody to look as if he were dead. And when he reviewed the findings, Troy quickly realized there were several good candidates for that.

He then checked to see if the doc had ordered any. What if that's what the doc was doing with the women? Particularly the two they had found photos of. Troy wondered what had happened to the third rape victim. And what if it was just a case of using the date-rape drug? That's why he wanted Lionel's body to go back with him, but, after they'd moved it, somebody else had moved it again. Or did Lionel have a friend working with him, and they were in cahoots over something?

Troy liked the idea of another person hiding on the rig somewhere. He really liked that idea. When a knock came on Berkley's door, he froze. The knock came again, harder. He walked toward her and gently tucked the blanket up over her ears, so that she could sleep a little longer. If this had been Axel or Mason, they would have used a particular knock, so he knew it wasn't them.

"Stupid bitch!"

When he heard that, he immediately dove for the door and stepped out. Standing there, sure enough, was Jonesy, who looked at him, looked at her bedroom door, and sneered.

"Like I said, she'd spread her legs for anybody."

He didn't get another word out before Troy's fist connected with Jonesy's jaw. His head snapped back, and he hit the hallway wall and slid down into a puddle on the ground.

"You didn't have to do that," she said, standing beside him.

He looked at her and groaned. "Dang it. I wanted to let you sleep."

"I'm glad you caught him," she said, "because that's exactly what happened the last time."

He nodded, tucked her close to him. "Is this the kind of abuse you've been getting?"

"It didn't used to be like this," she said softly. "But, after the women were raped, yes. They should do DNA testing for everybody who works here," she said.

"And yet they won't because most of the men will protest that it's against their rights."

"So, is that his blood on your fist?"

"It is," he said, with interest. "Do you want to keep some?"

"I so want to keep it." She walked back inside, grabbed a washcloth, and quickly wiped the blood off his knuckles. Then she bagged it. "I'll send this to the DNA lab, where I sent everything else. Of course it takes weeks to get answers."

"Interesting that you're paying for it."

"It's international waters, so the company won't cover it," she said. "And I think that's just wrong too."

"It's very wrong," he said.

She looked again at Jonesy as she walked back into her room. "Do we just leave him out there?"

"I would," he said, "unless you know which room was his."

"It's down about six doors," she said. She thought about it and then said, "Let me get dressed real quick."

He turned around and gathered up his laptop, then put it all away. By the time he was done, she was dressed. They stepped out and found Jonesy still collapsed on the ground. Troy walked over, checked for a pulse, and picked him up. "Which room is his?"

She led him down the hallway and opened it up, and Troy walked in and dumped Jonesy unceremoniously onto the bunk.

When they headed back out, he said, "I need to wash up though."

She stepped into the bathroom, showed him where he could wash up, and waited for him. Then together, they headed back to the dining area.

"I hope you're not coming back to this place," he said, his tone dark.

She looked at him and smiled. "Quite protective, aren't you?"

"Obviously, under the circumstances, but I also care," he said. "The environment here is not healthy for any woman, much less one I'm starting to really care about."

She reached over, slipped her fingers in his, and said, "Thank you. That's one of the nicest things anybody has said to me in a long time."

He chuckled and said, "Well, from what I've seen around here, the bar hasn't been very high."

She giggled and punched him in the arm.

Just as they walked into the dining area, something delicious smelling came from the oven. She walked over to the counter to see what Denny had made. It looked like bear claws.

"Yum. Those look lovely, Denny," she said warmly.

He smiled. "When I'm stressed, upset, depressed, or whatever, I find baking soothes my soul."

"Well, I hate to say it," she said, "but I really hope you're upset a little more often."

He stopped for a moment, then realized what she meant and burst out laughing.

As she walked over to get some coffee, she noted the rest of the dining area was empty. Pouring two coffees, and taking the treats Denny offered, she walked to the small table by the window, where she and Troy sat down.

CHAPTER 13

"IT IS REALLY pleasant in here when it's empty," Berkley whispered. "I know the others will arrive soon, but it's quite nice right now to sit and relax and to do something halfway normal."

Denny walked over with the coffee carafe. "Romance is in the air, I see."

"Maybe," she admitted. "Let's just say, we're happy to get to know each other at the moment."

"Take the moments when you can," he said. "They are over too damn fast."

"Denny, I'm sorry about your history," she said. "I've always been a plain talker. Please don't feel you have to hide your past from us. Clearly you've turned your life around and should be really proud of that."

He stopped, looked at her in surprise, and then slowly nodded. "Thank you," he said. "Not many people know."

She shrugged. "I don't think it matters to a whole lot of people. We've got enough ugliness going on here right now."

"Which is why I figured everybody would be pointing the finger at me," he said. "I'm a convicted felon and all."

"That doesn't mean that you killed anybody here," she said, "or that you were involved in the rapes."

"I wasn't," he said, his tone sincere.

She believed him.

"Got no truck with anybody who was either. I got into a bad spot with gangs and ended up in a real ugly scenario. I got caught for it and paid my price," he said, "but I've been clear ever since."

"Right," she said, "I'm not sure there's anything else we can do here."

"Well, you can find out who the hell is killing those men," he said. "I'm pretty damn sure it's all related to the rapes though."

"Got it," she said. "The trouble is, whoever it is, why would they also do the sabotage?"

"I was thinking about that," he said. "They're amateur jobs, if you think about it."

At that, Troy froze and looked at him. "You're right because, if they wanted to take out the whole rig, they could have. If they had gone down onto the platforms, a couple C-4 discharges would have done massive damage—especially if they'd hit the drills too."

Denny nodded. "That's what I mean. So an amateur job means somebody who's causing trouble but doesn't really know how to do maximum damage."

"And who would that be?"

"It could be any of them," he said. "Anybody here now but hopefully not Winslow and Chucky. I'd hate to see them involved. It just wouldn't make sense."

"Me too," she said. "Hopefully they aren't."

"I can't see it. They've seen too much over the years, and I think they just want to leave this time and not come back. They are really looking forward to retiring."

"What about Jonesy? Or Idiot."

He laughed at that. "Jonesy. He's always just Jonesy. I think it's the drugs in his system. They're supposed to do drug testing on the crew, and somehow he got free and clear this last time around. It must have killed him to stay off long enough to test clean, but he's definitely on drugs. I've seen the science."

She thought about it and said, "I don't know the science."

"Highs and lows," he said. "Too happy, too shiny-eyed, and then down."

"I get it," Troy said, "but you're right. These are supposed to be drug-free zones."

"Which just means it's underground, but it's always there," Denny said. He walked back to his coffeepot and replaced the carafe. "You guys eat up and enjoy. The rest of them will be up here soon enough."

"We could hope they will be," Troy said. "It looks like the storm has abated."

"Maybe you guys can all get out of here today," Denny said. "Me, I'll stay if I can."

"Why?"

"This is home for me," he said. "When the next crew comes in, they'll still need food, and I'll be here, waiting for them." And, with that, he added, "I'll take a short nap and come back before the rest of the crew expects a real breakfast."

As soon as he left, she looked at Troy. "I don't think Denny is involved in this."

"I don't either," Troy said quietly. "Like he said, this is his home. It hurts him to see people abusing it. He knows what bad is, and, in comparison, this is pretty good. He doesn't want anything to ruin it."

"True enough."

The guys arrived soon afterward. Mason walked in and

took one look at the treats. His eyebrows shot up, and he hurried over to the pan to snag one of the bear claws. Just as he went to grab it, Axel reached down and swooped it out from under his hand. When he glared at his big friend, Axel just chuckled with laughter.

She smiled up at them. "Glad to see you guys got some sleep."

"We both caught a couple hours," Mason said. "What happened to you?"

"Yeah, ask Troy about that," she said in disgust.

Troy explained what Jonesy had done.

"Interesting."

"Yeah, so I think we should go back to the medical clinic," Troy said. "I want to check for something else down there."

"Go for it," Mason said. "Go alone if you like. Berkley can hang out with us."

"Perfect."

"You want to tell us what you're looking for?" Axel asked.

"A date-rape drug," he said. He quickly disappeared out the door.

BACK IN THE medical clinic, Troy was happy to see that at least power had been restored inside the room. With the lights on, and the door locked, he quickly went through all the cabinets. Not only were they devoid of any personal things from the doctor himself but he found no sign of the date-rape drug he was looking for. He went through every drawer and every cupboard.

It wasn't until Troy got to the guy's computer system

that he finally hit pay dirt. In the little computer desk drawer, at the very back, he spied a bottle of it. He stared at it, realizing the bottle was half empty. He swore gently.

"Well, that explains that," he said. He grabbed a pair of gloves, pulled out the bottle, and stuck it into a little baggie, which he stuffed into his pocket. They had searched the bodies last night, and there hadn't been anything, but, once on the doctor's computer system, Troy logged on and came to a password screen. He sat here and stared at it for a long moment, then typed in the name of the date-rape drug. Instantly the screen opened up.

He shook his head at that, wrote a text message, and sent it to Mason. And then he went through the photos. Photos and emails, all communications in and out. And his heart got sadder and sadder as he worked. The doctor was involved, and, according to this, he had given the women each a dose, though he hadn't been the one taking the photos. As such, the one taking the photos hadn't been administering the drugs. Then together, they had charged the men for access. When each woman woke up—broken, beaten, and bloody— of course she couldn't remember anything.

But here the doc listed the three recent women, and un- fortunately he listed two others from a couple years ago. The photos were here too, and the dates that they were raped, and then the dispersion of all the related photographs too. He quickly downloaded it all and sent everything in a file to Mason, copying himself too.

When a knock came on the door, he waited with the monitor off. The knock came again, but, when Troy heard somebody rattling the doorknob, he quickly raced to hide behind the door. He heard sounds of metal scraping metal, and then the door was pushed open. The light flicked on, and a man stepped in. The door was gently closed behind him, but he didn't turn to see Troy standing there. He walked forward as Troy studied him from the back, unsure who it was.

But when he walked to the monitor and sat down at the computer to log in, Troy stepped forward and asked, "What are you looking for?"

The man turned and looked at him in shock.

Troy realized who it was. "Hello, Lionel."

Lionel's face flushed with anger. "What the fuck do you know?" he roared, standing upright.

Then the last of the tumblers clicked in Troy's head. "I know that you were abused," he said gently. "I know what they did to you."

Lionel's eyes filled with tears, and he angrily wiped them away. "You don't know anything. You don't fucking know anything." He raised his fist, as if he would fight off Troy, which was highly unlikely since Troy was at least sixty pounds heavier and another six inches taller.

"I'm not here to hurt you, Lionel."

"Everybody on this damn rig is here to hurt me," he said.

"Did you have anything to do with sabotaging the rig?"

"No," Lionel said.

"Are you sure about that?"

"Is that what this is about? Haven't enough people died already?"

"Haven't enough people been abused already?" Troy said instantly.

"I don't know what you're talking about," he said, and he sat back down at the computer. Realizing that Troy had gotten beyond the log-on screen, he turned to look at Troy, profoundly sad. "What did you find?"

"I found a lot, and all of it makes me sick." Troy watched him intently but from the far side of the room. Lionel was a wild card, and he'd been through a lot. "Are you okay from the drugs?"

Lionel shrugged. "Maybe," he said.

"Where is your brother?"

"He's fine, sleeping off the drugs I gave him," he said. "He's in my room, under the bunk."

"Why would you drug your brother?" And of course they hadn't searched Lionel's room. There hadn't been any need to. They'd taken a cursory look but that was all.

"It was an easy way to prevent him from stopping me."

"What are your plans?" Troy asked, leaning his back against the door, his arms over his chest.

Lionel glared at him. "You don't know anything," he said. "I have a plan. At least I will have."

"So, explain it to me," he said. "Try me. I'm here, and I'm listening."

"So what if you are?" Lionel said, his voice suddenly weary. "Nobody gives a shit. Nobody gave a shit all this time, and I doubt you'll give a shit either."

"Why, because I work for the company?"

"The company is the worst," he said. "They're in on it, you know?"

At that, Troy straightened. "Are they?" He wanted to keep Lionel talking, but he also didn't want to scare him away yet. He still needed information.

"Yes," he said. "At least some of them, probably not all."

"Did you have anything to do with all those deaths?"

"No," he said, and then he gave a broken sigh. "But I'm not upset at all that they're dead."

"Were they the ones who abused you?"

Lionel stared at him, tears once again in the corner of his eyes. "How do you know?" he asked, in a broken whisper.

Troy had his own phone on, recording the video and the audio on this discussion. However, he held up the other phone he had in his pocket, one of the managers' phones. "Because, after figuring out what they did to the women," he said, "it wasn't a far leap to figure out that maybe you were next."

"Yeah, I was next," he said. "I didn't have a clue about what had happened. At least not the first time. And then, after the second time, I wondered."

"Jesus." Troy swore several times fluently. "I'm sorry, man. That really sucks."

Lionel started to weep. "No," he said. "It's more than that, more than it sucks. I wanted to die when I realized what happened."

"But how did you figure it out?"

"You mean, besides the pain? One of the guys showed me a picture," he said, "I was completely buck naked, and, … and they took photos."

"Shit." Troy couldn't imagine the betrayal he felt. "Do you know who it was?"

"I know a bunch of them, but I don't know all of them. And I don't know how many people saw those photos," he said.

The shame in his tone ripped at Troy's heart. "Lionel, it's not your fault. You know? They're abusers. These guys, they're just abusers who get off on power trips like this, knowing they can do something to you while you can't do anything about it."

"It wouldn't have been so bad, not knowing and all,"

Lionel said, "until I saw the photos. And then they started to show people the photos. They started taking money for the next time."

Troy swallowed hard. "The next time? Any idea how many times?"

"No. I never knew when it would happen. I didn't know if it was in my food or my coffee. I didn't know if it was in my water. For all I know, I got shot up with it too."

"So you have no idea if it was more than three or four times?"

"No, but the last time I woke up, … bleeding," he said. "More than the other times. It was brutal. I could hardly even move. I managed to get to the doctor, and that's when I realized he was part of it."

"How did you find that out?"

"Because he wasn't even surprised. He said, 'They shouldn't have …' and then stopped talking." Lionel was too choked up to continue.

"Jesus," Troy said, "I'm sorry. The doctor is dead now."

"Yep, he is," Lionel said, standing up. "And what will you do about it?"

"I'm not doing anything about it," Troy said. "When daylight comes, I'm getting on a helicopter, and I'm leaving this place."

"You better take her with you."

"Why is that?"

"She was next," he said. "I heard them talking about it. I was trying to figure out what to do for myself, when I heard them saying that they wanted a woman again, and they wanted her."

"Do you know if they still have any plans for her?"

"Well, the four managers are dead, and I don't know

who else is involved," he said. "But I can guarantee you, it will be at least one of the guys who's still here."

"Maybe," Troy said, "I hope not. But I don't have a problem taking them out either. The ocean can have them, for all I care. Sick bastards." Troy stared solemn-eyed at the young man who'd been so painfully abused by the people he worked with. "But, Lionel, I need you to stop punishing them."

"I didn't kill them," he said quietly. "I applaud whoever did, but I didn't do it."

"Seriously?" Troy felt the shock all the way through his bones.

"Yeah, seriously. I came here looking for evidence to prove what had happened, because I'm going after the company for millions. This happened on their watch, under their atmosphere of assault and abuse, and they turned a blind eye," he said. "All I need is evidence to get money for help to get over all this," he said. "I don't even know if I'll be okay ever again. The doc couldn't do very much, and I'm still bleeding."

"Why didn't you run when the explosion happened? Why didn't you take your chance to get off?"

"I wanted to," he said, "and then I realized that, with everybody gone, I'd have a better chance of finding out who all was behind this. I've got one of the managers' phones, and that told me a lot. It's bad news, all of it. Those three women and me, and now I know they've been stalking Berkley." He pulled a phone from his pants pocket. "Look at this." Quickly he opened several photos, and they were all of Berkley. Unfortunately they were from her office, outside her door, and even in the bathroom.

"Damn it," Troy said. "Is there any of her in her bedroom?"

Lionel nodded, switched to another set of photos, finding a picture of her bed, Berkley lying in it. And Troy knew that meant somebody could quite possibly have seen him with Berkley last night.

She was in more danger than ever.

CHAPTER 14

"AND HOW ARE things going between you and Troy?" Axel asked.

She beamed up at him. "Great," she said. "He's a good guy."

"That he is," Axel said.

Mason nodded, a knowing grin on his face; then he looked down at his phone and swore. He bolted to his feet. "You two stay together, okay?"

"Will do," Axel said and watched Mason disappear.

"Where is he going?"

"Either Troy or Nelson must have texted him," Axel said. He got up and walked over to the pan of bear claws and grabbed another one. "Do you think Denny will mind if we eat them all before breakfast?"

"Well, since he's not here to stop us, he'll probably be upset, but, at the same time, he'll be thrilled," she said. "It's one of those cases where you want people to enjoy them, but you don't want them to enjoy them so much that you don't have enough for everyone else."

"Good point," he said, yet he still grabbed another one. He sat back down with her, but she stared at him nervously.

"Do you think Troy is okay?"

"Why wouldn't he be?" Axel said.

"Just the way that Mason bolted out of here."

"I'm sure he'll be fine," he said, as he took a big bite. "There's a lot of bolting in our world."

She looked around the empty dining area. "Where is everybody?"

He stopped, looked around the room, then back at her, and said, "Do you really think something has happened to all of them?"

"I don't know," she said. "Like I really don't know."

"Shit," he said. "You really know how to ruin a treat, don't you?" But she stared at him nervously. "Okay, what do you want to do?" He picked up his phone.

She grabbed hers and sent Troy a text, asking if he was okay. The response came right back. "Well, Troy says he's okay." With a smile, she texted back. **Good. I was just checking.**

At that, a little heart emoji came right back. She chuckled.

"I'll say again that everything is good with Troy and me," she said.

"Make sure you take some time to get to know him," Axel said.

"Yeah, right," she said. "Like we've had a whole lot of time, haven't we?"

"You can learn a lot about a guy in a situation like this," Axel said. "Seriously."

"Yep, absolutely. And, like I said, he's a good guy."

"Well, in that case," he said, "instead of the barbecue on the weekend being at Mason's, it'll be at my place. Why don't you bring him?"

She looked at him in delight. "You know what? I just might manage that."

He grinned. "Good, because you never know. We've got

to take these things one day at a time. Life is over way too fast in some cases."

"I hear you," she said quietly. "It's not exactly how I want to think about life, but you're right." As she sat there, nursing her coffee, she sent Troy several more texts. **Can I come down there?**

No.

Please.

No.

Okay, I'm coming.

NO!

Laughing, she texted back. **Okay, just teasing.**

Make sure that you are.

Not in any danger here.

How do you figure that?

Nobody even around. Just Axel and me.

Where's Mason?

Took off in a hurry.

I'll call him.

"Troy will call Mason to make sure everything's okay."

"Well, I tried myself, except he's not answering," Axel said, staring down at his phone. "I'll try Nelson." He lifted his phone to his ear, trying to call him. But, when he got no answer, he looked at her, clearly concerned.

"Go," she said.

Immediately he shook his head. "Hell no, I'm not leaving you behind."

"Well, you should," she said. "We can't have any more people hurt."

"Exactly," he said with emphasis.

She glared at him. "If I order you, will you go?"

He burst out laughing.

She sat here, her chin propped on her palm. "Then let's

both go," she said.

"No," he said. "That's not happening either."

"Are you sure?"

"Absolutely I'm sure," he said.

Just then the door opened, and Troy walked in, but he wasn't alone. She looked over at the man beside him and bolted to her feet. "Lionel," she cried out and raced toward him.

He gave her a wan smile but let her hug him. In fact, as she held him close, he wrapped his arms around her, and what started off as a gentle hug, ended up with the two of them almost supporting each other upright.

She looked at him and whispered, "Are you okay?"

He shook his head. "Not sure I'll ever be okay again," he whispered.

She led him to her spot and sat him gently down on the chair. "I was so afraid they'd done to you what they did to Tabitha."

He looked at her with huge puffy eyes.

"Oh, God," she whispered.

He nodded slowly.

"This is an outrage," she whispered to Lionel. She grabbed another chair to sit down beside him and looked at Troy to see if he understood but could tell from the look on his face that he did.

Axel stood, went for coffee, and brought a stout cup of black coffee to Lionel, sitting across the table from him. Without saying a word, Lionel seemed to calm down some.

She patted Lionel softly on the shoulder as she got up and huddled with Troy, to have a private conversation. "Evidence of it?"

"Date-rape drug," Troy whispered, as he nodded, then

turned his back to Lionel, drawing Berkley closer, so the poor guy couldn't hear more. "Lionel was knocked out several times and then attacked. They used him, took photos, and when he woke up again, he had no idea except that he'd been abused and sometimes beaten. It happened at least three times, possibly four or five. He's not even sure. The last time they left him bleeding pretty badly. He went to the doctor, and that's when he realized the doc already knew about it, even made a comment about something they shouldn't have done."

"That little bastard." She straightened, her hands clenched into fists.

Troy grabbed her and said, "Slow down. He's already dead. Remember?"

"Too bad," she growled. "I'd like to punch him into the ground myself."

"And we also have the doctor's phone and the other manager's phone, plus the doctor's computer," he said, "and it's more damning than anything. I have emailed the photos and the schedule."

"Schedule?" she said, in a horrified voice.

"Yes, schedule."

"Let me see it," she said. He brought it up on his phone, and she studied it in shock. "They planned these attacks? And they organized them in advance?" Something was almost familiar about it, but she didn't really understand why.

"Yes," he said, "they did."

Berkley was shocked. "That's pretty low for anybody,' she said. "But to plan something like this, over and over again? That's sick."

"Oh, it gets worse," Troy said. He brought up the calendar again, tapped a day several days ago, and said, "This was on the schedule before the blast."

She looked down at it and slowly sank back against the wall, looking dumbfounded. "It's got my name right there."

He nodded. "They were done abusing Lionel for a while, and they wanted a woman again."

She stared up at him, feeling heartsick. "They would do to me what they did to Tabitha?"

"Yeah," he said. "You were on the schedule. So whoever caused the sabotage kept you from being drugged and raped. You could have been really hurt."

THERE WAS NO easy way to tell her, but Troy figured blunt and straightforward was the best. But then the look on her face about did him in. He wrapped her up in his arms, and she curled up against him. He could feel the shudders rocking through her. He looked over at Axel, the two of them sharing a look, still amazed to be shocked at the depravity of some people.

Troy gently moved Berkley over to the table with Axel and Lionel.

"What was it Denny said? Something about a group of men like this?" Troy asked.

"I think that was Chucky," Axel said. "I think those two knew more than they let on."

"Maybe so," Troy said. "And maybe that's why they wanted out. Maybe that's why they were so sick of life here and what they were seeing and hearing evidence of."

"Probably," Axel said. "Bastards."

Now with Lionel and Berkley here, both of them shattered by the news and revelations, Troy wasn't even sure what the next step was. He had to keep them both safe before whatever group of assholes decided to try to hurt them again.

"We can't know who all is involved though, can we? Are they listed?" she asked.

"Quite a few of them are listed, yes," Troy said. "They paid for the honor."

A shudder racked through her as she stared at him. "Why? Why are men so horrible?" she asked, her voice barely above a whisper.

"Only some men," Troy reminded her. "Lionel has confirmed those he can ID."

Lionel gave a nod, his expression grim, but he seemed to be sitting taller now that he was surrounded by people to support him.

She leaned up against Troy's chest and burrowed against him. "I don't even want to think about it," she said

"The thing is," Troy said, "Lionel says that he woke up in the body bag and doesn't know how he got in there."

She stared at Lionel. "Seriously?"

He nodded. "Yeah, I woke up in the body bag. In the freezer. That was unnerving, I tell you. I managed to get out of the body bag and realized where I was and got out. I thought I was dead for sure, but it was so similar to every other time, only this time it didn't feel like I'd been raped."

"Can you remember what you might have ingested?" Berkley asked him. "They drugged my rum one night."

"I don't really drink alcohol," Lionel stated.

"Any idea otherwise how you might have ended up drugged?"

"No," he said. "I've racked my brain about it, but I don't know."

"Your brother is still here," Berkley said. "You know that, right?"

"I really wanted to tell him," he said. "I've been worried about explaining this to him, but then I didn't have the guts to."

"I get it," Troy said. They stared out over the oceans as the sun rose. It was still stormy and ugly outside, but a little bit more daylight was breaking through.

"Can we get off the rig today?" she asked.

"I hope so," Troy said. "I presume you're done with wanting to stay."

"I'm very done," she said, in a quiet voice. "I won't be coming back here again."

"No, this culture is not good for anybody," he said.

"I know," she whispered. "But we still haven't found who's behind all this."

Just then Mason and Nelson walked in.

"So, what the hell's going on?" she asked Mason, hopping to her feet.

He studied her face for a long moment. "Well, we appear to have brought something to light," he said, "but you won't want to hear it."

"If you're telling us about Lionel here," she said, stepping back so they could see Lionel, "and that I was on the calendar as being the next victim for their nasty pay-to-play events, I already know."

He nodded. "Glad I didn't have to tell you that," he said in a clipped voice. "Chucky and Winslow are up, and they'll join us here," he said. "I stopped in to talk to Denny, and he's on his way back here too."

"What about the others?" Troy said.

"Well, Bruce, as we know, is dead, so we need Jonesy

and Idiot to join everybody too," Axel said.

"Right," she said. "Well, Jonesy is a little worse for wear, after Troy beat the crap out of him. What's up with the pilot?"

"He's fine. He's staying with our men."

"And Daniel, the foreman?" she asked.

"Right, that's who I was looking for. Where is his room?" Mason asked.

Lionel gave it to him. Then added, "But he's in my room."

"We'll go wake him up," Mason said.

"What about the company man, Gregor?" Troy asked.

"Yeah, we knocked on his door earlier," he said. "If he's not up, we'll rap on it again, after we wake up Daniel." Mason and Nelson both left.

"I'll put on more coffee," Berkley said.

Troy got up to walk over and check on her. "Are you okay?"

She looked at him and gave him a dark look. "Just rattled. It's a little hard to realize that you've been targeted, and they had you on a calendar, scheduled for that kind of abuse," she said. "It's pretty upsetting."

"It is," he said, as he helped her put on another pot. "It could get really ugly coming up. You know that, right?"

"Uglier?" she asked, skeptical. "I'm not sure that's possible."

"Yes," he said, "it actually could."

She shrugged. "If you say so."

Just then several more blasts came, and the four of them stared at each other in shock. Troy and Axel were at the door instantly. Berkley went back to Lionel and waved at them. "Go, go, go."

Troy hesitated, then shook his head. "We stay together. Both of you come on."

Lionel looked at him. "Leave me here," he said, his voice broken. "Maybe they'll blast me into the ocean too."

Troy wasn't having anything to do with that, and he grabbed one of Berkley's hands and one of Lionel's arms and hauled them down and outside.

They could hear creaking steel and metal as the rig suffered.

"I don't think any of us are intended to get off this rig alive," she cried out.

"It'll be fine," Troy said. "We have a navy ship close at hand," he said, "so we've got a way off. But I want to make sure that whoever is here has another way to get themselves off too. We can take everybody, but we need to all be in one place."

As he spoke, another huge crash came, and one part of the rig started to collapse. She screamed as Troy pulled the three of them underneath the shelter, as the steel railing from above came down.

"We didn't get up to check the top of the rig, did we?" Berkley asked.

"No," he said. "It probably wouldn't have made a difference anyway, because whoever did this has been working all night to get around us."

"One guy can get around pretty hidden from sight in this rig," Lionel said, but his voice was faint, and he looked terrified.

"What about the helicopter?" she asked.

Troy nodded. "We'll take you both up there right now."

They headed toward the chopper. As they got up there, Chucky and Winslow were already there, waiting. They looked relieved when they saw them.

"Please tell me that you've got a pilot for this bird."

"Not at the moment, but we will have," Troy said. "We're getting everybody up here. I'm not sure what's going on, but everybody needs to be evacuated."

Just then another blast rumbled throughout the rig, and the part they stood on listed and dropped about six inches.

CHAPTER 15

BERKLEY SCREAMED AND hung on to the railing.

Troy looked at Winslow and Chucky. "You two keep these two here and stay together. I have to go help the others."

The two men nodded, grim but determined, as they reached out and grabbed hold of Lionel.

"You knew, didn't you?" Lionel asked.

"We suspected something," he said, "but, no, we didn't know. We would have stopped it if we'd known for sure, and we just found out a couple days ago."

"Just before the first blast?" she asked.

He nodded. "Yeah, somebody was posting pictures, and we accidentally saw them."

"Jesus," she swore, feeling sick.

Chucky looked at Lionel. "We're so sorry."

"Yeah, I am too," Lionel said. "This isn't exactly something that you walk away from."

"No, it isn't."

The wind picked up just then, carrying everybody's words away. They clung to each other beside the helicopter, which was still strapped down, as more blasts continued to erupt around them.

"This whole place will go down," she screamed.

Chucky nodded. "It will." He looked over at Winslow.

"How is your helicopter flying?"

"Hell no," he said, "I can't stand to fly anyway. I do it under duress only."

The two men looked at Lionel and Berkley. "Either of you know how to fly?"

She shook her head as several men climbed up the ladder on the side, and one of them was the pilot. "Here's our pilot," she said, and they all cheered.

He hopped into the helicopter as Gregor arrived, and then Troy came up, carrying Jonesy over his shoulder, who was still unconscious or perhaps passed out. Troy laid him down not-so-gently on the deck and disappeared again.

Axel came up, dragging Idiot and Denny.

Denny was shaking. "Oh, my God, oh, my God," he cried out. "Why would somebody do this?"

She reached out a hand and grabbed his. "I'm so sorry," she said. "The next place will become home too. You'll see."

He looked at her sadly. "No," he said. "It won't."

The pilot started the rotors on the helicopter and began his usual preflight procedures.

The others were gathered to get access to the helicopter, and she realized that there weren't enough seats. She looked up and swore, then looked at the pilot. "We have too many people."

"I know," he said grimly.

Gregor hopped in and said, "Well, this is my helicopter, so you can damn well be sure I'm going in."

At that, Denny looked over, and Gregor nodded and said, "Denny, get up here. Chucky, Winslow, let's go."

It was almost as if he were picking and choosing who he would save. And she knew in her heart of hearts it wouldn't be her. She hadn't had anything to do with him all this time that he'd been here. But would he let Mason, Nelson, Axel, and Troy die too?

Just then a big life raft was tossed over the side. She stared at it in shock. As she looked up, Troy and Axel were coming up onto the top deck. Axel picked up Jonesy and tossed him into the life raft and Idiot too, screaming the whole way. "Keep a close watch on those two," Troy yelled to someone below.

Berkley heard the life raft take off.

As Troy ran over to her, he reached for Gregor and pulled him out of the helicopter. When she turned to look back at Axel in shock, he had somebody in his grasp too. It was Daniel. Lionel still stood beside her.

"Daniel," he called out, and he raced toward him. Daniel gave him a big hug and then stepped back.

"Go, save yourself," he said.

Lionel shook his head. "No," he said. "I need you to come too."

Daniel gave him a gentle look. "No, buddy. This time you'll have to take the trip alone."

"Why?" Lionel cried out, not sure what Daniel was trying to say.

"I'm not coming," Daniel said.

And then Berkley understood. "It was you, wasn't it?" she said. "You saw the same pictures that everybody else did, and you found out what they had done to your brother."

He looked at his brother and nodded. "I didn't know, buddy. I would have done anything to have stopped it. I'm the one who drugged you and put you in the body bag. I was trying to get you away from those assholes, hopefully off the rig, while I made them pay. The fucking supers were damn easy to take out with an overdose of the same drug they used on the others. But I was looking for an opportunity to get rid of the rest, those sickos who paid for the photos, when these new guys arrived."

"How did you score the C-4?" Berkley asked, understanding his rage. She'd felt the same over her girlfriend's rape at the hands of her coworkers but had been helpless to go Daniel's route. She'd planned to make the men pay through the law.

Daniel looked at Lionel. "I told Jude what happened. He offered to score the C-4 and to bring it to me as he was close by. He wanted to stay and to make the men pay too, but I didn't want him to know just what I'd done or how far it had gone. He still loves you, kid. He didn't have any part in this, … but he wanted to protect you."

Lionel started to cry.

She reached out and held him tight. "So you killed them all?" she asked Daniel. "Even Bruce? Was he involved?"

"No, he wasn't, but he saw me kill the doc. I had no choice then. I was already too committed. I'm sorry about killing Bruce. … At one time I wondered if I could get off here alive and have them all be fish food. However, with the new arrivals, it was great in one way but not in others. … Besides, my job isn't quite done," he said. "I've got a beef with one still," he said. "I just had to wait for him to arrive." He turned and glared at Gregor, who immediately started screaming.

"You're fucking nuts," Gregor said. "I didn't have anything to do with it. I don't even know what you're talking about!"

Then the rest of it clicked into place for her—why the schedule had seemed so familiar.

"That's why they were planning the dates," she said. "I

saw the schedule. It was the same dates you were flying in."

"This was not a scheduled flight," he said. "What kind of an idiot are you, anyway?"

"No. It was scheduled, but you canceled it, and then, when the blast blew, you came anyway," she said. "But you were also scheduled to come in for my rape," she said. "The same as you were here every time they drugged Lionel and before that, with my friend Tabitha."

He straightened and glared at her. "You don't know what the hell you're talking about! Do you really think I would have brought these guys in with me if that were the case?"

"Of course," she said. "It was a perfect cover, wasn't it?"

"Well, it was," Daniel said. "Except for one thing that I know. I've got the pictures of you doing my brother."

Gregor's face twisted with disgust. "I'm not a fucking gay homosexual," he said.

"No, and that's why you did it. To put him in his place as, what did you say? *The scum and an abhorrence to this world.*"

Gregor straightened and said, "You can't prove a thing," he said. "You're full of shit."

"Actually I can," he said. "I've already given Axel the proof. And what I don't have, I'm pretty sure Troy and Berkley have already got." He glanced at the two of them, and they both nodded.

"Yes," Berkley said. "I can coordinate his schedule with all the rapes. He was part of it right from the beginning."

"That's what I thought," Daniel said. He walked closer to his brother and gave him a big hug.

Troy was hanging on to Gregor, who even now was trying to get back up into the helicopter.

She looked over at Troy and Axel and said, "There's no room for all of us."

"I know," Troy said. "And we don't have much time now."

"Shit," she said. "I don't have to go into the water, do I?"

"No," he said, with a gentle smile. "At least I don't think so." He said to Lionel, "Come on. Let's get you up into the helicopter."

Lionel shook his head. "Not without my brother."

"No, I'm not going, dude." He looked over at Lionel, smiled, and said, "Remember, I love you, brother." He then made a flying tackle at Gregor, the company man. Picking him up over his shoulder, he made a crazy-ass jump and dove off the edge of the rig.

She screamed, and Lionel screamed, and everybody raced to the edge, where they could see that both men had hit and were speared onto an open piece of metal, swinging free from the blast. Lionel's screams turned into wailing cries.

Berkley grabbed him and held on tight. "I'm so sorry, Lionel, but he'd killed a lot of people over this, and his life would have been a nightmare in prison. I am so sorry for your loss, but you have to go now." With one last hug, she pushed him toward Troy, who picked him up, loaded him into the helicopter, and buckled him into the last spot. "Get going," he shouted at the pilot.

The pilot looked at him in shock and looked down at the company man. "What about you guys?"

"We're covered," he said, jumping off the runner of the chopper and signaling the pilot to go.

In moments the rotors were turning faster, and the pilot lifted the helicopter straight up, then took off, heading toward land.

Then Berkley noted another helicopter coming toward them from a navy ship in the near distance. "How will we get us all on that?" she cried out.

"Well, our other two guys took Nelson and Mason with them, already in the big lifeboat, and they'll deliver Idiot and Jonesy to the authorities for us," he said, "so it's just the three of us left."

When she saw a long strap dangling from the helicopter, hanging down with hooks, she groaned and said, "Seriously?"

"Do you trust me?" Troy asked with a big smile.

She threw her arms around him. "Absolutely."

Axel quickly buckled them up and tugged the rope, so they would start to winch them up.

She looked down at him and panicked. "You have to come," she said. "Jump on right now. The helicopter can carry us, but this rig is going at any moment."

Just then another blast came and a massive creaking sound followed. Axel made one jump and grabbed the winch and the hook that was on the bottom. Troy reached down and grabbed his hand, and together they were swept upward as the winch in the helicopter pulled them higher and higher. Axel was the first one helped in, as the most precariously positioned of the three, and then they were looped over, and both Troy and Berkley landed inside the helicopter. She stared in shock as the blasts continued on the rig, with fires now shooting up from multiple areas, as it self-destructed. Of Daniel and Gregor, the company man, there was absolutely no sign. That part of the rig had fallen under the heavy waves, never to be seen again.

TROY QUICKLY BUCKLED her in, not sure how much of the look on her face was just her body going into shock to protect her from what had happened or simply a total overload of her brain. He sat down beside her, as they were quickly swept back over to the naval ship. "Are you okay?"

She looked at him, still in shock, and then slowly nodded. "I think so," she said. "It was Daniel all the time."

"And it makes sense, right?" Axel said. "There's no love like family."

She nodded. "And poor Lionel, I still can't believe what they did to him."

"And the women," Troy reminded her.

She nodded. "At least now we have an idea of who and what happened, so maybe we can get some closure for the victims."

"The company will have a hell of a time bailing themselves out of this one," he said.

"Not necessarily," she said, "but, if you guys give us a hand, then maybe we can get them. There won't be any criminal charges because it seems all the main players are dead," she said in a broken tone. "But Idiot and Jonesy? Surely they can land some hefty jail time. And maybe the victims can get a settlement so they can get help to move forward."

"Exactly," he said. "Stay positive. These things take a lot of time, but this will work out."

She reached over and slipped her hand in his. "Thank you."

He grinned. "Hey, remember that date part?"

"Yeah, didn't we say Italian?"

"Nope," he said. "We said Japanese."

"We said Italian," she said, staring out at the water. "I

distinctly remember Italian."

"You know something? I'm pretty sure it was Japanese," he said, "but that just means we'll have to go out twice."

She smiled, looked up at him, and said, "I think I can manage that."

As soon as they disembarked, he helped her to a room on the destroyer, where they were quickly debriefed and then given a bunk room for their own use.

As she walked into the small room, she shook her head. "So how long will we be here?"

"Just a couple days," he said. "Once we get a little closer to land, we'll fly you back in again and head home, down to the base."

"I'm from San Diego," she said. "You're from Coronado."

"Same diff," he said. He dropped his bag on the floor.

"How come you have gear?" she asked suspiciously. "And I lost everything?"

"Not quite everything," he said. "I did scoop up your laptop and a few things. It's in my bag," he said. "Mine is full of the extra weapons we brought. We didn't want them to go under if they didn't have to."

"I didn't get a shower. Do you mind?"

"Not at all," he said, then he explained the navy's shower system to her, so they could make the most efficient use of the water on board.

She came out soon afterward, wearing a robe. "It's strange. I know I'm physically clean," she said, "but, on the inside, I feel dirty."

"Come on. Let's lie down and relax," he said. "You've got a couple hours to yourself," he said. "Then we'll have to go talk to various people, particularly once we tap into land—the bosses and the military police."

"Right," she said, "not to mention the local police and the company reps."

"Exactly," he said.

She laid down on the bed with a blanket over her and said, "You know something?"

"What?"

"I think I'd feel much cleaner if you were with me."

He looked at her for a moment, puzzled. "How does that have anything to do with being clean?"

"Forget *clean*. Let's say, *renewed*. Maybe *refreshed*. How about *restoring my faith*?"

"Now that," he said, "I can get behind." He walked to the door, made sure it was locked, and then stripped down in front of her.

"I'm barely dressed as it is," she said, throwing back the blanket. "I only came out in a robe and my underwear."

"Still way too many clothes," he said, and, completely nude, he climbed in beside her.

She sat up, quickly divested herself of the robe and her bra and panties, and looked at him. "I didn't really expect this to happen when I put out that SOS."

"But you did ask for help, and you never know what you'll get back." He laughed. "Besides, I don't think there's anything I like better than helping damsels in distress."

She reached up and placed a finger on his lips. "As long as this isn't the typical result from all that rescuing."

He chuckled and pulled her down. "No way. This is a first."

"And the last," she whispered as their lips met.

He kissed her, first gently, then hard, deep, and passionately, as she twisted beneath him with joy in her heart.

She realized that it was finally over. They were safe, and everything in her world would be okay again. She would have to mourn the loss of innocence in Tabitha and Lionel, plus the loss of Daniel in her own way. And she would have to help deal with the aftermath for Tabitha and Lionel. That would not be easy. The inquiry and investigation into this nightmare would go on for weeks, months, or perhaps much longer, but she hoped the entire industry would take steps to ensure that such a terrible thing would never happen again and that no one would have to work in such an atmosphere of abuse on the rigs—or elsewhere—ever again.

She was also thankful to not have to go back to that same rig. She knew it was billions of dollars' worth of rig now buried in the sea and that the environmental hazard was also something that would take a long time to mop up, but she couldn't be at all upset that it was destroyed. It represented such evil.

"Stop thinking," he whispered. He kissed her, his tongue sliding along the edge of her lips before delving deep inside.

She wrapped her arms around his neck and held him close. He slid his hands in hers and pulled her arms up over her head, and she moaned as their bodies linked and twisted together. "You feel so damn good," she said.

"There's just something about danger, something about coming close to losing your life."

"I think it's more than that," she said. "It was seeing the depravity of humanity and realizing that, once again, Mother Nature wins. She'll completely absorb all that nastiness, feed it to the fish, and try to move on. I can only hope that I can too."

He kissed her again and again. "You will," he said. "We'll make sure of it."

She smiled. "You're the best thing that came out of that place, you know?"

"No," he whispered, trailing kisses across her cheek, breathing heavily against her ear and her neck. "I'd have to say, you are."

She could feel shudders rocking her body. "Oh, my God, that feels so good," she whispered, twisting beneath him.

He held her hands tight and firm.

She groaned as she tried to touch him but couldn't move. He slid down her body, his kisses leaving a hot moist trail everywhere they went. He latched onto one nipple and suckled deep, and she could feel a response pooling in her abdomen. She groaned, raising her hips, her pelvis pressing against him, as he slid from left to right, giving the other breast the same treatment. Finally he slowly slid his hands down her arms, all the way down her hips to reach underneath and to cup her buttocks and squeezed them gently, all the while his mouth explored her ribs, her belly, and down to the moistness at the heart of her. When he reached for a taste, she shuddered and cried out.

He placed a hand gently over her mouth, and she realized that she could be heard. It was all she could do to keep back the cries as he tasted and delved and teased, until she was a liquid pool of mind-numbing jelly. When he finally rose up, she grabbed him by the hair and tugged him all the way up and then down to her lips. She kissed him deeply, and he finally slid all the way inside her body.

"Now that feels like a welcome home," she whispered, smiling.

He lifted his head and smiled back at her and said, "I think that's the nicest thing I've heard yet."

"I mean it," she said. "It's been a long time of traveling and feeling like I was missing something in my life."

"Well, hopefully we can find it together," he said, "because I'm sure as hell not letting you go back to an oil rig like that one again."

She smiled and wrapped her legs around him. "Agreed. How about we find a place and sort ourselves out for a bit and figure out our future together?"

He started to move, building up the pace faster and faster, diving deeper and harder into the heart of her. It was all she could do to hang on and to not let her cries rip out through the destroyer they were on. When she finally crashed over the edge of the cliff, he cried out gently above her and then slowly sagged down.

Wrapping her up in his arms, he whispered, "How about we figure out our future together every day, knowing that we have all the tomorrows ahead of us?"

With tears in her eyes, she whispered, "That sounds beautiful to me."

"So sleep now," he whispered. "And, when you wake up, it'll be a whole new day."

She did exactly that. She slept deeply and beautifully peaceful, feeling safe with him at her side.

Dale Mayer

BOOK-25

PROLOGUE

AXEL SALISBURY ALMOST leaped out of the office building; he was so happy the day was over. He'd been training on a software inventory management system. Office work. *Ugh.* As far as he was concerned, it was a load of crap. But their skill sets had to be updated on a regular basis. He'd much rather go out for target practice or for a workout in the gym or even for basic maintenance on their gear, but it wasn't to be. Today was all about paper-pushing. He was a fighter, not a writer. He shuddered at that. As he threw his bag into the back of his Jeep, a shout came across the parking lot. He turned to see Mason. Axel walked across, shook his hand, and said, "You look like you recovered from that lovely trip we just completed."

Mason nodded, his face grim. "That was a mess, wasn't it?"

"The place wasn't so bad," Axel said, "but the people? Wow."

"The company's going through quite the headaches right now, between the government court cases and overhauling their employment practices, not to mention dealing with the fallout from the sabotage and the lawsuits from the sexual assault victims."

"Sounds like they needed to do something about it a long time ago," Axel said, shaking his head. "And, so far, it's been quiet since we got home."

"Not anymore," Mason said. "I need you on a team with me right now."

Axel looked at him in surprise. "Now?"

"Somebody'll be in front of your place in thirty minutes," he said. "We've got a submarine down with eleven men and one woman on board."

"One of ours?" Odd that it would have so few crew.

"It's a new generation sub, smaller, more agile. Crew went down, doing some testing on it. And they're stuck. We're flying out in ninety minutes."

At that, Axel nodded and said, "I'll go home and grab my to-go bag." He walked back to his Jeep, hopped in, and drove toward his apartment. He parked, grabbed his laptop bag, went in, his mind already sorting through what he might need to add to his already prepped to-go duffel. He prided himself on being ready in minutes. Lives often depended on it.

He was outside and waiting as a truck came by and picked him up. Mason wasn't among the crew. Someone said he had taken an earlier flight with Nelson. Both would meet them on the next leg. Axel nodded and took the last empty place in the vehicle. "Do we have an update on the sub's crew?"

"Last communication said they were alive, but that was over an hour ago," the driver stated, "but they've been beached on the sea floor."

"Anybody know why?"

"An onboard explosion." came the driver's terse answer.

Axel nodded and thought about that. "So oxygen's the issue." He studied the three guys with him. He knew Dane and Cooper from Mason's crew. But the guy beside him, he didn't know. He reached out a hand and said, "I'm Axel."

"Baylor Massey."

Axel nodded and didn't say anything. He'd heard a lot of names before, but that one was a first.

They hit the naval airport, loaded onto the cargo plane, and were airborne within another twenty minutes. Sitting in the back, it was noisy, and nobody did any talking. Axel wished to heck he had a little more intel. He hated walking into a scenario blind, but, in these rescue situations, it often came down to a need-to-know basis. When they landed, he knew they would hit the ground running. He tried to nap as much as he could, so he had some energy for what was about to come.

CHAPTER 1

O NCE THEY LANDED, they were picked up and taken to the dock area.

"Are we ready to head out to sea?" Axel asked Mason, who stood, hands on hips, studying their new surroundings.

Nelson remained silent beside Mason, only a chin lift as his greeting to Axel.

Mason gave a hard, clipped nod. "Yes." With that, they all marched down the dock, jumped onto the Zodiacs, and headed out to a destroyer.

As he climbed on board, Axel asked, "Any briefing?"

"Not much to tell you, as the information is thin on the ground," Mason said. "Looks like we'll have to go down in the rescue subs to see what's up."

Axel nodded at that. This six-man team would all ride in one pressurized submersible for the initial search. Other rescue subs were available as needed. Hopefully the rescue subs would have more occupants on the way back up. However, only one rescue sub could attach to the downed sub at a time. "Are we expecting to actually see something?"

"We will. They're not all that deep," Mason said. "But we're hoping this rescue mission is not a recovery one. And, if we can save the sub itself, we need to do that too."

"Got it. Any communication with those on board?"

"Not for two hours."

Axel winced. There could be a lot of reasons for that, but none of them were good. He'd never been in one of these new subs and was thrilled to check it out today, except for the reason why he was here. Fully geared up and ready to hit the water at a moment's notice, he stood inside the rescue sub as they slowly descended.

"We're twenty-four minutes away," Mason said, as an aside.

Axel nodded, watching out the windows as the ocean moved around them. Down here, they were the ones out of their element. They were the intruders. Everybody else resided here. But, just like going to a foreign country, here they were the ones who stood out. Axel heard the engine puttering gently inside and saw the lights of the other subs as they came down.

When they finally found the sunken sub, Axel leaned forward, looking for any available information. They were using powerful lights to see what they could, but, as they slowly skirted alongside the sub, there was nothing to see. "So where is the damage?" he murmured, through the intercom in his helmet.

Everybody stared outside, and communications were sporadic among them. "I'm not seeing any damage to the exterior," Mason said.

"No," Axel said, "so the problem's got to be internal."

He nodded. "We're going in," Mason said.

Their sub had a special lock that attached to the hatch of the disabled submarine. As theirs descended, they quickly prepared to board. As it locked around the bottom hatch, with the water draining out, they opened the hatch into the grounded sub. Axel was the first to jump down. Fully geared with oxygen, he slowly made his way into the new prototype sub. Behind him, the other five men were coming just as fast.

Once they were in, Axel headed forward. He wasn't even sure what he would find at this point. As he got closer to the engine room, where they expected to see people, he found two men, both dead. As he slowly checked them over, he saw bullet holes in their foreheads. He held up a hand, stopping the men behind him and pointed downward.

Mason was right behind Axel when he saw the bullet holes. Mason stared at Axel, who responded with a grim nod and moved forward. Now it was a whole different story. This didn't look like an accident at all; this was sabotage. What he didn't know was if any of the twelve-person crew was alive. With the other men spreading out, Axel would check the engine room. Two more dead had been found aft, and, as Axel went down, he found another four bodies. Now they had eight, all dead, all shot with a single bullet hole in the forehead. He came back up to find the rest of his group standing together. "So we're missing four then?"

"Nope," Mason said. "I found two in the kitchen, so we're only missing two."

"One's dead in the bathroom as well," Dane said. "So we're missing only one."

"Looks like the same gun took out the ones I've seen," Axel said.

"Exactly," Mason said. "I'm assuming our missing man is the one who did this."

"Then where is he?" Axel asked. He looked around at the sub. "And what did he do to bring it down?"

"Looks like the navigation system is fried," said Cooper in the back, as he worked on the instrument panel.

"Can we get the sub to rise?" Mason asked.

"Not by its own power, but we can do a rescue mission

and lift it to the surface," Cooper said. "We'll have to replace this entire panel before we can figure out what's going on."

"So how did the last man get out?" Baylor asked.

"Likely from the torpedo tube," Mason said, his tone grim. "It would take a bit of a trick though."

"Meaning, they needed somebody inside to actually operate it?" Axel asked.

Mason frowned. "I don't know for sure. We'd have to check on how these new torpedo tube launchers work. Usually the idea is that they're locked and loaded, then fired. If the last man was inside a missile tube, he couldn't have done the job by himself."

"Unless there were two saboteurs," Axel said slowly. "And one killed himself on board."

"It's possible." Baylor added, "One man here is sporting a broken leg and a bullet down low."

"Does he also have a bullet in his forehead?" Axel asked. "Where is he?"

"Outside the torpedo room," said Baylor.

"Let me take a look," Axel replied.

"We'll all take a look," Mason said, "but we also need to relay what we found."

"So we either do a recovery or take the entire sub up as it is," Axel said.

"We'll bring down a repair crew to see if they can get this mobile. We'll move all the bodies into one area," Mason said. "But let's check this one out first." Upon closer review, they confirmed that this man had, indeed, been shot low and had a broken leg, with a crutch close by. "I'll say this was the guy. He was attacked, knew he wouldn't make it, and took his own life. That bullet's in the temple, not in the forehead like the rest."

"Right, so we need to gather all the information we can on him," Axel said.

Mason nodded. "There'll be a full investigation into this," Mason said, "but that'll come later."

"Do we know for a fact that our shooter is gone?" Baylor asked.

Mason turned, looked at him, and said, "Do you have reason to believe somebody else is on this ship?"

"You've got to wonder," Nelson said.

"Check it out then," Mason ordered.

And, with that, the four men took off, leaving Axel and Mason. "What about the other rescue subs?"

"They can't come in while we're locked onto the hatch," Mason said. "While we're doing recon and relaying the information upward, they'll prepare a crew to come down and see if they can fix this enough to make it rise. Otherwise, they'll have to use the balloons to bring it up."

"That will take a couple days. But, if nobody in here is left to save, the timing won't particularly matter, I guess," Axel said. He shook his head. "Damn, boss. I don't know what I expected, but this wasn't it."

"No, it's not what we wanted at all," Mason replied.

"So, the last communication was recent, like, two hours ago?"

Mason nodded. "According to my intel anyway. More like three hours plus now," he said. "And that intel hasn't been too accurate so far."

"Do we know who sent the last communique?"

"Private Hostettler," he said. "I've got the rest of my team topside gathering all communications to and from this sub."

Axel bent and checked the name tag on this last man.

The one with the injured leg and the gunshot in the temple. "Hostettler, that's this guy," he said.

"So we're assuming that he wasn't calling for help then?"

"It was a garbled message," Mason said. "Sounds like the radio guys couldn't make much sense of it."

"I'd say it didn't," Axel noted with a frown, "but, at the same time, we have no way to know what really went on down here."

"Well, we do know a lot more now," Mason said, "but none of it's good. Eleven dead men on board. Damn it."

"What do you want to do with the bodies for now?" Axel asked.

"Let's put them in that one stateroom," he said. "Makes for an easier recovery. That way the new crew can come in here, see if they can fix the sub, and bring it to the surface." And that's what they did. When the others rejoined them, Mason looked over and asked, "Did you find anything else?"

The men shook their heads, but a frown was on Baylor's face. "No, but—"

"What made you think we aren't alone?" Mason asked.

"I thought I heard something earlier, but we couldn't find anything."

"Anything else?" Mason asked, trying to clarify this issue.

Baylor shook his head. "No, but—did you ever just have a feeling somebody was there?"

"We can't let another crew down here without resolving this," Axel said.

"Let's do a full sweep then," Mason ordered. "We've all had that feeling enough to know not to discount it."

They started at the aft and slowly worked their way through, checking everywhere—up and down, shafts, compartments, looking at every possible hiding place. With the blueprints in his head, Mason quickly directed them through every section. When they came to the engine room, he stopped and said, "Okay, so there should be a twelfth person on board," he said, "and it's possible that's the person who left the sub," he said.

"Wait. Something's not right," Baylor said. "Damn it all, I should have put this together before. That twelfth person isn't a guy."

"Right. One woman is on the crew," Axel stated.

"Exactly. But not just a crewman. It's Dr. Ally Minga," Mason said with a nod.

"So, if she's here, do we really suspect she's the one who's done all this?" Axel motioned to the devastation behind them.

"I wouldn't think it likely," Mason said. "Tesla's worked with her some before."

"Well, she's obviously not one of the bodies," Baylor said. "So where is she?"

"We haven't exactly identified ourselves," Axel said. "If she's alive, she could be hiding and thinking this sub is still under siege."

"True enough," Mason said. He walked over and hit the sub's PA system, and, after first identifying himself, he continued, "Dr. Minga, let us know where you are. If you're injured, we're here to help. Eleven dead men are on board. We have a downed sub, and you're the only one unaccounted for. Oxygen will be a problem soon, so we need to locate and remove you quickly."

When he stopped speaking, they all were silent and listened. Within seconds, an ever-so-slight tapping sound could be heard. Axel looked up and headed toward the main hallway. Up above was one of the tunnels for the HVAC system. A little farther on, he found a somewhat removable screen. With a tall stretch he could just about lift it. Behind him, Baylor gave him a boost, and Axel popped the screen off to the side. Jumping, he grabbed hold of the edges of the opening with both hands, and, with a little more help from Baylor, he lifted himself into the tunnel.

"Dr. Minga?" Axel called out. More tapping came from farther down. He slowly worked his way through the HVAC system. Subs were meant to be highly efficient, and every square inch was important, so maneuvering in the tight space was not an easy chore. He didn't get very far when he saw something up ahead. "Dr. Minga?"

Again the tapping.

As he got closer, he realized she faced him, her head and arms mostly visible. But she was pinched in where the system narrowed. He reached out a hand and squeezed her fingers. "Are you hurt?"

She squeezed back twice.

"Can you move at all?" He heard a slow exhale.

"Yes," she said, "with help. It's my leg."

"Okay," he said. "I'll back up, and I want you to come toward me." He slowly shifted her arms until they were stretched out in front of her. He backed up a few inches at a time and slowly dragged her toward him, clearly causing her pain. When he got to the opening, he knew Baylor would be there, ready to help. Alex slid down partially and found Baylor ready for him.

"I've got Dr. Minga here, but she's hurt. I'll have to pull her down headfirst." Immediately, willing hands reached up, and Axel slowly lowered the woman from the hatch and passed her headfirst to Baylor. Mason and Nelson were there as well, supporting her torso as it appeared. With Axel slowly moving her out of the shaft to the men below, he tried to support her legs, but one was clearly badly broken. He could see her wince and could feel her shudder. He heard her whimper as her leg went over the edge and down.

Even with his best efforts, Axel couldn't stop her from taking a jarring blow as gravity took over. But, when she was fully down, Axel hopped down too, shifted her so she was seated, and gently propped her up against Mason. Then Axel slapped Baylor on the back and said, "Thanks for the hand."

"Not a problem," Baylor said.

Axel hadn't really realized before just how big the new man was, but he stood a good four inches above him, and Axel was six-two himself. He crouched in front of Dr. Minga. In the darkness of the sub, their flashlights all shone to check out her leg. Axel winced. "That's not a pretty break," he said.

She gasped, and yet it was more of a broken laugh. "You think?" she said. "It's more of a bullet, less of a break. Or a break caused by a bullet to be precise."

"The shooter got you?"

"Yeah, twice."

"You've got a second bullet wound?"

"Well, three actually, but who's counting? One in each leg, plus this. It's a graze, I think," she said, pointing. As the flashlights traveled over her, she tilted her head, and all along her temple and hairline a bullet had carved out a bloody path that had barely missed taking her life.

"Jesus! You were damn lucky on that one," Axel said.

"I'm damn lucky you guys showed up when you did," she said. "Hopefully you have a way to get me out of here. My future wasn't looking too bright."

"We have several small rescue subs," Mason said. "We'll get you up there."

She nodded. "I'd be very grateful," she whispered. She leaned forward, and whatever had been holding her hair up lost its grip, and a shock of brilliant bright-orange hair dropped over her shoulders and face.

Axel looked at it and smiled. Just something about gingery hair that he loved. The fact that she was broken and in so much pain was not something to smile about though. He studied her pale but sweaty face quickly and, after a look at her eyes, realized that the head wound may have knocked her out for a time. "Listen, Doc. When did you get the head wound?"

"At some point in the fray," she said with a one-arm shrug. "He fired a bunch, and it was a mad scramble for everyone. After I took the shot in the leg that blasted apart the bones, I knew I wasn't running anywhere and would be a sitting duck. So, while I still could, and the shooter was distracted elsewhere, I climbed into the vent shaft system. The other shots came from below, at some point, while I was up there. It was a good hiding spot, but, by then, I was pretty well stuck there."

"Who was the shooter?"

"No clue," she said. "Twelve of us were on this mission," she said, "but the shooter was dressed in black with a full head mask. I don't know if it was one of us or somebody else who had hidden on board."

"Either one is possible," Mason said, "but you're the twelfth that we've found now, and we have eleven bodies."

She nodded, then winced. "I was afraid of that when everything went silent."

"Anybody you'd suspect on the crew?" Axel asked.

"No. I only ever had trouble with one of them, Hostettler."

"Well, he's dead too, with a broken leg and a bullet low in his belly. It looks like he may have taken his own life after he took that first bullet. While the others might be shot up a bit, they also each took a bullet in the forehead."

"Wait, but Hostettler wasn't doing the shooting," she said.

AFTER A BIT of silence, Mason asked gently, "What do you mean? Are you sure?"

"Positive," she said. "Completely different body types. Hostettler is squarish and shorter, five-nine maybe. The shooter was six foot, or more, and skinny. Long and lean. At the time that I saw the chaos going on, I wondered where he'd managed to hide. Not much spare room in this place."

"I'm surprised you managed to get away," Baylor said, his tone neutral.

She looked up at him and gestured to her leg and her head and said, "Funny, I don't feel like I got away."

"But he didn't come up after you."

"No," she said, "I thought for sure he was, after all the shooting had stopped. Then I felt something secured to the sub."

"What? How long ago was that?" Axel asked urgently. "Because we just secured to the sub. Are you saying he disappeared at the same time?"

She frowned. "No. It was longer ago. Well, I don't know," she said. "It's all fuzzy, like a distant dream. I suppose it's possible, but I would have said it was hours ago, but I don't really know."

"Interesting. We thought maybe he went out in the torpedo tube."

"Couldn't have. They're not functioning," she said.

"Well, let's get you up and out of here, so that the repair crew can come down and see if they can get this sub up again," Axel said.

"The instrument panel took some heavy fire," she said.

Axel nodded, pulling some bandages out of his pack. "Can you guys give me a hand? Let's deal with the bleeding and splint that leg."

"Sure thing," Baylor said, as he and Nelson jumped in to help. "How bad is the other leg, Doc?"

"The other leg? Oh, I don't really notice it compared to the shattered leg and my head."

"Do you know if this attack was targeted at the submarine or if this was about somebody on board?" Mason asked.

"Captain Tronson is a great leader, so it seems unlikely that he was targeted," she said.

"Interesting," Mason said. "Well, let's get you out of here. That's the priority."

"No," she said, shaking her head. "Finding out who did this is the priority," she said. "These were all good men. What a terrible waste."

Axel said, "The bottom line is, in order to do them decent, we will find who did this, so their deaths aren't in vain."

"It's all in vain," she said.

"What do mean?"

"This was sabotage," she said.

"Were these men targeted and assigned to this project specifically, or were they just the unlucky ones?"

"I don't know," she replied.

"Were you picked for this?"

"I was testing the navigation system," she said, "so I needed to be on board. We'd had some glitches with it earlier. My understanding was that a skeleton crew was taking it out for a test run."

"So where did this shooter guy come from?" Axel asked.

"Exactly." Using Axel's hand for support, she slowly stood on her better leg. As she did, she wavered. He reached out, grabbed her, and said, "Whoa. Just take your time."

She smiled weakly. "I'd do better if I had a crutch or something. Trying to get around with either leg won't be easy."

"You're not going far," Mason said. Just then his communication device went off. He stepped off to the side. She looked up at the others. "Can we get out of here now?"

Axel nodded. "Let's get you topside." It took another fifteen minutes to get her into the small rescue sub up above. They had deliberately come down with room for a couple extra people, just in case.

"Are other subs out here?" she asked.

"Yeah, we've got a couple teams standing by," Axel said. "We didn't know what we would find and wanted room to shuttle everyone out."

"Glad to hear that," she said. "I can't believe I'm the only one going home alive."

"Just glad we found you in time," Axel said.

CHAPTER 2

ALLY WOKE UP, hazy and confused, wondering where the hell she was. Everything was white. Like seriously white. She slammed her eyes shut against the glare coming in from the window. As she shifted, she moaned. Her leg wasn't screaming, but her head was killing her.

"Take it easy," a female said, her voice full of warmth. "You're in the hospital. You've just had surgery to fix your leg, among other things."

Her eyes popped back open again. "Surgery? My leg?"

"Yes," the nurse said in that same gentle voice. "Both legs actually, and we did a little work on your head while we were at it."

"My head really hurts."

"You were on a sub. Do you remember? There was an attack. You were rescued, but you sustained some injuries."

"I barely remember," she said. And she had a vague, hazy memory of gunfire, screaming, and sounds of fighting, and yet she still wondered what she had been doing back then. She remembered being deep into the problem on the navigation system, pretty sure she had just figured out the problem, when she discovered the real trouble. She'd sent off an alert just before everything had erupted around her.

When she'd taken the first bullet in the leg, she knew immediately her leg was badly damaged. The shooter had moved on to other targets, and she knew her leg was too badly injured to run. So, with adrenaline assisting her, she scrambled into the hatch above and moved through the vent shaft. She had no idea what the hell was going on though by then, as she heard a hell of a firefight taking place—but she couldn't see anything.

Without a weapon of her own, she had been completely useless. She remembered moving as best she could until the shaft narrowed, and it was much harder to move there. More shooting occurred. At some point she realized her other leg was burning in pain and that she must have been shot again. And still another shot grazed her head. She must have been unconscious after that.

She lay here in the bed after the nurse left, wondering how she'd even got out of the sub. She didn't remember that at all. Just then a knock came at the door to her hospital room.

"Come in," she said, after a moment. She looked up to see a face that she vaguely remembered. But instead of a smile she gave him a frown. "Do I know you?"

His smile was bright. "Well," he said, "if you remembered getting out of the sub you would," he said, "but I suspect the pain may have blotted out the clarity of your thinking at the time."

"Oh, God, I hate to say it," she said, "I do vaguely remember you but not very clearly."

"Good, Axel Salisbury at your service," he said. "It was a painful trip for you."

"I'd just as soon forget it then," she said. She motioned at her leg. "Apparently I've just had surgery."

"Yeah. The bones didn't want to align properly," he said, "and some of the chips and fragments would give you trouble, so they went in and cleaned it out to make sure everything was good to go. I haven't heard any results myself. I just heard them talking when I was standing in the ER with you."

"Why were you in the ER with me?" She studied him, wondering at the weird tug she felt inside. "Oh, you're the one who dragged me out of the ceiling shaft," she said suddenly.

"Ouch," he said, "and here I was thinking it was more like a rescue. You know? Saving the fair damsel in distress. *Dragging you out of the ceiling* sounds like it lacks finesse."

"Well, whichever it was," she said in a dry tone, "I don't remember much."

"Both," he said, that grin flashing again.

Something about his grin was very endearing. "Thank you," she said suddenly. "I know the circumstances were dire, and I appreciate you finding me."

"We almost didn't," he said. "We had eleven bodies and figured the twelfth was the shooter who had somehow escaped, only to realize that all of the dead were men, which meant that one Dr. Ally Minga wasn't among them."

"No, I wasn't among them," she said softly. "And I was the only female on board."

"So it was easy to figure out who we were missing," he said. He walked closer, leaned his hands on the edge of her bed, and stared down at her leg. "That'll take a while to heal."

"Yeah, it will," she said. "Hopefully I won't be in the hospital for too long though."

His gaze went to her head.

She reached up and patted the bandage around her head and asked, "How bad is that?" She groaned. "Did they cut off all my hair?"

He grinned. "I'm pretty sure they had to cut some of it," he said. "I didn't think it was all that bad when I first looked, but honestly, it was caked with blood, so I couldn't see it that well. You probably got some stitches."

"Maybe so." She nodded slowly. "It is sure pounding." She reached up with both hands, immediately wishing she hadn't. "The pain is excruciating."

"I'm sorry. Head injuries are like that. Trust me. I know."

"Not your fault," she said, with a wave of her hand. "I just need to lie here dead quiet for a couple days."

"Can you even do that?"

"Well, maybe, if I don't talk to anybody," she said. "Dang it, I almost started shaking my head. It's instinctive."

"You're about due for more painkillers. The nurse told me that I only had a few minutes to talk to you before she'd be back with your meds."

"Great," she said, "so I get to spend the next forty-eight hours drugged up."

"It's either drugged up or in terrible pain."

"I don't like the drugs," she said abruptly.

"I don't either," he said, and enough sympathy was in his voice that she believed him. Then he added, "But I prefer it over being incapacitated by pain."

She had to agree. "You've got a point there," she murmured. "How are you guys doing on the investigation?"

"Not sure we'll be investigating," he said.

Her eyes flew open, and she stared at him. "I hope you do," she said, "because it had something to do with that coworker."

"Well, it might have," he said gently, "but it might not

have either."

"I told you that the shooter I saw was tall, lean, and a very different body type."

"And I hear you, but, according to what we've heard so far, there's no sign of him."

She frowned. "So no one'll believe me. Is that it?" She hated to hear that note of bitterness in her tone. But it was always a case of being that one female up against a dozen men. She was either imagining things or overreacting. "He was there," she said forcefully.

Axel picked up her hand and asked, "Are you certain?"

She stared at him. "Yes. He also had a faint limp."

"Which side?"

She shut her eyes for a moment, recalling the memory. "Favoring his right," she said. "I don't know if it was from an injury that occurred on the sub," she said, "or something else."

"Weapons?"

"I don't know exactly," she said. "He had a small snub-nosed-looking handgun. I hadn't really seen anything like it before."

"But you're licensed for weapons?"

"I've done basic training," she said, "but I don't carry. I'm a navigation IT specialist," she said. "I was looking for bugs in the actual coding."

"So you don't have much action experience."

"None."

"You can't say that anymore," he said grimly. "You've got experience now."

"Not the kind of experience I want," she said.

"None of us do." He patted her hand and said, "Think back now. Can you tell me anything else about him? Did you hear his voice?"

She closed her eyes again and thought about it. "It was such a panic of multiple people screaming. And so much noise," she said slowly. "Such a freaky experience, turning around, and he's firing at people. It's chaos. Somebody yelled out, 'What are you doing? Who are you?'" With that, she stopped. "He said something." She frowned, focused.

He patted her hand again, just waiting.

She said, "It's like that line out of a B movie. He said something like, 'I'm your worst nightmare.'"

"Interesting," he said.

"Why?" she asked.

"Because, for most of us, our worst nightmare is betrayal. Somebody we trust turning on us."

"Well, if he wasn't one of the men on the crew," she said, "how does betrayal fit in with this?"

"We're wondering if Hostettler was working with him."

Her gaze widened; she hadn't thought about that. "I didn't like him. But that doesn't mean he's a part of this."

"No, but he's the only one who we figure committed suicide."

She stared up at him. "It was pretty ugly down there, once we realized we couldn't get the sub back up. We didn't know what the hell was going on, and we were wondering how long before a rescue could be done. How much air we had was a big concern. Then it got really crazy when the shooting started. So who knows what Hostettler thought. Everybody would soon be dead with us short on air. Then the shooting came, with everybody lying there, shot up and in pain. Maybe his suicide was the easy answer for Hostettler."

"Maybe," he said with a nod. "It means though that

we'll be looking into his background pretty carefully."

She winced. "I imagine you'll be doing that for all of us," she murmured.

"But it's not an issue, unless you're trying to hide something," he murmured. A moment of awkward silence passed. When it went on, he squeezed her fingers. "Is there?"

Her eyes flew open, and she stared at him. "Me personally? No more than anybody else," she said. "It's not that I'm trying to hide anything. I just don't want some things aired."

"Okay, so why don't you just air them to me right now," he said. "Maybe I can head off some of it. We don't want to waste our time and resources on stuff that isn't relevant anyway."

"It's probably already too late," she murmured. "Four years ago, my ex posted a bunch of photos on the internet. Nude photos of me. He was trying to get revenge for the breakup."

"Asshole," he said in an irritated tone.

"Exactly," she said. "I went to the cops, but they never would do anything with it."

"No. Once a photo's up on the net," he said, "it's out there."

"And it's not that the photos were pornographic or anything," she said, "just more along the line of sexy. Maybe that made them more appealing." She shook her head. "I don't know. It was pretty bad. They're out there. I was just hoping this wouldn't inspire a new round of interest in them. That's really not who I am."

"Thank you for telling me," he said. "I'll just tell the guys up-front and take the news out of it."

"That just means they'll all instantly look for them," she said bitterly.

"So how did you handle it at the time?"

"I posted a dozen photos of myself, like in a bikini and in a thong. I figured if more pictures were out there of my own choosing, maybe they'd stop looking for the others."

"An interesting point of attack," he said in surprise.

She opened her eyes, stared at him, and said, "I'd much rather play offense on my terms than sit back on defense and wait for something to happen."

"Unless you're hurt?' he asked.

"Hurting and facing impossible odds," she whispered.

Just then the nurse came bubbling back in. "Time's up," she said. "This young lady gets to go back to sleep for a while."

"She'll be happy for that, I'd wager."

AXEL WALKED OUT of the room, knowing she'd probably be asleep within ten or fifteen minutes, if not sooner. He stood at the doorway and waited till the nurse came back out and then checked through the window of her door. Ally had curled up as best she could, with her leg in traction, and went right to sleep. "Will she be okay?" he asked the nurse.

"Yes, we think she'll do well," the nurse said. "You can probably come back in another four or five hours, if you have more questions for her."

"I'll see," he said. "Thank you." And, with a smile, he headed off. As he walked out the exit door of the hospital, he contacted Mason. "Just talked to Dr. Minga," he said. "She's out of surgery and awake, although they just gave her meds, so she'll be back under any minute now."

"Apparently the one leg was quite a mess," Mason said. "The other was a soft tissue injury through and through, didn't hit anything major."

"From the looks of her, she won't be moving too much very soon."

"They did give us the x-rays to point to the trajectory. For the bad one, she was shot as if she were seated and stood up as somebody was above her and fired downward, so it went down at the top of the thigh through the femur and out just above the knee."

"That's not good," he said.

"It shattered the bone top and bottom, so the femur will not support anything for a while. And that's if it heals properly. It took them a while to pull out all the chips and fragments."

"Oh, that's worse than I thought," he said. "What about the head wound?"

"Stitches. It was a deep graze, split the skin, and ran along her skull. She'll have a hell of a headache for a few days."

"She doesn't remember getting off the sub," Axel said. "She vaguely remembered me, but that's it."

"You are kind of forgettable," Mason said, with a smile in his voice.

Axel grinned at that. "Hey, I can be unassuming and discreet, if I need to be."

"I'd like to see that just once," Mason said.

"She is still adamant that another person was on board though," Axel said abruptly. "I told her that the general consensus is Hostettler was likely the shooter and then took himself out at the end. She disagreed and made the point that he might have taken himself out because he had no hope for help and because he had nothing ahead but terrible pain until he finally ran out of oxygen."

Mason made a small noncommittal sound.

"I told her, if that were the case, chances are there would be an even bigger investigation."

"Nobody believes a thirteenth man was on board," Mason said.

"I know that," he said, "but she's pretty adamant."

"But how did he get out then?"

"She did say that somebody locked on to the hatch before we did. Remember?"

"And that's possible," he said. "A pretty shitty deal though."

"Killing all twelve on a submarine—or trying to—and making it look like one of them was actually the killer who'd gone rogue is also pretty shitty too," he said. "It's just a bad deal all the way around." Axel now stood outside the hospital in the parking lot beside his Jeep. "It's not our investigation though, is it?"

"No," Mason said cautiously. "At this point I don't think they'll be doing too much of an investigation. It's fairly low-key at the moment, as they try to keep it out of the media."

"What if she's right?"

"How will you find out?"

"I don't know," he said. "Any chance we can get access to the cameras for the loading of the sub? See if anybody around there fits the description?"

"What, tall and lean?"

"She said he had a bit of a limp, favored his right side, though that could have happened in the fight on the sub," he said.

At that, Mason hesitated. "It'll have to be on your own time," he warned.

"You know what? I'm okay with that," he said. "I saw those men in there. Shot all to hell, then one between the eyes for good measure. They were butchered. That's not fair. They went out there in good faith, serving their country and testing the new sub. They didn't expect to die that day."

"Nobody ever does," Mason said. "I'll see what kind of access I can get you for those cameras. Head on home, and I'll contact you soon."

With that, Axel walked to the burger joint on the next block, got himself something to take home for dinner, returned to his Jeep, and headed for his apartment. As he walked in, his phone rang. He hurriedly put everything down and answered. "Mason?"

"Yeah, I sent you a link," he said. "It's got security data on it. Listen. Don't share it with anyone, and, if you find anything, you tell me and only me." And, with that, he hung up.

Axel loved this cloak-and-dagger stuff, but this one was particularly sensitive. If a thirteenth man was on board, somebody had been lax in letting him get there. Axel was good to blame Hostettler for it, but that didn't mean the guy had a part in it. Where had the thirteenth man hidden onboard? In the HVAC system, like Ally? It would make sense why the gunman shot up the HVAC system, in case anyone else had had the same idea as he had. And sometimes, when shit hit the fan, *sometimes* it was nobody's intention and nobody's fault.

Carrying his burger, he headed to his laptop, turned it on, brought up the link, and clicked on it. It was one of the cameras on the loading dock, where the submarine was being loaded. And the feed started four days earlier. "Interesting timing. Thanks, Mason."

Axel checked his own watch, thinking it would take a while to get through four days of video. He set the speed three times faster and moved through the video, slowing it down when anybody was coming and going, and took screenshots of faces for later. When nothing was happening, he sped it up, then slowed it back down again. Finally he was up to the day the sub left. Still more supplies were loaded and some equipment. He watched as Dr. Minga walked up and got on, followed by the rest of the crew. Hostettler was there. He was laughing and joking with the others. He carried a simple duffel bag, like everybody else did. Minga herself had a small bag, not a duffel, but more of a suitcase without the wheels. They were supposed to be out for seven days. They were out for three before things blew up. He kept watch, but nobody else came on board.

He shut off the video and sat back, considering this, then got up and pulled a beer from the fridge. Sitting back down again, he backed up to the twenty-four hours before, focusing especially on the night before launch, and set it at normal speed and then slowed it down even more and watched. He leaned forward when he thought he saw movement. Everything was pitch-black, and it was hard to see anything leading up to the sub. He leaned forward again, slowed it down, and took another look.

And, sure enough, there was something, someone, wandering around in the dark. Studying the guy's movements, Axel didn't see any method to his madness, until he pulled his phone from his pocket and held it to his ear, then moved quickly toward the sub. Was there some kind of a security lock on the sub that had now been unlocked? Someone else who helped him gain access? Axel watched as the man quickly boarded the submarine, having absolutely no trouble opening the hatch and getting inside. Axel waited and watched. "Where are you, you little bugger?"

But nobody else was here. And at no point in time—from that moment until the next day when the submarine left—were there signs of that man leaving the sub. Axel sat back, then reran that same video feed of the man answering the phone and then walking into the sub, watching at a very slow speed. Axel noted a slight hitch in his stride, indeed, an odd little movement that he made, favoring his right side.

"Bingo," he said, and he picked up the phone to call Mason.

CHAPTER 3

A LLY WOKE UP again, this time more aware of where she was, her thoughts less hazy, though the pain was still overwhelming her. The nurse walked in a few minutes later. "You must have an instinct for knowing when your patients wake up," she said.

"That's easy," the nurse said cheerfully. "Your meds should have worn off about twenty minutes ago, and usually the pain kicking in wakes you up."

"Well, why don't you just keep the pain meds coming," Ally joked, "and then I don't have to wake up until this is healed."

"Well, wouldn't that be nice," she said. "I'm sorry to tell you, but it won't be that simple."

"Of course not." She looked down at her leg. "How long do I have to stay here?"

"It's not for me to say," the nurse said, "but, when the doctor can get you out of here, rest assured that he will."

"Got it," she said. "I was just hoping to get out sooner rather than later."

"Maybe," the nurse said. "As long as the x-rays show the bone is set properly and the blood circulation is fine. You are nicely casted, so you'll probably be good to go home before too terribly long, if it heals well."

Ally watched as the nurse checked her blood pressure,

temperature, and took her pulse. "I'm still alive, I presume," she said. "Alive and in good health, from the sounds of it."

"The doctor's doing rounds at nine. He'll pop in then." And, with that, she headed to the door.

"Wait. Is there any chance of getting a coffee?"

"Sure," she said. "How do you take it?"

"Black, please."

"It will have to be coffee from the nurses' station, until breakfast is delivered in an hour."

"What time is it anyway?"

"It's seven," the nurse said. She walked back into the room and moved the small table used for meals closer to Ally. "Your phone is here too."

When she saw it, she smiled with relief. "I hadn't even thought about it," she said, "but I'd be very sad to lose it."

"You and the rest of the world," she said with a smile. "I'll get you a coffee."

Ally reached for her phone, grateful that the movement didn't seem to wake up the trolls in her head that she'd pictured doing the pounding against her skull. As she lay back down again, phone in hand, she realized that she felt a whole lot better. Taped to the top of her phone, she saw someone had left a phone number. And no name. She knew only one person who would do that. *Axel.* She smiled when she saw it.

"So there you are," she murmured, knowing instinctively that this was the man who had helped get her out of the submarine. She added his phone number to her contacts, then sent him a text. **Cute move, leaving your number like that.**

Next she checked her emails, wincing at the seventy-five that downloaded when she brought up the app. "That's not fair," she murmured. She didn't know if anybody had heard she was in the hospital or not, but most of these appeared to be business oriented. One was from her mom, and she doubly winced at that.

"Sorry, Mom. I don't dare talk to you right now," she said to herself. "I have no idea what I'm supposed to tell you."

As far as everybody knew, she was still out in the sub and wouldn't be home for another few days. She checked out the news, frowned at the political climate of anger and angst taking over the country, and then checked the weather, simply because, when there's nothing else to talk about, there was the weather. She had a few favorite sites that she whipped through, just browsing the internet, wondering what had happened while she was out of it, only to realize that basically nothing had, and it was still the same old crap like always. Just as she went to put down her phone, a text message came through. She smiled when she saw it was from Axel.

How'd you know it was me?
You're the only one who came to see me.
Are you alone?
Kinda stuck in the hospital. Never alone here.
Can I come visit?
It's pretty early.
But, if you're awake and I'm awake, does it matter? Can I come?
Sure, I guess. Can't promise they'll let you in though.

He sent her a happy face. **I'll make it in.**

She trusted him on that too. Hearing no more from Axel, she put down her phone, just as the nurse walked back in with a cup of coffee. "The same guy who was here the other day is on his way back," she said. "He has more questions."

"Not surprised," the nurse said. "I'll send him up."

"Thank you," Ally replied. Then she sat here and waited, sipping her coffee. With any luck he wouldn't be here too early. When he walked in ten minutes later, she looked at him, surprised. "How'd you get here so fast?"

"I live on base," he said.

She nodded. "Did you follow up on anything?"

He looked around behind him and then closed the door.

Her eyebrows rose. "Is that a safe thing to do?"

"I'm not sure," he said, "but it'll have to be. I need to talk to you about something," he said, "and I don't want anybody listening in."

"Top secret, huh?" she said lightly. But, then again, that was her world too.

He walked forward, looked at the coffee cup, and smiled. "That coffee any good?"

"It's hot and bitter and strong," she said. "I haven't had any in a couple days. I figured it might clear off the rest of my headache that's still pounding."

"Yeah, caffeine is tough that way," he said. "But a caffeine headache? Really? That's kind of a stretch for somebody with God-only-knows how many stitches in her head."

"So I suppose you don't drink coffee and the like?"

"Hell no," he said. "I probably drink twice as much as you do."

Her smile got brighter. "No wonder you're here so early. So what did you want to talk about?"

He looked at his watch and said, "It's not that early. When will we be interrupted?"

"Breakfast comes around eight, I was told," she said.

"It'll be close," he said, "but we still have twenty

minutes."

She nodded. "And you're still evading the issue."

"You can't say anything to anybody," he said.

She stared at him, perplexed. "That's fine," she said. "I don't exactly have anybody to say anything to, in case you haven't noticed." He walked over, held up his phone, swiped the screen to get to something, and showed her a small video clip. The angle was wrong for her to see very clearly, so she brought his hand closer and twisted it, so she could get a better look at the video playing.

He said, "It's dark at the time of the video too, so keep that in mind."

She watched as the shadowy figure answered a phone call and then walked down the approach to the sub. He got in without any trouble. "There's security on that sub," she murmured.

"Keep watching," he said.

She watched as the video sped up, and finally she could see herself and the others approach, and then the sub took off. She handed the phone back, wondering what she was supposed to see. Then she got it. "He didn't get off, did he?"

Axel shook his head. "No," he said, "not that I could find."

"So I was right," she said softly. She looked at him and took another sip of coffee. "Have you told anybody?"

"Mason," he said with a nod. "I left it with him."

"Are you anticipating a problem?"

"Well, it's possible," he said. "I'm not sure. I think it's nice and tidy for the navy to keep it the way it currently appears."

"Meaning?"

"Hostettler shot everyone and then himself."

"Unless he didn't, in which case hard questions need to be asked. Yet it's all wrapped up, but for the ramblings of some woman with a head injury."

"Except for that video," he said.

"You found it, so, if anybody's looking, they should find it too, right?"

"And that, of course, is another question. Whether they look and find it or not, I don't know. But Mason will take it to them, and hopefully that will force an investigation."

"I hope so," she said. She paused, looked at him, and said, "So, the guy. Who is he?"

"Don't know yet," he said cheerfully, "but I'll find out."

She leaned back in the bed, studied his face, and gave a quick nod. "Do. I want to know who that bastard is."

IT WAS ONE thing to want to catch this guy, but it was another thing entirely to figure out who it was. They had absolutely no evidence or anything else other than the stark figure moving in the darkness. Black on black was never good for identification. But it had to be somebody with access, somebody who had security credentials, with a level of clearance to get in, and somebody who knew the timing of this mission and when the sub was going down. Those parameters should reduce the numbers of suspects to something manageable. As he walked out of the hospital, he called Mason. "Any update?"

"Of course not," Mason said, a note of humor in his voice. "You know how this works."

"I know," he said. "I was just hoping."

"Did she recognize him?"

"No, but I think she feels vindicated. At least the presence of that one shadow gave credence to her account."

"Here's the problem," Mason said. "I'm getting the impression from someone above that, because she's still alive, she was likely to be the person in partnership with Hostettler."

Axel froze, stared at the parking lot, as if suddenly seeing it for the first time. "Seriously?" He tried to think back to everything he'd learned about her, which was damn little. How she had conducted herself, where she'd been hidden, and what she was like now that she was awake. And none of it jived with that theory. "I don't believe it," he said.

"The question is, do you believe her?"

"Yes," he said instinctively. And then he frowned. "But I don't know why."

"Sometimes our gut is all we have to go by," Mason said.

"I know. She feels honest." And he stopped "You're right. It's just gut. It's instinct. I trust her."

"Well, the brass wants a full investigation into her history, background, connections, because they think that, through her, they'll find him."

"That's possible," he said, grasping at straws, "but that doesn't mean she's aware of the connection or that she played a role in this somehow."

"You mean, somebody was doing this to get back at her?"

"Or used her somehow as a way to get in to where he needed to go."

"It's possible," he said thoughtfully. "We do tend to see only what's in front of us. And people are looking at her as the sole survivor and potentially the only one who can tell them anything. The problem with that is, they won't be looking at anyone else."

"Sure," Axel said, "but that doesn't mean she can tell the investigators anything useful."

"Anyway, I suggest you stick close to her and see what you can find out."

"The navy is doing their investigation already as well?"

"An investigation is going on right now, yes," he said, "but it'll be at a different level. You know that."

"So, I'm to do this on an unofficial level?"

"Yes," Mason said. "It's kind of half-cleared, let's say." He chuckled, adding a note of humor. "So it may take a bit of your free time."

"I don't give a damn about that," he said. "Besides, now you've got me going, I'll be pissed if she's involved."

"Ah, she's gotten to you, has she?"

He frowned at that. "I don't know that I would say that," he said cautiously.

"I would," Mason said cheerfully. "Get to know her. See what's behind this thing."

"She won't like that I'm buddying up with her to investigate her."

"You'll have to figure out the best way to handle it," he said quietly. "If she is found to have played a part, you know what'll happen to her."

Axel winced because being a traitor to your own country, sabotaging millions of dollars of equipment, and causing the deaths or being directly involved in the murders of a eleven countrymen and fellow military personnel would never be a good end. "I still don't think she could have anything to do with this," he said.

"Then prove it," Mason said and hung up.

The question was how, why, and where to even begin. Did he tell her about it? She'd be more open if she thought she was helping him clear her. But she also might get her back up and not want to contribute anything. That wouldn't be to her benefit, but people weren't always reasonable about things like this. He wanted her cooperation. It was by far the easiest way to get what he needed to find out.

He turned and stared up at the hospital. He was here already. He could just go back in and see what she had to contribute. As he stood here, another vehicle drove past. And then another and another. He realized the workday was starting, and the hospital's day shifts were coming on as it got busier and busier. That also meant a lot more other people would be walking in and out of the hospital. His mind automatically went to the guy who had the access to get into the sub when he shouldn't have. If he got onto the sub, he could easily get into the hospital. But why would he? The only reason he would care if she was alive or dead was if he'd heard about her surviving—and if he thought she could identify him.

Frowning at that, he slowly walked to his Jeep. He need-ed his laptop, and he needed to do some background checks on who she was, who her friends were, and what was going on in her world. No point in going up there blind without any intel before looking for her assistance.

She would just get angry and hurt.

Whereas, if he had a case to present, it would be a lot easier. Not feeling good about the situation in any way, shape, or form, he figured he'd camp out in her hallway as he did research. Then he'd approach her.

This time he didn't go into her room, finding a nearby empty hospital room to use temporarily. If the nurses needed it for a patient, he'd find another empty room.

He accessed her personnel file, at least what he was allowed to see, and found she was thirty-one years old, single, and never married. Her family consisted of a brother and her parents, who lived in Australia. Her father was an engineer, working in building construction. Her mother had been a stay-at-home mom but apparently was heavily involved in charity work. Axel made a few notes, but not a whole lot was here.

He focused his efforts on her again and checked her education. He could see her path between degrees, until she finally ended up in her specialty. He frowned at that. She had gotten a lot of her training in the military, which was not uncommon, but she had excelled and was always at the top of the class. She could do very well in the private sector, but instead she stayed in the service.

He knew a lot of people made the military service their career, and others just stayed until something in their life caused them to move on. He wondered what she would do after this accident. Apparently she had always been a fanatic about submarines, so she was technically doing what she loved to do. But then people would say things like that, but it didn't necessarily hold true. Over time, all these ideals and goals could change. Career interests changed as well. He wondered just how much hers had changed and how much they were changing now.

He searched on Google to see what else he could find. He found her Facebook page with very sporadic posts. He checked a few of the dating sites, but nothing was under her name. Of course she could have used a different name. She looked like the straight-shooter kind of person, but then what did he know? According to Mason, an awful lot of questions were being asked about her role in this as it was.

Axel decided a few hospital sandwiches were in order, so

he got up, found the lunchroom, and was just about to get a cup of coffee, when his phone rang. "Hello?"

"He was here," she said, her voice tense, sounding thin and high.

"Who was here?" He could hear her gasping in the background, realizing that, even though she hadn't stated who she was, he had no trouble recognizing Ally's voice. "Ally, what's the matter?"

But her breaths were raspy and harsh.

"Come on. Talk to me. You're okay. Talk to me."

She gave a high-pitched laugh. "What do you mean, *I'm okay?*" she said. "I just told you that he was here." And the phone went dead. Having heard the emphasis on *he*, Axel snatched his laptop and his phone and was out the cafeteria door in seconds. As he barreled up the steps, then through the hallway to her room, one of the nurses stepped forward from the nurses' station and said, "Sorry, sir. She can't have visitors right now."

"Oh, she's having a visitor," he said, his voice hard. "She sent out a call for help. I need to know what the hell is going on."

The nurse looked at him in shock. "What are you talking about?" she asked. "She had her checkup not even forty minutes ago."

"And lunch?"

"Yes. Her lunch was delivered probably about five to ten minutes ago," she said, checking her watch. But he still walked rapidly down the hallway, the nurse racing to catch up. When he finally got to Ally's door, he pushed it open and stepped in. He didn't care about knocking. She sat there with her arms wrapped tight around her chest, curled up into a tiny ball at the headboard, as much as she could with a cast. At least her leg wasn't in traction at the moment. He raced forward and, without even thinking about it, scooped her into his arms, turned to sit down with her in his lap and wrapped a blanket around her.

The nurse caught up with him and immediately looked at her. "Dear God," she said. "What happened?"

"She's in shock."

The nurse quickly checked her vitals, but Axel wasn't really concerned about that. He just held her close and spoke softly to Ally. "It's okay. I've got you. You're safe now."

She started to shake her head, and she couldn't seem to stop.

And he knew exactly what that was—shock. And that it would take a lot for her to calm down. Looking at the nurse, he said, "I'm just holding her for now. Give us a few minutes."

She frowned, nodded, and said, "I'll have to report this though."

"That's fine," he said. "You and me both."

She gave him a startled look, then left the two of them alone.

CHAPTER 4

W HEN ALLY SLOWLY became more aware of her surroundings as the shock wore off, she realized she was wrapped up in Axel's arms. Still on her hospital bed, her bad leg in a cast, just stretched out in front of her, she shivered as soon as the stiffness receded.

He grabbed another blanket and awkwardly threw it around her.

"I'm fine," she whispered, her teeth chattering.

"Sure you are," he said.

Obviously he didn't believe her, but then she didn't believe herself either. She snuggled closer. "I-I saw him. You know?"

"Who?"

"The shooter," she whispered. "From the sub."

He stiffened and then relaxed.

"You knew that's who I was talking about."

"But I still needed you to say it," he said. "Did you get a good look at him?"

She shook her head. "He was walking away. But I'd seen him the same way, walking away on the sub," she whispered. "So I knew it was him."

"Same body type, same coloring?"

"I don't know about coloring," she said. "He had a black mask on in the sub."

"So you said. How can you possibly know it's the same man then?"

"Same hitch to his leg," she whispered. And the shivering got worse for a few moments. He rubbed her arms and her back, waiting for her to calm down. "I'm not normally like this," she said. "But seeing him, it was such a shock. It was like seeing a ghost. I knew he was here for me."

"Wait. Did he hurt you?"

She shook her head. "No, and he didn't come far into the room," she said. "Neither did he have a weapon, that I could see."

"So what did you see?"

She frowned. "Well, he was leaving the room, pushing the trolley." She shook her head. "So I guess he did come into my hospital room. I didn't think to ask anyone about him."

"So he works here?"

"I assumed so at first sight, but now I think it was just a ruse," she said. "He didn't turn back for me to see his face though. Maybe he was checking out that I was there and how easy it would be to gain access to me." It was pretty damn hard to stay calm and to discuss this as everyday conversation. The truth was, she was freaked. And yet part of her worried she'd imagined it all. Maybe it was a new orderly, and he was just lost.

"When was that?" he asked, checking his watch.

"Just before I phoned you," she said. "Why?"

"I can check the camera feeds."

She tilted her head back from his chest to look up at him. "Would they let you?"

"If it's connected to this case, you can bet they will. If not, maybe somebody else can get it for me," he promised.

"Chances are this guy hid his face from the cameras though."

She frowned at that. "I wouldn't be at all surprised. He probably had a hat close by or something."

"Maybe, but as long as we can connect that same hitch in his step, it will identify him."

"I can't believe I froze like that, but, when I saw him, I freaked out."

"Do you think that gait is natural or put-on?"

"What? Why? Somebody would have to be really good to do that all the time," she said.

"A lot of people step into these roles," he said. "And they play them very well. Sometimes they forget to step back into them too, so that, when you see them walking without something like that hitch, it's disconcerting, and you're left figuring out what's going on. Just think about it."

"I suppose it's possible," she said, sagging against him. "Anything is possible at this point. Anyway, I'm fine now, really."

"I'm not," he said cheerfully. And he squeezed her gently. "That phone call took ten years off my life."

"Sorry," she whispered, then just relaxed against him, wondering about the connection that had sprung up between them. "I didn't even know what to do. I just reached for my phone and dialed."

"Well, I'm glad you called my number. It's a good thing I left it for you."

"Maybe," she said. "But I don't know, I probably should have called the MPs."

"Maybe. But then they aren't up to speed on the case, are they?"

"I think that's why I called you," she said in a wry tone. "You also said you lived on base, so I knew you'd be nearby."

"I was here still. Right out in the hallway for a while. Then headed to the cafeteria for lunch and coffee, while continuing my work on the investigation."

"Did you get official permission?"

"I've asked," he said with a smile.

She nodded. "I hope they find him."

"Oh, we'll find him," he said.

The absolute surety in his tone made her realize that, if this guy could help her out in any way, he would.

"But I suspect," he said, "that you're not telling me the whole truth."

She stiffened and slowly pushed herself away from his chest and glared at him.

But his gaze was steady and held hers true. "And you need to," he said. "All of it. I don't care how dirty, how ugly, or whatever, it needs to come out."

Her breath caught in her chest. "Nobody likes to talk about unpleasantness in their world," she said.

"It doesn't matter," he said. And this time he was adamant. She wasn't getting away from this. "What the hell is going on? What's going on with this guy?"

"The only thing I can think of," she said, "is because of the submarine. He knew I was here. Somebody must have leaked that I survived somehow."

"I don't think too much leaking would be required," he said. "You're here in the hospital. How many hundreds of people work here?"

"Meaning that he could have just checked to see if anybody came in?"

"I would," he said. "Wouldn't you?"

"Well, potentially, yes," she said, realizing the common sense of that. "Still," she said, "it can't be." She closed her eyes.

"*What* can't be? What do you know?" he asked urgently.

She shook her head. "I don't know anything," she said.

"Then what is it you are trying to hide?"

She stared at him, wondering if she dare tell him.

AXEL COULD SEE it in Ally's eyes; something was there. He didn't know how to get the truth out of her. She clearly had something she needed to say, and she needed to do it fast. If this was the same man who had been on the sub, her life was in danger. And it could happen at any point in time. He didn't know how to get the truth from her. He waited a long moment, shifted on the bed, so that she could lie back down normally. "Was your life in danger before this incident?"

She stared at him in confusion. "Before the sub was sunk?" She shook her head. "How would I know?" she asked in surprise.

"I guess I'm asking if you knew of any other threats against you before this. Any boyfriends or ex-husbands?" He knew she hadn't been married, but she didn't know he knew that.

"No," she said. "I've never been married. And, no, I don't have any vindictive exes."

"And yet the one ex posted those nude photos of you."

"That was his revenge moment," she admitted, "but it's hardly likely he is going after my life now, some four years later."

"What was his punishment?"

"He lost his job. The police were on his case, but the judge just gave him a thirty-day sentence and a slap on the wrist," she said bitterly.

"That doesn't seem like very much."

"But still," she said, shrugging, "I guess I'm glad he got any kind of reprimand."

"Losing his job might have hurt though."

"Maybe, but I doubt it. He got another one right away."

"I'm gonna need his name, phone number, and address," Axel said.

She frowned at that. "I don't want him involved."

"Too bad," he said. "What's his name?" And he stared at her, waiting.

Finally she grudgingly gave it to him. "He's married and has a little girl now," she said.

"Good," he snapped.

"He probably won't want to mess up his new world then, will he?"

"I'm not intentionally trying to mess up his new world either," he said. "And maybe he did serve his debt to society," Axel said, "but he hardly served his debt to you."

"The pictures can never be taken down anyway," she said stiffly.

"I know," he said, "but he certainly didn't do any restitution for you, did he?"

She shook her head. "What can anybody do?"

"Maybe I'll ask him that," he said thoughtfully.

She looked at him in alarm.

"So, besides him," Axel said, "who else and what else?"

"Nothing," she said. "Isn't that enough?"

"Only if it's the truth," he said. "As I find out, most of the time, a lot more is in people's background than they're willing to tell me."

"Okay, come on now," she said. "I don't know this guy."

"Maybe not," he said. And he studied her intently because something remained there. And when she dropped her eyelids, he knew. "You may not know this person," he said, "but you're afraid you do." Her gaze flew open, and she gasped. He nodded. "Yeah, so enough of that crap," he said. "Let's hear it. You need to tell me who you think it is."

"But I could be wrong," she said.

"And you could be right. It's easy enough for me to check to make sure you're wrong, if you'll just give me something to work with."

"No, it's not that easy," she said. "He went through a lot too."

"Spill," he ordered.

She frowned, and her gaze turned stubborn.

"Either that, or I'll turn it all over to the naval investigation team," he said. "And they'll rip apart your life."

She paled at that threat.

At least she understood he had the power to make it happen. And maybe he had another weapon to use too. "You need to understand," he said, "that, as far as the military is concerned, you're the only survivor. And, therefore, you're likely involved with the shooter. And since you're the one they have, you could find yourself in the position of being held responsible."

She gasped, staring at him in shock.

He nodded. "You had to have seen it coming."

But she shook her head. "No. I didn't," she said. "I barely survived a horrible event with my life. If you guys hadn't come when you did, I would have died on board," she said. "How could the navy possibly think I was involved? And what about Hostettler?"

"They're looking into him too. But the fact of the matter

is, he died. You didn't." She seemed to shrink in on herself at that. He understood. He reached out, grabbed her hands, and said, "Ally, you need to talk to me."

But she lay here, almost catatonic as she stared at him.

"Smarten up," he ordered. She frowned and blinked. And he was glad that the anger was getting through to her. "This isn't the time to curl up and die," he ordered. "This is the time to fight back. To muster your defenses. To get all your information and present it in a clearly laid-out manner, so that you're completely outside of this investigation."

"And how do I do that?" she said.

"I don't know," he said, "but you need to start by being honest with me. And you need to stop wasting time and do it now."

CHAPTER 5

A LLY LAY IN the hospital bed, staring up at him. She'd never thought it would come to this point.

"Who was this man who entered your hospital room, who you didn't know, yet you may know, but you don't want it to be him?" he asked.

"I don't know," she said dully. She reached up, and, like a child, scrubbed her face with her palms. "Somebody was in my life a while ago," she said. "Similar build. Every time I see this new guy, on the sub and here in the hospital, I was reminded of … him. But there was no limp back then."

"Accidents, surgery, and all kinds of other moments in a person's life can create a limp like that," he said. "Even faking it."

She frowned, nodded, and said, "And I considered that, but it still made no sense."

"And why is that?"

She stared at him, her eyes glazing over. "You won't understand, and you won't believe me."

"Try me."

Something was implacable about his gaze. And yet the hand that held hers was gentle, strong but soothing. She desperately wanted his help. She desperately wanted to tell him that it was all foolish but to check into it first to make sure. She squeezed his hand, and he held firm.

"You need a friend right now," he said. "And I don't see anybody else here."

She winced. "That's a low blow."

"It's the truth. I don't sugarcoat things. You're in trouble right now, with a clock ticking at the shooter's whim, and I'm here, and I can help."

"Or you're working for the military," she said. "You are waiting for me to strangle myself with my own lies."

"Are you lying?"

She stared at him. "No, but you'll think I am."

"I can't help if you don't tell me," he said. When she didn't speak, he let go of her hand.

Something was just so symbolic about that, as if he were cutting the tie between them, and she knew it was this moment or not at all. "When I last saw him," she said, "he was dead."

He looked up, startled.

She nodded. "That's why I know it can't be him."

"Tell me," he ordered. "Better start at the beginning."

"It's my brother," she said. She took a slow deep breath. "He was killed by a bullet wound a couple years ago, along with his best friend," she said sadly. "He and his best friend, they were both of a similar body type. I considered whether it was his friend, but I don't think it was."

"Details, please. And start with, why is your brother's death not in your file?"

She glanced at him, startled. "You read my file?"

"Of course I did," he said, brushing that off to the side. "It doesn't mention your boyfriend either."

"No," she said. "I worked hard to keep that out."

"And your brother?"

"I had two brothers," she said. "This one was from the

wrong side of the blanket. My father had an affair quite a few years ago," she said. "And Rory was the result. We found out just a few years ago. So that's why he's not in my file."

"And does Rory hate your family?"

"No, he was getting to know us, and I thought everything was fine. We worked really hard to create some kind of a relationship. My mother was a bit on the standoffish side, but that's to be expected, since her husband brought home a love child from a time when they had had marital problems," she said. "But, before Rory's death, I think we'd all made great progress. And then he died, and it seemed like everything just kind of disappeared."

"What's his name?"

"Rory Granger," she said. "He died with this friend, Thomas Hardy. They were gunned down on the streets of New York City."

"Deliberate?"

"As far as I know, nobody was ever charged with their murders. So I don't know anything from the police investigation. I tried to get answers, but nobody would talk to me. Finally I had to walk away because it was destroying me."

"So, both of the men, Rory and Thomas, had a similar build, tall, slim?"

"Both were tall and slim. Both were light-haired, somewhere between dark blond or light brown. Whatever," she said, "They were more than just friends."

"And that could be another motive for the murder too then," he said. "An awful lot of hate is in this world."

"Possibly. I was totally accepting. My father was too. I think Mother was getting there."

"What about your other brother?"

She shrugged. "He didn't say much either way. He

didn't seem to care."

"What's his build?"

"Short and stocky," she said. "He's five-ten, two hundred."

"Fat?"

She shook her head. "No, not at all. He works out. He's a bit of a gym junkie."

He nodded. "What else can you tell me?"

"Not much to tell," she said. "That's what I mean. Nothing's there. I know that build. Just something familiar about the look of him."

"Did he have anything to do with your world?"

"No," she said. "Not in my work world. Not at all."

"Any chance the death was a fake?"

"I don't see how it could be. We buried Rory," she said, bewildered. "Neither do I see a reason for him to fake his death."

"Both of them?"

She shook her head. "No. My brother's friend Thomas, his family took him and buried him in their hometown."

"So you didn't attend to his funeral?"

"No. I'm not sure there was one," she said. "He was cremated and only left behind a sister at the time anyway." She watched as he jotted down the notes. "It's way too convoluted to think either of them would be involved in this," she said. "There is no reason."

"There's always a reason," he said. "What we don't know is the reason for killing a submarine crew and downing a sub like this."

"That's got to be the work of another country," she said. "It can't be our own people."

"And why is that?" he asked, lifting his head to stare at

her. "Or is it just you want it *not* to be our own people? We have friendly fire happening on bases where somebody we're doing training with turns around and shoots a dozen of our own men," he said. "How is this any different?"

"But then it would be another country's soldiers," she said, nodding.

"And again, it doesn't matter, works either way," he said. "Somebody just needs a motive. They might make it look as if it was you. They might make it look as if it was Hostettler. But that doesn't mean it was either of you, particularly if there's a connection to somebody else on board."

She frowned. "To have a connection to somebody else and me would be too big of a coincidence."

"Well, I agree with you there," he said. "So, unfortunately for you, we're about to turn your life upside down."

"Didn't you say the formal investigation was already doing that?"

"Yes," he said. "And they'll be looking to prove you guilty," he said quietly. "I, on the other hand, will be looking to prove you innocent."

Her eyebrows rose at that. "Seriously?"

He reached over, grabbed her hand, and said, "As long as you're honest with me," he said, "I'll be honest with you." He squeezed her hand, hopped off the bed, and said, "Now you need to rest."

She shook her head. "I'll never rest again," she said, "because I keep seeing him. I keep seeing that physique."

He walked to the door and stopped, then turned and said, "Call me if you think of anything else," he said, "or if you see anybody else."

"What if I see him again?" she asked bitterly.

"I'll have one of our guys come in to check to see if your

visitor left anything.”

She gasped. “Like a bomb?”

“No,” Axel was quick to say. “More like a bug or even a tracking device.” He turned back around. “Where are your clothes at?”

She pointed to the bathroom. “In a cabinet in there.”

He stepped inside and was gone a few minutes. He exited, his head shaking. “No tracker in your clothes, your shoes.”

“But a listening device makes sense.”

Axel nodded, stepping toward her. “He must think you know something.” He held up his finger and pulled out his phone. He stepped outside her room, saying, “I’ll just be a minute.”

She nodded.

“Mason, can you see about getting Ally’s hospital room swept for bugs. Her visitor was here for some reason. And he had ample time to kill her but didn’t.”

“Right. I’ll send Dane. And since her intruder didn’t kill her, he must want her to be the scapegoat.”

“She already is,” Axel huffed.

“For the murders, yes. But what if the point was to steal that sub? It’s worth a ton and is the newest technology the navy has to offer.”

“But it was sunk, wasn’t working. If it takes us two days to lift it, how could the killer do it?”

“Maybe it wasn’t supposed to sink.” At that, Mason hung up.

IT WAS HARD to understand how Ally had gotten caught up in this. She’d headed out on a job to test the navigation and the computer system on board. Yet somehow she'd ended up as the suspect in a mass murder. She shook her head.

Axel returned, as promised. "Dane's coming." Axel pointed his finger, making a circular motion.

She nodded. *Checking for bugs.* "Good."

He walked toward her, whispering in her ear, "We'll do everything we can to keep you safe and to find out who's behind this."

She nodded, remaining quiet, knowing she shouldn't speak of anything important at this time.

Axel stood next to her, holding her hand. When Dane entered within minutes, toting a small black box, he immediately got to work.

Hmm. It looked like a walkie-talkie to her.

Dane took a minute or so to sweep her room, finding nothing. With a smile and a wave, he was off again.

"How about you put a guard on this door?"

"I'd be happy to," he said, "but I already know that everybody above isn't on board with that."

"Because they don't believe me, do they?" she said bitterly.

"Even if you did see somebody with that same build here at the hospital," he said, "you weren't attacked here. Nothing happened. Which is odd for him to make this move and not leave behind a bug or a tracker or poisoned food or drink or whatever. Sounds like recon to me, which means he'll be back. And we'll watch for that. But the brass will just say that you're paranoid and trying to deflect attention from the truth."

She sagged back in her bed. "Life sucks."

"It does," he said, "but it's also full of good things. So remember that too."

She shook her head. "Says you. Right about now, I don't see too much good about it."

"Stay alive," he ordered. "That's your job right now." And he turned and walked out.

AXEL DIDN'T TELL her that he was camping out here in the hospital for a while. Thought it was for the best right now. The element of surprise, for her and for her limping man. He snagged an empty hospital room nearby, sat back down, and called Mason. He clarified what was happening on her end, despite interruptions caused by Mason repeatedly swearing and interjecting comments. Finally Axel said, "So I'll start running down the half brother and his friend, while you guys do your official investigation into whoever had access to both the sub and now the hospital. If not a limping navy man, our limping man has contacts to compromised seamen, I'm sad to say."

Mason swore again. "Well, they've shut me out of the investigation now too," Mason said, his voice hard.

"I wonder why?" Axel asked.

"More protocol than anything, I think."

"Well, the navy's bound to come after her soon, aren't they?"

"Certainly they'll come to her for questioning," Mason said. "I'm a little surprised they haven't already."

"Oh, and Ally thinks a foreign country could be stealing our sub," Axel noted.

"*Hmm.*"

"Yeah, well, she was in shock today when I got here after the guy visited her. Legit shock. Absolutely no way she was faking that."

"But it could be for a lot of different reasons," Mason warned. "You can't get so sucked in to the scenario that you don't keep your head about you."

"No, that's not a problem," he said. "Better to spend the afternoon here doing research."

"If you have trouble getting information," Mason said, "let me know."

"Will do." After he hung up, he settled down and started researching. Not a hell of a lot was accessible. That was the problem. The half brother, Rory, was a pretty open-end deal. Raised by a single mom, he'd gone to a poor school and had lived in a poor neighborhood, yet he appeared to have turned out okay. He'd gone to college to get a degree in IT. Interesting that it was the same field as his sister, though IT was a pretty broad topic these days. They had connected a couple years ago, according to Ally. Axel wanted to contact her folks and get some confirmation on that but figured he could wait until he was done with this kind of research.

He plowed through as much as he could, then got the NYC coroner's office on the phone. They were busy, didn't see his case as a rush—not compared to their other rushes—were happy to rerun the DNA samples of Rory and Thomas and to reconfirm those samples taken from the dead bodies matched up with other medical records gathered on the two men. Axel should expect something in eight to twelve weeks.

With a sigh, Axel turned his focus on Thomas Hardy. Axel found even less on this guy than had been online on Rory. Axel snorted. Here were two twentysomething males who were not on social media, were not on the dating sites, weren't even posting reviews on Amazon. But, then again, if these guys were gay, even in the 2020s, some people were not open to this lifestyle.

Maybe Axel needed to check for police records. Seems Rory and Thomas had moved around a bit. Not so surprising with job transfers and the like, much less for their chosen lifestyle. Axel didn't want to call some twenty local PDs, checking out where both Rory and Thomas had individually lived over the past decade, before it seemed they finally moved in together, nearby here in California. Unfortunately they died soon thereafter.

At least they were together, Axel thought.

Problem was, the individual PDs didn't share every offense to contribute to the NCIC national database, not unless it had to do with missing persons or felony-level offenses, like serial killers or serial rapists and the like. With that thought, Axel checked the sex offender list. That was national. Still no luck. Rory and Thomas were either under the radar for privacy or just were not criminals, at least at the federal level.

Axel finally ended up sending Mason a text. **Nothing popping on the half brother Rory, practically nothing on the friend Thomas. Almost as if they didn't exist.**

Let me take a look. Mason came back a little later. **California license. Thomas would have been 28 years old.**

Axel replied right away. **Right. So, the brother was 29. They were both about the same age.**

Mason continued, **Went to the same elementary and middle schools but not the same high school. Reconnected afterward.**

Interesting. Where are you getting that from?

Mason phoned him. "Thomas and Rory were both in the navy."

"Well, well, well," Axel said, "there's your connection."

"Both confirmed deceased, with death certificates, cremations, burials."

"Shit," Axel said. "Do we really believe they both died though?"

"I'm not sure," he said. "I'll have to dig in to look further."

"I've asked the NYC coroner's office for a redo on the DNA to confirm IDs. They said it could take up to three months, so I'm not expecting anything for at least four months. So if you can speed that up …" Axel said.

"I'm just trying to work out the justification for this," Mason said, with a note of humor.

"But, in this case, eleven dead navy men is pretty good justification."

"Very true," Mason said. "But the brass already thinks they have their man—woman. Remember? So they don't want any more evidence. Their minds are made up, and they don't want anybody to distract them from Ally. They think they have enough as it is. Any connection to Hostetler?"

"I was just going to ask if you want to keep looking into that."

"Yep. Will do. You keep digging too."

"I'll chase that one down next," Axel said. When he hung up, he got up for another sandwich run to the hospital's cafeteria and sat down there for a quick break. As he did so, his phone rang. He didn't recognize the number, but answered it.

"You were talking to my daughter," said the man on the other end of the phone.

"And your daughter is?" But deep inside, he knew.

"My daughter is Ally. She said you were there today."

"Yes, I was," Axel said, speaking slowly. "Did you have a specific reason for calling me?"

"Her brother Rory," he said. "It's a bad stage to set for a life, and it ended up even worse. But I can confirm what she said."

"Well, you can't actually," he said, "because you don't know what she said to me."

"I didn't know about my son Rory's existence until later in his life," he said. "The affair happened during a bad time in my marriage, and my wife and I had split up for a time. Rory's mother never told me. When my son came looking for me, he was already twenty-four or twenty-five years old."

"Interesting," he said.

"We tried really hard to make a family relationship. My wife obviously had a much harder time with it than I did. Ally welcomed him with open arms."

"She seems like the type," Axel said.

"Her heart is big," her father said. "Unfortunately she trusts a little too easily, like that ex-boyfriend of hers."

"Right, he seems to have been a number one pain."

"Lawyer fees, court case, it was ugly, very nasty, and she's still paying for it," he said. "That man has no honor and is just drainage under the sewer. If you ask me, he deserves everything coming to him and more. So I hope you go pound him into the ground," her father said in frustration. "Unfortunately I'm not living near my Ally, still reside here in Australia, and I'm not physically fit enough to do it myself. But, believe me, I've wondered about hiring someone else to."

"Leave that be," Axel said. "It's not something you want to get into."

"No, but he shouldn't be out walking around after what he did," her father said.

"Can't disagree with you there. Now tell me what happened with Rory's and Thomas's deaths."

"They were visiting New York City, walking through one of the worst areas of town. It was a drive-by shooting, and two other people were on the street. They were shot as well. Both my son Rory and his friend Thomas were shot. Neither survived. Of the two other people shot, one survived, and one did not."

"So there's obviously a police file somewhere then?"

"Yes, they were visiting at the time. You'll have to contact the police department there for a case file."

"Anybody ever convicted?"

"Gang war," he said. "Nobody convicted. Probably a dozen suspects, but nobody they can pin it on."

"Got it," he said. "Typical, isn't it?"

"Unfortunately it's the innocent who suffer all the time," he said. "And I'm getting damn tired of it. First, my daughter was victimized by her boyfriend—or fiancé at the time actually. And that was followed by her brother being victimized as well."

"I'm sorry," he said. "We'll see what comes out of this."

"No, we can't," he said. "The problem is, she is being victimized all over again," he said. "I can't just sit here and let that happen." Ally's father got very emotional.

Axel rushed to assure him. "That's why I'm trying to help, sir," he said. "I can't guarantee what'll happen though."

"Of course not. The navy does what they do, but that's no excuse for picking on her. She wouldn't hurt a fly."

"Then we'll have to prove it, sir," Axel said. "I have to trust in what I'm doing. I have to trust that this is possible."

"Maybe," he said. "The problem is, when the military wants something to go away, they make it go away. And, if they want a scapegoat, they make a scapegoat. My daughter's already been traumatized by men in her world," he said. "I don't want it to happen again." Something about the tone of his voice made Axel lean forward.

"What was her relationship like with her brother?"

"Which one?" the father hedged.

"Don't mess with me," Axel snapped. "You want my help to keep your daughter safe and to get her out of all this? Then you need to come clean." There was a moment's hesitation.

"Rory resented her," he said. "He was still paying student loans, whereas I had helped her through school, and she'd gotten scholarships most of the way. So she was free and clear of student debt and had already made it to the military. I think, drawing parallels with her academically—and seeing the potential difference in his finances, lifestyle, and career path—he saw how different it would have been, had he been part of our family from the beginning. The whole thing took a toll."

"And he resented her specifically?"

"Yes, though I'm not exactly sure why. I think because they were both in the same field, and that bothered him too. Plus both were in the navy, but she was fast-tracking up, and he wasn't."

"Was he a bit of a sexist?"

"He was gay," her father said. "I didn't mind, but I do think he resented women. He had a tough relationship with his mother as well."

"Interesting," he said. "And you're sure he's dead?"

A bark of laughter came from the other end of the call. "I saw his body myself. He took one full round to the chest. There was no saving my boy," he said. A moment of hesitation came before he cleared his throat, and he added quickly, "Please save my daughter." And, with that, he hung up.

CHAPTER 6

WHEN THE DOCTOR showed up in the late afternoon, Ally immediately asked him, "When can I leave?"

He frowned at her, but she just glared right back. "I'm not sure that you're being allowed to leave," he said in a mild tone.

She froze, and her eyebrows slowly lifted. "What? What are you saying?"

"This is a military hospital on a military base. There is some question as to your involvement in the scenario that put you here," he said, "but that's not my department. However, two naval guards are outside your room now."

"Are they to keep me safe or to stop me from leaving?" she asked in a low voice.

"I can't answer that," he said. "I was kind of hoping you would."

"I didn't have anything to do with it," she said, "but I did think that I saw the shooter here at the hospital."

At that, he froze, staring at her. "Are you serious? And you didn't tell anyone?"

"I did tell someone," she said. "I told the SEAL who was here this morning."

His fingers tapped on his upper arm. "I wonder if that's what the guards are about."

"I don't know," she said, "but that shooter visit was also

why I was hoping to leave."

"Meaning that, he knows you're here, and you may be safer out there?"

"I was hoping so," she reached up, rubbing her face again, "but I feel like shit. So I'm a sitting duck either way."

"That wasn't just a simple break, young lady. The bullet did terrible damage to the femur. It'll take quite a while to heal. We had to put pins in there and a steel bar."

"I know," she said. "And I'm very grateful for what you did."

"But you're only grateful in little ways," he said, with a note of humor. "Understood? That head of yours, on the other hand," he said, "must be giving you a crazy headache."

"Well, it was doing okay," she said. "And then it came back again."

"Your painkillers are probably wearing off," he said, checking his tablet. He nodded. "Yeah, you're due for more."

"So, that's what it is?" She groaned as she stared out the window. "I was hoping it was just a temporary setback, and I could get up and leave."

"Have you tried walking?"

"Yes," she said. "To the bathroom."

"And how did that go?"

"I've been better," she said.

"Yes, I'm sure you have," he said.

"I used both crutches, and it was slow going."

"The crutches will be a help temporarily," he said. "We can change that cast to a walking boot after a few weeks," he added. "But, for now, I don't want you moving around much or putting any weight on the good leg. And that casted leg needs to be elevated. Meanwhile, we must watch that other leg wound too. There's always a chance of infection setting in."

"I could do that at home," she said hopefully.

"And who'll look after you?"

Her face fell.

He nodded. "Look. You live alone. You don't have any-body close who could come and look after you."

"There are people I could call to help," she said slowly. She looked down at the leg and winced, thinking of trying to get to the bathroom or getting in and out of bed at her place. "The setup here is better. I get that, but—"

"Stay here for a few more days," he said. "Whether the guards are here to help you or to keep you contained," he said, "they'll stop anybody from trying to get in here."

There was some wisdom to that, so she sank back against the bed and nodded. "How bad is my head?"

"Considering how close you came to being dead right now, I would say, it's not so bad," he said. "However, the bullet ran right along the skull line," he said, "and packed one hell of punch. But you're alive."

"I know," she whispered. "Sometimes I forget to re-member that."

"Focus on that," he advised. "There will be another day after this," he said. "Tomorrow is bound to be better."

"It can't be much worse," she whispered.

"None of that," he said. "From where I stand, this *all* could have been a lot worse."

And, with that, he turned and walked out. She realized she was being selfish and feeling sorry for herself, remember-ing the other men from the sub. Besides, it wouldn't help anything. But all the thoughts of everything that had gone on continued to circle in her head. Nothing made any sense, and she desperately needed it to. She liked things that were logical—like code, where she could see a problem and fix it. Lines of code made sense, or they didn't. And, as soon as she saw something wrong, she could apply her knowledge and figure out how to make it right. But this? There was no making it right. She didn't know what the hell was going on, but something was seriously wrong that defied logical explanation, and she couldn't see her way out of it.

Just then her father called her. "I spoke with him," he said abruptly.

She frowned. "I only told you about him being here," she said, sitting up straight, "so you wouldn't worry."

"Well, I know how this works," he said. "I've watched my children go through hell like this and have a bad end," he said. "I wanted to make sure that I put in a pitch to see that you came out on the right side of this."

"Oh, Dad," she said, with a heavy sigh, as she sagged against the headboard. She reached up a tired hand and brushed her hair off her face. "Did you tell Mom?"

"Not the details," he said. "I didn't want to upset her any more than I had to."

"She'll have to know sometime though," she whispered.

"Maybe not," he said. "Maybe this will all be over, and she won't have to know anything about it, until it's done with."

Her father was nothing if not an optimist. But, after his son Rory's death and what happened to Ally with her lowlife boyfriend, her father was no longer the same believer in humanity. Not like before. "I think Axel is working in my favor," she said, "but you know how these guys are. It's just so hard to know what they're thinking."

"I know," he said. "I'll keep an eye on it, and I'll hound him too."

"I doubt if that'll help," she said.

"It can't hurt," he replied. "Somebody's got to look after you, and I can't do much from Australia."

"Dad, I'm fine," she whispered.

"You're stuck in a hospital bed with busted-up legs," he said. "They won't even let you leave the hospital because you can't look after yourself," he said. "You probably have to be in traction with your leg elevated, don't you?"

She chuckled. "Did you talk to the doctor too?" she asked.

"No, but maybe I should."

"Don't bother. I just spoke to him," she said. "He repeated almost exactly what you just said."

Her father chuckled. "Medical advice is pretty well universal," he said. "I am concerned about the head injury though."

"I'm normal. I'm talking. I'm rational. I don't even have a concussion. I just have a bunch of stitches on the side of my head. And, of course, they shaved my head. At least that strip."

"That's to be expected," he said. "Right now, it's probably still numb too. That'll hurt and itch like hell before long. Guaranteed to drive you crazy."

"Great, thanks," she said. "I'm really looking forward to that."

"It will be fine," he said humorously. "At least you'll know you're alive at that point. Right now, you probably feel like you're half dead."

"I do," she said. "It's kind of frustrating. But I'm working on it. I just want answers."

"We all do," he said. "We all do." And, with that, he hung up.

AXEL GOT WATER-COOLER word from Mason that the navy had two guards on Ally's hospital room. *Well, I don't need to stick around here so much then*, Axel thought. Now, besides digging into Hostettler, that ex-boyfriend of Ally's was a piece of information Axel wanted to deal with personally. But how the hell would he get to the bottom of that?

Then he decided that the best tactic was forward movement. He'd look up the ex's address, remembering that he had a wife and a little girl, as Ally had said. Finding the directions, he hopped into his Jeep and left the base's hospital and headed into San Diego. It was another fifteen minutes across traffic to get to the small bungalow. He walked up to the front door, and a woman answered. He smiled and introduced himself. "I'm looking for Carl. Is he home?"

"Yes, he's out back," she said, frowning.

Axel nodded. "I'd like to speak with him," he said easily.

Still frowning, she closed the door partially and called out, "Carl, somebody's here to see you."

"Can't even get a day off, can I?" he said humorously. She opened the door when Carl arrived, and Axel stared at him.

"Who are you?" Carl said, frowning.

"I'm involved in the investigation of an accident that happened recently," he said and introduced himself with his name and base.

"So, connected to the base?"

"Yes, that's correct, related to the base," he said. "And it involves Ally."

With that, Carl's face drained. He looked nervously at his wife and then said, "Well, maybe we should take this outside and not disturb my wife with it."

"Oh, I'm pretty sure this is something your wife needs to know about and to deal with," he said, taking a step inside. He looked over at her and smiled. "Ma'am."

She looked at him hesitantly and asked, "Why would you come after Carl?"

"Just some questions," he said. "I need to know his whereabouts during this incident." He quickly noted the date with a notepad and a pencil in his hand. "So where were you during this time?"

Carl stared at him and said, "I was here at home," he said.

"The whole time?"

He frowned. "Well, I was at work too."

Axel jotted down where he worked and who could vouch for him at the job. And then he said, "And the rest of the time. Who can vouch for that?"

"My wife, Mary, here," he said. "I was here with my wife and my daughter."

"The entire time?" Axel asked, looking at him.

Carl looked at his wife, the two of them frowning at each other, then he turned back to Axel and said, "Yes, I believe so."

Axel kept quiet for a moment.

"Why? What happened?" Carl asked.

"I'm afraid that's classified," he said smoothly.

"And why would you come here?" Mary asked. "What's this got to do with Carl?"

"Well, ma'am, his animosity toward Ally in the past has made him a suspect in this case," Axel said. "His court case and his method of revenge led us back to check him out to make sure he wasn't involved in this."

"That was a long time ago," Carl said quickly.

"Four years ago," he said. "Yet you served only thirty days."

"Yes, but that was a trumped-up charge," Mary protested.

"Trumped-up?" Axel looked at her with interest. "You are aware that he took nude photos of his fiancée and posted them all over the internet in revenge, right?"

She gasped and stepped back slowly.

"*Revenge porn* is what they call it."

She looked at her husband, clearly stunned.

"Look," Carl said, holding up his hands. "That's who I was back then. That's not who I am now. I was really angry." Mary stared, her gaze going between the two men. "You did what?"

Carl took a slow, deep breath. "Mary, calm down."

"Me, calm down?" she said. "You did that to Ally?"

He took a deep breath, and then he slowly nodded. "I did. I was really, really, really angry."

"Why did you break up?" she asked suddenly. Carl was silent. "Do you know why they broke up?" she asked, looking at Axel.

He turned to Carl and said, "Carl, why don't you just tell her the truth and be done with it."

With obvious reluctance, he spoke. "I had an affair, and she found out," he said heavily. It was easy to see from the look on his face that he thought his whole world would come crashing down.

"*You* had an affair. She broke up with you, so you got revenge by posting private photos of her on the internet?" Mary's voice rose higher. She took several steps back, looked at him, and said, "Do I even know who you are?"

"Mary, I'm a different man," he said. "I went through hell over that. I made a mistake, and I paid for it."

"You paid for it, yes," she said, "but Ally is still paying for it. Every day. Those photos will never be gone," she said, her hand over her mouth, as she stared at her husband, shell-shocked. "God, Carl," she said. "That is an action that goes on forever."

"I know," he said. "And, as you can see, I'll be hounded forever because of it too," and he pointed at Axel. Then he turned to Axel and said, "Thank you very much for destroying my marriage," he said. "I had nothing to do with whatever's going on with Ally now."

"Maybe not," Axel said, "but I hardly think it's fair that your wife doesn't know what you're capable of. After all, she's now got to know that the nude pictures you have of Mary are likely to end up on the internet too," he said. He turned to Mary and said, "I'm sorry, Mary. That's not how I would want you to find out such a thing. But you're much better off understanding what your husband is capable of." He turned back to Carl. "And the bottom line is this—if you have any connection to this attack on Ally, you won't be walking on a thirty-day sentence." And, with that, Axel turned and walked away.

He could hear Mary behind him, screaming at her husband. With grim satisfaction, Axel realized life would not be quite the same for this man who had tried to hide from what he did. Maybe there was a point in time where Carl had paid his price to society for what he'd done.

But for Ally? That invasion would never go away. Mary had called it when she had said that it was a life sentence for Ally. Back in his Jeep, Axel wrote off Carl as being a suspect.

CHAPTER 7

STUCK IN HER hospital room, it seemed like Ally could do absolutely nothing. She had her phone, and she spent her waking hours researching all the members of the team that she had gone into the sub with. At least when her mind was clearer of drugs she could do this. There had to be a connection somewhere. She'd given the list to Axel, though surely somebody else was around who could have given it to him.

Knowing Axel, he probably had it five times over from different people. He seemed to be thorough and was always double-checking and cross-checking. But every time somebody walked past the window to her hospital room or her door, she glanced up, and, of course, it was always too late to see who it was.

She was becoming paranoid now that she'd had the one visitor. That it looked like her brother's friend didn't mean that it was. She knew her brother Rory and his friend had to be dead. And there was no reason to suspect that same body frame meant that it was actually the same man. They say there are like thirteen archetypes of people in the world. But it was just too damn easy every time she saw that slight angle to his head and, in her mind, to replace it with her brother's friend Thomas. But how was that even possible? Because Thomas really died. And his body had been cremated, right?

The fact is, her brother's friend also had another sibling.

It all just made her sick to her stomach. But why would anybody go to the sub and kill everybody? And that was the point she kept coming back to. If it was revenge, why didn't they take them out one at a time, each in a different way? Then there would be no outright connection for the police or the navy to follow, right? Surely a major killing spree event like that on the sub took a lot of planning all at once. And, sure, the shock of multiple killings would then completely stymie most people as they tried to figure out what was going on, but the investigators would get to the bottom of it eventually.

She just didn't know when that would happen. The sooner, the better, but it felt like it was her against the rest of the world. Yet she needed to heal. She needed to get that "good" leg capable of holding her weight so she could at least be mobile. She didn't want to stay in the hospital. And the guards? Well, the guards were a whole different story.

Axel had come with his diagram of the sub, wanting to verify the position of all the men. She kept going over and over it in her head, wondering if she could have seen something differently, if she could have done something differently, but it was just so hard to remember.

As she lay here, fighting the frustration, she could hear footsteps, multiple heavy footsteps coming down the hallway. And she knew the navy was coming to her. She froze in the bed, wondering if she could pretend to be asleep. When the door was pushed open, she knew there was no hope of that either. Two men, both MPs, stepped forward, and another man followed them. A colonel but she didn't know which one. She saluted from the bed.

"I understand that you were a part of this submarine

mess," he said, his voice clear and hard. "I have some questions for you."

"If, when you say, I was *part of it*, you mean that I was there as assigned and attacked at the same time as the others were killed, then, yes, that is correct, sir," she said, her voice clear and her diction concise. "However, if you are implying that I was part of the murder of my fellow crew members," she said, "then that is an absolute and clear no."

"In that case, you won't mind us asking you some questions, will you?" he said smoothly.

In the same tone she responded, "Of course not, sir. Please proceed."

And there followed one of the most grueling hour-long sessions that she'd ever endured. And it only broke off when the doctor stepped into the room.

"That's enough," he said. "She's exhausted. And look at her. She's clearly traumatized, and now she's looking feverish again from all this," he said. He walked over, checked her temperature and pulse, glaring at the colonel. "I can't have a decline in her healing," he snapped. "She was very seriously injured. If she should have a setback, she's at risk ..." and, with that, he let his voice trail off.

The colonel shrugged. "If she's a traitor to our country, her death won't matter anyway," he said, as he shot her a hard glance. "If you're lying, it will be much worse for you."

"I'm not lying," she said with some heat but desperate to not degenerate into a weeping female. "My record stands for itself. I'm not prone to fits of hysteria or imagination. Someone else did this. You need to find him."

"And why should we, when you look good for this from where I stand." And, with that, he turned and the three men walked out.

She laid here, gasping for breath, feeling the heat over-whelming her. "I don't feel so good," she whispered. And almost instantly, her lunch came up and out of her mouth. She was shuddering and shaking by the time everything in her stomach had emptied. She hadn't even managed to lean over, so it was all over her and the sheets and blankets on her bed.

The doctor swore lightly at her side even as he called for a nurse to help clean her up. "This is exactly why I don't like anybody being questioned too early," he said. "That's just ridiculous."

The nurse arrived and took charge. Trying to follow the woma's requests as she wiped and mopped up her face before shifting to changing her bedding.

"I don't think he really cared," she said when she could wishing her stomach would calm down. It was roiling even now. "It's pretty obvious he thinks I'm guilty. He wants me to confess, whether it's the truth or not."

"If you had something to do with it," the doctor said, "then I'm sorry for your soul. But, if I had to decide, considering only your wounds," he said, "they need to find another suspect."

"Wouldn't that be nice," she said. "I don't think he's even bothering to look at actual facts like that."

The doctor stopped momentarily and then nodded. "I may need to send him the x-rays of your injuries then."

"What good would that do?" she asked.

"It might help him to understand how you got hurt."

"I don't think he cares," she said. "Somebody else is try-ing to help me prove my innocence, and I did a diagram of the submarine with all the bodies and where they found them," she said. "The trouble is, I blacked out after I got up into the HVAC shaft," she said. "So I'm not even sure it's possible for me confirm or deny where he found the bodies."

The doctor looked casually over at the side table, where she had the large piece of paper. "Come on. Even this adds to your stress, and that is the last thing you need to be doing."

"But I can't just lie here, doing nothing," she whispered. "You saw the colonel. I'll get court-martialed for the murder of eleven of my fellow crew members," she said. "Not to mention the sinking of a really expensive sub. But I didn't do it."

"Then we have to trust in the process," he said. "Help is out there. We just have to make sure that you get it."

"I'm glad you believe me," she said. "Obviously nobody else does."

"Hey, I saw your leg," he said. "You weren't doing any moving with that."

"I'm pretty sure they think I did everything before that happened," she said.

"But you couldn't have," he said. "The gunshot that shattered your leg so badly came earlier than the other two bullets."

She stopped and stared at him. "It did?"

He nodded. "Yes. The bullet holes clearly occurred at least an hour apart."

She continued to stare at him. "Maybe you could tell him that too," she said hopefully.

"That's what I was wondering," he said. "Obviously they're under a delusion as to what your role was in all this. Any of those bullet wounds would have incapacitated you. It's a wonder the blood loss alone didn't kill you."

Just then the colonel slammed back into the room.

"You're the one I've been looking for." He glared at her as if she were the one responsible for keeping the doctor from him.

"Good, I was about to track you down. She couldn't have done what you think she did. Her injuries wouldn't allow for it." He held up the x-rays and showed the colonel exactly what had happened, what the damage to her system had been at the time.

The colonel huffed and asked a few questions, obviously not ready to listen. He pointed at the file. "I want an independent medical team to look this over. I can't have her getting away with treason because you think she couldn't have done this." He snorted at that.

Her doctor stiffened. "Of course. That is your prerogative." He glared at the colonel. "In the meantime, you're adding to my patient's stress. So I'm asking you to leave now."

The two men stood glaring at each other before the colonel spun stiffly on his heels and left, his temper obviously brewing as he slammed the door behind him.

"He does have it in for you," the doctor said thoughtfully. "I wonder why?"

"I'm an easy answer. He's looking to close this and to get a few more accolades to decorate his uniform. He doesn't care about getting to the truth or catching the real traitor."

"Well, any doctor will see what I see, so not to worry. He can get all the professionals on his side that he wants. It's still a miracle the blood loss alone didn't kill you."

"And yet I was lying up in the ceiling shaft, bleeding to death, while my oxygen supply depleted," she said. "Even in the air venting system, I couldn't avoid the bullets. Thank heavens I was rescued when I was."

"That just means you were thinking on your own," he said. "Surviving is not something you should be penalized for. This whole thing is ridiculous."

"I'm glad you think so." And she did feel marginally better. "If you could show him that much, maybe he would at least start considering other options."

"I will," he said. "But now I want you to take some medicine and get some sleep," he said. "No more visitors."

"Except I need to see the guy who is helping me when he comes," she said, motioning toward the drawing. "I couldn't confirm or deny anything when he was here earlier. I was so tired that I couldn't do much."

"No," the doctor said. "It'll just add to your stress. You need to heal first and foremost."

"I need to get out of here," she said. "Can I walk on this leg?"

"No, and it needs to be elevated almost all the time, or you'll be in a real mess."

"I could get home and put it up," she said hopefully.

"Nope, not happening," he said. "At least not for a while."

"And what's *not for a while*?"

"At least a few days. You are still more fragile than you realize. You saw it for yourself with the colonel's visit."

"Fine," she said, giving in. "It's just not what I want to hear."

"Of course not," he said with a gentle smile. "That's why I'm the doctor, and you're not."

"I don't like that those guards are posted out there," she said. "Are they protecting me or just keeping me here?"

He looked at her, surprised, then thought about it and shrugged.

"And that's only one of the questions that keep rattling around in my head and making me sick," she muttered.

"Well, you've been injured enough without getting sick and stressed out more," he said.

She winced. "I'm really sorry about that."

"Don't be," the nurse said. "Being sick isn't something any of us want. Our bodily functions take over, and, for whatever reason, that needed to get out of you."

She nodded quietly. "I'm gonna need a new gown too."

"We can take care of that too," she said, and she quickly reached into the cupboard in the corner. The orderlies grabbed up the dirty bedding, made up the bed with fresh linens. Once only the two female nurses were with Ally, they exchanged her soiled hospital gown for a clean one. The other nurse helping Ally to stay upright helped her back onto the bed, and they hooked her leg back up so it was suspended. "Here, just rest," she said.

And, with that, Ally lay down, and, moments later, she collapsed back onto the bed. "Now I'm exhausted," she said.

"And, if nothing else," one of the nurses said, "that should tell you just what kind of shape you're really in right now."

"Meaning, it's shitty," Ally said bitterly. "I can't go anywhere, and I'm a sitting duck while I'm here."

"You're where you need to be," the other nurse said. "So just relax, and let us do what we need to do." Then gathering up their things, the two nurses left.

Ally pulled the blanket under her chin, willing the pain meds to hurry up and kick in. She didn't know what her stomach was up to, but she figured it was stress from the colonel. As she lay here, her mind kept going back to the bodies and to Axel. Did he understand that the brass had been here to question her? She'd so hoped to avoid having to deal with them. But, like any huge corporation, there were always bosses. And, in this case, those bosses were pretty scary. Curled up in a ball, at least on one side, as best she could with her leg suspended, she closed her eyes and let sleep overtake her.

AXEL HAD TO get back to the hospital and go over the diagram he had left with her. She hadn't talked about it very long or with any detail when he'd been there before. It seemed like, with the combination of the painkillers and her other medications, she was either too sleepy or in too much pain to have much comfort or clarity for a detailed discussion. He quickly sent her a text, asking her if she was up for a visit. When there was no answer, he called her. He didn't even stop to think until he heard her sleepy voice. "Oh, God," he whispered. "I'm so sorry. Go back to sleep."

"No," she said, yawning. "It's okay."

But he could immediately tell from her voice that something was up. "What happened?" His voice was sharper than he intended.

"Colonel someone or other showed up," she said. "He came with two MPs to ask questions. There was absolutely no doubt from his attitude and his questions that he believes I had something to do with it."

Axel winced at that. "Wish I'd have been there. I'm so sorry you had to go through that," he said.

"Well, we knew it was coming. The doctor ended up throwing him out. If all that wasn't embarrassing enough, once he left, I upchucked the contents of my stomach all over myself," she said. "It took a team of nurses and orderlies to come in and to put me and my bed to rights. The doctor also said I'm not getting out of here anytime soon. He said my leg needs to heal longer and that clearly my stamina is lacking, or I wouldn't have spiked a fever and puked my guts out over a few questions."

"That son of a bitch. He grilled you hard, didn't he? He must have if your body rebelled that way. Remind me to shake that doctor's hand for putting a stop to it."

"Wait though. I'm not done. The doctor said something else," she said. "I asked him to tell the colonel what the doc told me, but I don't know how that works. Then, as it was, the colonel came back looking for the doc. At that point, my doctor said that my injuries clearly happened an hour apart. And he doesn't see that I could have had anything to do with the killings on the sub because I wasn't capable of the kind of movement throughout the sub that your body chart would have demanded. I guess, after that first humdinger of a shot to my leg, the shock kicked in, so I could climb into the HVAC system. Then those last two shots were probably the gunman shooting up the HVAC vents overhead for good measure or just out of sheer anger or madness."

"Yes, that's good to know," he said. "Actually that's damn good. How did the colonel take the news?"

"Well, it's something," she said. "And the colonel didn't like it at all. He was pissed. Said something about an independent review of the medical file. His own medical team, I presume. Now my doctor did say it wouldn't matter who he talked to, the evidence was clear. Now if push came to shove, would he say that in the middle of a trial? I don't know."

"I hear you," he said, "but I'm sure the colonel will talk to another medical specialist. We just need that doctor to confirm the first doctor's assessment."

"Maybe," she said, "but I can tell you that the colonel didn't look like he gave a damn, and he'll probably get someone to back up his theory."

"Even if he does," he said, "that's why we have to follow up on all this. If he can't be convinced easily, we have more doctors to bring in as well. Let's let it play out and see how he does."

"It doesn't seem like it was anything any of the brass cared to follow up on," she continued.

He could hear the tears in her voice and searched for a change in topic. "Did you have a chance to look at the diagram I left you?"

"Not really," she said. "I'm awake again though, so maybe I can."

"How about I bring you a coffee?" he said.

"I don't know if you can get it past the guards," she said. "The doctor told me no visitors. I got too upset over the last one. I told him though that I needed to see you about the chart, and he was annoyed that I was even looking at it."

"*Hmm,*" he said. "Good point."

"What have you been doing?" she asked.

"I went and checked in on your ex," he said. "To make sure that he had an alibi for the date and times we are looking at."

She gave a laugh at that. "I'm sure he did," she said. "He was always one of those lucky buggers."

"Well, I don't think he's feeling all that lucky at the moment," he said. "In the course of our conversation, I did mention, while his wife was present, why it was logical for me to be asking Carl about an incident involving you."

She gasped. "What?"

"It made sense," he said smoothly. "Clearly he hadn't been honest with her."

"I still can't believe you did that," she muttered. "You didn't have to ruin his marriage."

"I didn't. He did," Axel said. "But, as somebody who has been vile toward you in the past, we had to know if he was involved in this now. It only makes sense that his wife would have to know about his history."

"Maybe," she said. "It just goes along with all the shitty things in my world."

"Shall I try to come up and see you?" he offered.

"I am still tired and exhausted," she said. "Maybe tomorrow." And just enough hope was in her voice that he agreed.

"Fine, I'll try again tomorrow," he said. "In the meantime, I'll keep digging deeper, doing research. All our witnesses, except you, are dead, so I'm at a dead end of people to see, other than your ex. Maybe if we can turn the tide on this," he said, "everything else will settle out and will be fine."

"Maybe," she said. "Somehow it feels like it'll never be fine again," she whispered.

"It will be," he said. "We'll do what we need to do and get out of this."

"I wonder," she said. "Honestly, I don't even know what that would look like or how it could possibly ever work."

"Keep the faith," he said.

When he rang off, he contacted Mason and filled him in.

"I knew they were planning on talking to her," Mason said. "It's to be expected."

"She said it was obvious that they were looking at her as the guilty party. Any new information on Hostettler?"

"We're working on a cross-check between all twelve crewmembers," he said. "We've found some crossover, like various missions, different departments, some friends, some friends at work only, some wives who are friends," Mason said, "but absolutely nothing pops as being a traitor."

"But that's part of the deal, isn't it?" Axel said. "Seems like it would be hard to be a successful traitor if you're letting people know about it."

"True enough, but, at the same time," Mason said, "usually something clues us in. Like I said, we're still working on it. If something should pop later, I'll send over photos for you to run by Ally."

"What about the security videos?" he asked. "Any idea who the trespasser was on the sub?"

"No. Voice recognition, facial recognition, body types, nothing's popping. I've taken it to several different places to see if anybody knew who it was, but we're not getting any confirmation on his identity."

"So, the only suspect is a dead friend of her dead brother?"

Mason's tone turned light at that. "We have to love ghosts when that's the theory we end up with, right?"

"I don't know," Axel said. "I'm not getting very far in this investigation."

"Don't worry. I've sent somebody to help you," he said.

"Oh? Why is that?"

"Because he's at loose ends, and he's got time off. And he thinks it can't be her."

"As long as we're not automatically dissing her from being involved just because she's a woman," he said. "Although the doctor did tell her—after he threw out the colonel, by the way—that she wouldn't have been physically capable of the crime. And this is more important—he told her that her bullet wounds occurred an hour apart."

"So, in theory, she took the shot that shattered her leg early on, and then took the second bullet much later."

"And the third," Axel said. "Don't forget the head wound."

"Correct," Mason said. "So, maybe she passed out with the first one? There is blood loss and shock to consider as well."

"Or, more likely, she managed to get away and hide after the first one. And then, as she said, he was firing up into the shaft later and tried to take her out then."

"And we also don't have any black box record because the sub wasn't fully functioning. But we have to consider that somebody came down to the hatch and opened it up to let the other guy out."

"I was wondering about a torpedo tube," Axel said, "but she said they weren't functional yet. I'd think another submersible was the most likely egress."

"Depends on what his skill set was and what the state of readiness of the sub was. She did mention, didn't she, something about feeling someone had been secured on the sub?"

"Yes, but she also said that she was unconscious and didn't remember a ton of what went on."

"Also not great," he said, "because that sounds like she's trying to get out of answering."

"Well, she might seem like that," he said, "but it's hardly fair, considering she was so badly injured."

"Yes," he said. "It is a fact of life though that, if you don't have the right answers, everybody looks at you sideways."

"Yes. I just feel like we don't have any information," Axel said.

"There's information," Mason said. "We just have to get to it."

"Have you tried fitting the framework of the brother's friend into the time frame that we have?"

There was silence on the other end. And Mason said, "Seriously?"

"I have no confirmation of his death and won't have any for at least four months. And I don't know what else to suggest," he said.

"I'm pretty damn frustrated myself."

"Understood," Axel said. "I know you're off the case, but can you approach the colonel with this medical timing for Ally's injuries?"

"Sure. Yeah. Why not? Haven't had my ass chewed out in like two hours." Mason chuckled. "When you get back to your apartment, you'll find somebody there waiting for you." And Mason hung up.

"Gotta research Hostettler. He needs some deeper investigation," Axel muttered to himself as he made his way back to his apartment. If he was going to have company, he better grab some food. He hadn't eaten either. He swung by and grabbed several burgers, fries, and a couple sodas. He had no clue who would be there and probably should have given them the opportunity to choose their own food, but Axel couldn't be bothered. As he pulled up and walked over to his front door, he saw another man leaning against the wall. "Baylor?"

"Absolutely," he said. "How're you doing, Axel?"

"Hey, did you volunteer to help us out on this?"

"Sure did," he said. "I've got the week off, and I'm bored

stiff. I had plans out of town, but it seems my girlfriend dumped me," he said with a shrug.

"Sorry, man. That sucks."

"Not that we were going out for all that long, but she apparently got a better offer, let's put it that way."

Axel chuckled at that. "Good," he said, "because I could use some fresh eyes. I don't have a clue what the hell's going on, and nothing is making any sense."

"What's this about a ghost or something?"

"Yeah, let me explain," he said, as he walked up to the apartment. "Have you eaten?"

"Nah, earlier," he said. "I just figured I'd stop by for a bit, see what the hell was going on, what I can do to help. Then I'd go out and get something later."

"You may want to rethink that," he said, "because I picked up enough burgers to last us a while."

"Sweet," Baylor said. "Let's hope that, by the time we get to the end of these burgers, and you've filled me in on this mess, we can find a different direction to investigate."

"I kind of like the ghost theory myself," Axel said. "Particularly since her shooter from the sub—who looks like her dead brother's lover, also presumed dead—was walking the halls of the hospital earlier today."

At that, Baylor stopped and looked at him. "Seriously?"

"Not the first time someone was declared dead who wasn't, right? But, yeah, she totally freaked out afterward because she's pretty damn sure she saw him."

"What was he doing?"

Axel stopped, thought about that, and said, "Pushing a trolley out of her room, dressed like an orderly."

"Why?"

He shook his head. "You know what? I have no idea.

Why would there even be a trolley in her room?" he wondered. "I'm assuming it was just a cover for a recon trip."

"There shouldn't have been a trolley left in her room," Baylor stated. "They would have left the cart out in the hallway and brought her a tray of food. They wouldn't have brought the food cart or a big trolley full of laundry in there either. They would have left it in the hallway, grabbed up what they needed, and gone in. But no one is checking that close to what others are doing. It would have looked completely normal to any passerby."

"So, the answer is, I don't know," he said. "But see? That's already a perspective I didn't have before. So I'm glad you're here."

"Glad to be here," Baylor said. "It's a damn frustrating crime. And right now, I could use a good puzzle."

"You got it. Come on in. Let's eat."

CHAPTER 8

ALLY WOKE UP the next morning and realized that she'd slept through dinner last night. When the nurse walked in early in the morning, she was surprised to see Ally awake. "What time is it?" she asked the nurse.

"Six-thirty," the nurse said, reaching out and checking her blood pressure.

"I missed dinner last night," she murmured.

"You did," she said. "And rounds. We came in and checked on you several times, but you were out."

"Maybe from the painkillers the doctor gave me?"

"Maybe," she said cheerfully. "At least you have an appetite now."

"I do, but I'd love a shower first."

"That'll be a little hard," she said. "The best I can do is bring you some water for a sponge bath."

"If I could just bathe myself, fine," she said. "But, if I can make it to the toilet, surely I can do a quick sponge bath in the bathroom."

"We might manage that," the nurse said. "Are you ready to try getting up and going to the bathroom?"

"Absolutely," she said, carefully removing her leg from the sling. "I do really have to pee." The nurse helped until she was vertical with the crutches in hand.

"Now take it really slow."

Ally took a few steps to the washroom, delighted that she was getting this far on her own steam. And the nurse said, "Don't close the door." So she closed it a little bit, just enough for some privacy. After she used the bathroom, she stood in front of the mirror and stared at herself. "Holy cow, I need more than a sponge bath," she cried out. "Oh my God," she said. "I had no idea my face was so dirty."

"It's not that bad," she said. "Don't forget you had surgery on that head."

"You sure I can't have a shower?"

"Absolutely," she said. "Hang on. I'm bringing you a stool. Let's see if we can get you sitting down in front of the sink, and then we can do a full sponge bath on you." And that's what they did.

It was awkward and uncomfortable, but, by the time she was done, with the nurse's help, Ally felt better. "And I suppose there's no way to do my hair either?"

"Nope, not right now. Can't get those stitches wet," she said. "This is the best we can do."

And slowly, with a fresh gown on and using her crutches, Ally made her way back to the bed, where she collapsed, exhausted. "Just that little bit," she said, "and I am so tired."

"Which is why you can't be on your own for a while," she said. "You need assistance to make sure that you get some healing in and to avoid hurting yourself worse with a fall."

"I get it," she said. "It just sucks."

"It doesn't matter if it sucks or not. It's a short-term deal."

"Right, I have to remember that," she said. When the nurse started to leave, she asked, "Any chance of a coffee?"

"You just said you were exhausted," she said. "Do you

want coffee? Or do you want to go back to sleep?"

"Coffee," she said. "Please."

"Will do," she said. "I'll be back in a few minutes."

The nurse returned ten or maybe fifteen minutes later with a hot cup of coffee and a cookie.

"That cookie looks great," she said. "Where'd you get that from?"

"Well, someone brought them in this morning for the staff," she said, "but I figured you might like the pick-me-up to tide you over."

"Yes, that'll work," she said. "Am I allowed to have somebody bring my laptop in here?"

"Sure," she said. "That might keep you from getting too bored."

"It would," she said. Knowing that Axel would be asleep, she picked up her phone and quickly sent him a text message, asking if he could pick up her laptop. When he responded immediately, she was surprised. And then when he asked where it was, she frowned. When she didn't answer right away, he phoned her.

"It was on the submarine," she said. "Damn. At least my work went well. I had figured out the problem."

"Yeah, we never discussed that. I know this was the new sub's maiden voyage and that you had some questions before you took off. So what was the final verdict?"

"That sub was not reliable. We had major work to redo on it before it could be put into action."

"So was it software-related or hardware-related?'

"A combo of both, as it is often found to be."

"But you saw no evidence of outright sabotage, did you?"

"I'm focused more on the software, so I'm qualified to

talk about the coding, which had some minor bugs in it, but I tweaked that. *Hmm.* In fact, I had to do that a couple times. However, on the hardware end, absent some engineer contradicting me, the batteries were all wrong."

"How so?"

"First, they shorted out. So we lost all nav, causing us to sink to the ocean floor. Second, these batteries are known to give off gases, both poisonous and deadly, generating chlorine gas if the sub were to fill with water. Third, the specs for this sub do not call for this type of battery."

"Okay, so a major fail on the part of the mechanics, I presume, which the navy will be all over. And something I don't have on my plate." He chuckled.

"So, could you go by my place? I have a spare laptop there as well."

"And where would I find that?"

"In the coffee table," she said.

"How about keys?"

"Crap," she said. "In my purse on the sub." She groaned.

"I can get the manager to let me in," he said, "if I can't get in on my own. I was coming to see you this morning anyway, so I'll bring your laptop with me."

"Woohoo! Thank you," she said. And, with that resolved, they ended the call. As she lay here, waiting for breakfast, the doctor popped in, a concerned look on his face.

"I'm fine," she said. "Much better than yesterday. That chat with the colonel really did a number on me. I got some good sleep though."

"That's great," he said.

"Somebody's bringing me my laptop too," she said. "I hope you don't have a problem with that."

"Nope," he said. "Anything that keeps you occupied and not worrying will help."

"Oh, and that also means you'll have to let me have a visitor." At his overdone expression of outrage, she laughed. "And, no, I didn't do that on purpose."

"Not on purpose, no," he said, "but it is a good excuse. And you look like you've gotten some good rest. Enough to be a little ornery anyway."

"I slept a lot last night," she said. "I actually slept through dinner."

"Yeah, you need to eat as well though," he said, frowning and looking at his tablet.

"But I slept," she said, "so surely that's worth something."

"Something, yes," he said, "but we have to maintain the balance. You need food and sleep."

"Well, I'm waiting on breakfast now," she said with a smile.

He nodded, checked her file, and said, "And you've been up and on crutches already, correct?"

She nodded. "And it was fine," she said.

"Okay," he said. "Spend the rest of the day with that leg up, and we'll see how it is this time tomorrow."

She smiled and nodded and didn't push him. But, if she could possibly see her way to getting home, she'd be one happy camper. As it was, her breakfast arrived at the same time that Axel did.

He took one look at the food and sniffed the air. "What's the food like?"

"It's food," she said. "I've had worse. We're both used to institutional food, right?"

He chuckled. "Got it." He helped her sit up by shifting

the angle of the bed and moving the table over. When he pulled the tops off the little bit of food, he frowned and said, "That's not enough to keep anybody alive."

She looked at it, surprised. "I even asked for extra because I slept through dinner last night," she said.

He looked at it, frowned, and headed back outside. When he returned with another tray, she looked at him, scandalized, and said, "Tell me that you didn't hijack my neighbor's breakfast."

"Nope," he said, "but everything comes portion controlled, it seems," he said. "So I grabbed you a second one. I think it might be different food." She looked under the lid and smiled. "This one's at least pancakes," she said.

"Do you like them?"

"Absolutely," she said. "So this is good. Thank you."

"If you say so," he said.

"It's great," she said, and immediately she dug in. He sat down beside her, and she realized he was holding a bag. "Is that my laptop?"

"IT IS," AXEL said. "I don't know how the recovery is going on the sub, but I presume, when it gets back up, you can get your purse and work laptop back again."

"I would hope so," she said. "I just don't know how that process is going."

"That is something I can probably get an update on," he said, and he quickly texted Mason.

"Who are you getting updates from anyway?"

He looked over and said, "Do you know Mason and Tesla?"

"I know Tesla," she said. "I've worked on several military

contracts with her."

"Her husband is Mason," he said.

She nodded. "I remember hearing something about him."

"All good things, I hope," Axel said.

She smiled. "I haven't heard anything bad about you SEALs yet," she said with a smile.

He looked at her plate and saw that it only had a little bit of food left. "You going finish that?"

"No," she said. "I'm done."

He quickly removed the trays and carried them outside. An empty trolley was down a couple doors. He put the dishes on there and walked back in, smiling at the two guards who'd let him in.

He said, "Now maybe we can set up your laptop." Pulling it out of the bag, he put it on the table and said, "I found your charger too." He hunted around for an outlet, then shifted the bed over just enough to reach it. With the bed positioned a little bit higher and the table lowered, she could actually work on the laptop. "Another question for you," he said. "Are you going to work, or are you just browsing and keeping yourself busy?"

"I can't really work," she said, "because my work was all about the sub. And now I have something else on my mind," she added with a wry smile.

"I don't want you worried about that," he said. "The doctor was very specific about you being stressed out. He was concerned about how sick you got."

"That's nice of him," she said, "but not very helpful, considering what I'm going through."

"Agreed," he said. "My thoughts were that maybe you could do a little bit of research into your brother and his friend."

"Maybe," she said with a smile. "I just wish there was something more substantial to go on. Just the fact that Thomas supposedly died didn't mean that he did. But what would be behind any of this? I don't even know what I can do," she said. "I don't know very much about them at all," she said.

"But," he said, "you're an IT specialist, and it's your brother and his friend. So why don't you do what you do and see if you can come up with anything at all?" He stood just then and said, "I'm under strict orders from the doctor to not keep you very long," he said. Then his phone beeped. "Mason needs me."

She shrugged but nodded. "Thanks for checking."

"So I'll take my leave. If you find anything on Rory or Thomas, let me know."

"Will do," she said with a smile. "And thank you very much for the delivery."

He nodded. "And if you see that guy again ..." he said. Immediately her face closed up. He nodded. "I know. I get it. You believe it was him. But the thing is, we need proof."

"What kind of proof can I give you?" she said. "I saw him, and then he was gone."

"What kind of trolley was he pushing?"

She looked at him and frowned. "One of those lunch trolleys."

"So it was laden with food?"

She stared at him. "Nothing was on it," she said, frowning.

"So an empty trolley."

"Maybe," she said, staring at him. "But why would he have a trolley in here?"

"That's what I've been trying to figure out," he said.

CHAPTER 9

ALLY WATCHED AS Axel left, wondering if he was right, if she could find something on her half brother and his friend. It didn't make any sense that she thought her shooter was Thomas. But, with a laptop, she somehow felt so much more freedom. Now she could start to ask the nurses about the trolleys. Because that really bothered her. There was absolutely no reason for the shooter from the sub to have been in her room with a trolley. Had she suddenly woken up or rolled over? Or maybe he'd left because she'd been awake, or maybe because a nurse was coming in? She didn't know. But was he still here? And could she get into the security cameras to see him?

The hospital staff said that trolleys are to remain in the hallways and that there hadn't been any sign of her visitor, not by any of the nurses on the floor or per the sign-in sheet at the front desk. She remembered something about a hat. But had he been wearing a hat through the entire hospital?

She quickly sent Axel a text, asking if she could get access to the hospital security videos.

Hold on, he texted. In a matter of moments, she had a link. And, with that, she could see the entire day. She watched everybody coming in through the front door that day, but she didn't find Thomas. Then she went to the other exits, and systematically she checked them all. At the one at the back, by the storage loading area, she finally thought she saw him, already dressed in orderly scrubs, as least the same color worn by the other orderlies in this hospital. She slowed it up and went back again ever-so-slightly, checking to see. And, sure enough, it was that same build and that same hair. She sent that section of the video feed to Axel and said, "This is him."

Now, with a place to start, she kept following him as he went throughout the building. She lost him on several other hallways and then picked him up again, only to lose him when her hallway camera feeds went out. But then she picked him up again as he left. Presumably after coming to her room. Still a group of nurses were standing outside her room in the same time frame. Maybe he left, thinking there would be a better time to attack her. Like when a group of women weren't standing around, talking. He didn't appear to talk to anybody and didn't do anything other than throw a lab coat over his standard orderly scrubs. Like a surgeon, just out of an operating room.

That gave him an elevated status as far as passing through the hallways, making it very easy to come in and out. She checked the parking lot feed, looking for him. He walked around the corner of the building and out of sight. Following that, she asked for access to the city cameras, after sending Axel a feed of the suspect leaving the building.

Axel called her then. "I'll pick it up," he said. "I can't give you access to that."

She frowned and struggled with that the limitation. "I'm better off to do this right now," she said. "I have the time."

"And I also have somebody helping me now," he said. "It's all good."

"Says you." Hanging up, she waited anxiously, thinking

what to do now. But she went back, trying to take any view that showed any feature she could get—his face, his profile. Then she sent it to her father. **Do you know who this is?**

Ally, you know you're supposed to be leaving this alone.

I can't, Dad. So answer the question. Do you recognize this person?

Sure. It's Thomas.

Yet Thomas is dead, right?

Yes, honey. And you know that as well as I do. Two years ago.

Dad, those pictures were taken since I've been in the hospital.

When her phone rang, she knew it would be her father.

"Are you serious?"

"Very," she said. "They say everybody has a double," she suggested cautiously.

He was quiet on that. "I know that friend of yours was looking into this. Did he find out anything?"

"Nothing definitive on this yet," she said. "And I got my laptop from home, so I decided to start digging myself."

"If Thomas is involved in this," he said, "you don't know what you're up against."

"I don't remember him being bad news though, do you?" she cried out.

"No, maybe he wasn't, but he loved your brother."

"And?"

"I don't think he loved you."

"I didn't do anything to Rory," she said in confusion. "Why would Thomas have anything against me?"

"It's hard to say."

"You're not making any sense. Or you're not telling me something," she said. "But I didn't do anything to them, so I don't know. It has to be somebody else in his family," she said.

"Actually that is possible," he said. "He had a younger brother. Maybe they blame you for Thomas being killed or something."

"Again, not something I had anything to do with," she said angrily. "Why would anybody blame me for that?"

"Well, I don't know if you remember, but the boys weren't supposed to go to New York," he said. "They were to come here and have some family time with us, but that didn't work out because you were graduating."

"And?"

"And what?"

"What was I graduating from?" she asked. "It seems like I'd have been done graduating by then."

He chuckled. "We had delayed the celebration because your mom had been so sick."

"So, they could have come for that."

"Yes, but your mother didn't want them there," he said, his voice heavy.

"Oh, don't tell me that she actually blamed me for wanting Rory and Thomas there? Did she?"

"Yeah, she did," he said. "I'm sorry about that."

"Great," she said. "I was quite happy to spend time with my half brother, yet apparently I'm the one who got blamed for this? That's not fair."

"No, it isn't," he said, "but I don't think anybody really thought about it at the time."

"So, instead of coming for the family event, they headed to New York City. Or I think that's where they were, weren't they?"

"Yes. And they ended up in a city hotel and got shot in

the midst of some gang turf war."

"So, maybe the younger brother is blaming me because I was more important than having them come visit? Isn't that a little thin?"

"It is, yes. Definitely," he said. "But what I don't know is how important it was to them."

"Right," she said. "So who knows?" She hung up from her father, not exactly sure what to think. Could she have been in trouble for something she had nothing directly to do with? And yet, why now, with everything else? That didn't make any sense to her. Just then she got another phone call. This one from a coworker.

Megan said, "Hey, I hear you had a pretty shitty week."

"That's one way to put it. What did you hear about it?"

"Only that something went wrong, and you are potentially involved."

"Great. Don't suppose they mentioned that I got shot up, three different times," she said. "Anyway, thanks for calling. And, hey, don't believe everything you hear, okay?"

Putting the phone calls out of her mind, Ally tried enlarging the hospital video feed, isolating the face. Now that she had a profile shot, a little bit better than the one she'd sent her father, she studied it for a long moment. She didn't have access to facial recognition programs, but she knew somebody who did.

She quickly contacted Tesla. **I'm in a spot and could use a hand.**

Tesla immediately came back. **What do you need, Ally?**

I'm trying to identify this man. Check out these pics. She sent Tesla various snips from the video. Then she sent her the best close-ups she had. **Any chance you have facial recognition?**

I can access some. Who do you think this is?

This man was in my hospital room, pushing an empty trolley.

Tesla replied right away. **He looks very familiar. I enhanced the video of the trespasser who entered the sub, so I'm wondering if it's him.**

Me too, Ally texted. Just when she was getting frustrated, thinking nobody would get back to her, Tesla called.

"Hi, Ally. I would definitely say it's the same person in the hospital as the one who was on the sub," she said with muted excitement. "No luck yet on tracking down who it is, but I'm still working on it. However, I need you to tell me if you have any idea who it is."

She told her the story about her half brother and his friend. "I don't know for sure that it's Thomas, but that's who I automatically thought it was," she said. "Even though I knew it was stupid. I knew it was wrong because how does someone who is dead come back and kill all the crew in a sub like that?" she asked. "And, Jesus, you'll never convince me it's all because they couldn't come for a family supper."

"Yeah, that one is pretty far-fetched," she said. "But listen. If they were looking for a fall guy to put this on, you might have been an easy one to choose."

She winced at that. "Maybe so, but why?"

"Lots of reasons to close something like this quickly. Gives confidence and make others feel more secure to know the navy has already found their terrorist. Unfortunately there could be any number of other reasons too. So hold tight. We'll get to the bottom of this." And, with that, Tesla hung up.

Ally sat back in her bed, frustrated that everybody else was out and about, doing stuff, yet she couldn't seem to get anywhere herself. She really wanted to just go sit in the hallway and watch the world pass by. She was so isolated in here, and it just seemed wrong. Still, she was sitting up at least and looking to find something else to do. Then the lights when out in her room. She glanced around, surprised. A power outage?

Well, power problems do happen. But wasn't a generator backing up the hospital power? And, sure enough, after a few minutes, the generator must have kicked in. The lights came back on but at a lesser power. Even so, she was surprised she had any power in her room, thinking they would save it for the surgeries and intensive care units. Still, she unplugged her laptop and put it off to the side in the bag that Axel had left. She thought about him and then realized she should probably update him. She quickly sent him an email with what she had found and what she had done with it.

Instead of getting an email back, he phoned her. "Are you okay?"

"Well, I was," she said. "Until this power outage. Now it just feels weird."

"Are you in darkness?"

"No, it's kind of like running lights," she said. "So, not full lights, giving a weird ambience to the place."

"Do you still think this guy in the hospital could be a family member of your brother's friend?"

"I don't know who he is," she said, "but he sure looks like Thomas, and even Tesla agreed it's likely the same guy who got on the sub."

"Well, that's something," he said. "Tesla's voice carries a lot of weight in the military."

"It doesn't get me off free and clear though," she said

bitterly. "All I want to do is go home."

"*Hmm*, with the power outage happening," he said, "I just want you to stay safe."

She froze at that, at something in his voice. "Why? Does that have something to do with it?" He didn't say anything, and her mind immediately started to fill in all the details.

"If the guy from the sub comes," he said, "you were never wrong from the beginning."

"Where are you?"

"On my way to you," he said. "Get up and lock your door."

"Easier said than done. I've got two injured legs. Remember?" she said, pushing the table away and throwing back her bedcovers. "How far away are you?"

"About ten minutes," he said.

"Perfect," she said. "I can make it that long."

"Says you," he said. "Anybody who is trained could take you out in seconds."

"Thanks for that," she snapped, "but I'm hardly alone here."

"You're alone enough," he said. "Now can you lock the door?"

"Are there even locks?"

"When you get over there, check," he replied.

"Fine, fine, fine," she said. "I'm just about up on my crutches, but I can't walk on the crutches and hold my cell phone."

"Leave the phone on the bed," he said, "but don't shut it off."

"Wow, you really are paranoid." And he was making her paranoid too. Awkward on the crutches, she made her way to the door, and, just as she was checking for a lock, it opened toward her.

AXEL COULDN'T STOP the anxiety coursing through him the closer he got. Something was seriously wrong right now. As he entered the hospital, he saw security everywhere. "What's going on?"

"Sir, you're not allowed in the hospital," said one of the security men.

"Well, I'm concerned about one of your patients," he said. "She was already part of a major attack, and I'm worried that somebody else has come after her now."

The security guard shook his head and said, "You're not going anywhere."

He picked up the phone again, still connecting to Ally's phone, and called out, "Are you there? Ally?"

But there was no answer. He said to the guard, "I need to make sure she's okay. But it doesn't have to be me. Send somebody else up." The guard looked at Axel and hesitated. "Look. I was talking to her. She was heading to the door to try and lock it. I don't know what's going on, but something is. She was supposed to have two guards looking after her."

"Something's going on all right," the security guard said.

Axel turned around as a team of men came through the door. "What's going on now?"

"Backup," the guard said.

Axel was shoved off to the side, while the guards had a quick meeting, and the men started searching, spreading out, looking for whatever it was they were looking for.

But in his heart of hearts Axel knew exactly what they were looking for. They were looking for an intruder, and he knew where that intruder was going. As the security guards' attentions were elsewhere, he quickly slipped down the hallway and hit the first set of stairs and bolted up toward her room.

As soon as he got there, he pushed on the door, hoping it was locked, but instead it pushed wide open. And he knew before he ever stepped inside that it would be empty. He called out, "Ally, are you here?"

Silence.

He quickly did a search of the room and realized he was right. But what really got him was that her crutches were lying on the floor, just at the door. "Shit, shit, shit." He bolted up the hallway and saw several soldiers walking toward him and said, "She's missing. Ally is missing."

One of the soldiers said, "We're looking for Ally Minga."

"This is her room," he said, "but she's missing."

The soldier looked at him and said, "Or she's escaped."

"Was she a prisoner?" Axel challenged. "Before you go too quickly down that path, she already reported sighting one of the men who looks suspiciously like the shooter who took over the sub. She's reported it to others as well."

"Such as?"

He quickly named Mason and Tesla and said, "You need to be talking to the brass."

The guy was already pulling out his phone and making calls.

But that wasn't enough for Axel. "She's gone," he said. "Somebody needs to track the video cameras." And then he stopped and said, "Crap! That's why the power is out."

The soldier looked at him. "What do you mean?"

"He caused the power outage so he could get her out of here and not be on video."

"Why take her with him?" the other soldier asked.

Axel stopped and thought about it and said, "I don't know. He could have just shot her from the doorway and been gone."

"Do you think her life is in danger?"

"Of course it is," he said. Then he stopped and said, "But that's the thing, isn't it? If, and I say *if*, it appears like she's escaped, then that just confirms she's involved in this mess. If he just shot her, the brass would know she wasn't."

"How would that help him?"

"It's a setup. It gives him a fall guy for the whole thing," he said. "Which is what he intended from the beginning." He pulled out his phone and quickly contacted Mason. Baylor, who'd driven over behind him was suddenly here as well. "It was pretty hard to get up here," he said. "I saw you slip away and worked my way in after you."

"They aren't very interested in helping us," he said to Baylor. "But her room is empty and her crutches are on the floor by the door. No clue what happened to her security."

"It was pulled off," one of the soldiers said.

Both Baylor and Axel nodded, then ignored them.

"Can she walk without the crutches?" Baylor asked.

"No," he said. "She can barely walk with them."

"Says you. Maybe the cast was fake too," one soldier suggested.

"Jesus. You need to get the x-rays from the doctor," he said. "That should convince you that she's in a much worse physical condition than you're thinking."

"Says you. We need you to stay here. We have questions."

Axel stared at him and said, "Sure, no problem. Of course I'll stay here." His phone rang then; it was Mason.

"I've been ordered to stay right here," he said, "but can Tesla get into the security cameras?"

"No. They went down with the power outage," he said. "She's onto the street cams right now, checking for how Ally may have been pulled out of there."

"A vehicle from the parking lot most likely," he said. "But I don't know what's going on, and I need to get out of here so I can help."

"And where would you go?" Mason asked.

"Her apartment," he said. "Because surely, if she is being made to look like she's part of this, this is her escape. Wouldn't that be the easiest? To take her home and then shoot her?"

"To make it look like a suicide, you mean?"

"Yeah," he said. "I don't know what the hell's going on, but we know that something is. How about the DMV?" Axel asked. "Any vehicles reported to these guys?"

"You mean, the dead ones?"

"Yes," he said.

"We'll check," he said. "And, Axel, cooperate with the military," he said.

"Of course," he said in a very calm tone.

Mason stopped and said, "Axel, I mean it."

"I do too," he said. "And I'll cooperate in the way I see fit. I'm going after her. I don't know where she is or what the hell is going on, but we have to find her."

"We're on it," he said.

"Just not fast enough," Axel said. Just then there was a shout, and the soldiers took off running down the hallway. He looked at Baylor and said, "I don't know about you, but that's my cue." They quickly disappeared down one of the back exits and headed outside the hospital, then around to the front parking lot, where they jumped into his Jeep. Baylor said, "Why would they take her to her apartment?"

"I don't know," he said. "Maybe they wouldn't. Maybe they'd take her down to the docks. Maybe they would just— I don't know," he said in frustration. He beat his hand on the steering wheel. "It just doesn't make any sense."

"No, it doesn't," he said. "But that just means we don't have the right pieces to the puzzle yet."

"At the moment, there aren't any pieces," he said. "And, right now, she could be one step away from death."

"Except for the fact that they took her alive. There's got to be a reason."

Mason phoned him back just then. "White delivery van, hospital logo on the side. It took off not long after the power outage began," he said. "Tesla caught sight of the vehicle. There's a passenger. Looks like she's unconscious or asleep. She thinks it's Ally."

"Where's it headed?"

"San Diego."

"Is she tracking it right now?"

"She is. Are you off the base yet?"

"Not yet," he said, "but I'm damn close." As it was, he reached the base exit, quickly pulled through, and took off. He didn't know what was going on at the hospital, but they hadn't shut down the base yet. And that was fine with him. He handed the phone to Baylor. "Put that on Speaker and keep track of what's going on. I just need to know where we're going and how to get there." With that, he focused on his driving and started pulling out of the traffic and weaving his way through. "Give me a destination," he said to Mason.

"Head down toward the loading docks," he said. "I don't know what's going on, but it looks like that's the direction the kidnapper took. It doesn't mean they won't take her off someplace from there, but that's where they're heading right now."

"I'm on it," Axel said.

The drive took fifteen minutes before Mason said, "They've taken a sharp right."

"Into the commercial district?"

"Into the shipyards," he said.

"That could be good news or bad news."

"No," Mason said. "I highly doubt there's any good news about it. You're too far behind to find out where she's gone."

"Can you switch to cameras in the shipping yards?"

"Tesla's working on it right now," he said. "Looks like the van has come to a full stop."

"And then what?"

"I don't know," he said. "You're still what, ten minutes away?"

He checked the clock and estimated, "Probably eleven," he said, and he started swearing. "Nobody's closer?"

"Maybe," Mason said. "A couple guys are in town right now."

"Well, see if anybody's closer," he said.

"I've already put out calls," Mason said. "I've got one coming in now." When he came back, he said, "Dane is in that area. He's already cruising the yards, looking for the vehicle. He said to keep moving. And he's looking."

"I'm coming," Axel said, shifting into a higher gear and said to Baylor, "Let's keep tracking this. We have to find her. Once she's gone into the shipyard, you know there's a good chance we'll lose her forever."

CHAPTER 10

ALLY'S PAIN LEVEL kept her sliding in and out of consciousness. She didn't have a clue where she was or how she got here. But she was being moved constantly—jolted from side to side, pushed forward and back. She didn't know what the hell was going on. And the more she cried out, it seemed like the rougher the trip. And it really was a trip. She was being transported somewhere. She just didn't understand where. Or why.

She tried to open her eyes, then realized she couldn't. Something was across them. She tried to move her arms and realized they were bound behind her. At that moment she understood. She had been taken captive. Shocked, horrified, and bitter, she determined she was in the bottom of some vehicle, her body taking every jolt as it went around corners. And every time it jarred her leg, the pain was horrible, sending her into another level of agony. The cast was still on her leg, which was about the only good thing. But, every time it was jarred, it hurt terribly.

She tried to shift enough that her other leg braced the broken leg, which helped a bit, but it also put pressure on the wound in that leg. On the next corner, she slammed against the vehicle floor and hit hard. She laid here, shuddering for a long moment, wondering what the hell had happened. Obviously she'd been taken from her hospital room, yet she couldn't seem to remember very much. She remembered the power going out. And that's when she remembered Axel telling her to lock the door.

She'd gotten to the door, and, just as she had tried to see if it locked, it pushed open right into her. She didn't know who it was, but her door opened hard and fast, then hands came up, and something was shoved over her face, and she'd gone down. *Chloroform.* She recognized the smell from the science lab. And once you smelled chloroform, absolutely no way you ever forgot it.

She wondered how they had gotten her out of the hospital. She couldn't open her eyes more than just a fraction, but it was enough that there was still darkness all around her. She rubbed her throbbing head against the floor to try to force the blindfold off, but that wasn't working either. She twisted her hands to see if she could get them free. But once again, she was stuck. She could try to get her bottom through her arms, but she wasn't sure with a broken leg in a cast that she could pull it off and could be left in a worse position.

She was, however, a long-time proponent of yoga. Taking a moment to breathe, then moving as softly and as easily as she could, she managed to pull her legs up against her chest, so her hands and arms could slide under her butt and then past her feet, so her hands were in front of her. The cast made it awkward and stretched her abilities but she made it. Not that it helped much, but it was something. Using her mouth, she tried to figure out just what was holding her hands together. It was some kind of a rope.

She grabbed onto part of the knots with her teeth and tried to loosen them, not even sure just what it was she was working with. Then she realized that with her fingers out front now, she could pull the blindfold off. Feeling stupid for not having done it immediately, she quickly pulled the blindfold over her head, then confirmed that she was inside a vehicle moving rapidly down a street. But it had no windows on the side or on the back door. But it was daylight since she could still see inside the vehicle.

She twisted to look up and couldn't see anybody in the passenger seat. She stared at her tied-up hands, wondering if she could use them to choke the driver. Could she actually hold him down long enough to take him out? Just then he turned into a corner, and she rolled to the side. She swore softly, and the driver laughed.

"Sorry about the ride, sweetheart," he said. "Still, you should be used to this kind of stuff by now."

She didn't know what the hell that meant. "What are you talking about?" she asked. She strained to listen to the voice but didn't recognize it. "Who are you, and why are you doing this?" she cried out.

"Well," he said, "you're just a scapegoat, but then you probably figured that out already. All those dead men in the sub. Oh, that was fun."

She said, "It wasn't fun at all. Are you the one who shot me?"

"I didn't say that, did I?" he said.

She stopped and froze. "Somebody else?" She shook her head. "Nobody else was on the sub." But did she know that for sure? Once up in the damn tiny space she'd been hiding in, she couldn't move, let alone see anyone.

"Keep guessing. You might get there," he said, laughing. He took another corner.

She cried out as she slammed against the wall again. There was no way to brace herself. "You don't have to drive so crazy," she said. "I'm already injured."

He said, "Well, the chance of you surviving this isn't good anyway."

"I thought you wanted a scapegoat," she said. "At least in prison, I'd still be alive."

"Oh, so you want to go to prison?" He paused to contemplate that for a long moment. "I don't think that'll work out for me."

"The least you can do is explain this," she said. "I was shot three times. Everybody on the sub but me was killed, and now here I am, kidnapped. What the hell is this all about?"

"Well, in theory, you should have figured it out already."

"Well, I'm trying to recognize your voice, and I can't," she said. "And I can't see you, so how the hell am I supposed to figure anything out when nobody explains anything?"

"Maybe that's true," he said, "but you'll still have to work it out from here on. I'm not giving you any help."

"Are you working alone?"

"Nope," he said. "Pretty hard to do a job like this alone."

"Right. Like who got you off the sub?" When he failed to answer her, she asked, "Are any of your coworkers still alive?" she asked.

At that, he burst out laughing. "What? Oh, that's a good question," he said. "I'm really not so sure about it. Some of them aren't," he said. "I know that for sure."

"Are you somehow related to my brother?" she asked softly.

He growled at that. "Your brother was an asshole."

She stopped and froze. "What? You're doing all this because he was an asshole?"

"Well, let's just say that it all works out to my advantage to have you and your brother blamed for this."

"My brother has been dead for years. He won't get blamed for anything."

"Maybe," he said, "but it's still about you and him."

"So this is about Rory and Thomas? Was Thomas your brother?"

"Don't even fucking say his name."

"Well, as confirmation goes," she said, lying back down again in the van, "that's not bad."

"But it doesn't tell you anything," he snarled.

"How much do I need to know anyway?" The fatigue was starting to hit her. "This is all bullshit."

"You live with the bullshit," he said. "You work for the government. Is there a bigger source of bullshit in the entire world?"

"I don't know," she said sadly. "I had hoped so."

"I guess you shouldn't have ripped out that navigation stuff on the sub."

She stopped and stared at the back of his head. "Were you there?"

"Partly. I was there for a lot of it."

"But I don't understand," she said. "The only navigation I ripped out was stuff that wasn't working. I was there to replace a lot of it."

"No, you were there to make sure it all worked," he said.

"Sure, but a bunch of stuff in there wasn't working well, so I was changing some of the wiring and codes."

"Says you," he said. "I figured you got wise to what I was up to."

"No," she said softly. "I wish I had though."

"I'm sure you do," he said, "but it didn't work out that way. So I had to go to plan B."

"What was plan A?"

"Well, to keep the navigation equipment, that's for sure."

She stopped, thought about it. "You were trying to steal the sub?" she cried out in wonder.

"Bingo," he said, "but you were not very smart about it."

"I had no idea you were in there doing that," she said. "You didn't have to shoot us all."

"Sure I did," he said. "I mean, it's not like I was prepared to leave witnesses around to rat on me."

"You could have locked everybody out," she said. "And just left us there."

"Oxygen was at a premium with twelve extra people breathing," he said cheerfully. "If a dozen people weren't breathing, it was better, and I had twelve times more air, if I needed it."

"Jesus," she said, "but you could have gotten the oxygen system back up and running again."

"I could have," he said. "That was the plan. But then you did something to the navigation."

"I figured *you* did," she said, confused all over again.

"No. I just told you that I didn't."

"But some of it was really messed up. In fact, I had to correct the software, twice, when it should have been fixed the first time," she said, reaching up with her hands to rub the side of her head. "This makes no sense."

He stopped talking for a moment, as he drove the van through the afternoon traffic, and then he gave a short bark. "That fucking Hostettler. If you didn't do it, maybe he actually did screw me over," he snapped.

"I did catch him at my station a couple times, and, when I asked him what he was doing, he always just gave me that halfway smile and said he was interested in what was going on."

"Well, he was interested all right," the man said, "but he was a bit of a loose screw."

"Is that why you took him out?"

"Well, I didn't do it though," he said.

"You know what? I think you probably did take out Hostettler," she said. "They said that it looked like he committed suicide. But I suspect you grabbed the gun and put it to his head and pulled the trigger."

"Aren't you smart?" he said. "I made sure I shot him up a little bit first."

"So he was your partner?"

"Ex-partner."

Just way-too-much cheerfulness was in the man's voice. She only wished she could place it; she silently scooted over to get a view of his face, not wanting to get caught without her blindfold. "You look like Thomas," she said.

"What do you know about Thomas, and how would you know what I look like?"

"Because I saw the feed of you sneaking into the sub and later into the hospital," she said. "I figured it had to be you."

He swore up a blue streak, and she realized he hadn't been aware of those mistakes.

"They've got you all over the place," she said calmly. "Shadowed, sure, but that limp of yours is pretty describable."

"Took a bullet way back when," he said. "Never healed right."

"Sorry about that," she said.

Again, an ugly darkness filled the van as she waited for his reaction. But there was none. He just gave that bark of laughter and didn't say anything else. As if he knew something she didn't. Then what else was new?

But, with so many dead already, she knew that she didn't matter. She was just one more death to be had in this matter. So why the hell was he keeping her alive? "But you could have just left me in the hospital," she said. "Being there was killing me already."

"Glad you've got a sense of humor in all this," he said, chuckling, "but it won't do any good."

"In what way?" she asked, as if interested. All she was doing was desperately trying to figure out how to contact someone and get some help. She couldn't see her phone anywhere. Then she'd left it on the hospital bed when she went to the door. Damn. She had on only a hospital gown, and that made her feel even worse. As a matter of fact, she had no ID of any kind on her. Things were looking pretty rough. "Is there any heat you could turn on back here?"

"It's a hot sunny day," he said. "You'll be fine."

"Not really," she said, "it's freezing back here."

"I left your underwear and your hospital gown on," he said. "It's not like you can do anything with that cast on your leg."

"Some clothes would be nice." A chill was setting in.

"Some stuff is in the back there," he said. "Go for it, if you want."

"For that, I'd have to use my hands," she said.

"Well, that's not happening. So either make good use of it or don't," he snapped. And then he fell silent.

She had no clue how much farther they had to go, but she looked around and saw a bag. She reached for it and looked inside—a variety of clothing, mostly everything in a medium or large. There was a skirt, however. She managed to pull it on over her broken leg, her goodish leg, then past her hips. Now if she had something that she could put over her chest, she'd feel like she wasn't quite so vulnerable. But how she was supposed to do that with her hands tied?

When she studied the knots, one had loosened a bit, what with all the moving around and shifting. Not much but maybe enough to slip out one of her hands. It took her a bit, but she finally pulled one hand free. Not really knowing what to do from here, she went through the bag, pulled out a sweatshirt, and, with her back turned to the driver, she quickly pulled it on over her head. "Nice job," he said. Not sure how you got your hands out of that rope, but we'll keep it in mind for next time."

"You do that," she said. "I just want to go home."

"You're not going home," he said.

She looked up and saw that they were speeding along the highway as far as she could tell. And the speed was enough that, if she even tried to open the back door to jump out, she'd end up with another broken leg—or worse. Traffic was probably behind her too. "You could at least let me sit in the passenger seat," she complained.

He didn't say anything.

She stared at the rope in her hands, and she knew that Axel would have taken the rope and wrapped it around the driver's neck and choked him. She wondered about doing it.

"I can see what you're thinking," he said. "It's all over your face. I really wouldn't try that if I were you." He lifted his hand enough for her to see he held a handgun.

So, even if she tried to do anything, he could shoot her. Or she could get it free from his hand. Thinking over the horrors of the past few days, she realized she would rather go down fighting than be taken to whatever nightmare he had planned for her. But was this the best avenue right now?

When he slowed down and turned off the highway, she didn't know quite what to do. She figured she was almost out of time. Fighting the blinding pain, she shuffled up to the front seat, looking for street signs or anything to give her a location. Just when he reached up with gun, she snatched it from his hand and quickly turned it on him and held it against his head.

Hitting the brakes, he pulled off to the side of the road and lifted his hands in the air. "Okay," he said, in a totally different tone of voice. "That's not what I expected."

"You were turning the corner, and that's where your focus was," she said. "And you were still trying to keep your free hand on the gun."

"Got it," he said. "Now what?"

"Where is my phone?"

He motioned at the seat beside him. "It's right there. Good luck getting it and keeping that gun."

"Right," she said, and, taking a deep breath, she lined up her shot and fired it into his kneecap.

"You fucking bitch!" he screamed at the top of his lungs, writhing in agony. He rose, trying to twist in his seat.

But she held the handgun right between his eyes. "You'll get a second one," she said. "I owe you two more, after all."

He glared at her. "You don't know fuck," he yelled.

"Maybe not," she said, "but I'm learning." And, just like that, she pressed the gun hard against his forehead and reached out for cell phone. "Turn around and face forward."

"And if I don't?"

"Then forensics can go over your body," she said.

"I'm the victim here, not you." He shifted ever-so-slightly, groaning with one hand on his knee and the other holding his thigh. "I think you hit an artery," he murmured.

"Then you better hope we can get help fast," she said, "because otherwise you'll die right here."

"Bitch."

She just smiled.

AXEL HAD ALREADY met with shipyard security and the group of soldiers gathered outside in the shipyard. He quickly told them everything he knew. "We have to find her, and we have to do it now," he said. He'd already been dismissed, sent to one side, along with Baylor, who looked at him. Axel said, "We can't just stay here and do nothing." Axel stormed to his Jeep, Baylor with him. "There's got to be some way to get ahold of the gatehouse and see if they went through or not."

"We already know they did," Baylor said, getting into the Jeep as soon as Axel did.

"So no vehicle here came from the shipyards?" Axel slammed his hand against the steering wheel. "Where the hell are they?"

"Easy, take it easy," Baylor said.

Just then Axel's phone rang again. He answered without even looking at the display.

"It's me," Ally said in a rush. "I don't know where I am," she stated. "I was kidnapped, and I'm now holding the gun on the driver. I shot him in the knee so I could get my phone and call for help," she said. "I don't know where the hell we are though, and he's not talking."

"Shit," Axel said, spinning the steering wheel and pulling back out of the yard's parking lot. "Any idea if you were in the shipyards?"

"Not recently," she said. "We are on the highway, but I

couldn't figure out where."

Baylor interrupted. "Ally, I'm Baylor. Stay on your phone. I'll see if I can triangulate your location."

"Thanks, I'm not gonna be much help. I've got all I can do right here," she said.

"You don't have to do anything. We'll get within a block or two."

"Oh," she said, "I was hoping you could come right to me."

"Depends on where you are."

An odd sound through the phone.

"Is that your kidnapper?" Axel growled.

"Yes," she said. "He doesn't think much of me at all."

"Ally, take the butt of that gun, and slam that mother fucker as hard as you can across the temple. Do it now," Axel ordered.

"Don't you fucking dare," her kidnapper shouted.

Then came a hard *smack*. She was breathing heavily when she came back on the phone. "God, I hated doing that."

"Is he out cold?"

"I think so, but I don't want to touch him."

"Don't you relax your guard," he said. "This guy is a killer, and he won't think anything of turning the tables on you, even with a shot-up knee."

"I know," she said, trying to hold on.

He could hear her bravery through her tears. "We're on the way," he said. "You hold that thought. We'll be there soon."

"How soon?" she asked.

"If he makes a move against you," he said, "shoot him again, and this time you kill him. Do you hear me?"

"If I have to, I will," she said. "I'm just trying to stay awake. The pain is pretty bad."

"Don't you black out," he said. "That could be the end of it."

"He's out cold," she said, "and I'm not far behind."

"No," he roared. "Do you hear me? He'll come to faster than you."

"It's so hard to hang on," she said.

He could hear the fatigue and her tears. "Get yourself as comfortable as you can," he said. "You keep your eyes on him and that gun trained on him. We can't be too far away now, and, if we aren't, we'll get somebody there who's closer."

"I want to believe you," she said. "God, this has just gone to shit."

"Did he tell you anything?"

"He's got a team. Some of them are dead," she said, "I can't remember half of what he said. Something about me being a scapegoat. I said jail was better than being dead, and he sounded surprised at that idea, so I think he thought that I would end up dead eventually."

"I imagine that's the plan," he said. "Then you can't repeat whatever tale he spins."

"He is related somehow to my brother's friend, or at least he knows them," he said. "He took a bullet that didn't heal right, and that's where the limp came from."

"Did he say whether he was military or anything official?"

"I don't think so," she said, but he heard the tremor in her voice.

"Ally, buck up."

She growled. "I'm here, aren't I?"

"Yes, but I can't have you go to pieces."

"I haven't gone to pieces yet," she gasped. "That's not fair."

Her breathing was scaring him. "Ally, I can tell that you're fading in and out," he said, his voice gentler now. "Remember. This is coming to an end very quickly. You can't afford to have him take over while you're asleep. Either shoot him again or stay awake."

"You're such a hard-ass," she muttered.

He grinned. "I love that tone in your voice."

"The one that says you're an asshole?" She said it, but this time there was humor in her tone.

Axel looked over at Baylor to see him grinning. "Maybe I am," he said, "but this asshole is trying to keep you alive."

"It seems like you're the only one," she whispered. "Everybody else just wants me to die."

"Not happening," he said. "Come on, sweetheart. Stay awake."

"Ha, you only say 'sweetheart' when you want something."

But her tone was fading in and out again. "Ally," he snapped. "Talk to me."

"I don't want to," she said. "Holy shit, this hurts."

"It's just a leg," he said.

"I think it's just a leg," she said, "but my head's pretty fuzzy, and I might have busted some stitches."

He sucked in his breath. "Did you hurt your head again? Are you bleeding?"

"Bleeding some. Don't know about my head," she said. "It was a pretty rough ride in the back of the van. I still can't believe I got myself free."

"Yeah, you got yourself free, overtook the killer, shot,

and incapacitated him. Now all you have to do is stay awake for the rescue."

"Why the hell should I wait for a rescue?" she said indignantly. "I'm the one who did all the work."

He burst out laughing. "You keep saying that," he said, "and you did do everything right. We're just coming in to clean up the mess."

"And that you can do," she said. "He's bleeding everywhere." She started to get worried. "Will they think I murdered him?"

"You were the kidnap victim," he said drily. "I don't think so."

"But they already want to convict me for something I didn't do," she said, "so why wouldn't they convict me for this too?"

"Don't even think about it," he warned. "This guy attacked you, kidnapped you from your room, threw you in the back of a van, and was driving you away. Of course you fought for your life."

"But I shot him," she said. "I guess I should have shot him in the head, huh?"

"Well, that would have been one way, but maybe this way we can get some answers out of him," he said reassuringly. "Come on." He looked over at Baylor. "We're almost there."

Baylor nodded. "We are," he said. "I have the district she's in." He quickly set up the GPS. "We're on the way, Ally, just hold steady."

"I'm here," she said. "I'm slumped behind the passenger seat, hoping he doesn't wake up."

"If he does, he's likely to be stronger than you, so you'll have to shoot him," he said.

"Except for the knee," she said. "And the rate he's bleeding, I'm not sure he'll ever wake up."

"We've got an ambulance coming too," he said, "and law enforcement. This guy won't get away again."

"He's heavily involved in whatever this shit is," she said. "I just don't know what it's all about."

"Did he give you any clues?"

"Oh, yeah," she said, pausing to catch her breath. "They were trying to steal the sub, but something went wrong, something to do with my navigation system," she said. "I don't remember exactly. Then I think he decided that Hostettler might have betrayed him."

"What?" Axel said, trying to get through the convoluted explanation.

"It was really confusing," she said, "but I think they were trying to steal the sub, which is state-of-the-art, so it makes sense, and they needed the navigation system, but something went wrong, and I don't know what."

"Did he think that Hostettler might have just changed his mind?"

"Maybe. Maybe Hostettler saw the shooter kill everybody and realized just how volatile the guy was. Or maybe Hostettler didn't realize that it would be murder for everyone. Or that he would end up the victim of a gun shot himself."

"Only a fool goes into a battle like this without realizing that potential," Axel said. "Betrayal seems to be the number one game in town."

"About six more blocks," Baylor said.

Axel quickly made those turns, as instructed by the GPS, then realized nothing was here. "How close does this navigate to?"

"Not nearly close enough," Baylor said.

"We'll have to drive around a few corners here. Ally, are you there? Can you hear me?"

"I'm here," she said, but her words were slurring.

That worried Axel more than anything. That wasn't fatigue as much as it could be was a brain injury thing. When she didn't answer, it worried him even more. "Ally, talk to me," he said. "Where are you? Can you see if you're at a corner? Can you see if you're on a side street? What can you tell me about what you see?" He spoke urgently, his voice hard, clipped. Trying to get her attention.

"Apartment building," she whispered, "across the street. I don't know what's beside me, a mailbox maybe, something big, but it's green."

"We're coming around the corner, trying to find you."

"White van," Baylor said, pointing. "At that corner."

Racing toward it, Axel parked his vehicle at an angle in front of the van, and they both jumped out and raced forward. Axel went around to the side where the large passenger door was and pulled it open. There she was, but she was barely conscious. She was still holding the gun, but her arm wavered. He took the gun away from her and quickly emptied it and shoved it into his belt. "Take it easy, sweetie. Take it easy."

She looked up at him with a lopsided grin. "I waited," she said proudly, then promptly collapsed onto his arm. Meanwhile, Baylor checked over the gunman and said, "She's right. Looks like she did nick an artery in his leg. He's in bad shape."

"He's also a tricky bastard," Axel said.

"I know, but I don't think he's too far gone."

"Give the ambulance the location, and make sure they

get here fast. See if we can check his ID and anything else on him before we get bumped out of this."

"Already on it," Baylor said, as he busily checked the shooter's pockets. He found a wallet with a driver's license and a little bit of cash. He quickly took photographs of all of it and said, "A license is here, but it's not likely the driver. It says he's forty-seven years old. This guy doesn't look like he's more than early thirties." He shoved the wallet back into the pocket and checked the rest of them.

"What about the dash and the glove box? I can't check anything," Axel said, holding onto Ally, "but I'm taking photos of the rest of the interior here, just in case there's anything."

By the time the cops and the ambulance arrived, Axel and Baylor had done as much as they could. The gunman was transferred to a gurney and taken up into the ambulance, but, since only one ambulance was here, and they took off with the murderer, it pissed Axel off to know that Ally would have to wait. "We'll drive her to the hospital ourselves," Axel said to the cops. And, with Baylor driving this time, Axel carried her in his arms to the back seat of his Jeep, and they took off.

"How bad is she?" Baylor asked.

"Blood's pouring off her head," he said. "It's her second head injury in as many days, and that's bad news. Looks like she busted the stitches in her good leg somehow."

"At least the bad leg is in a cast, so hopefully nothing there got messed up," Baylor said.

"Yeah," Axel said, "but she doesn't look very good."

"Hold on," Baylor said. "We'll be there in a few minutes."

As Axel stared down at her, his fingers gently stroking

her cheek, Axel murmured, "What the hell did they do to you? Hang tight, sweetheart. We're almost there. You're almost safe." And in spite of every warning inside him not to, he leaned over and kissed her gently on the cheek.

CHAPTER 11

W HEN ALLY WOKE up, that same damn sledgehammer pounded in her head that she remembered from days earlier. She groaned and shifted in the bed, chilled and then hot, chilled and then sweating. And she couldn't get warm. As soon as she did get warm, she couldn't stand the blankets on her. She heard a voice talking to her on the other side, but she didn't know which side. Was this death, or was it life? She didn't know if she cared anymore. But she remembered something about the voice; it was soft, but it had been yelling at her last time. She frowned. "Are you still yelling at me?" she murmured.

"Maybe," he said, no laughter in his voice. "I want you to wake up to make sure you're okay."

"Of course I'm not okay," she said. She opened her eyes briefly and then gasped at the light pounding against her eyeballs. She quickly slammed her eyelids shut. "And apparently I won't be okay for a few more days yet." She groaned. "Who let the sledgehammers back into my skull?"

"I'm so sorry, sweetheart. That's another head injury."

"Just because I'm smart, people don't need to try to kill off the little gray brain cells," she murmured, and she shuddered again.

"Are you cold?"

"I go cold and then hot," she said. "I can't seem to get

warm, and then I just sweat."

"That's the shock," the nurse said from the other side of her. At least she thought it was a nurse. Why the hell was the nurse here anyway?

"Plus, it looks like you're running a bit of a fever," she said. "We'll try to keep you warm, while you wait for the doctor."

"You'll probably need an x-ray," Ally said.

"Why is that?" the nurse asked.

"Because it hurts way worse than last time. It hurts like really, really bad," she whispered. "I'm about to be sick." And, with that, both Axel and the nurse jumped into action, and Ally was gently rolled to the side of the bed, where she threw up into the bag the nurse produced out of nowhere. Ally groaned as she lay here, her whole body shaking with dry heaves. "I could do without that."

"That's from the pain and shock," the nurse said. "Here's some water to rinse your mouth with." When Ally rinsed her mouth and spat it back out again, they helped her lie back gently on the bed. Once again the shivering started, and the nurse responded quickly with a heated blanket.

As soon as Ally felt it, she almost moaned in relief. "I didn't know I could be so cold," she whispered.

"Well, this will warm you up," Axel said. "The problem is, you'll start sweating again."

"Right now I don't care," she said. "It just feels like there's no heat in my body at all. Even my face is freezing." He gently laid some of the warm blanket across her cheek. She moaned and brushed into it. "Did you get him?"

"We've got him," Axel said, "but he's unconscious, and he's here in the hospital with you."

"I probably damn-near killed him, didn't I?"

"There's a good chance he could lose that leg," he said.

"That's the least of what he should be worried about," she murmured.

"I agree," he said.

"Oh my, does that mean Thomas's brother, Webber, was in the navy? I mean, active navy?"

"Seems he was," Axel said, "but dishonorably discharged for stealing. We're looking deeper into his file. But it looks like the seeds of discontent were already there. And stealing? … Well, stealing a sub is just a bigger item than whatever he was kicked out for. And he might have wanted to get his own payback."

And that's when she realized Axel was holding her hands. She squeezed his fingers. "Thanks for finding me," she said. "I don't know how much longer I could have hung on."

"Somebody probably would have found both of you unconscious in that van eventually," he said, "but it wouldn't have been a pretty sight."

"No," she said, "I can't imagine it would have been. Anyway, I'm grateful."

"It's all good," he said. "Now what we have to do is track down the rest of what's going on in your world."

"There shouldn't be anything," she said. "It should have been a simple IT job."

"So maybe you need to tell us a little more about what the job was?"

"We were just testing out the sub," she said. "It was a maiden voyage, and we were doing—Wait. I can't remember all of what he said to me," she said, her teeth chattering, "but I remember some of it. They were planning to steal the sub. They had one guy inside, Hostettler, and Webber, who got on board without anyone knowing—Webber is Thomas's brother. None of that should be possible. You know that, right?"

"In theory, none of this stuff is ever possible," he said. "Checks and balances are in place for all of it, but, when people really want to get around it, we know all too well that they can."

"Right. So Thomas's brother is the extra man on board, probably hiding in the HVAC system. He'd seen me pulling out some wires from the navigation system and mistakenly thought I was tearing it up. I was just changing out components, fixing the problems. His partner was Hostettler, who apparently was part of this whole thing, and somewhere along the line, he got to my navigation equipment, and I assume sabotaged the sub, although I'm not positive it was him. I had found something was wrong and sounded an alarm that we were in trouble. So we end up going down and sinking. Then this guy, Thomas's brother, takes over and shoots everybody, not yet realizing what Hostettler's done, and, instead of Thomas's brother piloting the sub out, we're stuck on the ocean floor." She stopped. "Wait. But that means he had to have that kind of experience. Could he pilot a sub?"

"You've got a point there," Axel said. "Not very many people know how to man a sub. But he had been navy anyway, so that training is certainly possible."

"I think Hostettler was probably supposed to do it with him. And maybe they had another team coming or something to pull them from the sub at the bottom of the ocean."

"But then what? When their rescue came, they decided to leave the sub behind?"

"Maybe Hostettler or Thomas's brother couldn't fix it.

Maybe they decided there was no time or," she said, "I had sent out an alarm," she whispered. "Several actually."

"So maybe the two bad guys knew the alarm would bring help, so they decided to abort and live to steal another day."

"Maybe," she said softly, with a tired sigh. "I don't know."

"The fact that you sent out the alarm should go a long way to clear you. If there's any proof of that?"

"No clue. I sent it, but it doesn't mean the transmission went anywhere. I just couldn't understand why nobody came. It seemed like it was forever."

"You were really badly hurt, sweetheart. It's a wonder you managed to stay alive."

"Well, the whole thing made for a couple really shitty days," she said. "I've had about enough of those."

"Hopefully this guy survives his surgery," Axel said, "and maybe we can get some answers from him."

"I got the feeling that he didn't really care. Like he was out of here either way, but I don't know exactly what that meant."

"It does make sense that a foreign country was behind this," Axel said thoughtfully. "Either that or somebody with deep-enough pockets to steal their own sub."

"It was small, as subs go," she said. "More of a research vessel—that's what we would use it for. But, when I was testing it, I kept getting a stealth error."

"Well, with stealth features, it could be desirable for a lot of people," Axel said, frowning at the thought of a broader pool of potential suspects. He'd need Mason's help on that.

"With enough private money, they could certainly have paid these guys to steal it," she said.

"American bank accounts were checked. It will take longer to look at offshore accounts though. And, of course, Swiss banks aren't helpful in any way."

"But money talks, and—for something like this—big money would be required. So sounds like a foreign government financing such an effort."

"Interesting that it wasn't stolen though," he mused. "A lot of investigations are ongoing into foreign powers right now. Wonder who'd pay and be bold enough for something like this. I favor Russia myself. Seems like they've always been there, and that threat has never quite been removed."

AXEL STOPPED AND thought about it, then quickly sent Mason a text, asking about the alerts. Mason replied that he hadn't heard anything about it but would check. While he was busy texting Mason, he noted that Ally appeared to be falling asleep. A sound at the door caught his attention. Baylor was there and motioned to him. With another look at Ally, Axel got up and walked over.

Baylor nodded toward the bed. "How is she?"

"Pretty trashed," he said. "Really tired and pretty sore. A little shocky still."

"Is her head okay?"

"I think we're waiting on x-rays," he said.

"Okay. I took a photo of Thomas's brother before in the van, and we ran him through some databases. We already knew he's former US Navy and known to work for the Russian government at times."

"That's interesting," Axel said. "He doesn't look or sound Russian."

"No, although the Russians have a decent force of American and English agents they use."

"Well, that sucks," he said. "You'd expect a Russian agent to sound that way at least."

Baylor chuckled. "I know, right?"

"Any sign of connections to Ally?"

"That's what I need to find out," he said. "If you're okay in here, I'll sit out in the waiting room with my laptop and work on that."

"Sounds good. Send what you have to Mason, will you? Tesla's got access to all kinds of databases."

He nodded. "Sure. I'll do that right now."

With that little bit of a progress, it didn't take long to get some history back. As Axel sat here by Ally's side, his phone buzzed constantly. Finally Mason called him.

"So there was a connection. Ally's shooter and kidnapper looks to be Thomas's brother."

"So why was he so upset at Ally and her half brother Rory?"

"Rory and Rory's friend Thomas were gay and were a couple," he said. "And while Ally's family was somewhat okay with the relationship, Thomas's brother had more of a challenge with that."

"And the limp?"

"The limp is Webber's alone, per his US Navy record."

"Right," Axel said. "She told me that Thomas didn't have a limp, but this new guy, at the sub and at the hospital, looked like Thomas, who is dead, but also had a limp."

"I agree with her. According to this, it looks like her shooter is also her kidnapper and is actually Thomas's brother."

"Exactly."

CHAPTER 12

ALLY WOKE UP, once again feeling like the sledgehammers were at work inside her head. But the snakes had calmed down, and she didn't appear to have any abrupt sharp, searing pains. Just that constant hammering. She shifted restlessly in the bed, feeling her hand picked up almost immediately. "Axel?"

"Absolutely," he said. "I've been here off and on all night."

Her eyes flew open at that. She rolled over slightly, wincing at the pain as she stared up at him. "I didn't plan for you to do that."

"I didn't plan for it either," he added, "but I did it because it's what I needed to do."

"I wouldn't have thought I was still in any danger."

"I'm not taking any chances," he said with a smile. And he leaned over, kissed her on her uninjured temple, and said, "How are you feeling?"

"Rough, but better than whenever that was." Then her gaze widened. "Do you guys still have him? Is he alive?"

"Yes, and yes," he answered. "He is alive. He's under guard." He could see the relief on her face.

"And the connection with my half brother?"

"Apparently Webber was also in the military," he said. "Your brother's friend Thomas had already left the service when he was killed, but his brother was still in active service. He ended up getting drummed out for bad behavior at some point. Yes, it's Thomas's brother."

Her gaze widened at that. "What kind of bad behavior?"

"Stealing, of all things," he said. "They didn't have enough proof to do a complete trial, so he was given a dishonorable discharge."

"And that probably pissed him off," she said.

"I'm sure it did," he said. "A desire for revenge was probably boiling in his gut."

"But why take it out on his brother's friend?"

"Maybe his brother Thomas turned away from Webber because he refused to accept the relationship between Thomas and Rory."

"So then, when Thomas and Rory are killed, he blames Rory even more. So Rory was an easy target for his anger, and, when they saw my name on the list, I became the perfect scapegoat?" she asked in disbelief.

"If you have twelve random names, and you recognize one as that of someone you don't like already, doesn't that make a perfect person to take it all out on? Or to set up to take the fall?"

"I suppose," she said. "It's still a shitty deal though."

"An awful lot in life is shitty," he murmured.

She yawned. "It is, indeed. I really don't want to stay in this damn hospital."

"Wait until your head gets checked," he said. "Then, I don't know, we might get you back home again. We'll see. It depends on what the doctor says."

Just then the door opened, and the nurse came in. She bustled forward and said, "You're looking much better today."

"I feel better too," Ally murmured. "When is the doctor coming around?"

"Not until nine," the nurse said. "We'll get you fixed up and get your meds and some food in you before he gets here."

"I really want to go home," she said.

The nurse stopped, shook her head, and said, "I don't think that'll be possible. You must get stabilized again."

"It'll be doubly hard for me to sleep here," she said. "I'll be seeing kidnappers everywhere."

"But now that we know," she said, "it won't happen again."

"Except there's no guard, is there?" Ally asked in a dry tone.

"No, that's true," she said hesitantly, as she looked toward the doorway. "You'll have to talk to the doctor about all this."

"I will," Ally said, sinking back against the pillows. "Any chance of a coffee?"

"Sure enough, when I get the rounds done," she said. "Otherwise, your buddy here can go to the cafeteria and can get some." The nurse waved as she left Ally alone with Axel.

Ally looked over at Axel. "How about it? Coffee run?"

"Baylor's outside," he said cheerfully. "He'll go get us some."

"Baylor is hardly your errand boy," she said in protest.

"But he doesn't mind, and I'm not leaving you alone," he said with a smile.

She stared at him. "You're still that worried?"

"I'm absolutely still worried. But it is what it is."

"Fine," she murmured. "I so want to go home, but I need somebody who can help me."

"You can come back to my place," he said. "I have a two-bedroom apartment, and I'm only using one."

She gave him a lopsided smile. "I'm not sure that's a good idea."

"I think it's a great idea," he said, sitting down. "Who else has been at your side these last few days?"

"But I might need a little more help than I'm quite willing to let you provide," she said in a dry tone.

"What? You mean, like a shower or bath?"

She nodded.

He grinned, shaking his head. "It could be fun though," he said. "Something to consider at least."

She laughed. "Is that all you ever think about?"

"Hey," he said, "that's the first time it's ever even come up with you."

"If you say so," she said. "I did think you were cute from the first moment I saw you." But her eyes were closed, and her head was turned slightly away.

Strong fingers reached over, tapped her gently on the cheek. "Do you want to open your eyes and look at me?"

Her eyes flew open, and she rolled her head to the side, then looked at him and smiled. "What?"

"Do you want to repeat that?"

"Repeat what?" But the corner of her lips curled up.

"That's what I thought." And, with that, he leaned over and kissed her.

When he pulled his head back, she stared. "Why did you do that?"

"Why did you say you thought I was cute?"

"Because I like you."

He nodded. "Fair enough. And I like you. Glad that we've got the niceties out of the way." And lifting her chin a little more, he kissed her again; this time it was deeper, more passionate, and a whole lot more stirring than before.

When he pulled back the second time, she closed her eyes. "That was a deadly kiss."

"Maybe so," he said, "but personally I think you're a deadly woman."

She opened her eyes, looked at him, and smiled. "Sounds like a meeting of the minds here."

"Agreed." And, with that, he lowered his head yet again.

A MEETING OF the minds there might be, but damn Ally was potent. Axel had left soon after that last kiss. "Why can't there be a guard on her?" he roared into the phone.

Mason's voice was calming on the other end. "I put in a request. You know that. My hands are tied."

"They had guards on her before."

"That was when they felt she might escape their wrath," he said in a dry tone.

"Well, I guess I'm gonna have to stay here then?" he snapped.

"I figured you might say something like that," he said. "So I've cleared it with the hospital. But you'll have to watch your step."

"Why?"

"Because technically you're not authorized. They only allow family members."

"Which I'm not," he said.

"I know. That's why I said you were her fiancé," he said. "Are you still at the hospital?"

"Yes. Baylor's here with me."

"So leave him as the guard. You go change clothes and

grab some food. And then I would suggest you sit either in the hallway or in her room."

"Probably both," he said. "But damn it. This is a shitty situation. She's been attacked twice now."

"And they have guards on the shooter," he said, "because that is somebody the brass does want to talk to."

"Yeah. Not impressed."

"But they also don't believe that there's any other danger to her," Mason reminded him. "She escaped her captivity and captured her own kidnapper. So, if anything, she might get a commendation."

"I don't think she wants that either," Axel said slowly. "She just wants this over with."

"It isn't, of course."

"No, but the military, if they can make it seem like it is, they will. She didn't seem to think it's over at all."

"But there's no reason to come back after her," Mason said. "Which is why the guards are on the shooter."

"Right, they need him taken out."

"Right. So, depending on who's on guard," he said, "and how many shifts there are, you may want to keep an eye on the shooter too."

"I'll talk to Baylor about that," he said, "but I still don't believe she's not in danger."

"What would they get by taking her?" Mason asked.

"Her skills."

"Maybe," he said. "Not sure it's much of an issue at this point though."

"It is. They were trying to steal a sub," he said. "That's not exactly a one-man job. Plus, however big this crew was to begin with, to steal a sub, it's been reduced. So maybe whoever's out there who wants to kill the shooter, maybe they want Ally to fix and to pilot the sub off the ocean floor for him."

"But trying to catch the shooter's contact, now *that* would be worth something," Mason said. "But who is it likely to be?"

"Well, let's track his movements," he said. "That's what Baylor and I can do from here. We'll backtrack and see if we can come up with somebody the shooter's met recently or several times."

"You do that," Mason said. "I approve."

"Can we use Tesla's skills then too?"

"If you need to," he said in surprise. "I also have some pull with the investigation again. We might get some help from them."

"I doubt it," Axel said, trying to keep the bitterness out of his voice.

"Remember. They have to follow the rules," Mason said in a mild tone.

"I know," he said. "It doesn't mean I have to like it."

"Of course not. Nobody likes being told we can't do something."

Axel hung up just then and looked over to see Baylor already working on it. "There's got to be some trace of a contact," he said.

"There's more than a trace," Baylor said. "The white van was a rental. That hospital stuff on the side was fake. It was rented to a Bulgarian."

"Do we have a name?"

"We have a name," Baylor said. "But, when I type in the name, it comes up as somebody in the morgue."

"He did tell Ally that some of his partners were dead. So now we need to check this Bulgarian for other contacts. Send me his name."

"I'm on it," Baylor said. "We'll also need food some-time."

"I don't want more hospital food," Axel murmured.

"We can order pizza," Baylor said with a grin. "I can meet them down at the front door."

"You do that," he said. "I want a double pepperoni, large. And that's just for me, by the way."

Baylor chuckled.

Axel soon heard him making the phone call, but Axel was on track with the Bulgarian because now they had somebody to track. Everybody around Webber was being taken out. So, the question of the hour was, *Would somebody come to take out Webber too?* It made sense. And it was something that Axel would do, should he be in that position himself.

With a long list of names of known associates for the Bulgarian, he started cross-checking against anybody in Ally's world. Then, as an afterthought, he checked against Hostettler. And bingo. "We've got two brothers," he said, almost an hour later. "We've got a Brian and a Marshal Karsnav, both Russians."

"Oh, I like that," Baylor said.

Axel looked up to see his partner walking toward him, just a few feet away, holding two pizza boxes. "I didn't realize you left," he said.

"Not an issue," he said. "I just wanted to make sure we got food." He set down the pizza boxes and said, "Who are these guys and how are they related?"

"Friends of Hostettler."

"The dead guy from the sub?"

"Yeah, the guy who was made to look like he killed himself but didn't, yes. Instead, it was the hidden shooter onboard who shot him."

"So we have a traitor within the twelve-man team that went on board," Baylor recapped. "That's Hostettler. And Ally's kidnapper, Webber, stated that Hostettler helped him, as the thirteenth person, get on board. However, Hostettler changed his mind—for whatever reason—to not continue with this plan to steal the sub for the Russians, and Hostettler caused the sabotage that grounded the sub, and then he was shot dead anyway."

"It was quite possible that he had an inkling about it being his demise in the first place," Axel said.

"If that were me, I would probably end up shooting the shooter," he said. "And then maybe even taking myself out too."

"I can't see either of us in a situation where we would betray our country for money," Axel said, "but it's certainly a likely scenario for a lot of people. So Ally survives. Webber comes back after her to see if she survives. To make sure she doesn't know anything about what happened maybe? Then he returns and kidnaps her?"

"Why not take her the first time?"

"Maybe he needed to recon the hospital. You and I would do recon first. He needed time to set it up better, to make it look like she escaped the hospital, and he would plant evidence pointing to her as being the shooter from the sub."

"That could work," Baylor said. "It's shitty, but it could work."

"The trouble is, in these cases, the powers that be want a fast and easy answer," he said. "So it was definitely possible that it would work."

"So what do we do now? We can't get a hold of the shooter while he's in the emergency room," Baylor said. They quickly discussed the ins and outs of the investigation as they munched their way through the pizzas. "The problem is," he said, "how do we get these two Russian guys?"

"Yeah, and they may not even be the people we're looking for ultimately," Axel reminded him.

Baylor nodded. "A good lead though."

"On that note," he said, "I'll see if we can do any rundowns on these two names. I was doing an internet search," he said, "but not coming up with anything." He quickly texted the names to Mason and Tesla. **Two known associates of Hostettler's and both Russian. A Bulgarian owned the van used to kidnap Ally, but he's in the morgue. These two brothers were in his known circle.**

There wasn't any immediate answer, and that was fine. When the guys finished eating, Axel grabbed his laptop. And then, before he got back to his research, he stood up and checked on Ally. As he walked into her room, she was sleeping still. She hadn't had dinner again, but there didn't appear to be any need for food right now. He checked to make sure everything was good. Checked on her windows, the closet in her room, and the bathroom, then he stepped back out again.

Baylor looked up at him and raised an eyebrow.

"She's sleeping," Axel said. He frowned and looked back at her. She looked so lost and forlorn in that big bed. He stepped back inside, reached down, picked up her hand, and kissed it. "Just heal," he whispered. "You'll be fine now." And then, because he couldn't help himself, he leaned over and kissed her gently on the cheek. He stood here for a long moment, wondering at his actions, then finally admitting that just something about her tugged at his heartstrings, something he hadn't expected but was happening anyway.

When he finally went back outside again, he was moody and slightly disoriented. He hadn't expected to care about her. And he didn't know if it was just the scenario or if this was something much more. When he sat down with a heavy sigh, Baylor looked over at him.

"Well, you obviously care about her," he said.

"Yeah," he said. "Man, I wasn't expecting that."

"You should have been," he said. "It seems like everybody in Mason's world gets hit by some damn Cupid's arrow or something."

"Nah, that's everybody else," Axel said. "Never me."

"Guess what?" he said. "Looks like it's you this time."

Axel sat here and wondered. Because, of all the things that he hadn't expected, it was strange to find somebody who he really liked and respected. He would never forget seeing what she was like in that van—valiant, hanging on, and injured, but struggling to make it until he could get there. "She's worth fighting for," he murmured.

Baylor looked at him, smiled, and said, "I never said she wasn't. But she's obviously your waterloo."

He looked at Baylor. "What does that even mean?"

"She'll bring you down, boy."

"Is that what happens in relationships?"

"Unless you want to go down," he said. "In which case then, she becomes your partner. Anything else isn't good enough."

CHAPTER 13

LONG AFTER AXEL left, the warmth in Ally's heart remained. It was hard not to think of anything else. But at least it gave Ally something to think about other than the damn kidnapping. And the fact that the asshole who'd done it was still under military guard. She had no idea who had jurisdiction, but she doubted the navy would hand him over anytime soon. She hadn't heard whether he'd had surgery or not, but she presumed he was getting the treatment he needed. She should have just shot him in the head.

Lying on the hospital bed, she stared out the window, wondering at the point she'd come to where that was a better solution in her mind. But after all that she'd been through, she just wanted to know that it was over and that no one would come after her again. They still didn't know a whole lot about who was behind this. But she trusted Axel to do his best to solve this because he was on her side and working his way toward solving the problem.

The fact that they'd found a couple Russians and had made their connection with Hostettler was huge. If they could just track down those Russian brothers and bring them in for questioning, that would be great. When her phone beeped, she picked it up and checked. It was Axel again. She smiled at his message because a heart and a happy face emoji were beside it. Feeling like a schoolgirl with her first crush again, she chuckled and read the message.

Hey, aside from the fact that I miss you already, do you know the face below?

She scrolled up to see the photo, but it was small. When she brought it up full size on her phone, she stopped and stared. Instead of texting him back, she immediately phoned him. "I don't know this face per se," she said, "but he looks very similar to a man who worked on the submarine with us."

"Who?" he asked.

"Rodney Grant," she said. "The trouble is, my head is such a jumbled mess that I can't picture him in my mind to compare this to right now. I don't think they're twins or anything, but they could be family. I'm pretty sure of the resemblance."

"I'm on it," he said. "That photo came from Interpol, and he's a Russian spy on their watchlist. He was involved in a sabotage on a US destroyer. That's how he was brought to our attention. If he looks or perhaps is this Rodney Grant guy, then we have a new angle to follow." He hung up on that.

She tucked her phone beside her, thinking about that. Maybe Hostettler had been a diversion. Maybe that's why he'd ended up trying to fight back and to sabotage them. Or maybe he was just as much of a fall guy as she had been. All of it just sucked. But, if Rodney Grant was involved, had his death also been planned? Or was it another case of backstabbing? The one thing she did know was that stealing the submarine required a few people. They could have planned to take over the sub once everyone was dead, but they just picked up the shooter and left instead. As she went over it all in her mind, she realized she hadn't heard if the sub had been brought up and recovered or if they just removed the dead men. She sent Axel a text, asking. He replied right away, saying he'd find out.

Lying here with her leg aching and her head screaming wasn't helping. But she really wanted to know when she would be a little more mobile. She had to go to the bathroom, and, using that simple task as a test, she made her way to the bathroom to see how she handled it. It went better than she thought. As she came out, after straightening her hair and washing her face, the doctor stood in the doorway, frowning at her.

She looked at him and smiled. "I'm doing better than I expected," she said.

He looked at the heavy cast on her leg. "We can switch that out for fiberglass in another week or so."

"Fiberglass would be a lot lighter," she said.

"And you can have a shower," he said, "but you'll have to bag it. I can't have that getting wet inside."

"Right," she said, "but a shower would be lovely."

"I'm sure," he said, "but it's your head that has me worried now."

"That had me worried earlier too when the wound opened up," she said, "but I'm feeling much better now."

"Back to bed with you, and let me take a look," he said. As she managed to get back onto the bed, he helped her hook her leg back up and then asked, "How are the headaches?"

"When I woke up a bit ago, it was pretty bad," she said, "but, now that I'm up and moving, it's not too-too bad. I could really use some coffee again though."

"This isn't any old caffeine headache. Good try."

"I know," she said, "but the coffee is very soothing, and

it's a treat. So it's my go-to drink."

"I'll see what I can do," he said. When he was finally done checking her over, he nodded and said, "Maybe tomorrow."

"Tomorrow I can leave?" She bolted upright in surprise, wincing only a little.

"Maybe," he said, "I'm not sure about this cast though. It's looking sketchy, now that I study it. It got banged up pretty badly when you were kidnapped and tossed around in the back of the van." He looked at it, squeezed a couple spots, and frowned. "We better check out your leg before we get too carried away. I need to get that cast off and see how things are inside, and we'll go ahead and do the fiberglass cast now instead of waiting." He made notes on his tablet and said, "I'll see if I can work that in this afternoon."

"That would be great," she said. He nodded and disappeared. She sat back and quickly snatched up her phone and sent Axel a message. **Looks like I might get sprung from here tomorrow. New cast this afternoon.**

That's wonderful news.

His answer came back right away. She smiled because it was huge news. It would also free her up to do so much more. Sure, she'd be on crutches, but that was okay. And she could do so much more from home. Like that shower. She couldn't wait. She quickly Googled how to have a shower with a fiberglass leg cast, then laughed at some of the comments and the images that people had posted. She could do this.

With a smaller cast, a lighter cast, she would be so much more mobile. She knew her head was still an issue, but she was feeling okay. It hurt a lot, but what could she expect, having taken a couple blows to the head? Honestly, she was sore all over. Black and blue too. She'd busted out stitches in her good leg as well as her head. But the leg, once recasted, should be that much better again. It wasn't too long before the nurse walked in with a tray. She looked at it and smiled. "Is that coffee?"

"Doctor's orders," she said with a chuckle. "And we'll get you to x-ray and hopefully take off this old cast too."

"Why the x-ray?"

"Just as a precaution to make sure everything is still where it's supposed to be. It should be fine. The cast itself is damaged, but I can't imagine that your leg took too much of the damage."

"I hope not," she said, "because the doctor said that I might leave tomorrow."

"That would be wonderful news," the nurse said warmly.

When she was gone, Ally sat back, sipping her coffee. She sent her dad a quick text, letting him know the update. By the time her coffee was gone, she wasn't surprised to see an orderly come in to take her for x-rays. She smiled, happy to see him not hiding his face from hers—so she deemed him a real orderly—and he navigated her into the wheelchair, and he took her down. By the time she made it through the process, which was far easier this time, she was more than happy to get back in the wheelchair. "I can't wait for a lighter cast," she said.

"As soon as we get the x-ray results," he said, parking her in the waiting room, "we'll know what we're doing next. Should take about twenty minutes, maybe thirty, tops." Before long he came back with a smile on his face. "New cast it is," he said. "The leg's looking good."

"Are you allowed to tell me that?" she said with a grin.

"Nope," he said, "but the doctor will see you down at

the casting room."

She'd be surprised if it was the same doctor. When she arrived in a room that was obviously set up for a casting, the orderly helped her sit on the exam table. "Somebody will be here soon."

She nodded, and, as she suspected, it was another doctor, a younger one. He came in, shook her hand, and introduced himself as Dr. Perry. "Took a look at the x-rays," he said. "The leg is healing nicely. You didn't do any more damage," he said, "so we'll take off this plaster cast that took such a hit and get you a nice lighter model. Fiberglass."

She smiled with delight. "And I'll be happy to have it," she said. "This one's pretty heavy and clunky."

"It did the job though," he said. "It saved the leg." And, with that, he proceeded to cut off the old one, gently, because it was still so sore underneath.

By the time he got it off, she felt like her leg was a chunk of meat. "That was harder than I thought," she exclaimed.

"I know," he said. "Everybody's always afraid we'll cut them, but these saws won't do that." Peeling the fabric liner off, he gently washed the area, careful to avoid the healing incisions, and then let it air-dry.

As soon as he was done with that, she laughed at the fact that she would get a choice of her cast color. She didn't expect it, but very quickly she chose purple. Admiring her leg thirty minutes later, she was completely surprised at how silly and yet fun-loving it made her feel. With that done, she was taken back to her room. She was cold and tired now after that whole process, and, once in her bed, she realized she'd missed lunch as well. She groaned and asked the orderly, "I missed lunch, didn't I?"

"Not a problem," he said. "We'll get one delivered." He

disappeared, and she sank back into the bed. She held her leg out, still elevated, but it was cold, so she tucked a blanket around it, and, of course, the exposed part of her foot was very cold. She wondered what she was supposed to put over her toes. And realized she would need to get a very large sock. She quickly texted Axel. **Do you have any odd socks, old stretched-out ones?**

The response was a question mark.

New cast. My toes are freezing.

Back came a happy face and a thumbs-up. Surprised and a little delighted, she relaxed again. A lunch tray was delivered almost immediately. After Baylor confirmed it was safe.

He was always there in the background, keeping an eye on her. But not even he could stay twenty-four hours in a day.

She smiled at him before studying her lunch. Grilled cheese, tomato soup, and a small green salad that looked like it had seen better days. She stared at the food, wishing to God she could leave and go to a restaurant, but it wasn't meant to be today. That would be tomorrow's joy. She picked away at the food until she couldn't eat anymore and set it off to the side. She should have a nap, help the head to heal, and maybe then she can see her way to getting out of here.

With everything put off to the side, she got as comfortable she could with her leg elevated and closed her eyes. Sleep sounded like the best thing ever.

WHEN HE WALKED into her room midafternoon, Axel was surprised to find her sleeping. He frowned and stepped back out again. He'd stopped at the front desk, but nobody had been willing to give him any information. He laid the sock on the bed, staring at her foot that was completely covered up in a blanket. He'd also brought her a fresh latte. He wondered if he should wake her and then decided he didn't really want to do that and quickly stepped back out again. Just then he heard her murmur. He poked his head around the corner. "Sorry, I didn't want to wake you."

"Not a problem," she said softly. He studied her for a moment, but she appeared to be rapidly coming to awareness. She shifted in the bed and motioned at her leg. "Can you help me take it out of that thing?" He quickly eased back the sling, and she rested her leg on a couple pillows.

"It's much more comfortable on the pillows," she admitted. Just then she saw the cup. She lit up like a Christmas tree. "Is that for me?"

"Well, I can't drink two of them," he said with a smile and moved the table closer for her. "Is the doc still saying maybe tomorrow?"

She nodded, flipped the blanket back so he could see her new cast. "Look. It's much smaller," she said, "and I feel more mobile with it. It's lighter too," she said.

He nodded, and, setting down his cup, he moved to the edge of the bed where he'd left a big boot sock. Folding the top back, he gently placed it over her toes and around the cast. "How's that?"

"Oh, that's great," she said, as she moved her leg from side to side. "I feel like I can get out of here now."

His gaze went to the side of her head. "That still looks sore," he murmured. "How's the head?"

"It'll be a problem for a while, I'm sure," she said, "but I can rest at home as easily as I can here. Probably easier."

"How was lunch?" he asked, with a nod to the domed

plates.

"Pretty rough. That's another reason to go home. I can get real food."

He cracked a smile at that. "But you can't be on your leg very much."

"Ten, fifteen minutes. I don't need long to make a stir-fry," she said.

"Good to know," he said. "At least you can cook."

"I like to cook," she said. "I just don't have time for it, and it's not much fun just cooking for myself."

"I agree," he said. "I like to barbecue. Growing up, we used a smoker all the time. I'd love to get one again. I really enjoy working with that."

"That sounds awesome to me," she admitted. "I don't have much experience with either. Again, it's just me, so it hasn't been an issue."

"Well, maybe going forward, we'll plan a few Sunday dinners together."

"Backyard barbecues?" she asked hopefully.

"Sure enough," he said. "You know Mason and Tesla's house has a big pool in the back. We do an awful lot of get-togethers at their place."

"That sounds lovely," she said warmly. "I do miss having friends to do things with. I miss having family close."

"What about your parents?"

"I texted them the good news about getting out tomorrow," she said. "I don't think they're planning on coming over to visit anytime soon. I tried to dissuade Dad when I was first injured, but the only reason it worked then was because he hadn't told Mom the extent of my injuries." She checked her phone and said, "He hasn't answered me yet."

"Does that mean they could be headed this way?"

"With Dad, it definitely could be that," she said with a smile. "My dad and I are pretty close."

"And your mom?"

"Mom has always been a little less warm," she said. "She's just a little more, I don't know, independent, diffident. She's not cold by any means, and we're certainly close, but I connect more with my father."

"Understood," he said.

"Any update?" she asked, as she picked up her coffee cup and sipped through the little hole in the plastic lid.

"Your attacker is out of surgery, and he's under armed guard," he said. "His leg is repaired as much as they can at this point in time."

"Is he immobile then? I'm really hoping so."

"Me too," he said. "We're not too sure yet."

"And what about the two Russians?"

"Still tracking them down, trying to see where they are."

"Did you check the morgue?"

He gave a bark of laughter at that. "After the first guy, yes," he said, "we did. So far there hasn't been anybody with that name showing up."

"John Does?"

"They're checking," he added, "and, of course, we're on the hunt for Hostettler connections as to how and why. And that Grant guy as well."

She nodded. "It just seems awfully odd that he would look so similar."

"We pulled his picture from his military service record," he said, "and you're right. They do look a lot alike."

"So, family?"

"It's possible. Although they say everybody has a double."

"Yeah, but, in this case, that's just too much of a coincidence."

"I agree with you there," he said. "I want you to stay here and to stay safe, while we do all the running around and check this out."

"I have no intention of leaving until I'm cleared, and then I just want to go home and lock myself in my apartment," she said.

"And we can pick up groceries on the way."

"We?" she asked, a little delicately.

His smile started in his eyes and reached his mouth as he nodded. "I'm taking you home to my place," he said. "But I want to check out your apartment, make sure it's safe, pick up anything you need for a couple of days."

"Well, thank you," she said. "I appreciate that."

"Not an issue," he said. "I figured you can text me when you're clear, and I can probably be here within about ten or fifteen minutes, depending on what's going on at my end."

"Well, I plan to be right here," she said, "so that's not an issue."

He looked at the remnants of her lunch and said, "You want me to pick you up some dinner? You must be starving for something better than that."

She hesitated, and he studied her for a long moment. "You're not putting me out, you know?" he said. "I'm just running around and keeping an eye on you as it is."

"If you wouldn't mind then," she said, "there's even a little deli around the corner."

"Good, I know that place well," he said. "I'll go and get you a sandwich or something. That way you can eat it whenever." And, with that, he turned and walked out. He was more than happy to do something because the edginess inside was eating away at him. There was something he figured he should know but wasn't quite connecting to, and it was driving him crazy. They should have found answers. They should have found connections. They should have found something at this point in time, and they hadn't, and that was more bothersome than anything. He wanted to stay close because he just couldn't get rid of the feeling that her life was still in danger.

As he moved through the hospital, he walked past the room where the kidnapper was. Two guards stood at attention on the side. He stopped to talk to them, identified who he was, and asked, "Is he awake at all?"

They both shrugged and didn't say anything. He looked through the door to see the guy apparently sleeping. He frowned as he looked at him, wishing he could go in and beat the shit out of him. And then, with a muffled exclamation, he turned and walked away. He needed to retreat now before his anger got the best of him. That asshole didn't deserve to live for what he did to Ally in the back of the van. And, if the navy could prove that this asshole had anything to do with those eleven seamen dying, he should be dead already.

CHAPTER 14

I T WAS SO hard to do nothing. It was one thing when Ally was tired and exhausted and the medication was making her sleepy, but now that she was awake, aware, and knew that her time in the hospital was coming to an end, all she wanted to do was get out, and get out now. She had a laptop, but she'd already surfed sites, checked out a few YouTube videos and some TV, and she was bored stiff. She wanted to go home. She wanted to have a shower. She wanted to get her own clothes back on again. As she thought about that, she wondered. She had picked up some clothing from the inside of the van, and she had no clue where they had ended up. Maybe they had been taken in for forensics. She hoped so. Frowning at that, she quickly sent Axel a text, asking him about them.

"The MPs have them," he said. "Pretty sure they're running forensic diagnostics on it."

"Hope so," she said. "Who knows who they belonged to before. Maybe other dead people."

"It's possible," he said, "but I highly doubt it."

"A sweatshirt and a skirt?" she asked. "Where does that come in?"

"Maybe they were for you," he said. "If he had to take you any distance, he needed to have you dressed. Hospital gowns outside of a hospital would raise some eyebrows."

She sat back and thought about that. It was a pretty disgusting reality to even consider, but it kind of made sense. She wished she could talk to her kidnapper again. And that she'd asked a million more questions when she had had the chance. Now she knew she wouldn't have an opportunity for a private conversation again. And she also knew that, even if she asked to go down and talk to him, no way they'd let her in.

After shooting the guy's knee, he probably wouldn't be so talkative. Not to mention, Axel would freak out if he even knew she wanted to. But it was almost impossible to just sit here and wait for something to happen. To wait for other people to do what they needed to do to clear her.

Even waiting for Axel to come back with a sandwich was excruciating—so she could see him again. Just knowing he was doing this for her made her feel that much more special. She hadn't expected to have a relationship bloom at this point in her life. She'd been open to it but hadn't expected it. Particularly after all the nastiness that had happened. To see a light among all that dark negativity and the terrible happenings and accusations was huge. It made her feel like she wasn't completely alone in the world after all.

Sure, she had her parents, but that wasn't the same. And they were so far away that it just hurt that much more. She sipped away at her coffee, hoping Axel wouldn't be too long—for many reasons, but partly because she was bored and wanted to see him again. Nurses came and went and then finally Axel returned. He held up a large bag. She stared at him in surprise. "How many people are we feeding?"

"Just the two of us," he said. "I figured I might as well get something to eat too."

"Makes sense to me." She laughed. Axel took out several

individually wrapped sandwiches from the deli. "I've never eaten there," she said, looking at the sandwich bag logo with interest.

"I've had their sandwiches a couple times. They're really good." He held out two different kinds and said, "I didn't know if you wanted brown or white bread."

"Always brown, rye, or multigrain for me," she said, reaching for the darker bread.

"I ordered them filled, so they both have the works. I figured it was easy enough to take off something you didn't like."

"And again, very logical," she said with a smile. She was delighted. "I love veggies in my sandwiches," she said. She unwrapped one corner and took a bite. She sat back, chewing slowly, loving the mixture of flavors. "This is really, really good."

"It is," he said, "and they don't skimp on amounts. They were pretty reasonable too."

She nodded and watched as he grabbed a sandwich and plowed through it in no time. "I hope you bought yourself a second one?"

"I did," he said, lifting the bag that obviously wasn't empty. "And I bought you a second one." He put them both out on the small table.

"I'm not sure I can eat two," she confessed, "but I really want to. It's excellent."

"Sometimes it's just nice to know that you won't starve," he said. "I'll leave it for you, and you can eat it later tonight."

"Considering it's four o'clock already," she said, smiling, "I probably will."

With his sandwiches gone, he stood, grabbed the garbage, left the sandwich with her, and said, "I'll head out.

Baylor will take over, sitting in the hallway if you need anything. I'll check in with Mason, and hopefully we can get an update. I'll be back in a bit."

"Can you walk downstairs and see if there's any change in the kidnapper's condition?"

Axel nodded, his gaze intent. "What are you really thinking? Are you worried he'll get out of that bed and come up here and get you?"

She gave him a wan smile. "It's a little hard to forget that he already did that once."

At that, Axel winced and nodded. "You're right," he said. "I'll go check. I'll send you a text, okay?"

She nodded. "Okay." She watched as he left, feeling something inside her die down. It was hard to see him leave. There was a light in her life when he was around her, and it seemed to dim as he left. She waited for his text to confirm that the kidnapper was still thoroughly out and under guard. But, when it didn't come, she started to get antsy. She quickly sent him another text.

Did you check?

But there was no answer. She stared down at her phone with growing unease. The last thing she wanted was to think of anything happening to him. But it was hard not to, as there had been so much bad news already. It was impossible to not think of something ugly happening. Finally she phoned him, but the call went to voicemail. She called out for Baylor, several times. He should have been in the hallway. He never answered either. Then she didn't know what to do or who to call.

Finally she called Tesla, and, when Tesla answered the phone, she asked, "Is Mason there?"

"Sure," Tesla said in surprise. "I'm putting you on

Speaker. Go ahead."

"Mason, have you heard from Axel?"

Mason, his voice strong and comforting, came through the phone. "Not in the last hour or two. Why?"

"He left here at about four-twenty. Axel was going to check on the kidnapper downstairs on the way out, then text me to confirm that Webber was still under guard and unconscious, so there was no danger of the kidnapper coming after me again," she said, the words pouring out of her in a rush. "But Axel didn't text me. And I texted him several times and then even tried to call, and it's going to voicemail. Baylor didn't answer either."

"I'm trying Axel right now," Mason said, "but I haven't heard from him since he left your hospital bed."

"I have to admit I'm worried," she said.

"Last word we had," Tesla said, "was that your kidnapper wasn't capable of coming after you."

"Well, supposedly, yes," she said, "but I don't know about that."

"I'm checking with the hospital."

"I'm just—I just can't stop thinking about it," she said. "If anything happened to Axel, when he's done so much for me, I'll feel so terrible," she said in a low whisper.

"Take a deep breath," Mason said. "I'll track him down and get back to you."

And, with that, she had to be satisfied.

"Stay calm," Tesla whispered. "These guys really know how to take care of themselves."

"I know," Ally said, her voice breaking. "It just feels so wrong."

"You've really hit it off with him, haven't you?" Tesla said sympathetically.

"You could say that," she said. "I'd really hate to find something so special, only to lose it."

"No talk about losing it is allowed," Tesla said, her voice firm. "Just stop that right now."

"I know. I know. I know," she said. "I'm just—I'm trying to calm down, and it's so damn hard."

"Do you know exactly when he left?"

"Roughly," she said, "I'd say about four-twenty."

"Okay, I can log into the hospital video cameras and see where he went," Tesla said. "We'll get back to you as soon as we have something." And, with that, she hung up.

Ally knew how lucky she was to have people who could do this kind of stuff. If it was left to her, she wouldn't really know what to do. But if they could check the hospital video cameras, then maybe they could track where he went. It wasn't long, maybe fifteen minutes, before Tesla called her back.

"He went in to check on the kidnapper, went downstairs, and headed out to the parking lot. I lost track of him at that point in time."

"Does it show that he went to his vehicle?"

"No, not necessarily. It shows that he went toward it, but that's where the camera panned out, and he steps out of the viewing range."

"And what about his vehicle?"

"No sign of it leaving the base," Tesla said, her voice thoughtful. "I'm following street cams through town here. I'll get back to you." She hung up again.

But that wasn't good enough for Ally. She knew for a fact now that something had happened. She didn't know what. And that scared her even more. She quickly sent Axel yet another text, asking him to contact her. But, of course, there was no answer. She looked around the room, wishing she had clothes, but she didn't have anything to leave in. She sent Tesla a message, asking if she could get her some clothes.

"Sure, as long as you're not fussy."

"Hell no," she said, "but I'm leaving, and I'm going now, so it's either with a hospital gown and a spare or without."

"In that case," Tesla said, "I'm on it, and I'll be there out front in a few minutes."

Ally sat up on the bed, grabbed the crutches, made her way to the bathroom, and, by the time she'd used the facilities and washed her face and was coming out, she could hear Tesla's firm stride coming down the hallway. When she walked into the hospital room, Tesla had a worried look on her face. "Are you sure you should be leaving?"

"They were going to release me tomorrow," she said. "This is more important."

"And just what good will it do?" Tesla asked, her hands on her hips, her fingers playing over her hip bones in a rhythm as she pondered the problem. "It just means we'll have to worry about you at home too."

"But I was kidnapped from the hospital," she said, in a dry tone, "so it's hardly the safest place to be, particularly with the kidnapper right here too. Axel was the one standing guard over me. And Baylor's gone too. So that's not a help now."

"True, but I checked with the front desk when I came in," Tesla said, "and your kidnapper's still unconscious."

"But where are the two guys with the Russian connections? Axel showed me another image, and I told him how that one guy looked very similar to one of the men on the sub with me, a Rodney Grant," she said. "I guess I can't get past the feeling that something's going on, and I'm in danger here. Now I'm worried that Axel's already been hurt."

"Interesting," she murmured. "Well, let's get you dressed," she said, and she held up a loose flowing skirt. "I wasn't exactly sure what you could wear over that cast."

"That's fine," she said, and there was also a top and a sweater—obviously clothes from Tesla's closet. "Perfect." And within seconds Ally was dressed. Just as she was ready to grab her crutches, the power went out. She stared at Tesla. "You're in danger," she said urgently. "You need to leave."

Tesla stared at her and then gave a hard laugh. "You're the one who's in danger," she said, "and we're not leaving except together."

"I can get behind that," Ally replied with a deep breath. "The last time the power went out was when they came after me."

"I'll go to the doorway and keep it open," she said. Tesla walked over to the door, pulled it open, and stepped out. Seeing nobody bursting inside, Ally grabbed her crutches and slowly made her way, wishing she'd thought to ask for something for her feet, only to realize that Tesla was there, holding flip-flops. Grabbing up her laptop bag, she put one on her good foot.

"Thank you. I never even thought of that."

"I've been in a cast or two in my time," Tesla said. "This will make life a lot easier."

With the two women slowly making their way down the hallway, Ally stopped in front of the elevator and said, "Of course there's no elevator, is there?"

"Not without power," she said, "and you're on the third floor."

Ally swore lightly. "How hard can it be to go downstairs?"

"Really hard," Tesla said, "but let's give it a go." They made their way through the first set of stairwells, and she tried it with the crutches, but she felt like she would fall over every time. Instead, Tesla grabbed one of the crutches and said, "Trying using one and the railing." That worked better, so slowly they hopped their way down the stairs to the second floor. They still had to get down one more floor to the lobby.

"I need to tell the front desk that I've left," Ally said. "Otherwise, they'll put out an alarm, thinking I've been kidnapped again."

"True enough, and I've already told Mason," Tesla said. "I also want to get you off your feet before we injure your other leg even worse."

"It's better than being killed in bed. Hopefully Mason's on his way here."

"Yeah, as soon as I called him, he left," she said. "He should be waiting out front."

"Perfect," Ally said. "I'm definitely feeling a little insecure." Back down on the main floor, they slowly made the way to the reception area in front, and that's where Mason pulled up out front. When he saw them, he raced over to Tesla's side. "Did you guys see anyone?"

She shook her head. "Nope, and still nothing from Axel," she said.

Ally made it to the front desk and told the woman there that she was checking out. The woman shook her head and said, "You haven't been released."

"No," she said, "I understand. But this is the second power outage. I've already been kidnapped out of this place once after the other power outage," she said. "I don't feel safe anymore. The doctor told me that I could leave tomorrow anyway, so I'm checking out now. I'll sign the forms, or I'm leaving without them." It took ten minutes to get all the forms straightened out, and, by the time she had them signed, she felt pretty weak and woozy.

Mason stood there, glaring at her. "You know that you're probably safer right here."

"No," she said. "I might have been at one time but not now."

Mason frowned at that but said nothing.

"Did you find Axel?" she asked.

"No," he said, "I haven't."

"What about his vehicle?"

"We're still looking for it," he admitted. Just then his phone went off. He looked at it and said, "It's one of my guys. They found Axel's Jeep in the parking lot."

"Which parking lot?" she said.

"This one."

She stared at him. "He didn't even get out of the parking lot?"

"It's been moved is the problem," he said. "It's around the back."

"Let's go there first," she urged.

"We are. Plus, the two men who tracked it are on their way too." He helped her into the back of his Jeep, which was open air, and she could at least look around and see. With the crutches beside her, they drove around to where Axel's Jeep was. His had a hardtop on, so it looked more like a regular vehicle, not just a joyride. As they drove up, another vehicle came toward it from the far side.

But she already knew.

"He'll be inside," she said, "and he'll be hurt."

They looked at her hard. Mason hopped out, raced over toward the vehicle, and she knew it. There were shouts and yelling, as she watched a very groggy Axel slowly being helped from the back seat. Thankfully he stood on his own, though blood poured down the side of his head. Mason helped him walk to Mason's Jeep, where Axel sat down beside her. She reached out and gripped his fingers.

"Axel, what happened?"

He stared at her for a moment, as if trying to collect his thoughts. "You know? I'm not even sure I remember. I left you and was heading to my vehicle, but I don't know what happened after that."

"You went downstairs to check on the prisoner, and then you went outside. You never texted me, so I kept trying to reach you and finally contacted Tesla and Mason."

He looked at her in surprise, then looked at Tesla and Mason and said, "Thank you. I think."

"You were probably attacked on the way to your vehicle," Mason said.

Just then Dane and Baylor walked over. They took hard looks at Axel's head and said, "Looks like you got bashed over the head too, then they stuffed you into the back of your vehicle."

"Why bother," he wondered. "They left me alive, so they had to know I'd be coming after them."

"Chances are they were seen," he said.

"Or," Ally said quietly, "they had another mission to accomplish first."

The men turned to look her.

"Explain?" Mason barked.

"Our prisoner in the hospital," she said. "I highly suspect, if I wasn't being attacked, then my kidnapper was the target." At that, the two men who had joined Mason took off. She looked at Mason and asked, "Do they need somebody to go with them?"

"I'm going," Axel said, his voice stronger and sounding more pissed than anything, and he hopped out of the Jeep. She reached to stop him. Even Mason reached out to grab him, but Axel was already bolting toward the building door. She looked at Mason and asked, "Are you going after him? Or do I have to?"

"You are staying where you are," Mason roared. "Axel, get your ass back here."

But Axel was already around the corner, heading toward the front of the hospital. Mason glared at Tesla. She just shrugged and said, "You'll have to stay here and look after us, won't you?"

He rolled his eyes at that and pinched the bridge of his nose, and Ally realized that he didn't want to leave the two women alone either. She sat back in place. "They'll already be too late," she said, staring out across the parking lot. "Too much time has gone by. It was probably pretty easy for them to take out the prisoner."

"You think that's what the power outage was all about?" Tesla asked, turning around to see her.

She nodded. "They couldn't afford to keep him alive. You know that."

"And you?"

"I would have probably been the secondary casualty, but, between Axel and my kidnapper, they may not have had time to get to me. I was supposed to stay there until tomorrow, so, in their minds, they still had some time to take me out."

"Well," Tesla said with a bright smile, "looks like they missed their deadline."

"Because I changed it on them," Ally said, with a bright smile.

"And this is all supposition," Mason said, exasperation evident in his voice. But he was glaring in the direction the three men had gone. When his phone rang, he pulled it out, and she listened while he answered a call from Axel.

"What do you mean, he's dead? What about the guards outside his room? … They're still standing right there and didn't know? … Jesus Christ! What in the hell—" He swore up and down, now pacing outside his Jeep, but he had moved farther away so Ally couldn't hear the conversation. But the two women looked at each other.

"So that's exactly what it was then," Ally said.

"Looks like you were spot on," Tesla said.

Within a few minutes the three men came back around the side of the building, Axel on the phone with Mason. When they could see each other, they put away their phones. She looked over at Axel, when he, a little shaky, sat back down in the Jeep.

"He's dead, isn't he?"

He looked at her and nodded.

"So one attack on you, and they killed the prisoner, their primary target today, with the secondary one being me."

"Yes," he said. "I think that's probably accurate." He looked at Mason. "I suggest you take us back to her place. I'll stay with her and make sure she lives through the night," he said. "We need to get an APB out on whoever did this."

"Which means I need to get to my computer. We need facial recognition," Tesla said.

"I've already made contact, asking for the camera feeds."

"The navy should be on it themselves," Mason said. "What's the point of having guards if they let an orderly in who kills their patient and leaves, with nobody the wiser?"

"That's half the problem with security outside the room," Axel said. "Anything that happens inside the room, they don't even know about."

FINALLY BACK IN her apartment, though not exactly on the time schedule he'd planned, and hiding the fact that his head was pounding, Axel, with Baylor at his side, quickly checked out her apartment, then helped her inside and got her settled in the living room. He sat down beside her and said, "Sounds like takeout for dinner, huh?"

"If that means ordering in, yes," she said, "because I won't be going anywhere to take anything out."

He chuckled. "And I'd like a good whiskey, but I don't dare with my head."

"I can't believe you went back into that hospital," she cried out. "That's insane."

"Well, once you mentioned it, I knew you were right, and I had this fainthearted idea that maybe we could catch him."

"Well, you didn't," she said, "and it was pretty foolish in the first place."

He just rolled his eyes at her. Baylor came and stood in front of them. "I feel like I should stay too."

"We'll be fine," Axel said. "Honestly, we'll be okay here."

"You've got my number," he said. "Check in for the next couple hours. I'm a little worried about that head." He turned to look at Ally. "That head injury is nothing to be ignored."

"I hear you," she said, studying him and suddenly worried. "Maybe he should go to the hospital."

Axel snorted and said, "Like hell. I'm not going to the hospital."

"Why not?" she challenged. "You made sure I went."

"You also had gunshot wounds, a shattered leg, *and* a serious head injury that required stitches," he said in exasperation. "I'm fine." But he stood up, walked over to Baylor, and said, "Any chance you could make a food delivery?"

"Is that all you think about?" she cried out.

He turned and looked at her and said, "Yeah, when I'm hurt, I want food."

"Absolutely," Baylor said. "What are you thinking of?"

"That new Chinese place around the corner," he said. "I've got a hankering for noodles."

Baylor chuckled and said, "Well, at least if you're eating, I don't have to worry about the head as much."

"Absolutely," he said. "And I will check in with you a couple times just to make sure I'm still conscious."

"If there is the slightest chance," Ally said in a hard voice, "that you'll go unconscious, you're not staying here because I can't look after you."

"Which is why," Baylor said, handing her a piece of paper, "I'm giving you my number. You call me if you see him acting different, like blurred speech, falling asleep, not waking up. Anything suspicious and you contact me. You hear me?"

She nodded and grabbed the piece of paper, tucking it into her phone case.

"Just key it into your cell phone now," Baylor said.

"Then you won't have to worry about looking for it or punching it in." Obediently, as they watched, she entered his number into her Contacts. "And it's Baylor, right?"

"Sorry about that," he said with a grin. "Yep."

Axel smiled at the two of them. "Now food," he said, "and get lost."

Baylor gave a shout of laughter and left. Axel walked into the kitchen, turned on the sink and washed his face and hands quickly. Turning, he spied paper towels and used them to dry off. "Now do you have any coffee?"

"Yes." She gave him directions on where to find everything. By the time he had a pot brewing, she smiled and said, "There's nothing quite like the smell of fresh coffee."

"No," he said, "there isn't." Once the coffee brewed, he poured two cups, delivered them to the coffee table in front of her, then sat down beside her. He picked up her hand, laced it with his, and said, "I didn't expect to be two invalids together now."

She chuckled. "Well, according to you, you're not badly hurt. And according to me, I'm on the mend. So, if we're going to be invalids, this is the better way to be."

He squeezed her fingers and gently rested against the couch, leaning his head back.

"If you fall asleep," she warned, "I'll just poke you awake again."

He smiled, without opening his eyes. "I forgot you would follow Baylor's instructions to the letter."

"I have to," she said. "I don't want anything to happen to you." There was a catch in her voice as she said that.

He rolled his head to the side, looked at her, smiled. "I was thinking the same thing," he said. He lifted her fingers and gently kissed them.

"We're a fine pair," she whispered, but she leaned over and kissed him gently on the cheek. "I'm so glad you weren't badly hurt."

"And I think it sucks that we're home alone, and we're both injured."

She smiled. "We might be home and both injured, but we're hardly alone. Baylor'll be back anytime."

"Right," he said with a smile. "So I have a couple hours to get my strength back."

"Not for that," she said.

"Why not?" he asked with interest. She pointed at her leg. "Wow," he said, "do you really think something like that will stop me?"

She looked at him in surprise, then shrugged. "Well, maybe. The cast does go up pretty high."

"Not that high," he said, chuckling.

She grinned and said, "Well, I guess you are one of those can-do guys."

"For something like that, hell yes," he said. "I'll find a way to can-do you."

She burst out laughing at his ridiculous phrase, just when somebody knocked on the door.

"Food delivery," Baylor called out. Axel hopped to his feet, let Baylor in, and they both walked into the kitchen. Taking the Chinese food from Baylor, he quickly served up two plates. Baylor lifted a hand and said, "I'm out. Remember to call me." With that, he was gone.

Axel came back with forks and the plates laden with food and said, "Now we can eat." Like an old married couple, the two of them sat side by side and plowed through the food.

In between bites, Axel asked her, "So what will you do now?"

Ally gave him a one-arm shrug, chewed, and swallowed. "Get back to work as fast as I can."

Axel broadly grinned. A woman after his heart. This one would never tell him to give up his life's work, just like he would never tell her to give up hers. "For a tiny woman who isn't carrying, you are one tough lady."

She laughed. "I'll take that as a supreme compliment, coming from you."

"And it is." He nodded, staring at her. "I guess you've been surrounded by men in your life, being close to your dad, your brothers. Then in a field that is predominantly men too, joining the navy."

"*Hmm.* Never really saw it that way. You're right," she said. "It's not like I don't have women friends ..." She chuckled, not so much with mirth but with understanding. "Really, I guess they're more colleagues. *Hmm.*" When she lifted her empty plate, she shook her head in surprise. "I didn't expect to be that hungry after those sandwiches we had earlier."

"It's the adrenaline rush," he said, "then the shock and recovery."

"Says you," she retorted. "I'm just tired." She yawned.

"You're still dealing with the effects of the medications too," he said. "Thankfully I don't have that to deal with."

She looked at him and smiled. "A little bit of dried blood is on your forehead."

"Right," he said. "Maybe I'll have a shower at some point." He thought about it and nodded. "Actually a shower sounds awesome."

"Hardly fair," she said, "when I can't have one."

He looked at her, frowned, and said, "Can't?"

"No," she said. "Not can't," she explained. "I have to bag it up somehow." She frowned at that and said, "I don't even know that I could stand up in the shower. Not to mention try to keep my stitches dry."

"Well, I can fix that," he said. He got up and went into the kitchen. "Do you have any garbage bags? Oh, never mind." But he came back a moment later with a clear one.

She looked at it, frowned, and said, "What can you possibly do with that?" But before she realized what was going on, he had her full leg inside the bag, and, at the top, he used some duct tape he'd found and taped it right up under her skirt.

Smiling, he said, "There. You can have a shower now."

She looked at him with delight. "Do you think that'll work?"

He helped her to her feet and, with the crutches under her arms, led her to the bathroom attached to the master bedroom.

"Let's see what we've got to do to get you in there." He took a look inside and said, "You'll have to be careful getting into the bathtub." He frowned. "You could possibly even sit down and use the handheld."

"Well, that might not be a bad idea," she said, "as long as the drain is flowing," she said. "But, I still can't do it alone."

He looked at her for a moment. "I guess it depends on how badly you'll feel if you have some help?"

"How badly I'll feel?" She smiled and asked, "You mean, embarrassed?"

"Yeah. A lot of women wouldn't be comfortable if I were to help them in the shower."

"Well, I wouldn't be comfortable if you were helping a lot of women shower either," she joked.

He took a moment and then realized what she'd said and cracked up. "Does that mean you're okay to let me help?"

CHAPTER 15

"YOU KNOW WHAT? I think so," Ally said, "because I really do want to shower. I just feel grungy."

"We can do that," he said. "Let's get you stripped down and get the water going." Before long she had a steamy bathroom as the water sluiced down her, and she stood with his support against the wall. "I thought I would sit," she said.

"I figured it was better if we did this together," he said, with a smile.

"Says you." But she was holding on to him for support, and the shower was pouring hot water over her head, making her feel warm, comforted, and taken care of, despite the fact that the bullet path on her scalp stung terribly. The fact that she was standing completely nude, except for a cast in a plastic bag, with him standing next to her, also nude, was amazing. It was so intimate, exciting, and exhausting, but she just knew that this was where they were intended to be.

He held her close in his arms and said, "Here's the soap. Where's the shampoo?"

She pointed at the shampoo, and he gently lathered up her hair and slowly washed her head, giving her a soothing scalp massage at the same time while carefully avoiding the stitches alongside her head. "That feels so good," she whispered. "I checked out how much dried blood was still in my hair, and I got a horrid headache from it. The dried blood on my hair pulls on the stitches, and it's like these sharp stab wounds."

"I know," he whispered. "I've had my share of open head wounds too. I'm taking it easy, and we'll see if we can get your head clean and all that blood off your hair." After two shampoos and one bout of conditioner, he grabbed the bar of soap and proceeded to smoothly, carefully, and somehow without making it sexual, scrubbed her from top to bottom. By the time she stood here, squeaky clean and blush pink, she said with a chuckle, "I don't know where you got that experience from," she said, "but I feel completely cared for."

"Hey," he said, "have a seat on the side of the bathtub, and I'll take care of the rest of me." And he quickly shampooed his own damaged head and scrubbed himself down the same as he did her, and she watched with interest. "You're really gorgeous," she muttered.

He turned and looked at her in surprise. "I'm a fit male in his prime," he corrected, "so, if that is beautiful, thank you."

She smiled up at him. "I love the fact that you're completely not self-conscious about it."

"I was thinking the same about you," he said. He shut off the tap water and reached over and grabbed a towel. He quickly dried himself, giving his head a good scrub, and then stepped out of the bathtub and did his legs. "Now for you," he said.

He took the towel he'd already used and tried to dry her soaking head before taking a smaller towel and wrapping her hair up in it. Then he grabbed a second dry one and gently dried her off. With that done, he gently swung her around so that she was sitting with her legs outside of the bathtub. With her less-injured leg dry and as much of her body taken care of as he could, he slowly removed the plastic bag from her cast. "Look at that," he said. "Almost as good as new."

He helped her to her feet with an arm around her, and they hopped and hobbled their way to her bed. "Are you ready to go to sleep?"

"Absolutely," she said, feeling exhausted. "Who'd have thought a shower would do that to me."

"Of course it did," he said. "Your body is still healing."

"What about your body?" she asked.

"Mine is made out of cast iron," he said with a chuckle. At the bed, she pulled back the covers. He said, "Do you want a shirt or something?"

"No," she said, "I prefer to sleep in the buff anyway." She looked at him and said, "Are you sleeping with me?"

"Just waiting for an invite," he said, "but I don't want to pressure you."

"No pressure," she said. "Comfort." So, with the two of them in bed, arms around each other, she fell asleep.

IT ALWAYS AMAZED him to meet women who were so comfortable in their own body that they were okay with their nudity, and yet the rest of the world was the opposite. The kind of women who hid and tried to cover their breasts, even when they stood before him and they had been lovers for months. With Ally, she'd been completely unselfconscious, and it really blew him away. She'd let him help her, and together they'd taken care of a job that she desperately needed done but hadn't been capable of doing on her own. He knew her head had to hurt, and her hair was soaking wet, and he wasn't even sure if that was okay while she slept. But he figured it wouldn't be the first time.

The shower had helped him a lot too. His head was pounding, but he knew that he could nap and keep an eye on her, then nap a little more. He'd texted Baylor a couple times, and so far there had been absolutely no sign of whoever had attacked their prisoner. The base was on lockdown and a search ongoing, but Axel was out of that. When a text came, he reached for the phone to see a message from Baylor, saying all was well. **No further news?**

No.

Okay. We'll sleep, he typed. **If I wake up, I'll check in.**

With that, he closed his eyes. He wanted to sleep, but there was just something about being in the darkness with her, even breathing beside her. He tucked her close and thought about how special she was and how he had ended up in this position. It had been a few months since his last relationship, assuming you could call a week a relationship. It had taken that long for her to realize she didn't like him going off on his missions all the time and wanted him to quit his job and stay home. He'd made short work of that and had walked out almost immediately.

This job was who he was. He couldn't just walk away and separate himself from it the way people seemed to think he could. It was his life and his passion. And, for that alone, he needed to make sure he was true to himself. And Ally here, who had been out in the ocean, testing subs, knew and understood exactly what that feeling was. He reached over and kissed her on the forehead. Her eyes flew open. He frowned. "I'm sorry. I didn't mean to wake you."

She sank back in bed and snuggled close. "I don't know if you woke me," she said, "or if it's just that I'm not used to sleeping with somebody."

"I think I like that," he said.

She smiled, snuggled closer, and said, "I never have been one to have too many relationships," she said, "and the ones that I've had, I chose carefully because I wanted to make sure that everybody understood who I was first. I had a few wilder days before I went into my field, but that was a long time ago," she murmured. "Although Carl was a massive mistake obviously." She slipped an arm around Axel's waist and asked, "What about you?"

"A few months ago," he said, "I walked away from the last one because she wanted me to quit my job."

She tilted her head back and stared up at him in shock. "She didn't get you at all then, did she?"

"No," he said, sliding down as she rolled over onto her back. "I don't think she did," he said. "Do you realize that we're both awake? We're both in bed. And I think, though you can't really confirm it yet, but I think we're both not feeling too bad."

She slid her arms around his neck, and he could see the glow and the depth of her gaze. "So it's an interesting conundrum," she said, as she pulled him down toward her. "What do you think we should do?"

"I don't know," he said, "but you presented me with a problem earlier."

"And you promised me a solution," she murmured.

"I did," he said, "so maybe, just maybe, you should allow me to try that out."

"It might take a couple tries though," she said.

He gently brushed his lips against hers. "It might," he said, "especially to get it perfect."

Her lips flashed into a smile, and she murmured, "Well, I'm all about getting things perfect."

"Trial and error?"

"Practice makes perfect?"

"One never fails, one only fails to succeed?"

"Try, try again?"

He gave a shout of laughter and kissed her hard. She wrapped her arms around him and pulled him down against her. He could feel her warm plump breasts against his skin. He'd been holding back all the feelings, like trying to keep his body from reacting to holding a nude woman in the shower, but she'd been injured and so desperately in need of his care that he'd managed to keep his body from showing her just how much he wanted her. But right now, with her in bed and tucked up like this, there was no way in hell. With his erection prodding her thighs, she murmured, "I wondered where that was."

"Self-control," he muttered.

"Let's see if we can lose that," she whispered and pulled him down and kissed him passionately.

His brain melted as fire surged through his loins, and his muscles urged to take her in his arms and to crush her against him. He didn't want to hurt her though, yet, when her hand stroked down his body to find him, he knew he was completely lost. "You're playing with fire there."

"No," she said, "we both are. That means we are already in the inferno, and there's no playing anymore."

He lowered his head and kissed her deeply, his tongue warring with hers, as their bodies melted and surged against each other. He shifted so he could trail a line of kisses across her cheek and down her neck, while her fingers gently stroked his head, mindful of his injury no doubt, but firmly gripped his neck as she twisted beneath him. But he was heading for those breasts that he was so desperate to explore. Washing them was not the same as being able to cup and to gently enjoy their softness.

Then he kissed them, taking one nipple deep into his mouth and suckled. She twisted, moaning beneath him, and he knew that she would be so responsive to his touch. There was something freeing about that, and he allowed himself to forget about everything but the experience of being here with her in his arms as he teased, caressed, kissed, nipped, and stroked his way from one end of her body to the other, careful of her three wounds. When he came to the cast, he slid a finger past it, just to the inside of her thigh, and whispered, "This thing is not making me happy."

She chuckled. "Remember that saying about practice makes perfect?"

"Absolutely." And he nudged his hand upward to the tiny triangle of curls at the base of her thighs, and then he moved down her body and buried his face against them. She gasped, her legs opening wider, and he slid his tongue against the lips, finding the tiny nub hidden in the depths of the folds to suckle. She came off the bed, crying out for him, her hands reaching for his head, pulling him up to her. "Enough of that," she said.

"Enough or never enough?"

She moaned. "Both." But she pulled his hips down and almost instinctively his erection buried itself deep inside her. She sighed, lifting her casted leg. "I didn't think there was enough room," she said, "but you fit perfectly."

"The only thing is," he said, "you can't wrap your legs around me." She smiled, and they shifted ever-so-slightly to the side, her leg draped over his hips. She murmured as he grabbed her hips and held her in place, and she said, "I never even thought about it this way."

"Like I said," he repeated, "trial and error. And we can

keep on trying until we find the best way forward."

"We have like six weeks until I get this cast off."

"We have as long as it takes," he said, and he started to move.

CHAPTER 16

MAKING LOVE, NOT once, not twice, but three times in a few hours, was a new experience for her. Making love with a cast was definitely a new experience, and that it was Axel with her just added to it. By the time she crashed again in the wee hours of the morning, he crashed with her. She woke up suddenly, and it was probably not even an hour later. She realized that the apartment had taken on a little bit of a chill, but then they didn't have a sheet on them either.

As she shifted on the bed to reach for a sheet, she thought she heard something out in the living room. She froze and reached down a hand and gripped his side and hip hard, pinching deep. He came awake instantly. He sat up, and she held a finger to her lips and pointed to the living room.

She reached over and grabbed the sweater that Tesla had brought her earlier. That's all that she had, but at least it was long enough that it went down to her hips. Axel jumped into his jeans and a T-shirt and bolted to the edge of the door. He motioned at her to lie back down. She nodded, stretched out, and pulled the sheet up over her. As she did so, a shadow approached the doorway.

She stopped and froze and then slowly pretended to come awake. "Hello?"

"Hello," came a strange male voice. "I'm really glad to

find you here."

"Oh my God, who are you?" she said, crying out and pulling herself up against the headboard.

"Somebody who has been looking in the hospital for you, so very smart of you to leave. But you just messed up my plans."

"What plans?" she asked. "Once there was a second power outage, I left of course," she said. "I got kidnapped the first time."

He chuckled. "And then he messes up the job," he said. "He was supposed to deliver you to us, so we could finish setting the scene and leave you holding the bag."

"Well, that's what you say, but I was already being looked at as the traitor," she said bitterly. "Obviously you're part of that whole submarine mess." She flicked out a hand and turned on the night light.

He roared as he stepped forward. "You shouldn't have done that," he snapped.

She stared up at him. "You look so much like Rodney Grant from the sub," she said in apparent wonder. "Are you his brother?"

"Cousin, our mothers were sisters. His came to America. Mine stayed in the mother country," he said. "And he didn't want to have anything to do with us, so it was really no hardship that we took him out on the sub."

"You did or that asshole you killed in the hospital?"

"Well, actually Hostettler did it apparently," he said. "Hostettler always hated him."

"What a devious web you weave," she said bitterly, staring at him. She could see Axel behind him and wasn't sure what he was waiting for, but she was determined to get as many answers as she could before somebody else died, and she couldn't get what she needed. "Why were you doing any of this though? The sub, I mean?"

"That sub is valuable," he said, surprised. "What's so hard to understand about that?"

"Well, who told you it was even happening?"

"Well, I heard about it from my cousin first, and then we contacted several people to see if anybody was interested in being our inside man. Hostettler was the only one in a financial spot. He needed money for a divorce coming up, and his wife was trying to take him to the cleaners. He needed some money she couldn't get to."

"So he arranged to help you steal the sub and kill everybody else?"

"Yep," he said, "and, of course, the idiot in the hospital just got a little too cheeky for his britches. Once he failed, he knew what would happen."

"So is it just you left now?" she asked.

"Me and my partner," he said, "but he didn't want to do this part. He's out in the vehicle, waiting for me," he added.

At that point in time she shifted in the bed, trying to distract him when she saw Axel with his phone out. She knew it was important that they get the guy outside as well. "I still don't understand why you had to kill everybody," she said. "Wasn't there another way to do it?"

"Maybe," he said carelessly. "But it's not like those few men are an issue."

"And me?"

"You weren't intended as the target, but, once we realized you were on that list, somebody pinpointed you as someone they had a grudge with. That just made you an easy target and, being the only female, just doubled that."

"Females are always the weakest?"

"In a case like this, yes, so you made the perfect target. Plus, you'd also gotten away on us, so it was an even easier answer."

"So simple," she said, shaking her head, "and so brutal."

"Absolutely," he said. And he slowly pulled out his gun.

She swallowed hard. "Why do you have to kill me now?" she asked. "At least if I'm the patsy, the navy has a reason to look at me," she said. "If you murder me, they'll know it wasn't me."

"On the contrary," he said, "we're putting money into your account now to make it look like you were paid off for this. We're setting up emails and leaving incriminating evidence in your apartment," he said. "Not to mention at your work. They can look all they want. All they'll see is that you're guilty and that you had a major role in killing all your coworkers as you tried to steal the sub."

"My God," she said, "that's terrible."

"Of course it is," he said. "That's what we do, and that's what serves our purpose."

"You don't care about how many lives you've ruined," she said bitterly.

"Not particularly," he said. "We're talking about millions and millions of dollars each for the sale of that sub," he said, "enough for all of us to retire."

"For you guys to retire, yes, but not me," she said. "All you care about is making sure you get to walk away."

"Absolutely," he said with a smile. "Why should I care about you?"

"So that's it? It's all about you?"

"Absolutely." And, at that, he smiled and took several steps closer. She wished to God that Axel would make a move, but she had to trust that he had a plan. She spun her legs out on the far side of the bed and then hopped to her feet. "Interesting outfit," he said, "and the cast in purple?"

"They gave me a choice," she said defensively. "Purple seemed like a good color."

"Right," he said, with a note of mockery. "You'll look great as somebody who betrayed them. They won't even know what to think about you," he said. "Look at you. You look like the most unlikely traitor in the world."

"So why would you even choose me?" she cried out in frustration.

"Because it's so perfect," he said. "Their psychologists will analyze this for decades to come, and they won't understand what they did wrong because, to them, you were just not somebody who they suspected of treason."

"What makes you think you can present a good-enough case that they'll believe you?"

"Not a problem. When you think about it," he said, "they don't want to work at it. They just want to see things closed. As long as they have somebody to present as being the guilty party, they can be absolved of their own sins."

"There isn't a whole lot of what you're saying that I want to hear," she said, "so, if this is what you're planning on doing, just shoot me now and be done with it."

"I can do that," he said, and he raised his arm to shoot her.

Just as his gun arm came into alignment with her, she dove under the bed, slamming her good leg underneath. But she could hear Axel come down hard on the gunman. Shots were fired, but she heard them hit the wall on the far side, and there was a fight that she could only see from underneath the bed—watching Axel's bare feet versus the gunman's heavy boots—but she heard the sound of fists and grunts and blows as they fought consistently; then, all of a sudden, the gun fell to the ground beside her. She snatched it up, dragged herself out from under the bed, and held it on the intruder, from her position on the floor. "Stop, or I'll shoot."

The gunman looked over at her and raised an eyebrow. "Like fucking hell," he said. "I'll kill this guy first."

But just then Axel came with a right uppercut, crunching the gunman's nose underneath his fist. The gunman screamed, but Axel's left that followed hit the guy's jaw just as hard. The gunman went to his knees and then, almost in a comic move, Axel slapped the back of his head, and the intruder fell forward to collapse unconscious on the floor. Axel raced to her, helping her off the floor, and he wrapped her up in his arms and held her close. "We have to get the guy outside," he said. She nodded. Just then his phone rang. He pulled it out and answered, putting it on Speaker so she could hear.

"Hey," Mason said. "He's been surrounded, the question of whether he'll give up or not is still up for grabs."

"Put a bullet in his head for all I care," she cried through the phone. "How many times do I have to be attacked before somebody believes me?" Through the phone they heard a shot. "Oh my God, did somebody shoot him?"

"No," Mason said heavily. "I suspect he took his own life. But nobody's approaching the vehicle just yet."

"Well, the one up here's alive," she said. "You can get your answers from him."

"There'll be a team at your door within minutes. This is your warning."

She looked at Axel and walked gingerly without her crutches to her clothes and got dressed as quickly as she could manage. She grabbed her crutches and headed to the front door. "You don't open that door," he said, "until you ID who's on the outside."

"Right." Just then a pounding came on the door. She asked, "Who's there?"

But it was Baylor. "Open the door, Ally," he said. "Let me in." She quickly opened the door and said, "Careful," as she tried to back up with the crutches. He led four other men into her apartment. She said, "They're in the bedroom." She followed the gang back and hobbled over to Axel's side. He pulled her close, and she watched the men check out the one on the ground. "Is he alive?"

Baylor nodded. "Yes, and we want to keep him that way," he said. "This is the only one we have left out of the gang."

"I know," she said, "and dammit, they killed everybody just to sell that stupid sub."

"We've seen men killed for a lot less," Baylor said quietly. "In this case we're just grateful to have one alive." He looked over at Axel. "How are you doing, man?"

"I'm fine," he said. "Now that it's all over …"

She snuggled in close. "Is it really over now?"

He nodded and held her close. "It is. So now you can get back to the business of living."

They waited and watched while the guy was picked up and carried out. Baylor smiled at them and said, "Now you can get back to what you were doing."

"Sleeping," she retorted.

Baylor chuckled and said, "Sounds like a waste to me." And, with that, he was gone.

Axel held her close and said, "In a way it was a waste but maybe not," he said, "because we made good use of our time earlier."

"And we're still tired," she said.

"So I suggest we go back to bed," he said, "and grab a little bit more sleep."

"I can't sleep after all this excitement," she said.

He smiled down at her. "What do you have in mind?"

She winked at him. "I don't know. Maybe a little more of what we had before," she said, sliding her arms around his neck. "This time we won't have to worry about interruptions."

"Isn't that the truth." And he leaned over and kissed her gently. "Now we have time for us."

Kissing him back, she agreed. "All the time in the world."

EPILOGUE

B AYLOR WALKED OUTSIDE the apartment, knowing full well that those two had crossed some kind of invisible line into a relationship. Outside he met Mason and motioned to the one gunman they had. "He's unconscious, but he's okay. It looks like Axel broke his nose and maybe shattered his jaw."

"Axel's got a hell of a set of hooks. He used to be a boxer in his day and a dirty-ass street fighter."

"Well, I can relate to the street fighting," Baylor said.

Mason looked up at the apartment. "Are they coming down?"

"Nope, I don't think so," he said. "I suspect they'll go back to bed and not to sleep."

Mason grinned. "Good for them," he said. Then he chuckled.

"What's so funny?" Baylor asked, looking at him, completely puzzled.

"Nothing, just the magic again. It seems to still be working."

"You and your bloody matchmaking," he said. "Good thing you haven't started in on me yet."

"Oh, your turn will come," he said.

"I'm okay to not have a relationship," he said. "This kind of life isn't for most women."

"No, and yet the funny thing is, several of us have found partners, and it's worked out really well," Mason said with a smile.

"Yeah, but you've got Tesla. That's different."

"And what about Ally?" he asked, motioning to the apartment.

"She's different too."

"Well, I can name another twenty women," Mason said, "who are just as good and the good kind of different."

"Yep, but that's the thing," Baylor said. "All the good women in the world are gone."

"Oh, I don't know about that," Mason said, chuckling.

"Nope," he said. "Not happening."

Mason looked at him with a smile and said, "You know what? I've never intentionally set out to do this," he said, "but, in this case, challenge accepted."

This concludes Book 25 of SEALs of Honor: Axel.

Read about Baylor: SEALs of Honor, Book 26

Author's Note

Thank you for reading SEALs of Honor, Books 23–25! If you enjoyed the book, please take a moment and leave a short review.

Dear reader,

I love to hear from readers, and you can contact me at my website: www.dalemayer.com or at my Facebook author page. To be informed of new releases and special offers, sign up for my newsletter or follow me on BookBub. And if you are interested in joining Dale Mayer's Reader Group, here is the Facebook sign up page.
http://geni.us/DaleMayerFBGroup

Cheers,
Dale Mayer

About the Author

Dale Mayer is a *USA Today* best-selling author, best known for her SEALs military romances, her Psychic Visions series, and her Lovely Lethal Garden cozy series. Her contemporary romances are raw and full of passion and emotion (Broken But … Mending, Hathaway House series). Her thrillers will keep you guessing (Kate Morgan, By Death series), and her romantic comedies will keep you giggling (*It's a Dog's Life*, a stand-alone novella; and the Broken Protocols series, starring Charming Marvin, the cat).

Dale honors the stories that come to her—and some of them are crazy, break all the rules and cross multiple genres!

To go with her fiction, she also writes nonfiction in many different fields, with books available on résumé writing, companion gardening, and the US mortgage system. All her books are available in print and ebook format.

Connect with Dale Mayer Online

Dale's Website – www.dalemayer.com
Twitter – @DaleMayer
Facebook Page – geni.us/DaleMayerFBFanPage
Facebook Group – geni.us/DaleMayerFBGroup
BookBub – geni.us/DaleMayerBookbub
Instagram – geni.us/DaleMayerInstagram
Goodreads – geni.us/DaleMayerGoodreads
Newsletter – geni.us/DaleNews

Also by Dale Mayer

Published Adult Books:

Hathaway House

Aaron, Book 1

Brock, Book 2

Cole, Book 3

Denton, Book 4

Elliot, Book 5

Finn, Book 6

Gregory, Book 7

Heath, Book 8

Iain, Book 9

Jaden, Book 10

Keith, Book 11

Lance, Book 12

Melissa, Book 13

Nash, Book 14

Owen, Book 15

Hathaway House, Books 1–3

Hathaway House, Books 4–6

Hathaway House, Books 7–9

The K9 Files

Ethan, Book 1

Pierce, Book 2

Zane, Book 3

Blaze, Book 4

Lucas, Book 5

Parker, Book 6

Carter, Book 7

Weston, Book 8

Greyson, Book 9

Rowan, Book 10

Caleb, Book 11

Lovely Lethal Gardens

Arsenic in the Azaleas, Book 1

Bones in the Begonias, Book 2

Corpse in the Carnations, Book 3

Daggers in the Dahlias, Book 4

Evidence in the Echinacea, Book 5

Footprints in the Ferns, Book 6

Gun in the Gardenias, Book 7

Handcuffs in the Heather, Book 8

Ice Pick in the Ivy, Book 9

Jewels in the Juniper, Book 10

Killer in the Kiwis, Book 11

Lovely Lethal Gardens, Books 1–2

Lovely Lethal Gardens, Books 3–4

Lovely Lethal Gardens, Books 5–6

Lovely Lethal Gardens, Books 7–8

Lovely Lethal Gardens, Books 9–10

Psychic Vision Series

Tuesday's Child

Hide 'n Go Seek

Maddy's Floor

Garden of Sorrow

Knock Knock…

Rare Find

Eyes to the Soul

Now You See Her

Shattered

Into the Abyss

Seeds of Malice

Eye of the Falcon

Itsy-Bitsy Spider

Unmasked

Deep Beneath

From the Ashes

Stroke of Death

Ice Maiden

Psychic Visions Books 1–3

Psychic Visions Books 4–6

Psychic Visions Books 7–9

By Death Series

Touched by Death

Haunted by Death

Chilled by Death

By Death Books 1–3

Broken Protocols – Romantic Comedy Series

Cat's Meow

Cat's Pajamas

Cat's Cradle

Cat's Claus

Broken Protocols 1-4

Broken and... Mending

Skin

Scars

Scales (of Justice)

Broken but... Mending 1-3

Glory

Genesis

Tori

Celeste

Glory Trilogy

Biker Blues

Morgan: Biker Blues, Volume 1

Cash: Biker Blues, Volume 2

SEALs of Honor

Mason: SEALs of Honor, Book 1

Hawk: SEALs of Honor, Book 2

Dane: SEALs of Honor, Book 3

Swede: SEALs of Honor, Book 4

Heroes for Hire, Books 10–12

Heroes for Hire, Books 13–15

SEALs of Steel

Badger: SEALs of Steel, Book 1

Erick: SEALs of Steel, Book 2

Cade: SEALs of Steel, Book 3

Talon: SEALs of Steel, Book 4

Laszlo: SEALs of Steel, Book 5

Geir: SEALs of Steel, Book 6

Jager: SEALs of Steel, Book 7

The Final Reveal: SEALs of Steel, Book 8

SEALs of Steel, Books 1–4

SEALs of Steel, Books 5–8

SEALs of Steel, Books 1–8

The Mavericks

Kerrick, Book 1

Griffin, Book 2

Jax, Book 3

Beau, Book 4

Asher, Book 5

Ryker, Book 6

Miles, Book 7

Nico, Book 8

Keane, Book 9

Lennox, Book 10

Gavin, Book 11

Shane, Book 12

Bullard's Battle Series

Ryland's Reach, Book 1

Cain's Cross, Book 2

Eton's Escape, Book 3

Garret's Gambit, Book 4

Kano's Keep, Book 5

Fallon's Flaw, Book 6

Quinn's Quest, Book 7

Bullard's Beauty, Book 8

Collections

Dare to Be You...

Dare to Love...

Dare to be Strong...

RomanceX3

Standalone Novellas

It's a Dog's Life

Riana's Revenge

Second Chances

Published Young Adult Books:

Family Blood Ties Series

Vampire in Denial

Vampire in Distress

Vampire in Design

Vampire in Deceit

Vampire in Defiance

Vampire in Conflict

Vampire in Chaos

Vampire in Crisis

Vampire in Control

Vampire in Charge

Family Blood Ties Set 1–3

Family Blood Ties Set 1–5

Family Blood Ties Set 4–6

Family Blood Ties Set 7–9

Sian's Solution, A Family Blood Ties Series Prequel
Novelette

Design series

Dangerous Designs

Deadly Designs

Darkest Designs

Design Series Trilogy

Standalone

In Cassie's Corner

Gem Stone (a Gemma Stone Mystery)

Time Thieves

Published Non-Fiction Books:

Career Essentials

Career Essentials: The Résumé

Career Essentials: The Cover Letter

Career Essentials: The Interview

Career Essentials: 3 in 1

www.ingramcontent.com/pod-product-compliance
Lightning Source LLC
Chambersburg PA
CBHW071400200726
48294CB00004B/1232

* 9 7 8 1 7 7 3 3 6 4 0 6 3 *